"Weeds!" Starris grabbed a handful of the sweatpants threatening to fall around her ankles and shot an incredulous look at Jordan. "You brought me out here to look at a bunch of weeds?"

Pursing his lips, Jordon gazed at his flower plot. His plants might not win any prizes, but she did not have to insult them. He used the too-big pants to propel Starris toward him. "My plants are not weeds, and they are very, very sensitive. So, if you are going to hurl insults, please lower your voice. And that's not why I brought you out here."

With one hand securely holding her pants, Starris used the other to swipe back auburn wisps of hair from her forehead and tipped her head back to meet Jordan's gaze. "It's not?"

"No." Jordan lowered his head. "I brought you out here for this." Matching their lips together, his mouth closed over hers. It was a good thing that he held her pants or they would have fallen to her feet when Starris lifted her arms to encircle his neck.

Lifting his head, Jordon locked his eyes with hers and smiled. "Now, I truly am full," he said. "I've been wanting to do that ever since you walked practically naked into my study."

SUBTLE SECRETS

WANDA Y. THOMAS

Genesis Press, Inc.

Indigo Love Stories

An imprint of Genesis Press, Inc.
Publishing Company

Genesis Press, Inc.
P.O. Box 101
Columbus, MS 39703

ISBN-13: 978-1-58571-218-2
ISBN-10: 1-58571-218-3
Manufactured in the United States of America

First Edition 2001
Second Edition 2007

Visit us at www.genesis-press.com or call at 1-888-Indigo-1

DEDICATION

This book is dedicated to my mother and father: Pearlie Mae and Morris Lee Thomas. For your spirit, love, guidance, and determination to raise seven children to be productive adults, I say thank you.

PROLOGUE

Denver, Colorado

"How old is the child?"

Delbert Marco's dark eyes shifted to the man standing at the windows in his office before returning to the picture of his family. It sat on the corner of his polished, cherrywood desk, and at times like this, reminded him of how lucky he was to have them. He glanced down at the letter in his hand. The contents had shocked them both, but Delbert, a seasoned professional, had already mentally begun charting a strategy on how to handle the situation. As appalling as the news was, Jordon needed to snap back so that they could make some decisions. Since it didn't look as if that would happen any time soon, Delbert repeated the answer he'd already given three times. "According to the letter—twelve months."

Anguish joined the tension swarming in the lawyer's office as Jordon Randolph Banks turned away. His heartbeat sped up, then slowed almost to the point of nonexistence. He rested his forehead on the windowpane and stared through a sheen of tears at the street five stories below. "Why, Gloria? Why would you do something like this to me?"

The barely perceptible words sounded like a painful moan, and Delbert winced. As a celebrated divorce lawyer, he had witnessed his share of the awful things people did when ending loveless marriages. Just when Delbert thought he'd seen and heard it all, something else always came along to top even the most horrendous story. But this last vengeful act perpetrated on Jordon Banks by his ex-wife ranked as the most disgusting thing he'd come across in the twenty years of his career.

Having handled Jordon's side of the divorce, gut instinct had told Delbert that Gloria Banks spelled bad news. It wasn't enough that Jordon had gone against his advice and agreed to her list of demands, uncontested. Gloria had seemed determined to break Jordon in the process. That she'd been found dead, murdered by the hands of suspect unknown, did not surprise Delbert. And if what the letter stated proved true, bad didn't come close to describing Gloria Banks or the repulsion he felt for her at that moment.

Heaving a deep sigh, Delbert flung the letter down on his desk and leaned back in his chair. "J.R., I know how bad this is for you, but we can't take this letter as gospel. Our first move will be to authenticate the validity of this letter and, secondly, the claims made therein."

"How do I get my daughter out of that place?"

"Let's not jump the gun here, Jordon. This letter is not proof that a child exists. Even if she does, we cannot make the assumption that she is your daughter."

Jordon turned from the window, a ruthless expression twisting his handsome face. "She's mine!"

Delbert sat up. "You can't go flying half-cocked across the country on a hunch, J.R. I'll get a detective on this right away, and in a few weeks, after blood tests, we'll know for sure."

Jordon stalked to the door. "You do that, Del. In the meantime, you can reach me in Atlanta. My daughter is not an orphan, and she does not belong in an orphanage. And I do not intend to let a child of my flesh and blood spend another day in a place where she does not belong!"

Atlanta, Georgia

The same day Jordon Banks received his letter, another lay crumpled on a rickety brown table littered with overflowing ashtrays, half-smoked butts and the feathery remains of white lines left in someone's hasty indulgence. Brown, half-closed and glassy eyes surveyed their surroundings in disgust. A few friends, he'd said. They'd play a few rounds of cards and end the evening early.

The eyes took in the bits of trash and crushed potato chips littering the dark brown carpet. One of the cheap-looking sheers covering her windows had been knocked from its rod. Bottles—some empty, some not, one tipped and leaking on the carpet under the table—added to the foul smell in the room. The gathering that had crowded into the tiny apartment had been so loud the neighbors had called the police. Now, she had to clean up this mess. The eyes stopped on the man, so stoned he probably didn't even know that he was asleep on the floor. As much as she hated the tiny apartment and the poverty that cloaked the community where she lived, she hated him more.

Just one year ago, she'd finally gotten herself together and pulled herself up to the next rung on the ladder. He'd offered her pretty words and promises, then dragged her back down into the gutter.

Lying on the couch, Lisa curled herself into a despondent ball and tried to fight off the memories that had surfaced after she'd read the letter. But like an annoying itch needing to be scratched, she couldn't stop herself from remembering or staunch the flow of the tears of rolling down her cheeks.

As the older of the two, she remembered the mother they had shared and the fathers they did not. She remembered the sickly baby and the long nights she'd held the frail infant in her arms while it fought against the effects of their mother's addiction to heroin. Held in the grip of the drug, their mother had neglected them both, and at the tender age of eight, she had stepped into the role of caregiver for her sister. When they needed clothes, she'd gone to the mission barrels. When they had no food, she'd begged or stolen what they needed. And though barely surviving, she had kept them alive.

She remembered the day the authorities came into their house. She'd been twelve, her sister four. Their mother had died, and though no one ever said, she'd known it was the drugs. They had been taken to a strange place, filled with lots of other children. The people there had not been nice and had separated her from her sister. She'd spent the long, lonely night crying on a lumpy mattress. The next morning, she'd learned that her sister had been taken away, and no one would tell her where. She'd searched for years, followed every lead. The only thing she'd gotten for her efforts was one picture a detective had found in an old police record. Her sister had been twenty. That was the last time she'd seen her sister alive. A woman had been found murdered in a hotel room. The local news had reported the incident as a drug deal gone wrong. The next day, Lisa had gone to identify the body.

Lisa believed her sister had come home and that she'd been looking for her. The letter she'd just received told her all she needed to know about her sister's life. Married and twice divorced herself, her life hadn't turned out any better, and it saddened her even more to know that neither of them had found the happiness they deserved.

Raising to a sitting position, Lisa sniffed up her tears and willed her mind to push back the pain as her hands tried to smooth the black hair standing wildly around her head. The first thing she needed to do was get away from this place. Second, check into rehab and get herself clean again. She may have been too late to save her sister, but she would not be too late to save her sister's child.

CHAPTER 1

Nine years and eleven months later...

The day started like any other for Starris Gilmore. Her alarm clock shrilled; she pounded it into silence with her fist. Then she pulled the striped comforter over her head, burrowed into her pillow and went back to sleep. Thirty minutes later, one nicely shaped leg swung over the edge of her sleigh bed, followed by a slender arm. Shortly, her head surfaced from her lair of blankets, and Starris squinted at the clock.

When she saw that it was eight-fifteen, she flipped back the covers and climbed from the bed. Taking a moment, she lifted her arms into the air, stretching her five-foot-eight frame, and after releasing a disgruntled groan, padded heavily in the direction of the bathroom. Standing at the mirror, Starris groaned again.

Gray-green eyes that sparkled when she was fully awake were heavy with sleep. Her naturally curly mane was a tangled mass and blanket wrinkles marred her smooth, golden-brown skin. In spite of the gruesome image reflected in the mirror, Starris felt a rush of exhilaration. Today she had an interview and, after three months of trying, what she felt was a real shot at finally getting a job.

Her friend, Shelby Reeves, had given her the lead for ROBY, an acronym for Rescuing Our Black Youth. The organization targeted teenage African-American males and provided mentors, job training and counseling on the value of education and goal setting. It hoped to steer some of the boys toward careers in corporate America where the presence of African-American males lacked shamefully.

Starris had already passed the first stage. Her résumé and one-page synopsis stating why she wanted to work for the organization had been good enough to make the first cut. Now, if her luck held, she'd make it through the interview, and by that evening she'd have a job. She stepped into the shower and felt immediately invigorated by the heated water steaming life into her body. Squeezing a generous dollop of scented body wash onto a loofah sponge, she tried for a note she had no hope of reaching when her off-key soprano voice lifted in song. Fifteen minutes later, Starris stepped from the shower and whipped a towel around her hair. She finished her morning toilette, then left the bedroom with a wide smile on her face.

Danielle Carter poured boiling water into a large mug, dropped in a raspberry Tea-Sickle, and stirred the mixture. "Morning, Mama."

"Good morning, angel." Starris kissed Dani's cheek, accepted the steaming cup of tea and took a seat at the breakfast nook.

Dani picked up her bowl of cereal and joined Starris at the table. "Have you decided what to wear?"

"Um-hmmm. The lavender dress."

Dani paused with the spoon in her mouth, then nodding her head in agreement, said, "That's good. You always look pretty in that."

"Thanks, angel. Let's hope someone other than you will be impressed."

"You'll get the job this time, Starris. I just know it."

Starris gave her a loving smile. Dani rarely expressed certainty of any kind and that she sounded so sure meant Starris was making headway with the child. "You know what, angel? I think you're right." She stood and picked up her cup. "But if I'm going to get that job, I need to get ready and get to my interview on time. When you've finished your breakfast, go directly next door. Mrs. Smith is taking you to school this morning, and I will be at your swim meet this afternoon."

Dani stood for a hug. "Okay, Starris. Good luck, but I don't think you'll need it today."

At ten-fifteen, Starris frowned as she watched another member of the competition step from the office where the interviews were being conducted. She observed the dreamy expression on the woman's face—the same expression she'd seen on the faces of those that had emerged before her. Starris lifted a delicately curved brow. She knew of only one thing that could put that type of look on a woman's face—a man.

The woman finally sighed and walked away from the door. Starris watched her go, then turned to stare candidly at the other people sitting in the metal chairs placed around the big empty space. All, including those already interviewed, had dressed in the standard corporate motif: dark suit, white shirt, power ties for the men and functional, low-heeled pumps for the women.

Starris looked down at her own attire and a niggle of misgiving slid through her shell of confidence. No one had dressed in a light color. As a graphics artist, Starris was used to working in small offices where dressing casual was the norm. She shrugged a shoulder. Well, it was too late to do anything about it now. If nothing else, she'd stand out from the crowd.

"Ms. Gilmore, you're next."

"Thank you," Starris replied, standing. After smoothing the front of the dress, she held her head high and made her way toward the office. Standing in the open doorway, she quickly surveyed the room. It was a large space with lots of potential, and the floor-to-ceiling windows on the back wall let in plenty of light. Two metal chairs sat facing each other in the middle of a cement floor. On a nearby chair, she saw a stack of manila folders and a stack of folders on the floor, as well.

I was right, Starris thought, bringing her eyes back to the windows. The interviewer was a man. Since his back was to her, she took a moment to measure him with her eyes. He stood well over six feet, had an athletic build, and he definitely knew how to dress. The tailored jacket of the black pinstriped suit stretched over broad shoulders. A white collar peeked above the jacket, meeting a well-shaped head, and the pants covered legs that seemed to go on forever. Starris was so busy giving him the once-over that she was unprepared when he suddenly turned and faced her.

Il est trés beau, she thought immediately. *Very handsome? Do you not see those dark curls on that head and that thick fringe of lashes framing those shining black eyes? What about that chestnut-colored face? And that body? Girlfriend, please! That man is not handsome. He's a god and a truly superb specimen of a man!*

Jordon Banks sucked in a sharp breath and quickly suppressed the urge to step closer. The electric jolts that started when his eyes collided with those of the woman standing in the doorway had now centered in one area of his body, and Jordon hoped like hell that Starris Gilmore didn't notice.

He hadn't thought he'd ever see her again. Even if he hadn't, Jordon would remember the oval-shaped face with skin that shone with a natural radiance, the high cheekbones that bespoke a Native American heritage and the luscious-lipped mouth. She had a small mole just to the right of her left eye, and the lavender dress emphasized the perfectly proportioned curves shaping her tall and willowy figure. The entirely feminine package had a billowy cloud of golden auburn curls that fell to her shoulders and light-colored lashes framed the hazel eyes that had haunted Jordon's dreams for months. They were eyes that should have danced with life, and while there was a measure of life in them, they still held a hint of the despair Jordon had witnessed when he'd first seen her, twenty-one months earlier.

Without the slightest inkling of who she was, Jordon had almost placed her application in the reject pile. He didn't consider himself judgmental, but Starris? The name had really thrown him for a minute. Then he'd read the one-page synopsis accompanying her résumé, and her heartfelt words had moved him.

It is not a choice, but a responsibility for the adult minds of today to impart wisdom and knowledge to the young minds that will control tomorrow. To ignore this responsibility is to throw away any chance of a decent future for any of us.

Of all the applicants, Starris was the only one Jordon felt had captured the heart and essence of ROBY. And if he could control the erotic thoughts tunneling through his mind, Jordon might have wondered why he hadn't made the connection earlier.

Almost simultaneously, Jordon cleared his throat, and Starris closed her open mouth. He gave her what he hoped looked like an easygoing smile. "Please, have a seat, Ms. Gilmore."

"Thank you," Starris replied, a flicker of recognition causing her brow to wrinkle. When he smiled, his face reflected chiseled planes, and the slight dimple in his chin became more prominent, too. Starris stared unabashedly, sure she'd seen this man before, but unable to place where. Gathering her thoughts, she made her feet carry her forward and sat in the chair. She had to focus on the interview, not the man, but now completely understood the dreamlike looks she'd seen on the faces of the women who had left his office earlier.

Jordon hastily took his seat and tried to buy some time to calm his racing heart by picking up a folder containing her résumé and scanning the page. Using the employment dates as a mark, he placed her age around thirty-five. That was good, because he would never consider dating anyone still part of the twenty-something crowd. Dating? Where the hell had that thought come from? He was supposed to be assessing Starris' potential as an employee for ROBY, not her potential as a woman for him.

Jordon's lips tightened in a slight grimace. *Get your mind back on business, Banks,* he chastised himself, glancing up just as Starris crossed her legs. The dress had a slit, and the peek it provided of a shapely thigh had Jordon's throat working convulsively. "Ah…Ms. Gilmore," he said after shaking his head as if to clear it. "My name is Jordon Banks, and I am the executive director of ROBY."

Starris leaned forward to shake the hand he extended. "*Bonjour, Monsieur Banks. Je m'appelle* Starris Gilmore."

Jordon released her hand and slouched back in his chair. "Excuse me?"

Mortified, Starris groaned and lowered her head. Speaking French came second nature to Starris, who had been born in France. She had lived in the country until the age of thirteen, and occasionally slipped into the language when she was extremely nervous or upset. Starris closed her eyes and made a desperate grab to regain her poise. She took a calming breath, then looked up and into the stunned expression on Jordon's face. "I am truly sorry, Mr. Banks. It's a nervous habit of mine—speaking French, I mean. Oh, never mind about that. My name is Starris Gilmore."

Jordon pressed his lips together and suddenly stood to his feet. He jammed his hands into his pockets and directed a pointed look at Starris. "No, Ms. Gilmore. I'm the one who should apologize. You see, as of this morning, all positions at ROBY have been filled."

Her mouth fell open again and Starris grabbed the edges of her chair. She held her breath to stop the topsy-turvy tumble of her stomach. Then tried to ascertain if the look on his face was a smirk or a scowl, because she was sure that this man, this Jordon Banks couldn't possibly be talking to her. Starris sat up straight and skewered him with a furious green glare. And if he was talking to her, she'd been looking for work for too long to be dismissed with a "howdy do" and a "see ya." In fact, she'd had it with the want ads, the agencies, the unsuccessful interviews, the "it's been a pleasures" and the "thanks for coming in, we'll let you knows." And this obnoxious jerk hadn't even had the courtesy to say that.

Her chin tilted upward, and Starris didn't even try to control the temper that as a child could flare with the slightest provocation. As an adult, she tried to conceal the trait by holding everything inside. Not a good habit, because without the relief of prior venting, when Starris did explode, it was a combining of the moment's situation and a long list of stored-up hurts. Lately, her temper had been threatening to rear its ugly head, and Jordon's rudeness along with every disappointment she'd been dealt during the last three months congested in her chest. Unfortunately for him, Jordon Banks had no way of knowing that or that he was about to become the recipient of the latest explosion to erupt from Starris Latrice Gilmore.

"Mr. Banks. There are fifteen open positions at this center, and I'm only interested in two—the executive assistant and the job acquisitions director. Okay, so I messed up and made a mistake. Mistakes are little slip-ups humans make because we are not perfect. But perhaps sitting on that throne in your isolated tower of power, you've forgotten how nerve-wracking it can be to be put in the hot seat during an interview. But let's not make more of this than necessary.

"Now, I've counted the people waltzing in and out of that door, and if the interviews started at eight, like the listing said, you haven't had the time to interview fifteen people. So, I doubt that what you've just told me is the truth. And I know I'm qualified to handle either of the jobs I've applied for with your little organization. I need this job, and I don't feel it's fair for you to reject me solely on the basis of one slip. So, I'll tell you what: why don't I go out and come in again, and we can start this interview over."

A muscle working in his cheek clearly indicated his annoyance, and Jordon drew himself up to every inch of his six-nine height. No one, absolutely no one talked to Jordon Banks that way. He stared down at the woman who'd just chewed him out royally and mentally capped his own temper. "No, Ms. Gilmore," he replied in a voice that sounded as frosty as the desolate plains of the Arctic. "When you go out that door, please continue until you've reached the exit sign. I'm sure you can find your way to the parking lot from there. It's been a pleasure. Thanks for coming in."

Starris stood and grabbed the back of the metal chair. She couldn't stop the waver in her voice as she made her appeal. "Mr. Banks, please. The least you can do is grant me an interview."

Jordon saw the sheen in her hazel eyes. His heart slammed against his chest. He looked away and made a silent entreaty that Starris not resort to tears. He was a sucker for tears. It was his daughter's most effective weapon. But this woman, beautiful though she might be, was not his daughter. She'd not only called him a liar, but had insulted his organization, as well. His baby. "Goodbye, Ms. Gilmore."

Jordon turned his back to Starris and didn't flinch when the door to his office slammed a few moments later.

"Is she here?"

"Quit pushing me, Jolie. I'm trying to find her." Danielle peered out at the bleachers again. "Okay, there she is."

"Where? Show me, Dani. I can't see her."

Danielle pointed her finger. "See, third row from the top in the blue jeans and pink sweater."

"She's beautiful," Jolie said, sighing dreamily. "You're so lucky, Dani. I wish Starris was going to be my mother, too."

"I know, but at least you have your father. If it weren't for Starris, I wouldn't have anybody," Danielle replied without rebuke. "And your dad's really neat."

"Well, I sure hope he gave Starris a job and that he gets here soon. Otherwise…"

Jolie didn't finish her comment and the two ten-year-olds, who shared the same birth date, chestnut coloring and curly black hair, also shared a secret smile. In girlish glee, large brown eyes, accompanied by a pair of dimpled cheeks, met shining black ones as the two friends linked arms and made their way back to the locker room.

Starris licked dry lips and firmed her shoulders as she went through a mental rite of building herself back up after the awful letdown of that morning. *This is a minor setback*, she told herself. *So, you didn't get a job at ROBY. There will be other opportunities, and soon you'll have your pick of several good jobs.* But even as Starris thought the words, her shoulders sagged forward just a bit. Three months had already passed. If she didn't find a job soon, she faced the prospect of starting the adoptive process over again or worse, losing Dani.

Starris emitted a sigh of frustration. In the year since she'd known Danielle Carter, the young girl had blossomed. She still felt a twinge in her heart every time she thought about the week-old baby left on the doorstep of the children's home. However, she could barely recall the bitter and sarcastic little girl whose defense it was to dish up scathing remarks upon introduction. Well, Dani had someone now, and although Starris knew that she was living on luck and borrowed time, she would do whatever it took to make sure that they stayed together.

Jordon saw Starris as soon as he entered the pool area and felt a shaft of guilt hit him center in the gut. She looked positively miserable, and it was his fault. Jordon prided himself on his honesty and couldn't understand why he'd lied to Starris. Added to his guilt was his attraction to a woman Jordon knew for a fact to be married. Slowly, he began to climb the bleachers. As his footsteps instinctively aimed in her direction, Jordon asked himself for the hundredth time that day what it was about Starris Gilmore that had prompted him to act so completely out of character and why he couldn't get her off his mind.

Except for her résumé, he knew virtually nothing about her. He'd only seen her one other time, and that was at a party celebrating the remarriage of Shelby and Nelson Reeves. Her husband had belittled Starris in front of a roomful of people, and Jordon had overheard the vulgar verbal assault she'd endured afterward. He still remembered the quiet dignity she'd displayed by walking away without responding. Jordon hadn't been able to forget that image of Starris. In all of his thirty-eight years, Jordon had never felt a pull toward a woman as strong as the one he'd felt that morning. Not even with Jolie's mother. And nothing in his mental dossier on women had prepared him for the power and female force of Starris Gilmore.

Her résumé suggested that she did not back down from challenges and that she was not afraid to take a risk—two things Jordon admired in himself and others. Given that, how had Starris come to marry a man who obviously did not appreciate her or her talents? Almost to her now, Jordon paused to steady his nerves. Nothing indicated that Starris had seen him. Maybe he'd come up with an appropriate greeting before he reached her.

Starris looked up, frowning, when she felt the heat of another body sitting unduly close to her. The bleachers were nearly empty. Why was this person trying to sit in her lap? She turned, a sharp retort poised on her tongue when her eyes came to rest on the handsome face of Jordon Banks. Up close, he was even better-looking than she'd first thought. He had a masculine bone structure, a strong square chin and underneath the neatly trimmed mustache, full, rosy dark lips made for kissing.

"So, we meet again, Ms. Gilmore," Jordon remarked, projecting a casualness he didn't feel.

His voice, a deep rumble, plowed its way through her body. Acutely aware of him and unable to suppress the sudden rattletrap beat of her heart, Starris rose jerkily to her feet. "Yes, Mr. Banks, we do. Please excuse me." She moved several feet down the bleacher and after releasing a deep breath, turned her attention to the young girls lining the pool for team introductions.

"Have I done something to offend you, Ms. Gilmore?" Jordon seated himself close to her again.

"Nothing that can't be rectified by a little more space between us, Mr. Banks."

"I like it here—next to you," Jordon drawled. He looked away and clapped when the announcer called Danielle

Carter's name. A dark brow rose when his gaze returned to Starris. She was jumping up and down and whooping it up like an audience member on the Arsenio Hall show.

"I take it that you know Dani Carter," he observed when she finally sat back down.

The light was back in her eyes when she looked at him. "Danielle is my daughter."

Jordon's heart dropped to his stomach where his tightening muscles silenced its beat. Things had just deteriorated from bad to worse than he could have ever expected. Why hadn't his daughter told him about Dani's mother, and that her name was Starris? If Jolie ever found out that he hadn't hired her best friend's mother, there would be hell to pay at home. He needed a way out of this mess—and quick.

Jordon was peeking at Starris with one eye and clapping his hands in announcement of his daughter's name when something occurred to him. If Starris was Dani's mother, why didn't they share the same last name? He waited until the noise died down, then scooted toward Starris. "I'm sorry, but did you say that Danielle Carter is your daughter?"

Starris shifted over on the bench. "Yes, I did. Why?"

Noting the space she'd again put between them, Jordon moved closer. "But you have different last names." As soon as the words left his mouth, Jordon looked down at his shoes. Stepchild, divorce, women's lib were just a few of the reasons that came to mind. Too bad he hadn't thought of them before he opened his big mouth. "That was a stupid remark."

Starris, trying to concentrate on the announcements about the swim team, didn't look at Jordon as she replied.

"No stupider than your lying to me about the job this morning."

Jordon's face heated. "About this morning, Ms. Gilmore. If I appeared rude, then I apologize. But I'm trying to put together a team at ROBY that will…"

Highly annoyed, Starris turned to face him and jabbed his chest with her finger. "Can it, Banks. The bull I don't need to hear, and I came here to watch my daughter swim. So, if you don't mind…" She moved again, this time several rows down the bleachers.

Jordon gritted his teeth and stood. That mouth of hers was definitely going to be a problem. If they were going to get along, she was going to have to learn to close it. Jordon sat next to Starris again and wrapped his fingers around her upper arm. His mind recorded the silky softness beneath his hand. Jordon ignored the tingling sensation it produced. He had something to say, and this time Starris Gilmore was going to stay seated and hear it. "Are you always this feisty, or is this a new trait you've developed just for me?"

Starris watched his lips curve in a tight smile and her normally quick-on-the-draw tongue stuck like glue to the roof of her mouth. Warm heat spread from the arm in his hand to her shoulders, and she just stopped herself from shuddering at the dark, sexy eyes fastened on hers. The devastating effect of that smile, even controlled, caused her stomach to roll. Starris tore her eyes away from his mouth. Her gaze roved downward over a large chest covered with a black sweater to meet a muscled thigh encased in a pair of heart-pounding blue jeans.

Starris absorbed a lungful of air and forced herself to remember that because of him she had failed to attain a job. "Let go of me, Mr. Banks."

Jordon secured his grip. "Unless you'd like to cause an embarrassing scene, why don't you just sit still and hear me out?"

Her eyes fired burning missiles at Jordon. "Oh, you mean like you heard me out this morning?"

Jordon relented by releasing her arm. "I had that coming, Starris. Look, let's start over and try and be friends—for the sake of our daughters," he added when Starris responded with a "why don't you drop dead" look.

"Our daughters?"

Jordon smiled. "Yeah. Jolie Banks is my daughter, and I believe, Danielle's best friend."

That's where I know him from, Starris thought. She looked from Jordon to the girls standing beside the pool and back to Jordon. She saw the mirror image, but until now, the child's last name had escaped her. Now, she felt a bit of a fool. Starris continued to stare, and her eyes grew even bigger as her memory abruptly cleared. This man wasn't just Jordon Banks. This man was Jordon Randolph Banks—J.R. to his friends—and the man Shelby Reeves had once said would be perfect for her. He'd also attended Shelby and Nelson's party and had witnessed the humiliation heaped on her by her ex-husband. What she'd felt then was nothing compared to what Starris felt at that very moment.

Jordon watched her composure crumble, and his heart melted. He was the one in the wrong, and Starris was the one feeling bad. "It's all right. I didn't realize who you were either until you mentioned Dani." Another lie. *Face it, Banks. When it comes to lying, you're aiming for king of the hill all in one day.*

"Please don't patronize me, Mr. Banks. I know when I've made a fool of myself."

So it was back to the sparring, Jordon thought with annoyance. "Look, Ms. Gilmore..."

"*Merde!* Will you please be quiet!" Starris said, cutting him off. "*Qu'est-ce que vous avez? Naturellement il est trés beau frére, mais ce elle n'en ai pas du tout besoin.*"

Jordon tsked his tongue. "Such language, Ms. Gilmore. But there is nothing wrong with me, and thank you for the compliment."

Her startled gaze flew to his face. "Huh?"

Jordon leaned closer, his finger tipped up her chin. "I said. Thank you for the compliment, but shouldn't you reserve that kind of flattery for your husband?"

"*Parlez vous français?*"

"*Oui. Je parle un peu, trés peu.*"

"If you speak only a little, how do you know what I said?"

"*Je parle trés peu.*" Jordon tapped his forefinger against his temple. "*Je comprends trés bein.*"

Zut, alors! A little French? The ease with which he'd spoken the language sounded like Jordon knew a whole lot of French, and he'd understood every word she'd said. If a hole had opened up just then, Starris couldn't have jumped in fast enough. She had cursed, told him to be quiet and called him a fine brother all in one breath, and he remembered Lonnie.

Mortified, Starris stood and looked down at Jordon. "Excuse me, Mr. Banks. I need to go to the ladies' room." She heard his deep chuckle as she walked away.

"A tout à l'heure, ma chérie."

Starris' back stiffened, and Jordon chuckled again. Served the little pretender right. He directed his eyes to the pool and his daughter, who had just mounted her block for the start of the four-hundred-meter butterfly relay.

CHAPTER 2

Pamela Shaw's tinkling laugh rang out. She stared at Starris with incredibly large and tear-filled brown eyes. "Girl, you have got to be kidding me. You did what?"

Starris squinted at her friend, irked that Pamela could find joy in her total humiliation. "This is not a laughing matter, Pam. What am I going to do? I was so sure I'd get that job. Now I'm right back at square one. What am I going to tell Dani?"

Pamela wiped the moisture from the corner of her eyes, then picked up her glass of Pepsi and eyed Starris over the rim. "I told you talking that fancy French would get you into trouble one day. Haven't I always said that?" Pamela cracked up again. "And with Jordon Banks, too. Girl, how much more embarrassing can it get?"

"A lot," Starris admitted. "Not only did I insult the man during the interview, I continued to do so at the swim meet yesterday."

Pamela sat up abruptly. "At the swim meet? This I've got to hear."

By the time she'd heard the rest of the story, Pamela was laughing so hard she nearly fell out of her chair.

"Can you believe it? Yesterday morning, I thought I had luck in my back pocket only to find that fate had me around the neck in a choke hold. And to top it all off, the man is Jolie's father."

"What!"

"You heard me, Pam. Jordon Banks is the father of Jolie Banks. That was Dani's best friend's father I insulted yesterday for heaven's sake." Starris pursed her lips. "I wanted to fall through the floor when I learned that little tidbit. What am I going to tell Dani?"

Bringing her giggles under control, Pamela looked around the restaurant. It was Saturday night. Families enjoying a meal of hamburgers, fries and colas packed the establishment. She spotted Dani in the video arcade. They had both dug into their purses and filled the child's hands with quarters to keep Dani occupied while they talked.

"Well, you'll definitely have to tell her about this latest set-back." Pamela laid her hand lightly on Starris' arm. "Now, don't start worrying. Dani's been in the system practically since birth. I'm sure she understands that sometimes plans get knocked off course. This isn't the first time an adoption's had problems, and I'm sure it won't be the last. Dani's strong, and as long as she knows you'll always be there for her, she'll be okay. As to insulting Jordon Banks, I'd let fate take its course on that one."

"It was fate that got me into this mess to begin with."

"True enough." Pam sipped through her straw before continuing. "But don't go borrowing trouble if it's never going to land on your doorstep, I always say. Or was that my grandmother? Anyway, if Dani does find out what happened, you can explain it then, and if she never brings it up, then she's none the wiser."

Sitting back, Pamela silently studied the effect of her words, waiting to see if Starris would shrug off the encounter with Jordon Banks. Pamela didn't think it was a big deal, but she knew Starris would place herself on the chopping block no matter who was at fault. If Starris hadn't blamed herself and tried to fix an unfixable marriage to Lonnie Gilmore, Pam felt sure she would have divorced the man a lot sooner than she had. Starris was loyal, and she had a large heart, but it was time she stopped running and found a man who would appreciate and love her for the person she was. Though Pamela's knowledge of Jordon Banks was sketchy, she knew he wasn't married and that the man had looks up the yin yang. Pamela suddenly giggled. Wouldn't it be a kick if Starris and Jordon Banks wound up as a twosome?

Starris glanced at her friend. "What's so funny now?"

Lifting her brows and shoulders in innocence, Pamela replied, "I was thinking about that lunch when Shelby said that you and Jordon Banks would make the perfect couple. Wait until she hears this."

Disbelief moved swiftly across Starris' face. "Pamela Shaw! Have you lost your mind? After today, I'd be lucky if I never saw the man again. Which reminds me. I need to have a little chat with our girl, Shel. She's the one who gave me that lead for ROBY. She knew Jordon 'J.R.' Banks was the executive director, but did she think to give a sister a hint? Absolutely not! She let me walk blindly into a situation that could have been avoided completely. Had I known…"

Both turned when they heard loud squeals coming from the direction of the video arcade. Starris wanted to scream in frustration and crawl under the table at the same time. Jordon Banks stood in the arcade doorway observing his daughter and Dani hug and dance like they hadn't seen each other in years. Looking at them, who would know that they had just seen each other yesterday and that they attended the same school?

Starris' gaze glued to the tan sweater hugging Jordon's solid back. Her eyes wandered lower, and she felt a definite rise in her pulse. There ought to be a law against wearing blue jeans the way Jordon Banks wore his. Even across the room, she felt the power of his virility and the crackling energy that seemed to surround him.

Feeling eyes on him, Jordon turned just as Starris looked away. As a former point guard for the Denver Nuggets, people noticed him all the time. He usually ignored the stares, but this time, he knew the eyes boring into his back were different, and that they were eyes he wanted to see again. Silently thanking the fates that had brought him to the restaurant, Jordon paused to hand his daughter a twenty, then made quick strides in the direction of Starris' table.

Pamela sat up straighter and patted her auburn locks into place. She ran a quick finger over her front teeth and looked at Starris. "Don't look now, sister-girl. But I believe Jordon Banks is on his way over, and by the look on his face, it's you he's coming to see."

No! She couldn't handle another encounter with Jordon; her nerves were already fried. Starris rose from her chair and turned to walk away from the table, but Pamela grabbed her arm.

"Sit down, Starris," she stated, watching as Jordon stopped to acknowledge a fan. "See, I was wrong. He's not even coming over here."

Starris chanced a glance up just as Jordon raised his head from the napkin he was signing and looked in her direction. He winked, excused himself and resumed his approach.

Starris looked down at her trembling hands. "I don't need this," she whispered.

Pamela glanced at her. "Girl, will you calm down before you start to hyperventilate, and smile because he's here." Pamela, taking her own advice, tilted her head back and grinned. "Hello."

"Hello," Jordon replied, his eyes on Starris. He waited for an introduction, but when none came, extended his hand to Pamela. "Jordon Banks."

"Pamela Shaw. It's nice to meet you."

Starris jumped when Pamela kicked her in the shin, but didn't raise her eyes from her lap.

Jordon took a chair. "It's a pleasure, Pamela. Good evening, Ms. Gilmore."

Starris stood again. "Excuse me, Pam. I need to go to the ladies' room."

This time, Jordon grabbed her arm. "Running again, Starris?"

Feeling herself backed into a corner, Starris raked a flustered hand through her hair as she sat on the edge of her chair. "I'm not running. I needed to…"

"I should tell you, Pamela, that Starris pulled this same trick on me yesterday," Jordon drawled. His hand slid down to capture hers, tightening its hold when Starris tried to free herself. "There we were enjoying the swim meet, or so I thought, until my date went to the bathroom and never returned."

Still tugging against Jordon's grip, Starris looked at Pamela, shaking her head in denial. "It was not a date. We bumped into each other."

Jordon pursed his lips. "That's not true, Starris. However, if that's what you'd like for your friend to think, I'm game," he said, winking at Pamela.

Starris used her other hand to grasp his arm with pinching fingers. "Why are you doing this?"

Jordon's expression didn't change. "Doing what? I thought we were having a loving and open relationship and now come to find out that you've kept our association a secret. That's probably for the best, though. I wouldn't want your husband to find out about us."

Pamela gave Starris a mock look of amazement. "Starris Gilmore! I thought I was your best friend. How could you not tell me that you were having an affair with the Jordon Banks? How long have the two of you been seeing each other?"

Jordon turned his head and ran an appreciative eye over the entire length of Starris' body, glad to see that he'd ruffled her feathers. After her little performance yesterday, it gave him a great deal of satisfaction, and it was fun. So much fun, Jordon decided to push Starris a little further by leaning over and kissing her cheek. He placed his arm along the back of her chair and looked at Pamela. "For a while now."

Starris made a silent appeal to Pamela not to believe anything Jordon said before turning to him and slamming her hand down on the table. "Look, you. I don't know what you're trying to prove by telling these lies, but this is not funny. You know good and well there is nothing between us. We met yesterday. Now, you tell Pamela that."

Jordon moved his arm to rest on her shoulders. "If you say so, baby." He looked at Pam. "Pamela, Starris says to tell you that we met yesterday."

Pamela giggled and stood. "Well, I do need to go to the ladies' room. While I'm gone, perhaps the two of you should get your story straight. You can start by discussing the fact that Starris is not married. I'll check on the girls on my way back."

Starris watched Pamela walk away, then turned blazing eyes to Jordon. "Why did you feel the need to do that?"

He leaned back in his chair, totally at ease under the hostile green stare. "I'm playing the game. Why didn't you tell me that you are no longer married?"

"What game, and it's none of your business, so why should I?"

"The Pretenders. You know, pretending to be something we're not, and it was important."

Starris would have responded except the girls chose that moment to run up to the table.

"Daddy," Jolie said, wrapping her arms around Jordon's neck from behind. "I asked, and Dani wants to go with us for ice cream. Can she come, Daddy? Please?"

Jordon unhooked and lifted his daughter's arms from his shoulders. He pulled her to stand in front of him. "Jolie Banks, while there may be some things that I have yet to teach you, manners is not one of them."

"Sorry, Daddy," Jolie whispered contritely. "Hello, Miss Starris. It's good to see you again."

For the first time that evening Starris smiled. "Hi, Jolie. Congratulations on your wins at the meet yesterday."

"Thanks." Jolie turned back to Jordon. "Daddy, can Dani come with us?"

"I'm afraid you're asking the wrong person, sweet pea. But if Ms. Gilmore has no objections, then it's okay with me."

Jolie turned back to Starris. "Can Dani go with us, Miss Starris? I-I mean will both of you come with us?"

Starris looked at Dani and knew by the way she deflected the glance that her daughter wanted to go. She also knew Dani would never ask. "Would you like to go with Jolie and Mr. Banks, Dani?"

Danielle nodded. "But only if you come too, Starris."

As much as she'd rather not spend more time in Jordon's company, Starris decided that for her daughter she could endure the man a while longer. "Okay, then we'll go."

"Great," Jordon murmured. He had observed the play of emotions on her face as Starris talked to her daughter. Gone was the anger she'd felt for him, replaced by a look of love. Maybe one day she'd look at him that way. As soon as he had the thought, a knot formed in his stomach. Jordon shifted uncomfortably in his chair. He didn't want her love. He didn't want any woman's love. "Jolie, perhaps Ms. Gilmore and Dani have other plans this evening."

Jolie looked downhearted. "But they don't, Daddy. You don't, do you, Dani?"

Danielle gave Starris a pass-the-buck glance. She wanted to go, but she would accept whatever decision her mother made. As she weighed her decision, Starris couldn't help noticing the similarities between the two girls. Both faces held the same rapt expression. Though their features were different, with their skin coloring and hair, they could easily pass for sisters. "Well, we were going to rent a movie." A sudden notion inter-rupted her train of thought, and Starris cast a knowing glance at Jordon. His gaze quickly diverted to the carpeted floor and confirmed her suspicions. If the answer was no, then the girls

would think she, and not he, was the bad guy. Because she
knew he'd set her up, Starris said, "But we can rent a movie
anytime, and I would love some ice cream."

Jordon's head rose sharply. Was that a challenge he'd heard
in her voice? The glimmer in her eyes told him it was, and
Jordon clenched his jaw. Okay, so maybe he could have helped
her out with the girls, but she didn't have to call him on it. And
besides, he wasn't backing down from any woman, especially
one with a mouth.

"So. Have the two of you gotten the story straight?"
Pamela asked, returning to the table.

Jordon stood and shoved his chair under the table. His eyes
bored into Starris. "Yes we have, Pamela. We're going for ice
cream. You are invited to accompany us."

Pamela looked from Jordon to Starris and smiled. "No,
no," she declined. "I have a hot date with a bubble bath and a
book." She gathered her things, hugged and kissed Dani, then
leaned over to place a peck on Starris' cheek. "Call me tomorrow with the details," she whispered. "I enjoyed meeting you,
Jordon Banks. Jolie, I'm sure I'll see you around. Ta-ta, everyone."

With a sinking feeling, Starris watched Pamela head for the
exit. She didn't want to be alone with Jordon. The verbal spar-
ing was tiring. She had hoped Pam would come along as a
buffer. She turned to face him again, but Jordon was talking to
the girls.

The girls! She wouldn't be alone. She had the girls.

Entering the ice cream parlor, Jordon spotted an empty booth and directed Starris and the girls toward the table. A teenage waiter set down four glasses of water and took out his pad.

"We'll get the ice cream," Jolie volunteered. "What would the two of you like?"

Jordon inclined his head toward Starris, who turned to Jolie with a smile, and said, "I'd like two scoops of pistachio in a bowl. Tell them to add whipped cream, sprinkle extra nuts and to top it off with two cherries."

"Got it," Jolie replied. "Daddy?"

"Vanilla. One scoop on a plain cone."

Jolie groaned. "Daddy, you're so predictable. You always get the same thing. Why don't you try something different this time? How about a banana split?"

Jordon's brow arched. "I like predictability. Things wrapped in fancy packages don't interest me. I repeat: Vanilla. One scoop on a plain cone."

Jolie rolled her eyes. "All right. All right. I've got it."

Starris looked away, knowing that somewhere in his response was a message meant for her. Jordon saw the frown wrinkling her forehead and felt instant contrition. The comment had been uncalled for, and Starris hadn't deserved it. In the car, she'd been pleasant and tried to engage him in conversation. He'd been brusque and short with her. She was making an effort, and he was acting like a jackass. Further, hadn't he been the one to suggest that they try and be friends for the sake of the girls. Jordon heard a throat clear and looked up to see his daughter staring at him as if he'd suddenly grown two heads.

He returned the stare, a question in his eyes. "What?"

Jolie held out her hand. "Money, Dad."

"Money! Aren't you the same little girl I handed a twenty to not thirty minutes ago?"

Jolie, taking offense with the remark, placed both hands on what would one day be a waist. "I am not a little girl, and that twenty was for the video arcade. This is the ice cream parlor, and you're paying for this date." She held out her hand again.

This is not a date, Jordon silently corrected his daughter as he reached for his wallet. He pulled out a ten.

"That's not enough," Jolie counseled. "Dani and I don't know what we want yet, and it could get expensive." Shaking his head, Jordon replaced the ten and pulled out another twenty. Jolie snatched the money from his hand. "Thanks!"

Jordon watched his daughter walk away with a frown. He heard the soft giggle as he replaced his wallet. "May I get in on the joke, Ms. Gilmore?"

Starris covered her twitching lips with her hand. "There is no joke."

His brow rose. "Then what is it that you find so amusing?"

Starris quickly composed herself and gave Jordon a blank stare. "Nothing."

"Oh, come now, Ms. Gilmore. I've never known you to be at a loss for words."

Starris plucked a napkin from the holder on the table and began folding down the corners. "You don't know me at all, Mr. Banks."

Jordon made a querulous sound deep in his throat. Why did this woman take offense at every word uttered from his mouth? He began to wonder if it was him or if she had it out for every man on the planet. Temper, he instructed himself remembering his self-talk just minutes earlier. Jordon forced a smile to his lips. "Touché, Starris. You're right, I don't know you. I'll tell you what, let's pretend we've just met." Jordon extended his hand across the table. "Jordon Banks."

Starris contemplated his hand, noting the long, tapered fingers and sparse clump of black curls beneath each knuckle as she weighed her decision. If Jordon truly meant what he said, she could try again, too. She smiled and placed her hand in his. "Starris Gilmore. I'm very pleased to meet you, Jordon Banks."

"Likewise. Now, back to my original question: What is it that you found so amusing a moment ago?"

"You and your daughter."

He and Jolie had been referred to as many things, but Jordon couldn't remember amusing ever being one of them. "Why is that, Starris?"

"Well, I couldn't help noticing how you came out on the short end of that exchange. Can I take it that little scene goes down often in your household?"

Jordon's cheeks heated both because of her remark and her intuition regarding him and Jolie. "Yes," he admitted sheepishly. "It does. And you want to know what the pitiful part is?"

"What?"

"I used to be a financial planner, and I can't teach my own child the value of money. Anything that little girl wants, she somehow manages to get out of me or my family."

Starris looked toward the counter where the girls stood placing their orders. "Well, daddies are known to be softhearted, and daughters have a natural ability to wrap them around their little finger. I know; I did it to my own father. My mother kept me from getting out of hand, though. If she hadn't, I'd have probably taken them to the poor house."

Sensing the pall that suddenly enveloped their booth, Starris looked up at Jordon. The black scowl twisting his face told her that she'd stumbled into forbidden territory.

"Jolie's mother is dead," he stated harshly.

A sense of sorrow stirred her heart, and Starris' attention shifted to Jolie. Losing a parent was hard. Not having a mother, especially at this stage in her life, had to be particularly hard for Jolie. Sensing his pain, but more of out concern for his daughter, Starris laid her hand on Jordon's arm. "I'm sorry, Jordon."

She just stopped herself from shivering when his expression hardened. "Why are you sorry? You didn't know my wife."

Though his voice, cold as a north wind, chilled her, Starris saw Jordon's attempt at anger as a cover for his pain. He must have loved his wife deeply to still care so much, and before she could stop them, her thoughts turned to her own marriage.

Love had played no part in her relationship with Lonnie Gilmore, although Starris had thought it had at the time. Her ex-husband had given her a harsh dose of reality in her value as a woman, and his very basic lessons had quickly adjusted her thinking. She knew her limitations in the love and romance department. And Jordon didn't appear to want her sympathy.

Jordon didn't miss the dispirited look on her face. "I owe you an apology, Starris. Gloria has been dead for more than nine years. I guess I'm still a little touchy about it. If it's all the same to you, I'd like to drop the subject?"

"If you'd like."

An awkward silence settled over their table. Starris picked up her napkin and began shredding it into little pieces. For a moment, they had really started to talk. Then as usual her mouth had gotten her into trouble. She glanced up, and finding his intense, dark stare on her, she looked away, seeking out the girls. Maybe it wasn't possible for them to be friends, but she truly hoped that their inability to get along didn't affect Dani and Jolie.

Jordon watched the little pieces of paper hit the table with a frown on his face. He'd done it again. He had practically jumped down her throat for no good reason, except that her innocent remark had reopened a painful wound he thought had healed permanently.

Glad to see the girls returning to the table, Starris took her bowl of ice cream from Dani. "Thanks, angel," she said, and without waiting for the others, dug into the gooey mixture. The faster they ate, the sooner she could part company with Jordon Banks. They were like two Chihuahuas snipping at each other, and he didn't interest her enough to keep up the effort.

Dani, noting that something was wrong between the two adults, leaned toward Starris, then gasped when the top scoop of her three-tiered cone toppled into her mother's lap. "Oh, Starris. I'm so sorry. I didn't mean to do it. Honest." Their hands tangled as both reached for napkins. "I'll clean it up," Dani said, just as a glass of water tipped over. Horrified, Dani looked at Jolie and Jordon. Whatever she saw in their faces caused her bottom lip to quiver right before she burst into tears.

Starris removed the cone from her hand and laid it in her bowl, then pulled Dani to her in a smothering hug. "Honey, don't cry," she crooned, smoothing her hand over the thick ponytail. "It's okay."

"But, I'm so clumsy. Now, they'll never ask us to go with them again. I'm s-sorry, Starris."

"Sweetheart." When Dani didn't respond, Starris took her face in her hands. "Danielle, listen to me. You are not clumsy. It was an accident. Everyone has accidents, and a little water and ice cream never hurt anyone, so there's no harm done. Are you listening to me, angel?"

Starris knew her words had not helped. Because Dani's self-confidence was almost nonexistent, Starris praised her for everything in the hopes of building her daughter's self-esteem. She desperately wanted her daughter to know and believe that she would always love her, no matter what. She squeezed Dani's slender body against her own and looked over her head at Jordon.

Understanding the silent plea, he reached out to touch Dani's arm. "Danielle," he said soothingly. "Li'l bit, nothing's been done here that can't be fixed with a little soap and water." Jordon pulled his arm back, purposely letting his elbow knock over another glass of water. "Oh, darn," he said. "Now, here I go."

Jolie reached for napkins. "Daddy, how many times have I told you not to be so clumsy."

Jordon laughed. "A lot, sweet pea. A lot. Watch out," he said right before another glass, tipped by Jolie, hit the table.

Jordon and Jolie looked at each other and broke out into laughter. Dani turned her head slightly to watch them mop up the water. When she giggled, Starris sighed.

"See, angel, I told you that everyone has accidents." She pulled another napkin and wiped the tears from Dani's face, then put her ice cream cone back in her hands. "Go on, baby. Finish eating your cone."

Jordon wiped up the last of the water and added his napkins to the sopping pile in the middle of the table. "Have I ever told you ladies about the time I helped my father paint the barn?"

Jolie heaved a sigh. "Only about a zillion times." She glanced at Dani. "But tell it again, Daddy. Miss Starris and Dani haven't heard the story."

Jordon leaned over to place a kiss on his daughter's cheek, then launched into his tale. When he paused to lick at his melting cone, Starris lowered her spoon and tried to identify what it was that made her insides tingle. She watched his tongue flick ardently at the melting cream. It was like a loving caress, and she would have given anything to trade places with that ice cream cone. Quickly squelching the thought, Starris lowered her head and stared into her bowl. What was the matter with her? She and Jordon couldn't exchange two civil sentences without deteriorating into a quarrel. Besides, she'd only known that man for one day.

She brought her attention back to the conversation when a bouncing Jolie said, "Tell them what Papiér said, Daddy."

Jordon observed the rapt expression on each of the three faces staring at him. Liking the attention, he smiled slowly, drawing out the moment. "Well," he finally drawled. "My dad took off his cap and scratched his head. I stood at his side, shaking in my shoes until he said, 'Son, I want to thank you for the colorful design you've painted on my truck. White is such a boring color, and I'd been thinking to do something about it. Now, you've taken care of the problem for me. But the next time I ask you to put the paint cans in the truck, I think it would be best if you checked the lids first. Now, go tell your mama we're home for dinner.'"

All three females sighed with relief and resumed eating. The girls were soon engrossed in a debate over the cutest boy in their class.

Starris furtively met Jordon's eyes. "Thank you," she mouthed. He acknowledged her words with a slight nod of his head.

As they walked across the parking lot to his car, Jordon moved closer to Starris and slipped his arm around her waist. It was a spontaneous move and one she didn't seem to mind. Starris wasn't always the sharp-tongued harpy she displayed to him. She'd handled Dani with a deep love and understanding that caused him to wonder about her marriage and what had happened to make her husband say those awful things to her. That she had divorced the man was, of course, good because now he didn't have to worry about having an unhealthy attraction for a married woman.

The other thing Jordon wondered about was Dani's constant referral to Starris by her first name. He knew some parents took a more liberal stance in child-rearing. However, he was not a believer in the practice. Not that he was anywhere near the perfect parent. Jordon glanced at his daughter, whose grip on his heart was strong. One day, when he knew her better, he'd ask Starris about it. But not tonight. He was much too wary of the verbal backlash.

CHAPTER 3

The following Saturday, Jordon thumbed a white tee into the lush grass on the eighth green and balanced his ball on top. He straightened and aligned his body and club with the ball. He went through a mental rite of tuning his mind for his drive: head down, shoulders back and arms straight. Then turning his body in a perfect twist, Jordon reared back and swung his club forward. Expectant black eyes watched the white golf ball sail through the air, only to land in a deformed, oblong-shaped sand trap three hundred yards away. With a grunt of frustration, Jordon let his driver slide through his fingers to his hand and headed for the golf cart. "If you value your life, Nelson Reeves, don't say one, single word," he muttered darkly.

Nelson hit the gas. Jordon's black mood had been their companion all morning, and it was starting to cast a pall on their weekly golf game. "J.R., if you don't want to date the woman, why did you ask her out?"

"I don't know," Jordon murmured.

"Well, the way I see this, you have two choices: You can show up and take the woman to dinner or call and cancel. But brooding about it will not give you any answers, and it's playing hell with your golf game. Make a decision, boy."

Jordon grabbed the top bar on the cart. "You know how I feel about this. I never want to get involved with a woman again. Why did I ask this one for a date, Nels? It was as if my mouth formed the words and spewed them out without my consent. I even kissed her. Me! I kissed a woman I hadn't known twenty-four hours, and you know what, Nelson? I liked it. I liked it so much I kissed her again. Christ, I feel like a seventeen-year-old with raging hormones. For God's sake, man, I practically attacked the woman. Why did I do that, Nelson?"

"What do I look like, your psychoanalyst? I'm in the cable business. If you need therapy, consult the yellow pages. But I'm sure you've managed to let your imagination make more of this than there is, as usual. If you had attacked Starris, the way you claim, why would the woman still want to go out with you?"

"Maybe she has a thing for sex-starved maniacs."

Nelson released a deep chuckle. "So, now we're getting to the heart of the problem." He stopped the cart and his laughter when he saw the beleaguered glower on Jordon's face. "Man, I know you think you have a serious problem, but if this thing you have for Starris is about sex, any woman would do. Hell, you have enough of them running after your sorry butt. I don't think it is. I think Jordon Randolph Banks has found a woman he could easily fall for, and now he's running scared."

Jordon jerked a club from his bag and gave serious thought to wrapping it around Nelson's head. Best friend or not, Jordon did not appreciate Nelson's quick analysis of a highly complex situation, especially when he was right. Nelson selected a club and walked to his ball, which unlike Jordon's had landed on the green. He birdied the hole, then leaned on the cart and watched Jordon try to defeat the sand trap without success. Giving up, Jordon picked up the ball and threw it on the green. He knocked it in the hole and returned to the cart. "Who the hell asked you anyway, Nelson?"

Nelson grinned. "You did."

Jordon peeked at his friend from beneath the brim of his golf cap. "Yeah. I guess I did, didn't I?"

Starris held the skirt of the dress in her hands and turned from the mirror. "What do you think?"

Pamela and Dani considered the dress. Insistent that she had to have a new outfit, Starris had dragged the two of them to Exterior Motives, an exclusive upscale boutique located in the heart of downtown Denver. Shelby Reeves had been rifling through the selections for the perfect dress for the past two hours. All three shrugged as they looked at one another, then Starris. "We think it's perfect," they said at once.

Starris twirled to the mirror again. "Really," she said, tilting her head back and forth as she examined the dress.

"Yes, really," Shelby replied. "I designed it, and I should know. Now go and get into your clothes and have Manny ring up the dress."

"That's right," Pamela added. "You're not the only one we're shopping for today. I have a hot date tonight, too." She turned to Shelby. "Now, what have you got to show me?"

"Something fabulous, sister-girl. Follow me."

Starris watched her daughter and friends walk away. Though they had tried to assure her, their words had not eased her troubled state and doubt dulled her eyes as she returned to the dressing room, doubt that had changed to outright fear by the time she reached the door. She hurried inside the stall and sitting on the bench, tried to breathe normally. She couldn't control the breaths, and when her nerves took over Starris knew that at any moment she would begin to hyperventilate. *Oh, God,* she thought, holding her chest in her hands when the dizziness began to make her feel lightheaded. Bending over, she placed her head between her knees and concentrated. It was a few minutes before she could sit up and lean back against the wall. Why was she doing this to herself?

Standing, Starris mulled over the question as she took off the dress she planned to wear on her dinner date with Jordon—if she didn't faint first. Replacing the garment on the padded rack, she hung it on the hook and reseated herself on the bench. You like him, her mind finally concluded in answer to the question. *Otherwise you wouldn't have stood there like an idiot when he kissed you last week.*

But she hadn't just stood there. Jordon's lips had touched hers, and a flame of passion had exploded through Starris. Their coming together had seemed natural. Their mouths had joined in a seductive dance until his lips had coaxed from her a basic and primitive response: her womanly desire for him as a man. Lost in the realm of sensuality he'd drawn her into, Starris barely remembered nodding her head yes when Jordon asked her out for dinner.

She fixed her eyes on the dress again. A classic chemise, the vibrant fuchsia silk had long sleeves and entwining beadwork that ran the length of the dress. Spring had come early to the Denver Metro area, bringing with it a wet and at times balmy March during the daylight hours. The nights were a different matter. But the dress had a rayon lining, and the stole would help ward off the chill of the evening. Matching pumps and multi-stoned earrings would complete the outfit, and if the hair stylist could do something with the wild mop on her head she called hair, she could quite possibly pull this off, however scared the thought of going out with Jordon made her.

Later that evening, Starris picked up her glass of wine and sipping from it, she leaned back in the bathtub and tried to catch the drop of water that leaked from the tap with her toe. She had been trying to relax for more than an hour. The warm water, two glasses of Chablis and the mellow sounds of Maze had done nothing to calm her nerves. Six years of abuse had done their damage, and when it came to being a woman who was sexy and fun, Starris knew she couldn't do it.

She finished the wine and rose from the water. Quickly drying herself, Starris reached for her robe and slipped it on. She belted the garment, stepped to the bathroom counter, and after removing the protective wrap around her hair, stared at her image. A rhinestone clasp secured the upswept style and the curling tendrils falling around her shoulders gave her a softer, more sophisticated look. Jordon, an unattached and well-known personality, would have women much more elegant and beautiful than she checking him out all evening. She didn't belong on the same playing field, and it might be best if she called and canceled their date. Starris left the bathroom satisfied that she'd made the right decision.

"You're not really planning to wear this, are you, Daddy?"

Jordon lowered the razor and looked in the mirror at his daughter. Jolie held his white dinner jacket from the tip of her finger as if it were diseased. Since arriving home from his golf game, she had been giving him nothing but grief. Though, that's not what she called it. She called her continuous stream of chatter helping him get ready for his date.

"So, now you're a fashion critic," Jordon replied sarcastically. "Jolie, will you please get off my case and find something else to occupy your mind? Like homework, for example?"

"It's Saturday, Daddy."

"Well, there's no use putting off till tomorrow what you can do today. Goodbye, sweet pea."

Jolie entered the bathroom and sat on the toilet seat, the jacket crushed in her hands.

"Would you mind putting my jacket back on the hanger and leaving? I'm trying to get ready for my date."

Huffing a breath that lifted curly black bangs from her eyes before they settled back again, Jolie ran a critical eye over her father. All the girls at school thought he was very good-looking. They also thought he was cool, and she did, too. She probably had the coolest dad around. He didn't preach to her, except about school, and when she had a problem, he listened. As fathers went, she probably had the best. But when it came to women, Jolie wasn't sure her father knew what he was doing. After all, it had been a long time since he'd gone on a date, and this one was too important to leave to chance.

"Daddy, tonight when you kiss Miss Starris, maybe you should put your arms around her."

"Now look, little girl. You've been pressing my buttons all day. I'll have you know that I already know how to kiss a woman, thank you very much."

"But you didn't put your arms around Miss Starris and hold her close to your body like you're supposed to."

Jordon was glad the shaving cream hid his embarrassment from his daughter. Because of their preoccupation with their still-going boys debate, he had wrongly assumed that the girls hadn't witnessed his indiscretion with Starris, and Jolie, finding him lacking somehow, had been critiquing the kiss all week.

"I don't need kissing tips from a ten-year-old. Besides, what do you know about it anyway? I hope you're not ignoring our talk and running around kissing boys at your age."

Jolie's face matched her dad's. "I, well. No, I haven't exactly kissed a boy yet, but I've seen a lot of people kiss in the movies."

"I don't remember any of the movies on your approved list that had kissing in them." His eyes took on a mischievous gleam. "I'll tell Alice that tonight you're only allowed to watch *The Little Mermaid.*"

"Daaaddy. This is serious. If I were a woman…"

"Which you are not," Jordon interjected, gliding the razor up his neck.

Jolie took a determined breath and persevered. "If I were a woman, I think I'd want the man kissing me to hold me in his arms."

That's it, Jordon thought ruefully. He pointed at the door. "Out, Jolie Kathryn. Go and find yourself something else to do other than drive me crazy."

Highly put out, Jolie stood and moved toward the door. "You're in a cranky mood. You should work on that before you pick up Miss Starris. I'll just go and find something else for you to wear."

"Stay out of my closet, Jolie Banks."

"But, Daddy."

Jordon closed his eyes and shook his head, his patience shot. "Sweet pea, please. Give it a rest, will you? I promise not to embarrass you with my dress this evening, but you have to give me a break." He walked over to Jolie and kissed her cheek. Then used his finger to brush a little of the shaving cream he'd left on her face onto the tip of her nose. "Turn up the stereo on your way out, and I'll see you downstairs in a bit. Okay?"

"He's here!" Dani ran to the front door. She flung it open and threw herself into Jordon's arms.

"What a greeting," he chuckled, returning the hug.

Realizing her error, Dani stepped back. "I'm sorry, Mr. Jordon. I guess I'm happy that I get to spend the night with Jolie."

"Don't worry about it, li'l bit. Jolie's just as excited, and she's cooked up a list of activities for the two of you this evening."

"She has?"

"Yep. I believe your first project of the night is baking chocolate chip cookies with Alice. That's something you don't want to miss because Alice makes the best chocolate chip cookies in the world." Jordon didn't understand Dani's sudden frown or why it reminded him so much of his daughter. "What's the matter? Don't you like cookies?"

"Um-hmmm."

"Then what is it that's bothering you?"

"I've never cooked anything before. Starris doesn't like to cook, and the people at the other place never made homemade cookies."

A dark brow lifted over eyes filled with questions. "What do you mean by 'the people at the other place'?"

"Good evening, Jordon."

One look at Starris, and Jordon forgot all about Dani and his question.

Dani smiled. "Doesn't Starris look pretty, Mr. Jordon?"

Her voice broke through his fog. Jordon blinked. He turned to Dani. "Yes. Yes, she does. As a matter of fact, Starris looks beautiful." He turned back to Starris. "Good evening."

Starris tried to smile, but her mouth refused to cooperate. Her heart continued to fluctuate at the sight of Jordon's tall, muscular build attired in a loose-fitting, dark amber suit. The color did wonderful things to his skin tone and highlighted his lustrous black eyes. She swallowed nervously and clasped her hands in front of her. "We're almost ready. Come in and make yourself at home while I help Danielle pack the rest of her things."

Jordon moved to a white couch. He waited until Starris and Dani left the room, then he sat and looked around. A screen divided one third of the large, pale green rectangle. The carpet, a swivel rocker and matching lounge were dusty rose; the furniture golden oak. Pink roses adorned the green accent rugs strewn over the floor, and the shelves of the entertainment unit were crammed with videotapes, books and other items. The room looked as if it had been tidied, but without the meticulous effort he knew Alice put into maintaining his home.

Curious about the screen, Jordon left the couch. Behind it, he found a desk and a white in-work placard on an easel. Several finished placards sat on a desk along with computer equipment. The scenes and images looked so real Jordon thought them pasted photographs until he pick one up and took a closer look.

It was an original drawing and recently done because the paint hadn't dried. Other images lined the walls and when he stepped from behind the screen, he saw still more. All had the words *RavenLove* scrawled boldly across the top and when he peered closer at the picture in his hands, he saw a tiny S almost hidden in a corner by the frame. Jordon left the office area and began making his way around the room. When Starris entered, he was staring, totally awed, at a *RavenLove* beachscape.

"Dani will be down in a few minutes, and then we can leave."

Jordon turned to her with a puzzled expression. "You're an artist."

Not knowing if the comment was a question or a statement, Starris moved to his side. "I consider myself more of a dabbler." She carefully removed the still-wet piece from his hands and took it back to her office.

Jordon continued his slow amble around the room. From the many pictures adorning her walls, Starris was much more than a dabbler, and modest, not a personality trait he would have associated with her. It also bothered him that she would try to diminish what was obviously an extraordinary artistic talent.

Starris watched Jordon, not liking the concentrated way he stopped and peered at each painting before moving on to the next work. "Um, Jordon. Would you like a tour of the house?"

He turned and after noting her closed body stance, smiled. He'd found out what he wanted to know. Except for the one picture over the couch, Starris had painted every other canvas and something about his interest in her work unsettled her. Why? "Yes," he responded. "I would like to see your home."

"I'll check on Dani and get us something to drink," Starris said as she led Jordon back into the living room. He sat on the couch again, trying to digest what he'd just seen. Rare, atypical, different and definitely curious were a few of the adjectives that came to his mind in defining Starris and the two-story floor plan she called home. While seemingly uncoordinated, some things had been constant throughout the home. The pastel colors on the walls had each been matched with dusty rose carpeting, and standing out as the focal point in each room was a snow-white item. The pale yellow kitchen had cluttered counters and a white refrigerator. The bathrooms, blue and peach respectively, had white shower curtains. White blinds broke up the monotony of beige walls in the guest bedroom, and Dani's aqua room, typical of a budding teenager, held a white armoire. The master bedroom had commanded his attention with its playful lavender and rose décor, and the things he could do with Starris in the white sleigh bed still held his mind in gridlock.

An unusual combination of colors, textures, kooky decor and accents, nothing in the house seemed to go together, and yet somehow it all did. Comparing it to his home, Jordon realized why: Starris' home was an extension of her personality. Each room had been designed to elicit a specific mood. In her home, he felt as if he could kick off his shoes and totally relax. His professionally decorated house had cost a bundle, and none of the rooms had any particular feel. Shaking his head, Jordon suddenly stood to his feet. His mental profile of Starris had just been shattered. Either his normally right-on-target assessment skills had disappeared or Starris had somehow bewitched him with some kind of alluring spell.

Dani's clumping on the stairs quickly pulled him from his musings. "I'm ready," she called to whichever of the adults was listening.

Starris met her in the hallway. She held a tray in her hands. "Take this into the living room and offer a drink to Mr. Banks. I'll be down in a minute."

Dani looked down at the tray and back at her. "I don't think we have time for drinks. Jolie is waiting for me."

Starris gave her a loving smile and a pat on the head. "I know Jolie is waiting, but we always have time to be polite and extend hospitality to our guests. Now, be a dear and take the tray into the living room and offer a drink to Mr. Banks."

Dani walked into the living room, her expression one Jordon had seen many times at his house. It was positively glum, and Dani was just as expert at it as Jolie. He moved to her side and took the tray. "What's the matter?"

"Nothing."

"Hmmm. A few minutes ago, there was a happy little girl here. Now, she's gone. Why don't you sit down here and tell me about it."

Dani sat. "It's just that I'm ready to go, and Starris says we have to have drinks. We're already late, and Jolie probably thinks I'm not coming."

"Well, I don't think it's as serious as all that, li'l bit. Jolie knows you're coming, and I promise to get you to the house in due time." Jordon affected a serious stance and held up a three-fingered salute. "You have my word of honor as a former Boy Scout. May I have my drink now?"

Jordon helped first Dani, then Starris inside the silver limousine sitting in their driveway. "Don't say anything yet. I'm trying to impress you," he said as the chauffeur closed the door.

At his house, both adults left the car to accompany Dani inside. Jordon opened the front door, and Starris preceded him into a plant-filled conservatory. What from the outside had looked like dark walls were actually colored glass panels. She looked up at the solar panels in the ceiling, then down at the center walkway paved in red brick leading to another set of dark polished doors. It felt like a small rain forest only not as damp or dank.

"This is lovely, Jordon."

"Thanks."

Starris bent over a lush fern and rubbed one of its leaves between her fingers. "These plants are so healthy. How do you keep the weather from affecting them, especially in the winter?"

"Energy-glass," he replied. "The panes are double-glazed to reduce heat loss, and the gaps between the sealed units are filled with an argon gas. The gas reduces the transference of heat from the inner to the outer panes." Tilting his head upward, he pointed at the ceiling. "The solar panels above us are specially coated to reflect heat into the space. Save your admiration, though. All I do in here is pay the water bill. I kill every plant I touch, and when I die, I'll have to answer for my crimes against nature."

Starris wanted to ask more questions, not only about the construction of the room, but the plants. Dani, who had no interest in the conservatory or Jordon's explanation, stood by the doors tapping her foot.

Seeing this, Jordon said, "I'll explain another day. Right now, I need to get this child inside the house."

Stepping into the foyer, a flowing and intricately carved maple staircase immediately drew Starris' eyes. It was a lovely piece, and she wanted to examine it closer. Jolie's throwing herself into her arms prevented her from acting on the urge.

"Thank you for letting Dani stay tonight, Miss Starris."

"You're welcome," she replied, returning the hug. "Now remember, both of you promised to be good tonight. Right?"

"Right!" both girls yelled in unison. "Bye, Starris. Bye, Daddy. Have a good time." They continued to scream as they ran off to somewhere in the house.

"Don't worry about the girls," a mature voice stated confidently. "I've been around young ones so long, hardly anything gets by me anymore."

With obvious affection, Jordon drew the woman forward. "Mrs. Gooden, I'd like to present Starris Gilmore. Starris, Mrs. Gooden, my housekeeper."

"Just call me Alice, child. Everybody does," Alice said, poking Jordon in the ribs with her elbow. "I don't know why J.R. is being so formal. We're quite the liberal household these days. I wear blue jeans now. And at the beauty salon today, I had all the gray rinsed out of my hair."

Starris smiled, instantly liking the sixty-something woman who barely came up to Jordon's chest. Alice Gooden, indeed, wore blue jeans behind a white apron tied around her substantial body. But whatever the stylist at the salon had used on her hair to rinse out the gray had colored the locks an interesting shade of blue.

"I know the girls will be fine with you, Alice."

Alice's face took on a speculative glow. "Would you like a tour of the house, child?"

"Oh, can I?"

"You just come with me," Alice said, taking Starris by the hand.

When they left, Jordon stood in the middle of the foyer, perplexed. Dani had run off with Jolie. Starris had gone with Alice, and here he was, supposedly on a date, without a woman in sight. He went into the library and poured a ginger ale. Then sat on the couch and tried to figure out just when he'd lost control of the evening.

CHAPTER 4

Except for Jolie's bedroom, Alice's and the kitchen, the interior of Jordon's house showcased a world of dark colors. Polished to a high gloss, the symmetrical and aesthetically designed furniture was no doubt expensive, but seemed much too fragile for his large frame. With the exception of the extraordinary pieces of African art in each room, Starris couldn't help feeling that the decor wasn't in line with Jordon's personality.

His suite, even with its wonderfully carved four-poster bed, seemed particularly somber. She'd seen many pictures of Jolie and others Alice had identified as his family throughout the house. None had been of his wife, and a picture of Jolie's mother had been noticeably absent in her bedroom, also. That seemed to contradict the deep emotion Jordon had displayed at the ice cream parlor. Yet, nowhere in his home was there a reminder of the woman who had caused those feelings.

Descending the staircase, Starris called a halt to her thoughts. Here she'd known the man for all of a week, and already she was conjecturing on what he should and should not have in his home. She tuned her mind to what Alice was saying, the name Gloria catching her interest.

"Now, I wasn't employed here when Gloria, the first Mrs. Banks, was alive, but from what I understand, the house was completely redone after their divorce."

Divorce? Jordon had divorced Gloria Banks before her death? He hadn't mentioned that. Then again, why would he? She was a virtual stranger, and he had no reason to reveal the circumstances of his personal life to her as she had none to reveal hers to him. And yet, Starris felt a strange sensation of hurt that the news hadn't come from him.

Unaware that she'd lost her audience, Alice continued speaking as she opened the doors to a sunken living room. Feeling guilty, Starris turned her attention to the room. The space kept within the confines of the dark décor. She crossed the floor, stopping before a waist-high, red marble pedestal. The Kuduo vessel, of Ashanti culture, had an elaborately fashioned lid and body and had probably once belonged to royalty. Kuduos, made to receive souls of the deceased, were filled with gold dust, jewels and the ointments used to annoint the body in the afterlife. The piece was exquisite. Starris could only conclude that Jordon either didn't know what to do with the art in his home or that he was perhaps trying to confer a part of his history in each room.

She followed Alice into the library, another room of dark colors, and glanced around the book-lined walls as Jordon stood anxiously to his feet. Not wanting to lie but unable to work up any enthusiasm for what she'd seen, Starris said, "You have a lovely home." The comment didn't match the confusion on her face.

Jordon smiled. *It's okay*, his eyes seemed to say. *I know this place is a tomb.* "Ready to go?"

Alice moved to the bar. "Perhaps Starris would like a drink."

Shaking his head, Jordon spoke up before Starris could respond. "There's no time for that. We need to get going. There is a special dinner waiting for us, and I don't want to lose the table." He took Starris by the hand and hustled her from the room. "I'll be late getting back, so don't wait up, Alice."

Starris barely had time to say a proper goodbye before Jordon had her out of the house and back inside the car. As soon as the car door closed, Jordon lowered his head and kissed her mouth thoroughly. Had Starris been thinking about what she was doing, and with a man she hardly knew, she might have stopped him. But in another world, a world filled only with Jordon, she parted her lips under the assault of his mouth.

Jordon's head reeled as he swiped his tongue inside the sweet, warm mouth beneath his. It was a soul-searching incident for him, but one he did not stop to explore, knowing that if he did, reality would spoil the tender moment. His hands glided up her neck to sweep over her hair. Finding the clasp, his fingers unclipped the hook, and he buried his hands in the glorious curls that tumbled down. Groaning a heartfelt sigh, he lifted his head and leaned back in the seat. He saw the passion shimmering in her eyes and heard the rasps of breath puffing through her slightly parted lips and knew she wanted more. He stopped Starris when she lifted her hand to her disheveled hair. "No, sweetheart. Leave it."

Her mind whirled. What in the world was she doing with Jordon Banks? She never encouraged or responded to men. But just being near Jordon made her forget who and where she was.

He pulled her closer, cradling the back of her head in his hands and stared deeply into her eyes. "What are you trying to do to me?"

Starris tried to look away, but found she couldn't. "Nothing," she answered softly.

"Then what is happening here, Starris?"

She closed her eyes. "I don't know."

He released her. "I don't know either, but maybe you should move across the seat before I try to find out." Starris started to scoot away. His hand on her arm stopped her. "On second thought. You'd better stay close to me where I can keep my eye on you."

Glad that she wasn't the only one flying without a net, Starris moved into his arms again.

Jordon smiled down at her. "We need to talk about something. It will help keep our minds off...other things."

"Okay," she agreed. "Tell me about the conservatory."

He shook his head. "I don't want to talk about that."

"Then let's discuss the art in your home. You have some really interesting pieces. Are you a collector?"

"Yes. I collect pieces from the Baule tribe that once occupied the African region of Ghana. I've traced my family to this tribe, so knowing about the culture also provides a personal history for me. Did you know that the Baule actually splintered off from the Ashanti and established its own kingdom in the beginnings of the eighteenth century?"

"Yes, I did. It was Queen Mother, Aura Poku, who fled her country with a host of followers and merged with the Guro and Senufo tribes. It was the Ashanti who brought the traditions of court and religious ceremonies to the others."

"Now I'm impressed. How did you come by your knowledge of my people?"

"In college. My minor was African history."

"Then you and I can look forward to some interesting discussions. But I don't want to talk about Africa or its art."

"Then what would you like to talk about?"

"This," he replied, lowering his head again. Starris returned the kiss with such fervor, his head spun. No one knew better than Jordon Banks how devious women could be. He pushed the thought aside and clung desperately to the belief that the woman in his arms and her response to him was genuine. Breathing scarce breaths, he lifted his head. "Enough, sweetheart. This is our first date, and we haven't even had dinner, so here's the plan: I'll try to control myself, but you have to promise me two things."

Struggling for air herself, Starris opened her eyes and scrounged her mind for an appropriate response. "What?"

"Stop looking at me as if you want to be ravished, and please—take your hand off my thigh."

In a million years and given as many hints, Starris never would have guessed the location of her dinner date with Jordon. She stepped from the limousine, her eyes wide with disbelief as Jordon led her into a semi-enclosed alcove. Along with a couple of space heaters, all the accouterments were present: a cloth-covered table, bone china, shining crystal, red roses, wine and candlelight. It was wonderfully exciting, incredibly romantic, and all the worrying she'd done had been for naught. Still, Starris couldn't believe that Jordon had insisted that they dress in evening wear to have dinner in Denver's City Park.

"I hope you don't mind, Starris. I wanted our first date to be without the interruptions that sometimes occur when I enter a public place."

Thoroughly fascinated, she made a sluggish turn to gape at him. "This is perfect."

Blushing in the glow of her smile, Jordon took her hand and guided Starris to a chair. Seated, she watched two men unload the back of a white van. Soon appetizing dishes of minestrone soup, salad, spinach-and-cheese-stuffed calzones, spaghetti and bread sticks, minus the garlic and dripping in butter, filled the table.

"I hope you like Italian cuisine. It's one of my favorites, along with Chinese, Mexican, Thai, French, Continental and especially seafood."

Starris laughed. "I love Italian food, and it sounds like there isn't much that you don't like."

"I'm not too fond of Indian fare or raw fish. And rabbit food turns me off totally."

"You're a man after my own heart," Starris remarked. "Eating is a favorite pastime of mine, but you didn't mentioned jelly doughnuts."

"I love jelly doughnuts! I like cherry the best. What about you?"

"Raspberry."

A man after her heart. The compliment pleased Jordon immensely. He raised the tulip-shaped glass, approved the burgundy Claret, then watched Starris encourage the waiter to fill her plate with portions of everything. She picked up her fork and glanced eagerly at Jordon. He picked up his own fork and watched approvingly as Starris dug hers heartily into the spaghetti.

Starris was a perplexing personality and a mass of contradictions, which like an intricate puzzle, Jordon felt compelled to decipher. He set his fork down and fired the first of his many questions. "What is RavenLove?"

She'd expected Jordon to bring up the paintings again and decided to answer honestly. "RavenLove is the creative imaginings and copyrighted logo for a line of greeting cards I designed because I was tired of buying cards for family members and friends with plants, animals or caricatures since the stores stocked no cards with images that resembled me."

Jordon picked up his wineglass and leaned back. "I can't say that I frequent gift shops all that often, but I have heard my sisters and Alice complain about the problem. I believe they solved it by mail-ordering their cards."

Starris nodded. "But why should we have to order our cards, when there are tons of stores selling greeting cards in Colorado. I'm hoping to be one of several people that change that."

"But all of your designs, at least the ones I saw, were African-American images in romantic settings. That would seem to limit your line."

"Our people fall in love just like anyone else, or don't you agree?"

Jordon smiled, noting the sparkle in her eyes. "Of course."

"Good. And I do plan to expand my designs. RavenLove has been test-marketed in four major cities, Denver included, and you know what?"

"What?" he responded, truly interested.

"The tests went extremely well. The line proved very popular with consumers. Right now, I'm supplying several gifts shops in the area, and I have a small contract with one of the main players."

"That's great," Jordon said, watching Starris attack one of the sausages on her plate.

Starris chewed and swallowed. "Yeah, it is. But one day, I plan to open my own specialty gifts and card shop."

"If you want to open your own gift shop, why did you apply for the executive assistant's job at ROBY?"

She swallowed the wine in her mouth and set her glass on the table. "Because I wanted the job."

"That doesn't explain the why, and that job is soon to be filled."

"I thought you said the job was already filled."

This was the reason Jordon didn't lie; he could never get away with it. "Okay, you've caught me, but I'm still not giving you the job."

Starris expelled a breath of exasperation. "Why not?"

"You're not qualified."

"Not qualified!" Starris quickly looked around and lowered her voice. "I'm perfectly qualified to be a gofer."

"The job entails a little more than that, Starris. I'm looking for someone with experience as an assistant. You have none. You are a graphic designer, and your marketing background is not a fit for any of the positions advertised. The hours are long and, as a nonprofit, the pay is lousy. Even if the salary was comparable, you're way too talented to waste yourself in jobs you're not qualified for in the first place."

Starris drew in a breath and let the air out slowly. "I know," she conceded. "But in order to adopt Dani, I have to find a job, and I've been looking for three months. I know that's not a long time and right now Denver is an employee's job market. It's a lot tougher out there than I thought." Starris didn't understand the pained look on Jordon's face. "I'm sorry, Jordon. I'm not trying to make you feel guilty. It's just that I thought for sure I'd have a job by now. But I'll find something. I'm sure of it, and Dani's adoption will go through without further problems."

The look Starris saw on Jordon's face had nothing to do with her revelations about the job market. It was the reminder of the time his daughter had spent in the child-welfare system. It had taken a year to get Jolie out of the system and then only after providing proof that he had fathered the little girl and submitting to a year of home visits.

Dani was a ward of the state, which explained her first-name relationship with Starris. Knowing what he knew now raised his respect for Starris, and at the same time added to the guilt he'd felt since running her out of his office. "Starris, I can't give you the executive assistant's job, and an offer has been extended for the job of acquisitions director. But there must be a capacity you can fill at ROBY."

Normally Starris, who prided herself on not accepting handouts, would have rejected Jordon's offer outright. But without a job, and with the looming prospect that she would soon lose her daughter, she was in no position to reject anything that would help her keep Dani. "What?" she asked, hoping she didn't sound too eager.

"What?" Jordon repeated to himself. He picked up his butter knife and positioned it as if to beat the table surface. He looked at Starris and laid it back down, then turned his gaze to the pond and the flock of ducks landing on the rippling surface to fish for their evening meal. Suddenly he smiled. "How about decorating my offices?"

The food in her mouth went down hard and Starris stared at him. "I'm not an interior decorator."

Jordon held up his hand to cut her off. "I agree, you're not. But you are an artist, which means that you're creative, and I've seen your home. I really think you'd do a great job."

"Why are you offering me a job now?"

"You really want to know for truth?"

"For truth," Starris answered.

"My daughter found out that I didn't give you a job, and I'm in the dog house. The other reason is that I'd like to help you and Dani. Despite what you think, I do not sit in a tower of power. I know how tough looking for and landing a position can be. So, what do you say? Do you want the job or not?"

Jordon Banks wanted something. Starris could tell by the avid way he leaned forward in anticipation of her answer. In the waning light, Jordon missed the astute sheen that came to her eyes. "What does the job as interior decorator pay?"

"First, state the amount of compensation acceptable to you, and we'll work our way from there." Jordon picked up his wineglass and relaxed in his seat. Starris Gilmore was as good as hired.

"Two hundred thousand."

Jordon swallowed, sending the wine down the wrong pipe. He doubled over in a fit of coughing. Starris smiled and waited until he'd caught his breath. Jordon eyed her when his breathing resumed. "Two hundred thousand? Dollars?"

Starris laughed. "No. Two hundred thousand ham hocks. Yes, dollars, silly."

"Starris, you can't be serious. You have no experience to back that type of salary, and I can hire an experienced firm for far less than that, I think. But that's neither here nor there. I'm only giving you this job because—" Jordon stopped and flushed warmly. He had almost put his foot in it. He couldn't tell Starris that he wanted her around, not yet anyway.

"I am kidding, Jordon. But I did want to see how far you'd go with this. Exactly why are you offering this job to me when you know I have no experience in the field?"

"Let me assure you that my intentions are honorable, and I have already explained my reasons. Now, as to the matter of salary…"

Jordon removed a pen from his pocket and wrote a figure on a napkin. He handed it to Starris. She shook her head no. He wrote another figure, and another when she vetoed that. Starris smiled and offered her hand across the table. She needed a job and, at the money he was offering, she'd be a fool not to take it, whatever his motivation.

"Jordon Banks, you've hired yourself an interior decorator."

Jordon returned the smile knowing a woman had outfoxed him, and since ROBY hadn't budgeted for an interior decorator, he'd have to pay her salary himself. He didn't care. He'd gotten what he wanted: time to explore the feelings Starris invoked and the basis for his attraction. She picked up her fork; he lifted his and began eating, too.

A plop on his head caused Jordon to look up at the sky. No, he thought as another fat drop of water landed square in the center of his forehead. Typical of Colorado in the springtime, dark clouds had rolled out from behind the majestic

Rocky Mountains and replaced the clear and starry night that had canopied them moments earlier. "Um, Starris. I think we're going to have to cut this dinner short."

No sooner had he said the words than the rain began pouring from the black sky in earnest. Jordon jumped from his chair and hurried around the table. By the time he reached Starris, it was too late. Soaked, he grabbed her hand and sprinted for the limo. They ducked under the umbrella the chauffeur held and climbed inside.

Starris took one look at Jordon and laughed. "You look like a drowned rat."

He reached out and flicked a drop of water from the tip of her nose. "You're one to talk, funny face. Maybe you should look in the mirror."

Tilting forward, Starris flipped down the mirror on the back of the seat. In the soft glow of light, she grimaced when she saw the mascara running down her face and hair plastered to her head. "Oh, Lord. I'm a mess, too." She began to laugh again.

It sounded so infectious, Jordon joined her. Another woman might be screaming her head off or complaining, but not Starris Gilmore. He liked that; he liked that a lot. "Yes, you are." He attempted to hide his grin when she turned black-rimmed eyes toward him. "But you're a lovely mess."

Jordon grabbed a hand towel and after drying her hair and face, did the same with his own. He sat back and wrapping his arms around her, pressed their bodies together until their wet clothing squished. With a necessity he didn't understand, he matched his lips to hers for a long, deep kiss. Just as she would have put her arms around his back, Jordon set Starris away roughly and scooted to the other side of the car. She heard his ragged breaths and watched his eyes close before he leaned forward and jammed his hands together.

For several silent, tense minutes, Jordon battled to abate the raging storm within him. For the third time, he'd been unable to control himself with Starris. He shouldn't have these feelings for someone he'd known for a week, but there seemed to be nothing he could do about the way he felt. When he saw her tremble, Jordon hit a button, and the car filled with warm air.

Admittedly, Starris felt chilled, but not a chill caused by the wetness of her attire. Obviously, she'd disappointed him, but she didn't know what she'd done wrong. She couldn't recall the number of times Lonnie had told her that she wasn't woman enough to satisfy a man. Jordon's reaction only offered further proof that her ex-husband was right. Maybe it was better this way. One disastrous shot at the elusive "forever after" had been enough her. Dejected, she turned to stare out of the window and sighed deeply.

Hearing it, Jordon's head jerked in her direction. He reached out and drew Starris to him, his mind a jumble of thoughts. It was a small concession on his part and an acknowledgment that he needed to touch Starris, too. Weakly, she leaned her head on his shoulder, glad for the warmth that settled over her again.

Long minutes of quiet passed as the car cut through the downpour toward Jordon's home. When it stopped, he quickly ushered Starris from the car and up the walk. In the conservatory, he didn't resist his need to hold her close once more. He pulled Starris into his arms and lowered his head. She tilted hers upward, giving him a clear shot at her mouth and closed her eyes. They flew open again when she felt his lips on her cheek.

"Starris, you are a beautiful woman, and you should be kissed. But I've had more than my fair share tonight. Taking any more will lead to something we won't be able to control nor, after only a week, are we ready for. It is not my habit to make love to strangers. I want to know you, everything about you. Then, and only when you're ready, will we take this relationship to the next logical level. I hope you understand what I'm trying to say."

Not only did she understand, Starris felt grateful, and the pull she'd been feeling toward Jordon strengthened with his words. He wanted to be her friend before they became lovers, if it ever came to that. "I understand completely, Jordon, and thank you."

Jordon would have said more except at that moment the front door opened, flooding the conservatory with light.

CHAPTER 5

Alice first stared at the two drenched adults, then, snapping out of her trance, quickly pulled Starris into the house. "Jordon Randolph Banks! What have you done to this child?" Without waiting for a response, she ushered Starris toward the staircase. "You just come along with me, Starris. We'll get you out of these wet clothes and into a nice, hot bath." She sent a look of reproach over her shoulder. "You take a beautiful woman out, and this is how you return her. It's no wonder you're a single man, J.R."

"I—we were caught in the rainstorm." Jordon stood, arms akimbo, feeling like a small boy caught with his hand in the cookie jar.

"Rainstorm! Where did you take the poor girl to dinner? In a park?"

Dripping, and noting that Alice had shown no concern for his welfare, Jordon followed the women up the staircase. Alice stopped outside a door a few feet from Jordon's suite. "You go right in there and get out of that wet clothing, Starris. I'll have a bath ready for you in a jiffy."

"That's very kind, Alice, but maybe Jordon could just take me home."

"After what he did to you this evening, I wouldn't trust him with my cat. Now, the matter is settled. You're staying here tonight. I won't have you going home to catch cold. Get along now. I'll be there in a minute."

Feeling very put-out by the whole affair, Jordon watched Alice mother Starris. He'd gotten just as wet. Where was her sympathy for him? Where was her loyalty? His eyes moved from Alice to Starris. She hadn't said one word to help him explain their predicament. Starris gave Jordon a "what am I supposed to do" shrug and stepped into the room.

Alice waited until the door closed, then turned to Jordon. "Why are you still standing here?"

His impatience forgotten, Jordon smiled. From day one, Alice Gooden had come into his home and, like a drill sergeant, taken over. She followed rigid schedules and expected him to keep them. She also expected him and Jolie to pick up after themselves, and when she needed help, they pitched in. At times, he felt as if he'd hired his mother rather than a housekeeper. However, Alice was much more than a housekeeper. She was a good friend, a confidant and quite frankly, a member of the family.

Alice tapped her foot on the floor and placed her hands on ample hips. "J.R., I need clothes for that girl, and I need them now. Move it, mister!"

"Yes, ma'am," Jordon replied, moving past Alice to his suite.

Inside his bedroom, Jordon opened a drawer in his bureau and took out a green T-shirt. He opened another drawer and removed a matching pair of sweat pants, then headed for the closet. Hearing his squishing shoes, Jordon grumbled as he crossed the room. "Can't even let a brother change out of these wet clothes first? No. Starris needs clothes."

He threw open the doors of a large, walk-in closet and flipped through the racks looking for a robe. Struck by a sudden thought, he stopped and looked up. Seeing the two white boxes, he dropped the clothes in his hands and crossed the space, reaching up to pull them down from the shelf. Jordon's

steps dragged as he left the closet. He sat on his bed, slowly
lifted the lid on one of the boxes and tried to sort through his
mixed feelings as he stared down at the hot-pink material.
Shelby Reeves had designed the gift he'd ordered, but had
never given to his wife. Jordon waited for the anger. When it
didn't come, he stood and removed the sleeper from the box.
He held it up, shaking his head.

Gloria wouldn't have liked the garment anyway. It was a
simple sleep shirt with tiny white hearts and a hemline that
stopped mid-thigh. There was also a matching wrapper.
Gloria had liked garters and lace, more along the lines of
Frederick's of Hollywood. He liked simple cuts and classic
lines and preferred the limbs of his women uncluttered by
hooks, feathers and spiked heels. Their differing tastes in
clothing had been only one of the many disagreements
between them. Jordon refolded the silk shirt, picked up the
wrapper and the box containing a sterling silver brush and
comb set. Gloria hadn't liked his taste in clothing; maybe
Starris would, and he left his bedroom in search of Alice.

Dressed in a navy sweat suit, Jordon stood in the doorway
and took in the scene in his family room. Mainly, he was staring at Starris. In the sleeper and wrapper, her face freshly
scrubbed and hair pulled into a ponytail, she didn't look any
older than the girls. His groin tightened, and Jordon quickly
tossed away that thought. His body's reaction was a clear sign
that Starris was no girl.

Dani and Jolie left the floor and sat on the couch beside
her. They placed their sock-clad feet next to hers on his
expensive Hepplewhite table as Starris wrapped both girls in
her embrace. His three women looked very cozy and comfort-

able. Jordon suddenly backed out of the doorway and strove to catch his breath. His three women! When had he started to think of Starris and Dani as belonging to him?

"You have a serious mental problem, Banks," Jordon muttered, and turning quickly he headed down the hallway. No way was he going into that room. Jordon had vowed that he would never get caught in the love-and-marriage trap again, and Starris Gilmore was wife material. If he let her, she'd come to him as a friend and lover, and with a ready-made sister for his daughter. Jordon grunted and entered his study. His long, thumping strides were angry as if he could somehow pound away the thoughts in his head with his feet. He dropped into his chair, pulled a folder toward him and tried to concentrate on his agenda for ROBY. However, deciphering how he felt about Starris and the fact that she was the first woman in more than twelve years to spend the night in his home took prominence in his thoughts. Jordon shoved the folder aside and left his desk. From a closet, he withdrew a gleaming gold saxophone. He stood facing the large bay window behind his desk and after hooking the strap around his neck began to play, his thoughts scattered.

The loss of his basketball career and discovering his wife's infidelity all in the same week had thrown Jordon for a loop, and he'd been wandering through life ever since. If not for Jolie, he'd probably be drifting about in the Himalayas or somewhere equally as distant. He could find no satisfaction in his professional life, and the constant metamorphosis had led to several career changes, including stints as a high school counselor, a financial planner and the formation of the DownTown Stock Club. His ability to predict the stock market had made it possible for himself, Nelson, and eight other investors to be financially secure for the rest of their lives. Because of his wife, he'd even pursued a law degree. Now, he was switching gears again.

At ROBY, however, Jordon felt that he'd finally found his match. He enjoyed working with the kids and the challenge of sourcing local businesses for internships or part-time employment. As word of the group spread, what had begun two years ago as a weekend program had grown into a fully funded organization needing a full-time staff. ROBY had signed contracts with companies providing employment for thirty youths and had a waiting list of at least fifty boys who had completed the training and counseling sessions. Jordon also had a list of more than seventy-five others waiting for entrance into the program. But without enough jobs or mentors, Jordon had temporarily suspended adding new names to the ROBY roster.

"Daddy?"

Jolie stood in the doorway, waiting for acknowledgment. They had a firm rule in their house: When her father was working, she was not to interrupt unless it was important.

Jordon turned when she called again and smiled. He unhooked the sax and laid it on the desk, then opened his arms. Jolie entered the room and walked into them. After an exchange of hugs, Jordon led them to the couch, and she settled herself in his lap. He kissed her cheek. "What is it, sweet pea?"

"How come you're in here instead of with us in the family room?"

Because Starris is in there and I'm afraid of what it might lead to, he answered in his head. To his daughter he said, "I needed to catch up on a little work and figured with you occupied with your company it would be a good time to do it."

Jolie pondered his answer as she studied his face. "But Daddy. My company is Dani. Miss Starris is your company, and I think it's rude to leave her alone by herself."

His daughter was right. It was rude to leave Starris to fend for herself, but Jordon also knew his limitations. He'd already proven that he couldn't keep his hands off the woman. Dressed as she was, sitting in the same room with her was a test Jordon knew he couldn't pass. However, he couldn't share these thoughts with his daughter, and he needed to give some type of response.

"You are absolutely right," he said, touching the tip of her nose with his finger. "I'll tell you what. Give me a little while longer to finish up in here, and when I'm done I'll come and join you and our guests in the family room."

The answer seemed to satisfy Jolie, and she climbed from his lap. "Okay, Daddy. I'll tell Miss Starris you'll be out in a little while."

Make sure you tell her it will be a long, little while, Jordon thought, watching his daughter skip happily from the room.

Starris became extremely anxious after Jolie's announcement that Jordon would join them later. She couldn't stop her eyes from straying to the doorway as if impatient for him to appear. Reprimanding herself, she forced herself to focus on the television screen and the movie she was watching with the girls. Three hours later, Starris reached over a sleeping Dani and picked up the remote. She clicked off the television and gently shook the girls. They had tried to stay awake, but forty-five minutes ago had given in to their drooping eyelids. Starris watched Jolie rub sleepy eyes with her fingers as she looked around the room, knowing she was searching for Jordon.

"Did Daddy come while I was sleeping?"

"No, honey. I guess he had more work than he thought."

Frowns of disappointment formed on the girls' faces. Starris couldn't help noticing again how alike they looked at times. She was careful not to let it show, but Starris was just as disappointed and felt a little silly that she had waited as eagerly for Jordon's arrival as the girls. She should have insisted that Jordon take her home. Keeping a firm arm around each girl's shoulders, Starris led them up the stairs and down the hallway to Jolie's room. Inside, they climbed into the matching baby-pink canopied beds.

Starris leaned down to kiss Dani good night. "I love you, angel."

"I love you, Mama. Thank you for letting me come tonight."

"You're welcome, angel. Sweet dreams, okay?"

"Um-hmmm," Dani intoned, snuggling down under the blankets.

Jolie sat up in her bed. "Miss Starris?"

Starris turned with a warm smile. "Yes."

"May I have a kiss, too?"

Starris couldn't cross to the bed fast enough. Jolie's voice had held a plea and the wide, black eyes, so much like Jordon's, pulled at her maternal heartstrings. Jolie's arms wrapped around her neck and, after receiving a big, wet kiss on her cheek she settled herself under the covers. She gave Starris a sleepy smile any mother would love.

"Thank you," she said, and closed her eyes.

Starris walked to the door and after a last look at the girls, turned off the light and closed the door. She walked slowly down the corridor to her room, her thoughts on Jordon and why he had elected not to spend time with the girls that evening. *Am I the reason,* she wondered?

Saddened, she climbed into bed and lay on her back, staring up at the ceiling. She told herself she was waiting for sleep, but she was really waiting for the sound of footsteps outside her door. A lone tear slipped down her cheek, and Starris wiped it away angrily. Jordon might not have wanted to spend any more time with her, but was it too much to ask that he show common courtesy? *He could have taken one minute to come and say he was too busy to join them instead of leaving me—I mean, the girls— sitting there waiting on him all night.*

Her next thought drew her brows together. Maybe he hadn't been able to come. Maybe he had fallen and knocked himself unconscious. Then, mad at herself for showing concern for him when he'd shown none for them, Starris sat up, punched her pillow a few times and flopped back down again. If he had fallen, it served the big lug head right. And she hoped the knot on his head was huge.

Unable to rid herself of the image of Jordon lying bleeding on the carpet, Starris rose from the bed and pulled on the hot-pink robe. She just wanted to make sure he was okay, and if he was, she had some questions and concerns about the job. She should ask Jordon about them, shouldn't she?

From the doorway, Starris quickly surveyed the study. Large, bulky furniture, more befitting a man of Jordon's caliber filled the space. Behind the sizable, antique desk where Jordon sat with his head bowed was a credenza. Its surface held a computer, a copy and fax machine and a picture of Jolie. An enormous, built-in, glass-enclosed case took up most of the wall across from him, its lighted shelves filled with plaques and trophies. Two carved tribal masks hung on either side of the door, but the small, orange hoops placed at varying heights around the room threw her. However, they did provide color in a room that exemplified the dismal effect of using gray, black and brown.

Starris knocked, then stood timidly until Jordon looked up.

His brow arched. "Yes?"

It wasn't an invitation, but Starris entered the room and sat in the chair across from Jordon. She stared intently at his head.

"Was there something you needed, Starris?"

Feeling guilty over her earlier thought, Starris uncrossed her legs and placed her feet flatly on the floor. "I was just wondering about the job. When do you need me to start?"

Jordon glanced at his watch before leaning back and balancing the pencil in his hand between his thumb and forefingers. At almost one in the morning, Starris couldn't possibly think he'd be fooled by a question that could have waited until tomorrow. If she wanted to be seduced, he'd gladly oblige her, since his thoughts had been running along those lines all evening. "Right away, of course, Monday specifically. Does this present a problem for you?"

She shifted in her chair. "In a way. You see, I'll need a few days to arrange after-school care for Dani. I'm not comfortable leaving her at home by herself. I'm also in the middle of completing a project for RavenLove."

"I understand," he replied. And he did. After five years, the man Alice dated had proposed marriage. She wanted to continue as his housekeeper, but would not be staying in the house. Jordon had been trying to come up with a solution for months. He looked at Starris. Jolie and Dani were good friends, and she appeared to like his daughter. "If there was a way to fix this so that you wouldn't have to put Dani in an after-care program, would you be open to hearing it?"

"Of course, but I don't see how. You're paying me for a full day's work. That means nine to five, and Dani gets out of school at three. That's at least two..."

Her voice trailed when Jordon yanked open one of the deep drawers on the side of his desk. Starris watched, mouth agape, when he began lifting and tossing small orange basketballs around the room. She tilted her body to the side when one whizzed by her ear, and her frown didn't appear to faze him. Jordon continued to flip balls until he'd used up his supply. Then he left the chair, gathered the balls and returned to the desk. He dumped them into the drawer, slammed it closed and dropped into his chair.

The man's definitely got a problem, Starris thought, watching, waiting and wondering what stunt Jordon would pull next. With his brooding stare on her, it was hard to keep from fidgeting, but Starris forced herself to sit still and wait him out. The silence went on for so long that she jumped when he began speaking.

"Starris, I hired you to decorate the offices of ROBY. That doesn't necessarily mean you'll have to put in full days on-site. In fact, now that I think about it, a lot of your work can be done from home. Initially, you'll come to the office to learn the layout and get a feel for the atmosphere I'd like to project, and you will, of course, need to discuss your selections with me." He gave her a lopsided grin. "It wouldn't be an efficient use of my time to run out to your place every time you have a swatch to show me. But outside of that, I think we could arrange something whereby your actual hours at the office could be, say, from nine to two, then you'd be free to pick up Dani and Jolie when they get out of school."

Starris' mind whirled as she began silently listing all the positives. This job was turning into a dream come true. Great hours, money and time to work on her designs. Her thoughts came to an abrupt halt. Dani and Jolie? Starris crossed her arms and fixed him with a knowledgeable stare. "Okay, Banks. Spill it."

Jordon pulled open the desk drawer again. Looking up and seeing the disapproving frown on her face, he closed the drawer and ran an agitated hand over his face. His eyes went to the pencil cup on his desk and his hand automatically followed. Glancing at Starris, he pulled the hand back and after a moment of squirming, leaned forward to place both elbows on the desk. He laced his fingers and propped his chin on top. Focusing on Starris when she changed position in the chair, his dark gaze landed and stayed on her thighs. Hearing his sharp intake of air, a waft of heat blew over Starris, and she tried to pull the shirt lower. Too late, she realized that she was woefully under-dressed in the presence of a man with whom she had zero control. Why hadn't she thought about that before seeking Jordon out?

No femme fatale, that one, Jordon thought as the last sheet of his Starris profile fell away. His stare became more intense as his mind visually defined the parts of her body the nightshirt did manage to shield. *Rein it in, Banks,* he finally chided himself, and grabbed a pencil. With it, he began to drum out a beat on the desk in direct correlation with the pounding of his heart. He heaved a deep breath. "Okay, Starris, here's what I was thinking: You know my housekeeper, Alice," he said, asking as if she'd never met the woman. Starris nodded. "Well, Alice wants to get married, and while I'm thrilled that she's found someone with whom to share her golden years, it does present a bit of a problem for me."

Forgetting her agitation, Starris leaned forward, unaware that the robe fell open and the nightshirt gave Jordon a full outline of her breasts. "Alice is getting married! How wonderful for her."

Jordon's eyes darkened with a hunger that, had Starris been more aware of her femininity and his thoughts, would have made her leave his study in a hurry. "Well, you can express your joy over the union to Alice later. I'm trying to explain my earlier statement," he growled in a deep, rumbling voice.

Having her thoughts pulled back to Jordon, Starris tensed in the chair. She fiddled with the hem of the shirt, then folded her hands and laid them primly in her lap.

"Anyway, Alice has always been here to pick Jolie up from school. With a new husband, she'll want more time off. I'd rather not start Jolie in an after-care program if I can prevent it."

Careful not to move from what she felt was a relatively safe position, Starris interrupted. "Jordon, when I agreed to take this job, I didn't know it came with strings. I'm not a babysitter, and you hardly know me. Why would you entrust your child's care to me?"

Concern wrinkled his brow, and the tempo of the drumming pencil picked up considerably. "Star, do you like my daughter?"

Her heart jumped in her chest. His shortening of her name somehow made their developing relationship seem more intimate. "I think Jolie's wonderful, but—"

Jordon stood, then sat and looked down at his desk drawer. Starris sighed with relief when he didn't open it and start tossing basketballs over her head again. He began drumming the pencil on the desk instead.

"Then what is the problem? Our girls are best friends, and I've personally witnessed the love you have for Dani. Now, I'm not asking that you love my daughter, just that you watch her for a few hours in the afternoon, for which I will compensate you additionally. You already have Dani, and the girls will likely entertain themselves, leaving you free to work on your designs for RavenLove and..."

"Jordon," Starris tried to interrupt softly.

"However, there is a downside to this proposal. When ROBY reopens for business, I'll be spending some late nights at the office. I can't promise that I'll always be on time picking up Jolie, but I'll try to maintain a schedule so that you're not overburdened—" Jordon continued to ramble along with his spiel, the pencil keeping beat with his speech.

He was nervous. Nervous and afraid she would turn him down flat, which had actually been her first inclination. She wouldn't, though, because she liked Jolie, and the girls were good together. It really wouldn't be a problem, unless it led to more duties of this type. "Jordon, stop. I'll do it."

When her response finally sank in, he rewarded her with a dazzling smile. "You will?" Starris nodded her confirmation. "Great! Now, as to additional compensation."

"I don't want any money, Jordon."

"Of course, you do, Star. Now, if I had to put Jolie in an after-care program, it would probably cost me about one-fifty a week. I'd want the best for my daughter," he added when he saw her eyes widen. "And since you'll be using your own car and gas, I think an additional fifty should cover those expenses. Does two hundred a week sound fair to you?"

Starris took a moment to collect herself before rising to her feet. Another of his bad habits had become glaringly evident. If Jordon Banks did listen to her, he had a way of dismissing her comments without consideration. She leaned down and placed both hands on his desk. "*Sois tranquille et faites attention!* Now, you listen to me, Banks. I said I don't want any money, and that is exactly what I mean. Just because I accepted your job does not mean that I am a charity case! I will watch Jolie for you, but only because I like your daughter, which is more than I can say for her father at the moment. But if you try to slip me so much as one extra dollar for the privilege, I'll…" She left the statement unfinished, spun on her heel and with as much dignity as she could muster in the too-short sleeper, marched toward the door muttering in French.

Jordon caught something about a head so hard it would probably repel a knot, but couldn't hear the rest. His eyes stayed glued to the brown set of slender legs walking away from him, while his mind began working on a plan to do something about that mouth.

CHAPTER 6

Despite the angry words she'd spoken the night before, Starris awoke feeling relaxed and refreshed. Being in a strange bed had not deterred her from falling asleep once she'd heard Jordon move down the hallway and the doors to his suite open and close. Not being in her own home and having no real reason to get up, she stretched her body languidly and languished in the bed, her brow wrinkled in thought. At one point last night, she could have sworn she'd heard someone in her room and thought she'd opened her eyes to see Jordon staring down at her. "Let's not get carried away with this, girlfriend," Starris muttered. "You dreamed about the man all night long. Is it any wonder you imagined that he'd come to you during the night?"

She stretched once more, then flipped back the covers and hopped out of bed. She grabbed the robe, turned for the bathroom and a pile of color in the chair caught her eye. She picked up the green sweatpants and T-shirt. Her clean and dry under things were there, also. "No," Starris murmured, dropping the clothing. "Alice put these here, not Jordon."

Coming out of his suite, Jordon stopped outside of the guest bedroom, his ears tuned to the noise coming from behind the door. He heard the sound of running water and unable to resist, cracked the door open. He'd left the clothes in her room last night, then watched Starris as she slept. With her mouth closed, she'd looked even more beautiful than ever. But was that god-awful racket supposed to be singing?

Chuckling, Jordon closed the door and continued down the hallway following the beckoning smell of Alice's coffee. He bounded down the stairs with the thought that it was a good thing ROBY wasn't a nightclub. Starris' voice, raised in song, could split an eardrum. *Well, Banks,* he thought, entering the kitchen. *Let's hope you find other flaws in the woman, otherwise you're a goner.*

"Morning, J.R." Alice set a steaming cup of black coffee in front of him.

"Good morning, Alice," Jordon all but sang.

"Nice day out today."

Jordon glanced out the window. "Appears to be."

"The girls aren't up yet. Thought I'd let them sleep. They were up rather late last night."

"That's your decision," Jordon replied. "You know I'm not about to interfere in the running of your household."

Alice stirred the batter in her bowl and poured three ladles of pancake mix onto the griddle. "Blueberry pancakes okay this morning?"

"Yep." Jordon picked up the paper and flipped to the sports section. He perused the basketball scores, then looked up frowning. "Alice, do we have any raspberry doughnuts?"

Alice laid the knife on the counter and arranged the cantaloupe slices she'd cut on a plate. "J.R., why would we have raspberry doughnuts? The baby likes cinnamon, and you eat cherry."

Jordon's face split into a silly grin. "Yeah. That's right, isn't it?" Lifting his cup, he stood and moved to the patio doors. He unlocked and slid the glass aside. "The next time you shop you might want to add raspberry to the list. When I find out what Dani likes, I'll let you know. Call me when the others come down, I'll be in the garden."

Alice watched Jordon go with a smile. Finally, she thought. She'd been looking forward to this day for many years. When he'd hired her, Jordon had not held back anything about his wife. She didn't like to think ill of the dead, but Alice felt fortunate that she hadn't been around when Gloria Banks had lived in the house. J.R. was as fine a man as any woman could hope for, and Alice couldn't even begin to fathom why the woman had tried to hurt him so badly.

Ever since he'd brought his daughter home, Alice had been hoping that he'd find a good woman, not only to help raise Jolie, but someone to love him. Meeting Starris Gilmore last night, she'd had a feeling about her. Jordon rarely dated, and when he did, he certainly never brought the woman to the house. *Starris is the one,* Alice thought confidently. Removing the pancakes from the griddle, she transferred them to the warmer, then went to wake her charges and the woman she felt sure would be the next Mrs. Banks.

One pancake lay on the platter and four forks stood poised in the air to spear it. Jordon looked at Dani, who looked at Jolie, who looked at Starris.

Alice clapped her hands. "Children! Stop this! There's batter in the kitchen; I'll make more pancakes." Ignored in the flurry of clinking forks, Alice picked up her coffee cup and relaxed in her chair. She smiled indulgently, listening to the sounds of laughter.

"Got it!" Starris smirked at the three faces staring at her and plopped the pancake onto her plate. "I have the fastest fork in the West," she stated. "So don't the rest of you ever try going up against me again."

Jordon wiped his mouth with his napkin and picked up his coffee. He leaned back in his chair and crossed one lengthy leg over the other. "I didn't want that pancake anyway, and you'd think that a woman who has already gobbled down five would think about her children and not take food from their little mouths."

"You can forget about making me feel guilty, Banks. I won this pancake fair and square." Starris reached for the blueberry syrup, making the mistake of glancing up at Dani and Jolie. The girls eyed her plate with gluttonous expressions. "Oh, all right." She sliced the pancake and placed a half on each girls' plates.

Jordon folded his napkin and stood up. "I'm proud of you, Star." He moved to her end of the table and held out his hand. "Come on. Let's leave the children to their breakfast. I have something to show you."

Starris looked at the hand. "But I was going to help Alice clean up."

Alice rose, her unwrinkled face shrewd with understanding as she studied Jordon. "Thank you, dear, but you go along with J.R. The girls will help me this morning. Won't you, girls?"

Their mouths full, Dani and Jolie nodded their heads in agreement.

"Weeds!" Starris grabbed a handful of the sweatpants threatening to fall around her ankles and shot an incredulous look at Jordon. "You brought me out here to look at a bunch of weeds?"

Pursing his lips, Jordon gazed at his flower plot. His plants might not win any prizes, but she did not have to insult them. He used the too-big pants to propel Starris toward him. "My plants are not weeds, and they are very, very sensitive. So, if you are going to hurl insults, please lower your voice. And that's not why I brought you out here."

With one hand securely holding her pants, Starris used the other to swipe back auburn wisps of hair from her forehead and tipped her head back to meet Jordon's gaze. "It's not?"

"No." Jordon lowered his head. "I brought you out here for this." Matching their lips together, his mouth closed over hers. It was a good thing that he held her pants or they would have fallen to her feet when Starris lifted her arms to encircle his neck.

Lifting his head, Jordon locked his eyes with hers and smiled. "Now, I truly am full," he said. "I've been wanting to do that ever since you walked practically naked into my study."

Starris had the grace to flush before she pushed him gently in the chest. "I was decently clothed last night, which is more than I can say for this morning. If you saw me undressed, Jordon Banks, it was those naughty thoughts in your mind."

Wanting to rub his hands up and down the slender body pressed so enticingly against his, but knowing if he let go of her pants they would fall and he'd be lost, Jordon pulled Starris closer. He ran his tongue from her jawbone to her ear where he whispered, "I'm not sure if my mind provided an accurate portrayal of these sweet curves. Show me the real thing, Star. I'd like to make a comparison."

Giggling at his antics, Starris gripped his shoulders tighter when she felt the definite grope of a hand on her bottom.

"What you have is a dirty mind, and I refuse to encourage you. However, despite your claim of being full, I don't think one kiss could ever satisfy you. So—"

Shock replaced the teasing light in Jordon's eyes when Starris placed her lips on his in a caress that she controlled. Held captive, he stood, pulses racing, responding to her directives and letting her lips empty his mind of everything other than the woman in his arms.

Astounded and highly alarmed, Starris held her breath and squeezed her eyes shut as the enormity of what she was doing made itself known in her mind. She first thought to pull away. Instead, she pushed her mouth harder against Jordon's and tried to remember some of his moves from last night. She nudged the tip of her tongue against the seam of his lips until they parted. Then stuck her tongue inside his mouth, and not sure what to do next, she stopped.

Her agitation trembled through her, and when she started to pull away, Jordon fisted his hands on the band of her pants, held her still and took over the kiss. He initiated the battle, wrapping his tongue around hers, then forcing hers back and plunging his inside her mouth. Starris snuggled closer as tingles moved swiftly through her body. Heated, shaking and breathless when their lips parted, she sought support on his muscled chest.

Giggles, soft, but distinct caused them to jump apart. Starris grabbed frantically at the falling pants. Both turned to the kitchen window. Jordon's face burned with the heat of passion and embarrassment. Starris could only stare at the ground.

Recovering first, Jordon grabbed her hand. "Let's get out of here. Little people have big ears and even bigger eyes."

"You two get out of that window and load the dishwasher," they heard Alice scolding the girls as Starris stumbled after Jordon.

Jordon led Starris around the side of the house, then stood in front of her and stole another quick kiss. "Close your eyes because now you're going to see why I really brought you out here." Jordon led her some ways from the house. He moved behind her when they stopped. "You can open your eyes now."

The profusion of color that met her gaze took her breath away. Enthralled, Starris moved forward until forced to halt at the red brick border. The intense hues combined with the bright sunlight almost hurt her eyes as she scanned the multitude and colorful variety of blossoms making up Jordon's wildflower garden. To complete the scene, a snow-white gazebo sat in the middle of it all. The rounded structure, settled comfortably on a small hill, almost preened in its backdrop of a grassy green knoll and assortment of various-sized blooms.

Starris gazed in wonder at the picturesque sight. Then ran laughing and holding on to the pants back to Jordon. "This garden is gorgeous! How did you do this when you told me that you couldn't grow anything?"

Bowled over by her reaction, Jordon grinned. One day, he vowed, she would smile this same way solely because of him. "I'd like to take credit for this wonderful creation, but I can't. The beauty you see before you is the result of a temper tantrum and Mother Earth. Remember that hail storm we had a few years back; the one that damaged all the roofs and cars?"

"Yes. I do."

"Well, it also destroyed the one and only flower garden I'd managed to grow in all my years of trying. I was so mad that I marched out here and scattered all the remaining seeds I had. The next year I had flowers. I thought it was pretty cool and every year since, I buy and scatter seeds, then leave it alone. It seems that as long as I have nothing to do with my plants and flowers, they thrive. These are the spring flowers, there will be more in the summer."

Hand-in-hand, Starris followed Jordon up the steps and into the gazebo. He sat on the wooden bench and pulled her down to his lap. In between long moments when they stopped exchanging kisses, she stared in awe at the utopia of splendor around them. This colorful place she could associate with Jordon. It was so unlike his home's dark interior.

"Jordon, I have a question that I hope will not offend you, and I'm only asking because I'm truly interested." She framed his face with her hands. "Do you promise not to get mad, Jordy?"

"I like that. Say it again."

Starris frowned. "Say what again?"

He kissed the tip of her nose. "My name. I like that way you say my name."

"Will you be serious?"

"Not until you say my name again."

"Jordy. Jordy. Jordy. Are you satisfied now?"

"Nope. I still need to see your body." He placed his mouth in the space between her breasts.

"Jordon, you said you'd wait until I was ready."

He nodded. "I did, and I will. Okay, shoot with the question."

"Well, it's your house. Out here, you've surrounded your-self with bright colors, but inside your home, it's so dark."

Gravely, he examined the expectant, multifarious eyes shining back at him. Starris lived in a world of colors. The decor in his home would never suit her taste or personality. "Some years back, I wanted everything changed, and I let the decorator have a free hand. I don't really like the results."

"Then why don't you have it redone?"

Jordon made a mental note to do something about his house. Starris had to feel comfortable in his home. He categorically ignored the notation his mind made that this was the first time since his divorce that he wanted to do something solely to please a woman. "Maybe one day I will," he said with a dismissive shrug.

Starris laid her head on his shoulder, and Jordon cradled her body. The droning buzz of pollinating bees didn't disturb the peaceful, companionable quiet they shared in the Edenic paradise. Jordon rested his cheek on top of her curls, his thoughts on breakfast and the laughter and fun that had flourished at his table. His gaze drifted down to the curly head lying comfortably beneath his chin. Idyllic thoughts of their short time together overruled critical mistrust, and for the first time in many years, Jordon relaxed in the presence of a woman. Starris was not an intrusion in his life. Rather she was an asset, one that Jordon had just come to realize he wanted to keep.

"If you don't have any plans, I'd like you and Dani to spend the day here with Jolie and me."

Something in his voice made Starris sit up and take notice. He tried to hide it, but she could see that her answer was important to him. However, the congenial host he'd played that morning did little to remove the doubts about herself or him. Jordon had been blowing hot and cold since she'd met him. Last night, he'd stayed away on purpose. Now, he wanted her to spend the day with him. She couldn't keep up with his constant flip-flopping. And if what she was reading in the inky depth of his eyes was any indication of what Jordon really wanted, Starris also knew there was no way she could satisfy it or him.

Feeling the slight tremble of her body and her indecision, Jordon tipped her chin and laid his mouth upon hers, tender and searching in his play to elicit a positive response from her. Lightheaded when the kiss ended, Starris made a desperate bid to gather her wits. "I can't, Jordon. I should...need to be getting home."

Her mouth said one thing, but her passion-drunk eyes and kiss-swollen lips said another. Quick to take advantage of his hold over her, Jordon kissed her again.

Starris felt her body swell with desire. "Jordon, please."

"Stay, Star," he whispered against her moist mouth. "Stay with me."

She heard the plea and fell under the spell of his jet-colored gaze. With effort, she managed to release herself from the stare and looked down at her attire. "I don't have anything to wear."

Jordon's eyes wandered her face until their gazes met again and fused in longing. "I can solve that problem for you, Star. If you'll let me, I'll solve all of your problems."

Using her teeth, Starris cracked open another pistachio nut and discarded the empty shell in the small trashcan at her side. She flipped another page of the *Essence* magazine in her lap and continued to observe Jordon and the girls, mostly Jordon. For a while, she had refereed the tennis game. The girls thought Jordon was cheating, calling some of their balls out of bounds when they were clearly in. Starris had to admit that she thought he was cheating, too, but couldn't back up the claim because instead of watching the ball she had been staring at the lithe brown body swathed in white. Upset by her lack of attention, the girls had dismissed Starris from her revered position as arbitrator. After which, she had returned to the patio and continued to watch Jordon.

Jordon had solved her clothing problem. A few hours ago, he'd gone to the store. He'd returned with new CDs for Jolie and Dani and a large package of steaks and a colorful silk scarf for Alice. For Starris, he'd purchased a red, sleeveless top, blue jeans and a large bag of pistachio nuts. He'd correctly guessed her size from looking at her or so he'd said.

It was a heady feeling knowing that Jordon wanted to be the one to solve her problems, and he was the first man ever to offer. She raised her hand to her mouth. Her eyes sought and found Jordon again, admiring the long strides and rippling muscles when he swung his racket to return a volley from Jolie. He'd been stealing kisses all day, and they had not exchanged a single angry word. Starris shivered and rubbed at the goose bumps on her arms. Jordon already had her walking on edge, and with the tiniest of shoves, she could easily fall in love with him. Then she really would have a problem.

Alice stepped onto the patio, calling a halt to her thoughts and the tennis game. The game ended posthaste, and Starris observed the self-assurance Alice displayed in her position as caretaker of Jordon's home. One word had Jordon and Jolie hopping like live wires. Even Dani had quickly fallen into line. How does she do it, Starris wondered.

Watching Alice, Starris couldn't help remembering how hard she tried with Lonnie, and his scathing mockery of her efforts. The first time he'd humiliated her in front of others had been just two weeks after their marriage, at their first dinner party. Starris had spent a week cleaning the house from top to bottom and had carefully planned and cooked the food on the menu. On the night of the dinner, Lonnie had seen one of the guests wiping his knife with his napkin. Cursing a blue streak, he'd jumped up from his chair and collected all the utensils from the table. He'd ordered Starris to the kitchen, then stood behind her while she'd washed and dried each piece by hand before putting them back on the table.

Before leaving, the man's wife had apologized profusely, saying that it was her husband's habit to always wipe his knife with his napkin. He had not meant to imply that the utensil was dirty, but Starris, already humiliated beyond belief, hadn't been able to respond. She soon came to learn that the incident was only the first of many that would plague her marriage. Starris lowered her head. There was no way she could ever step into Alice's shoes.

Stopping by her chair, and forgetting himself and their audience, Jordon leaned over and dropped a quick kiss on her mouth. "How are you doing, baby?"

Nonplussed when she saw the smiling faces of Dani and Jolie, Starris hastily left the chair and went into the house. Jordon watched her disappear through the patio door and exchanged a smile with Alice, then turned to fire up the electric grill while Alice shooed the girls into the house. Pacing the floor of the downstairs bathroom, Starris tried to bring her heightened emotions back under control. She stopped before the mirror and examined her heated face. Why had Jordon kissed her, so blatantly in front of the girls? She turned away and sat on the toilet seat. Starris was in trouble, and she knew it. Jordon was swiftly moving their relationship into a realm she couldn't handle. The sooner she gathered Dani and got away from him the better. She jumped to her feet when a rap sounded on the door.

"Starris? Are you okay?"

Sighing with relief, Starris crossed the floor and opened the door. Feeling the need to ground herself in a reality she could understand, she grabbed Dani in a crushing hug, grateful when the child hugged her back.

"Mama, what's wrong?"

Starris released Dani reluctantly, but purposefully. She couldn't use her daughter for comfort. She returned to the counter and, after splashing her face with cold water, grabbed a towel and dried herself. She replaced the towel and turned to Dani with a convincing smile. She wrapped an arm around her shoulders and walked them both from the room. "Nothing's wrong, angel. Let's go to the kitchen and see if we can help Alice."

Seasoned and cooked to perfection, the thick, juicy steak would have normally had her mouth watering.

Tonight, the meat sat on her plate along with the corn on the cob, baked potato and green beans, and Starris could only stare at the food.

"Mama, you're not eating," Dani pointed out. "Are you sure you're okay?"

Dani's use of the parental term caught Jordon completely unaware. More than pleased, he looked first at Dani, and then at the plate Starris hadn't touched. The joy fell from his face. Starris had been quiet all during the meal, and the animation that had accompanied breakfast was noticeably absent. It had to be that last kiss that upset her, probably because he'd done it in front of the girls. Briefly, he wondered why it hadn't bothered him, too. Although apprehensive of the rush of adrenaline that seized him in her presence, Jordon felt powerless to stop himself from commandeering them both into a relationship he wasn't sure he wanted either.

Starris looked around the table and felt a twinge of guilt for casting gloom on what had otherwise been a truly wonderful day. She picked up her knife and fork, but felt Jordon's hand on her arm before she could cut into the steak.

"Dani, your mother is fine. We've had a busy day, and I suspect she's just tired." Dani resumed eating, and Jordon leaned toward Starris with words for her ears only. "Baby, I know I upset you, and I'm sorry. If you don't want to eat, then don't do it on our account."

For the first time since sitting down to dinner, Starris raised her eyes to Jordon. The man was incredible, and all thoughts that she was not woman enough for him flew out the window. Maybe if she tried really hard this time, the kinship they had established could be something more than friendship.

You tried really hard with Lonnie, her mind reminded her.

No, this was different. Jordon was not Lonnie, and Jordon, after only a few days, had become attuned to her needs and feelings in a way her ex-husband never had. If she didn't try with Jordon, especially when it felt so right, when would she? Starris glanced at Jordon again and returned his smile of encouragement. *I will try,* Starris thought. She would try and she would learn, and if Jordon would help her a little bit, then Starris felt she might have a shot at a lasting, if not loving, relationship.

Jordon moved his last game piece to home. He looked up at the three female faces staring at him. "Soooorry," he said, and broke into laughter.

Starris watched him fall back against the couch, chuckling devilishly. He had won all but one of the five games, and each time had rubbed it in their faces. Jordon was a bad loser and an even worse winner. She reached for a pillow and winked at the girls. They reached for pillows of their own and before Jordon knew what was happening, three pillows came down on his head in rapid succession.

"Stop," he said, laughing as he tried to fight them off. "It's in the rules that you can't beat up the winner."

That earned him another pillow in the face. Jordon's hands grabbed the body closest to him. When he realized it was Starris, he pulled her into his lap and kissed her on the cheek. "There," he said. "That ought to pacify you. You've just received a most prestigious prize, a kiss from the king of Sorry."

"Hey," Jolie yelled. "That's not fair! You've been kissing Miss Starris all day. What about me and Dani? We lost, too."

"That's right, you did." Jordon rose from the floor and placed his hands on his waist. "Will all the losers please line up, and the winner will gladly bestow kisses."

There was much jostling and pushing before Starris and the girls finally formed a straight line, and Jordon smiled when he saw Starris standing proudly at the front. She stepped forward and lifted her cheek.

Jordon gave her a stern look. "You've already had your kiss. Move to the back of the line, and if there are any left, I might give you another." When she'd taken her place, Jordon said, "Now, listen carefully to these instructions because I am only allowed to say them one time. Each of you will step forward and bow. After you've repeated, 'Daddy is the king of Sorry,' you will receive a kiss."

Starris stepped out of line. "Is this really necessary?"

"Do you want a kiss?"

"Yes."

"Then get back in line. I'll have no dissension in the ranks."

Starris saluted. "Yes, sir."

"Jolie Kathryn, you may come forward."

Jolie stepped up and bowed. "Daddy is the king of Sorry."

Jordon kissed her on the cheek and sent her on her way. "Danielle." Jordon frowned. "What is your middle name, Dani?"

"Kathryn."

Only a raised brow signified Jordon's surprise as he cleared his throat and started again. "Danielle Kathryn, you may come forward."

Starris did let her surprise show when Dani stepped up without hesitation, bowed and repeated the phrase. Jordon kissed her cheek. When he sent Dani on her way, she ran giggling to Jolie. Still observing her, Starris jumped when Jordon's deep voice brought her attention back to him.

"Starris Latrice, you may come forward."

"That's okay, Jordy," Starris said, looking at the girls again. If Dani was three inches shorter, had black eyes and no dimples, she'd swear Dani and Jolie could be twins.

Jordon followed her stare and moved to Starris' side. "What's wrong, baby?"

Starris shook her head. The thought was crazy. "Nothing," she replied, looking at her watch. "It's time for us to get going, angel. Tomorrow is a school day."

"No!" Both girls groaned the word in unison.

If he wasn't supposed to be an adult, Jordon would have added his deep timbre to the ranks. He didn't want Starris to go either, but he had to back her on this one. "Okay, ladies. You heard what Starris said. Jolie, go help Dani gather her things and hurry back down."

Jordon and Starris began straightening the room. "Jolie's birthday is a week from Saturday. We usually start the festivities with a party just for family, then invite a few of her friends out for pizza and such the next day. I'm sure she's already invited Dani to that. I'd like the two of you to attend the family gathering with us."

Starris put the lid on the game box. "Thank you, Jordon. But we can't come. Dani's birthday is a week from Saturday, too. We're planning to take her shopping and then to dinner."

"I see," Jordon replied as a feeling of unease spread over him. Was the "we" she referred to another man? A light went off as a way to curtail any plans Starris had of going out with anyone other than him formed in his mind. He walked up behind her. "Why don't we make it a joint party for the girls? They're such good friends, I'm sure they wouldn't mind sharing their birthdays."

"That's a great idea," Alice seconded from the doorway. "I'll call your mother first thing in the morning."

"What's a great idea?" Jolie wanted to know, entering the room with Dani.

Starris stood mute as Jordon explained to the girls that they would be having a joint birthday party, to which they responded with squeals of joy. Starris looked at Jordon. They hadn't known each other long enough for family introductions. As she followed him to his car, Starris wondered why it was so important to Jordon that she meet his so soon.

Jordon didn't dally after dropping Starris and Dani at home. He saw them to the door, dropped a quick kiss on Starris' lips, and left. She suspected he left so quickly to escape hearing what she had to say about the joint party idea. In her bedroom, Starris undressed, climbed into bed and closed her eyes, sure that Jordon was rushing her, and not sure that she could handle the pace at which their relationship seemed to be accelerating.

CHAPTER 7

Starris had to concentrate to keep her mind on the Quad-E meeting going on around her. Almost impossible, since her brain had decided that it wanted to think about Jordon Banks and the effect he was having on her. She told herself the excitement she felt had nothing to do with him, but in truth, he had everything to do with it.

For the past week, he'd shown up at her door, with Jolie, on one pretense or another. On Monday, he'd returned a book Dani left at the house and brought the ROBY employment contract for her to sign. Tuesday, he'd wanted her opinion on when he should let Jolie start dating. Wednesday, he'd asked when he should buy Jolie her first bra. Thursday, they had talked about their backgrounds and exchanged very basic information about their ex-spouses. Last night, he didn't have a reason, but she let him in anyway.

Starris knew all he really wanted to do was cuddle on the couch and kiss, since that's what they usually ended up doing after sending the girls up to Dani's room. They were like two groping teenagers, and she didn't know how much longer she could hold out against the blaze that ignited every time Jordon touched her. And then there were the girls. What did they think about the developing relationship between their parents? Jordon had a good rapport with both of them. What concerned Starris was the strong attachment that Dani, so needy emotionally, had developed for Jordon. What would happen when Jordon was no longer a part of their lives?

While she wondered about the method to Jordon's madness, her awareness of him rose steadily. Each night, he left her mouth wet with kisses and her body filled with a desolation she could not voice for fear that he would try to move their relationship into the physical realm. Each night, she'd watched him leave, painfully aware of her growing feelings for him and too afraid to say anything that would mean the end of the friendship they had managed to forge despite their rocky beginning.

Starris redirected her thoughts from Jordon to ROBY, and the vision he'd shared with her for the organization's future. Jordon truly cared about the fatherless boys and had made a long-term commitment to the organization's success. That had not stopped her from voicing her opinion on the sexist role the organization played by not acknowledging the needs of the female gender. Using his own daughter as an example, Starris had pointed out that Jolie would soon reach an age when she would need female guidance. Jordon had jumped up from the couch and run from the house, only to return with his briefcase. The folder he'd pulled out had contained papers outlining his thoughts on a sister program for ROBY. He needed money and mentors, and had placed responsibility for sourcing women's groups under the job acquisitions director, a position still open because Jordon's first choice had declined the offer.

Quad-E was the natural choice to take the lead in the sister program, but Starris had been in the boxing ring too many times to believe that Carlotta Eldridge would readily accept anything she presented. However, Carlotta was the person she needed to convince. If she could, Jordon would have a sister organization, and Starris would prove herself more than qualified for the position.

Later that morning, Starris propped her bare feet on either side of a tall black stool and bent over her drawing easel, paintbrush in hand. Supposedly, she was putting the final touches on her latest RavenLove design. Actually, she was trying to rid herself of the anger she felt over Carlotta's flat refusal to provide mentors for Warren Village, a project that provided safe housing and day-care facilities for unwed, pregnant and teenage mothers. Seeing her hopes for a Quad-E and ROBY mesh dashed, Starris had angrily popped off at the mouth, which, in turn, had gotten her placed on censure—again. Resolved not to let the matter drop, she set her shoulders and began planning another approach. She sighed when the telephone rang.

"Hello," she answered dispiritedly.

"I knew it! I knew you'd be sitting there spitting nails over Carlotta and her refusal to consider the Warren Village proposal."

"I am not spitting nails, Shelby Reeves. I'm just deeply disappointed that thirty professional women can sit in a room and pretend all is right in the world and not feel an ounce of guilt over their complacent attitudes."

"I agree. But you know how adamant Carlotta is about calling the shots. You'll get your chance, so hang in there. Besides, how long can the woman hold out against the force of Starris Gilmore?"

"Apparently forever," Starris responded. "Every proposal brought before that woman is turned down for no reason other than that the idea didn't come from her and she wants to be queen of the hill."

"I know, but don't focus on winning a battle when there's a war at stake." There was a pregnant pause before Shelby continued. "Sooo, how are you and Jordon Banks getting on these days?"

Starris dropped her head to her hand. "Don't start with me, Shel. I'm not in the mood, and remember, I still owe you for setting me up in the first place."

"Like you care. Unless it is now your habit to spend all of your evenings with men you have no feelings for."

"Who told you that?"

"Who do you think? My 'can't keep a secret' husband."

"Nelson Reeves is a dead man, and I do not have feelings for Jordon Banks."

"That's not what Nelson said, and I'm of the mind to agree with him on this one. And you might want to rethink those death threats you're issuing. J.R. is Lauryn's godfather. He, and the four women with whom you share godparenting duties, may not like it."

"I don't issue threats," Starris gritted out through clenched teeth.

Shelby laughed. "Well, was I right or was I right? Is J.R. a slice of heaven, or what?"

"I wouldn't know."

"Starris, I realize you haven't known J.R. long enough to develop any feelings for him, but don't do anything to drive him away before you've had a chance to find out if you could love him," Shelby stated, her tone brooking no argument. "You could do worse, and there's none better than J.R. He's handsome, smart, successful and a good parent."

Starris sighed. "You don't have to promote the man's qualities to me, Shel. Jordon isn't the problem, and you know it. He doesn't need to be saddled with someone like me."

The long intake of air signaled the end of Shelby's patience. "Stop it, Starris Gilmore! I am not going to listen to you berate yourself over a jerk with the morals of a slug who didn't deserve to breathe the same air, let alone marry, you!"

"I know. Lonnie wasn't much of a man, was he?"

"Lonnie wasn't a man at all! However, Jordon Banks is, and it's been a long time since he's shown an interest in a woman, any woman, like he's shown for you. Both of you were badly hurt by people who were supposed to love you, but the two of you deserve to find happiness. So if you're truly not ready for a relationship, tell J.R. now before things go any farther. Don't let him find out later, after he's invested his emotions. I've known Jordon Banks for a long time, and he's the one person you don't want for an enemy."

Starris heard the deep voice and baby babble before Shelby said, "I need to go, girl. Nels and Lauryn are home and that rustle of bags I hear means that my husband is on his way back to the mall to return the mountain of toys he'll claim his daughter made him buy."

Shel had it all, Starris thought, hanging up with a wistful though unenvious sigh: a good man who loved and supported her, a gorgeous baby daughter, and she owned a successful fashion boutique. Though they'd had a couple of rough years, Starris had often wondered how, after so many years, Shelby and Nelson kept their love alive.

True love, she mused. Shelby and Nelson were the only couple she knew who'd ever come close to having what, to Starris, had become an out-of-reach fantasy. Once she had thought she'd found true love. What she had found was heartbreak. Not satisfied with breaking her heart, Lonnie had stripped her of her womanhood and the trust fund left to her by her father. Only recently had Starris begun to find her way back, and she dared not hope for anything more than a few good memories with Jordon Banks.

Giving up the pretense of working, Starris stabbed her brush into the cup of turpentine and left her office. She padded to the couch, lounged back and let her mind have its way with Jordon Banks. Everything Shelby had said about the man was true. Only Starris could add confident, opinionated and stubborn, loving, insightful, and for her, too much. And Shelby, her good friend and pal, had the nerve to worry about Jordon falling in love with her. What would happen if she fell in love with Jordon Banks?

Interrupted by chimes, Starris rose and went to the door. When a glance through the peephole revealed the lofty form of Jordon Banks, she shook her head in disbelief. Mental imaging sure was powerful stuff. And although she had somehow conjured up the man in the flesh, Starris wasn't prepared to see him; a moot point, unless she planned to keep him standing on her porch. She opened the door, and two large arms wrapped her in a bear hug.

"Hi, baby." Jordon kissed the top of her head and released her.

Starris stepped away and examined his attire. Everything about Jordon stated that he was a man comfortable in any setting. The hip-hugging blue jeans tapered down to meet the tops of a pair of snakeskin boots. Above the waist, two buttons of a tan cotton shirt opened to reveal a thickly corded neck. Starris turned abruptly and walked away, distress evident in her steps. Jordon looked too appealing; while she, on the other hand, looked a mess.

Jordon caught up with Starris, turned her around and lifted her chin with his fingertip. He stood staring at her for so long that she felt compelled to explain her rumpled appearance. "I've been working."

"You look fine," he replied, his voice dropping to a low huskiness that sent a shiver through her. Paint-spattered smock, hair piled in a knot on top of her head, face clear of makeup, except for the spot of orange paint on her nose, and she still looked exquisite, Jordon thought, releasing his breath. He didn't know which he preferred—the rumpled Starris or the perfectly packaged Starris. Both looked beautiful, and both made his heart race.

"Have a seat," Starris invited. She followed him to the couch where Jordon settled his muscular build into the thick cushions, and she took a chair. "Where are the girls?"

She's just been sitting here, Jordon thought, absorbed in her scent and warmth.

"Jordon Randolph Banks!" He looked at Starris and frowned. "Where are the girls?"

"They're outside. One of their friends stopped them for a chat."

"That has to be Brittany," Starris remarked. Her gaze turned pensive as she examined him. "I thought they were spending the day at your house."

"They were, except that I had to bring them along if they were to accompany us."

"Accompany us? We don't have plans today, Jordy."

Jordon wiggled his eyebrows, and a slow, sensual smile spread across his face. "Of course we do, and as lovely as you look with that orange paint on your nose, you'll need to change into a pair of blue jeans, a long-sleeve shirt and some sturdy shoes."

Shaken, Starris jumped up, but hadn't taken one step before Jordon reached out and brought her down beside him. "What's the matter, baby?"

Starris hid her face in the hard chest. "Why didn't you say something?"

Jordon pulled her closer, savoring the second time that Starris had touched him of her own accord. It seemed like forever that he'd had this want, this need to touch her, and he freely ran his hands up and down the small of her back. "Because it doesn't matter."

Starris sat up. "Of course it matters, Jordon. I always want to look my best for you, and today you've caught me at my worst."

A dark brow rose mockingly. "I've already seen your best, and the image of that next-to-nothing sleeper still plays havoc with my mind. However, if this is your worst, I think I can handle it." Starris rose from the couch. "Where are you going?"

"To shower and change for our date."

"Oh," Jordon said, watching her swaying hips disappear from the room. Five minutes later, he dropped the magazine he'd picked up and climbed the stairs. "Starris, you'll need to bring along an extra set of clothes," he called, making his way down the hallway. At the door to her bedroom, he froze and swallowed hard while staring at the completely unclothed body in front of him. He took two steps into the room; Starris, seeing the desire that leaped into his eyes, took two retreating steps.

Filled with deep and unfulfilled longing, Jordon observed her. It was there again, that look of stark fear. What, he wondered, had happened to make her fear him so? He stood still, his body taut with the stiffness of wanting her, yet knowing that should he dare try to touch Starris, he would drive her away, possibly forever. He held out his hand, his eyes holding a plea that dissolved into disappointment when Starris looked down at his hand, up to his face and fled the bedroom for the safety of her bathroom.

Following her path, Jordon bit back a need to pound on the door. Calming himself proved more difficult. With his lips, Jordon could induce Starris into a state of relaxation where she lay warm and pliant in his arms. But if his hands wandered anywhere near the parts of her body meant for sexual pleasure, her eyes glazed with panic. She acted like a frightened virgin or the victim of a rapist. Six years of marriage dismissed the virgin theory. However, the possibility that she'd been raped never strayed far from Jordon's mind.

Sexually, they were at an impasse, one he could not breach until she felt comfortable enough to confide in him. With a sigh, Jordon left the bedroom. Starris needed time, and he needed Starris, needed her so much he was willing to wait. He would figure out a way to break through the barrier and her aversion toward sex. Until then, Jordon also had to find a way to keep his own need from spilling over while helping Starris come to know the sensual being he knew she could be.

Hot, sticky and tired, Starris turned another shovel of dirt and chopped the clumps with its tip. She blew wispy bangs off her forehead, then stretched up, and with one hand flexed her back. "This is Jordon's idea of a date?" she asked quietly, cocking a brow in his direction.

Twice now, she'd gone out with Jordon Banks, and twice he'd astounded her with his choice of entertainment. Today's outing had included a comfortable, air-conditioned ride inside the cab of his luxury truck. Their destination: Colorado's Eastern plains.

Confused when he'd turned the truck onto a long, dirt-covered driveway and stopped in front of a white farmhouse, she'd watched him speak with the owners, then pull four shovels from the back of the truck. Jordon had explained what they were to do, then handed a shovel to each of them and pointed to a field in the distance. Starris figured he'd lost his mind, but this was their fifth stop, and the farmers had been generous. In exchange for digging what amounted to a few rows of dirt, they had filled the back of the truck with baskets of vegetables and fruit.

"How are my girls holding up?" Jordon asked, offering a ladle filled with water he'd dipped from a bucket.

Starris took the ladle, considered throwing the water in his face, then drank thirstily before holding out the utensil for more. "Just great," she muttered, crossing her arms as she waited for a refill.

Jordon regarded her from beneath hooded lids and shook his head. "Temper. Temper," he murmured. "But you'll be happy to know that this is our last stop." He turned away and dipped the ladle for the girls.

Starris lifted her shovel and trudged back to the truck. She hefted it and two baskets of green beans over the top and leaned against the side of the vehicle, huffing as she waited for Jordon.

"I'd have gotten those, Star," he said, easily carrying two baskets and three shovels.

"Thanks heaps," Starris replied sarcastically. She waited until he'd finished loading the remainder of the vegetables before asking, "Why, Jordon?"

"Alice," he replied as if the response explained everything. He opened the door of the truck. "Come on, girls. Let's go home."

Too tired to press him, Starris made her way to the front of the truck and climbed in. She wilted against the seat, grateful when he started the engine and the air conditioning came on full blast. In the few miles it took for her to recover and resume her inquiry, the girls fell asleep. "Would you like to explain what Alice has to do with your bringing us halfway across the state to spend the afternoon working like field hands?"

Jordon threw her a guarded glance before turning his attention back to the road. "Anyone listening to you would think you've been working on a chain gang."

"Anyone seeing me would think the same!"

"Keep your voice down, Star. The girls are asleep."

"Stop playing mind games, and I'll keep my voice down."

"I know you're tired, baby, but doing something good for someone else is supposed to give you a sense of fulfillment, not anger."

"Explain that, Banks, and this time don't beat around the bush."

Jordon sighed. Would there ever come a day when that mouth of hers would allow him the last word? "The fruits and vegetables are for Alice and her friends. When we get home, they will begin the really hard work of getting them cleaned, cooked, canned and delivered to homeless shelters around the city. They do it twice a year. In the spring, we dig, the farmers donate, Alice and her crew prepare, and we all deliver. In summer, we pick, they prepare and we all deliver."

"What a nice and generous thing to do," she replied, duly impressed. Starris returned Jordon's grin with one of her own, then turned in her seat and laid her head on his shoulder. "You're nice, too," she murmured, and promptly went to sleep.

Silken tresses slid down his bare arm in a gentle caress. Jordon smothered a grunt. The grunt became a loud groan when Starris shifted in her seat and nestled her body more fully against his side. Easing his death grip on the steering wheel, Jordon gave in to his desires and wrapped a muscular arm around her shoulders, pulling her closer. His hand splayed along her tiny waist, then moved upward toward her breasts. Starris shifted again, and Jordon snatched his hand down to rest on her hip.

He held his breath as an image of Starris, unclothed, rose startlingly clear in his mind. His body responded immediately. He sucked in air that seemed in short supply, wiggled in his seat, then fought the mental war, one he knew he had no chance of winning with her pillowed so comfortably against him.

To get his mind off the anguish Starris caused within his body, Jordon replaced his erotic thoughts of Starris with thoughts of the day they had shared. They had worked hard, and until she'd snapped at him a short while ago, Starris hadn't voiced a single complaint the entire afternoon. Admiration shone in his eyes as he thought about her bent over with her curvaceous bottom pointed toward the sky every time she encountered a rock. He'd had to work several rows over and in front of her to keep his mind focused on turning his own row. What a woman, Jordon thought, grinning, and as a reward for her good spirits and being a real trouper, tonight he'd take her out on a real date.

The earth-shaking sound of a jet flying overhead drowned out the sound of Starris' laughter. When the noise died, she looked at Jordon, and her laughter bubbled forth again. *"Je n'en reviens pas!"* she said, giggling helplessly.

"What, Star?" Jordon inquired with all seriousness. He tipped the bottle of wine to refill her cup. "What can't you get over?"

"You." Starris stopped laughing to catch her breath. "You are the strangest man I have ever met, Jordon Banks."

A fanciful expression crossed his face before his lips lifted and the roar of another jet muffled the tone of his laughter as he joined Starris in mirth. As suddenly as her laughter started, it stopped, and Starris settled back in the car seat, sipping from her cup while smoothing the pleats of her skirt with one hand. The sound of another jet and Jordon's concentration on its approach for takeoff gave her the opportunity to study the strong profile silhouetted against the twilight darkness.

After that afternoon's date, she should have been wary enough to question him when in the midst of shucking an ear of corn he'd asked her out again. She hadn't, and because of her inattention to that detail, Starris now found herself sitting in the middle of a field, sipping wine from a paper cup and watching airplanes land and take off from Denver International Airport. They had already eaten dinner, picnic fashion, on the hood of his car, and as odd as she felt, theirs wasn't the only vehicle in the field. It seemed that quite a few Denver residents thought the pastime a great way to spend an evening.

Jordon turned to her when the plane's taillights disappeared to the west and reached out his hand. Drawing her forward, his head lowered, and his lips claimed hers. The kiss was overdue and welcomed, and Starris launched herself into his arms enthusiastically. Jordon thrust his tongue forward, swiping the wine from her mouth until she moaned in abandonment.

His hands moved lower to tenderly caress her arms, encouraging a response that seemed to come so naturally from her. With tentative movements, he fitted his palm around the curve of one breast. When Starris didn't pull away, his heart cried with joy. He felt the shiver that passed through her body, and his questing fingers continued to tease, molding her nipple to a firm point beneath the linen blouse.

Breathing harshly, Jordon recognized her response as the breakthrough he'd been waiting for. A tremble coursed through his body, anchoring itself in his throbbing manhood.

"I want you, Starris," he rasped, covering her face in a blaze of kisses.

It was then something changed, and through his sexual haze, it finally dawned on Jordon that the low moans coming from Starris were born, not of passion, but of panic. And that the short, hot breaths against his neck were not meant to be provocative, but an attempt on her part to get air into her lungs.

Suddenly, she was struggling to get out of his arms. Her frantic movements brought a screeching halt to Jordon's ardor and moved him to action. He released Starris and then gently thrust her head between her knees.

"Baby, are you all right?" he beseeched, bending low to place his lips on her cheek. "Starris, I didn't mean to frighten you. Please, are you okay!"

Starris didn't respond. When her breathing returned to normal, she remained locked in the bent-over position, wishing that she could disappear. She couldn't face him. She couldn't! Not after the humiliating display he'd just witnessed. Jordon didn't know it, but he'd just seen her as she really was, a weak shell of a woman, afraid of love and afraid of men.

CHAPTER 8

Doreen Banks finished the yellow flower on Jolie's birthday cake and laid the tube of frosting down on the counter. She had been trying to pump Alice for information all morning and, thus far, Jordon's housekeeper had been very closemouthed. Deciding it was time for Alice to spill what she knew, Doreen poured two cups of coffee and took them to the kitchen table.

"Alice, why don't we take a break? J.R. and Jolie won't be here for a couple of hours, and everything's just about ready."

"All right, Dory. Just let me finish putting Danielle's name on this cake, and I'll be right with you."

When Alice sat at the table, Doreen wasted no time getting to the point. "You've been putting me off all day, Alice, and you know what I want to know. You've never clammed up on me before, so don't start now."

Alice sipped from her cup. "Well, Dory. I think that after all this time, the barrier around Jordon's heart is finally crumbling. Starris Gilmore may be the one."

"Is she a nice girl, Alice? I mean, will she hurt J.R.?"

"I don't think so." Alice got comfortable in her chair, and Doreen saw the light that lit her pale gray eyes. "No, Dory. I'm sure of it. Starris and her daughter spent a weekend at the house, so I had an opportunity to observe her real close. I'm not sure what she feels for J.R., but he spends most of his evenings with her. I can tell she likes him, too, and she appears taken with Jolie."

Doreen's eyes clouded with pain. "Appearances can be deceiving, Alice. Gloria taught this family that lesson well."

Alice reached out and took hold of Doreen's hand. "Dory, it's too early to tell where this relationship is going, but Starris is not the type of person that would hurt others intentionally. If these two fall in love, you have to put Gloria and what she did behind you and hope for the best."

Doreen stood and went back to the counter. "Alice, I know you're right, but I cannot allow another woman to hurt my son or my grandbaby ever again." She picked up her tube from the counter and turned back to the cake.

Dani and Jolie sat happily in the backseat of the silver Seville playing scavenger hunt, the car version. Jordon had made up the game boards the night before and had given them to the girls for the one-hour ride south from Highlands Ranch, a suburb of Denver, to Widefield, a suburb of Colorado Springs.

What had them so preoccupied was the money-making potential of the game. At stake: ten dollars, earned in quarter installments for every item found and marked on their boards. They could easily spot some of the items like two black-and-white cows, pine trees or horses. Others were more difficult, such as a specific make and color of a car, bumper stickers or a certain combination of people in a car. They could share information, but shouting resulted in a monetary penalty, and except for whispers and giggles, the girls were fairly quiet.

Starris, wishing she was anywhere except in the car with Jordon, sat in the front seat watching the shrubs and trees covering the hills and valleys along I-25 pass in a daze. She tried to keep her glances at Jordon, who wore blue jeans and a blue-and-white polo shirt that sent nervous jitters through her body, to a minimum. At his insistence, she'd changed out of a pale peach, linen pantsuit brought for the occasion into a pair of the blue jeans he seemed to favor. The short-sleeve, tangerine top and matching slip-ons made Starris looked all of sixteen. To combat the image, she'd twisted her hair into a French knot and used a little heavier hand with her makeup. Still, the outfit seemed too casual, and she was not pleased, especially meeting his family for the first time.

It wasn't only her outfit that had Starris keyed up or the horde of people waiting for them that had her stomach tied in knots. Her eyes slipped to Jordon again. All week, she'd waited for him to question her about the airport episode. So far, he hadn't said anything, but she knew the incident had shaken him; she'd seen it in his face. When she'd finally sat back in her seat, he'd acted so nonchalant about the whole thing that his normalcy had helped ease her discomposure, but he hadn't touched her since.

On the one hand, she wished Jordon would ask and get it over with. Then again, she loathed the thought of having to concoct an explanation that sounded plausible without revealing the very personal details of her life with Lonnie Gilmore. Of course, there was the very real possibility that Jordon didn't care enough to ask. Starris averted her eyes to the window again and tried to concentrate on scenery that suddenly became a watery blur.

Had it been any man but Jordon Banks, the sullen, quiet hindering his attempts to draw Starris into conversation might have made him edgy. However, the man was Jordon, and he understood her need for private time in preparation for the ordeal ahead. All week, Jordon had tried to work through his insistence that Starris accompany him today. At one point, he'd become so vehement that the matter was settled; Starris had swallowed whatever excuse she'd been ready to throw at him.

Finally, he'd had the last word.

"We'll be there in a few minutes," Jordon said to no one in particular. Exiting from the highway, he glanced at Starris. Last Saturday, she'd scared the hell of out him, but not enough to scare him off. Again he wondered why. What was it about her that kept him coming back for more? *Like you don't know, Banks. You want her with you because you're getting serious about the lady, and you're afraid to let her out of your sight.* Not liking the direction his thoughts had taken, Jordon asked, "Are my girls ready for their birthday party?"

"Yes!"

"Good. Jolie, I want to remind you again that you are not to leave Dani alone. All of your aunts, uncles and cousins will be there, and she doesn't know any of them."

"I won't, Daddy." Jolie turned to Dani. "You're going to like our family, Dani. Nommy is the best grandmother, and I'll bet she'll let you call her Nommy, too. Papiér will hug you a lot, and so will the others. But don't worry about that. We'll get lots of presents, and that's the best part."

"You'll get lots of presents, Jolie. They're your family, not mine. I don't need any more presents. Starris gave me this watch and a fifty-dollar savings bond. Aunt Pam got me these jeans and a shirt."

"That's all!" Jolie patted Dani's arm consolingly. "Well, don't worry. Daddy and I got some presents for you, and I'm sure Nommy got one for you since it's your birthday, too. I always get lots of stuff."

"I'm not worried, Jolie. I like what I got, and I'm really glad that my mom and Aunt Pam remembered my birthday. Your family doesn't have to give me anything."

Jordon glanced into the rearview mirror, then at Starris. If she heard the girls' conversation, she didn't seem to place much weight to it. He did, and he didn't like his daughter's materialistic perspective.

Ever since he'd brought Jolie home, his family had gone overboard in the spoiling department. He had to admit that he was just as guilty. Jolie would receive a mountain of gifts, most of which she wouldn't look at twice. Shamefaced, Jordon thought about Dani and how appreciative she was of the gifts she'd received. It was too late to do anything about it this year, but next year things were going to change for Miss Jolie Kathryn Banks.

"They're here," Alice said, watching Jordon turn into the driveway. The whole family stopped what they were doing and hurried to look out the windows at the four people exiting the car.

Five-foot-nine-inch Doreen Banks entered the room and took in the scene. Her mocha-colored face, smooth and free of makeup, looked much younger than her sixty-three years. Elegantly coifed and wearing blue jeans and a red striped shirt, she clapped her hands for attention. "Get out of those windows. There is no need to act as if J.R. has never brought a woman to this house before."

"It has been more than ten years, Mother." Rosalyn Banks, the oldest of the three siblings and the only one who took her looks after her mother's side of the family, hadn't stopped looking out the window as she responded. Her black, naturally curly mane had been permed into straightness, and her black eyes twinkled with mischief. She looked over her shoulder and shared a dimpled smile with her mother. "Anyway, we're waiting on Jolie, not J.R."

"Sure we are, Roz," Denise Banks-Pullman said with a smirk. "We can see Jolie any time. You might as well admit that we're waiting to pass judgment on the first woman in more than a decade our little brother cares enough about to bring down here to meet us."

"I don't care what you're waiting for," James Banks, an older and graying version of Jordon, asserted with an authoritative ring. "You heard your mother, get out of the windows! And if you can manage it, try and act like you're not a pack of vultures waiting to pounce on my son!" Bodies moved with haste when James stopped speaking.

"Thank you, dear."

James leaned down to kiss his wife's cheek. "You're welcome, sugar."

By the time Jordon moved around the car to help Starris, Jolie was halfway up the walk. "Hurry up, Dani! Everyone's waiting for us."

Dani had seen the faces appear, then disappear in the windows, and agitated, she ran back to Starris, who enfolded her in a hug.

"It's okay, angel. Go on. I'll be along after I help Jordon with the things in the trunk."

"I'll help," Dani offered.

Because she seemed to need it, Jordon gave Dani a quick hug, too. "No, li'l bit. We don't have that much. You go ahead with Jolie. We'll be there in a minute."

"Dani, come on," Jolie yelled from the porch. Too excited to wait for Dani as she dragged her feet, Jolie went into the house. "Nommy, we're here!"

A chorus of "Happy Birthdays" rang out from the large group gathered in the living room, but Doreen gave her grand-daughter a stern look. "Jolie Kathryn, didn't you bring a guest?"

"Yes, Nommy."

"Then why are you in here without her?"

Jordon, holding an armful of birthday presents, opened the door for Starris and Dani just as Jolie turned.

"Here she is, Nommy." Jolie went to Dani and pulled her forward. "Nommy, this is Danielle Carter. Dani, this is Nommy."

Starris watched the strange look that passed over Doreen's face before she stepped forward to welcome Dani. "Hello, Danielle. I'm glad you could come and help Jolie celebrate her birthday with us. Of course, it's your birthday, too, isn't it? You know, you're such a pretty girl. Who is it that you remind me of? Oh, right now I can't think of the name, but it will come to me, just you wait."

Noting his wife's rambling, James stepped forward and placed his hands on Doreen's shoulders. "Dani, I'm Papiér, and I'm very pleased to meet you."

"Hello, Mr. and Mrs. Banks," Dani responded in a quiet voice. "Thank you for letting me come today."

Jolie tugged Dani's hand, pulling her away to meet the rest of the family. Jordon placed his packages on the table and turned to his mother and father. "Mother, Papiér, I'd like you to meet Starris Gilmore. Starris, my mother and father."

The look she'd seen on Doreen's face when introduced to Dani came and went again quickly. "Hello, Mr. and Mrs. Banks. It's so nice to meet you. Thank you for having Dani and me."

Though Starris tried to pay attention, her eyes kept straying to Dani. Her daughter did not like strangers, and right now a roomful of people she didn't know was about to descend on her.

Jordon leaned down over her shoulder. "Don't worry about Dani, baby. Look at her, she's going to be fine, and my family will take care of her."

"That's one thing you don't have to worry about in this family. We take care of our own. Hi, Starris. I'm Rosalyn Banks. Call me Roz, though."

Starris shook the offered hand. "It's nice to meet you, Roz. I'm not worried about Dani's safety. It's just that she's not comfortable in large crowds."

Jordon put his arm around her waist. "She'll be fine, Star." He added when he saw his sister's frown, "Starris is experiencing a case of new-mother jitters. She's in the process of adopting Danielle."

"You are! How wonderful. There aren't many people willing to take in someone else's children. You must have a big heart."

"I don't think of Danielle as someone else's child. I feel like Dani belongs to me, and in a few months, I will truly be her mother."

"Well, don't drive yourself crazy. It won't be long until you'll have this mothering thing down pat."

"I hope so. There are so many things to worry about with children these days."

Rosalyn chuckled. "Girl, you are not preaching to the choir. I'm single, and I don't have any kids. I'm the favorite aunt. I prefer to visit with my nieces and nephews and send them home. If you need parenting tips or want to swap war stories, then talk to Denise. She has three rug rats."

"Which is exactly where we're headed. See you later, Roz," Jordon said.

Rosalyn winked. "By the way, J.R. I like her."

"Thanks." Jordon took Starris by the hand. "This way, baby."

Tapping the shoulder of a woman whose back was to them, Jordon said, "Neecy. There's someone here I'd like you to meet."

The woman turned, and Starris gasped in surprise. Denise, an exact, though shorter, replica of Jordon, held a wrapped bundle in each arm. Starris' hands itched to take them, and she struggled to quell the urge and pay attention as Jordon introduced his sister and twin.

"Denise, Starris Gilmore. Starris, my older sister, Denise Banks-Pullman."

"Hi, Starris. We've been looking forward to your arrival all day. Did you know that you're the first woman Jordon's brought to meet this family in more than ten years?"

Jordon put his fists on his waist. "It's not necessary for you to give Starris my complete history within seconds of meeting her, Neecy."

"Call it payback, little brother," she said in mock annoyance. "For the older crack."

"Well, I don't care who's older," Starris said, her eyes on the babies. "I'm pleased to meet you, Denise."

Denise did not take offense when Starris continued to stare at the babies in her arms. She'd grown used to the attention her twins generated. "I'm older by five minutes, but to hear J.R. talk, you'd think I'd beat him into the world by a year or more. If my arms weren't full, I'd give him a chop to the ribs."

Unable to restrain herself any longer, Starris reached for the babies, then stopped. "May I?"

Denise handed over one of the infants. "I never turn down a chance to lighten the load. That's Terrence. I'll hang on to Tyrone. He's not as receptive to strangers as his brother."

"No, I'll take them both," Starris replied.

"I hope you know you're a glutton for punishment."

"I don't mind." Starris settled Terrence in one arm so that she could take Tyrone.

"Hold it." Both women looked at Jordon. "Why are you aiding her, Star? If Neecy hands over my other nephew, it will leave her hands free to deliver that chop to my ribs. You're my friend. Protect me. Give back that baby."

Starris accepted Tyrone. "You deserve anything Denise cares to dish out. You're old enough to know better than to insult a woman with jokes about her age."

With both arms full, Starris sat in the chair behind her and gazed back and forth between the identical twins. She hugged the babies against her chest and crooned soft words to them. Jordon stood back and observed the warmth and love that beamed on her face. One look at his nephews, and she'd forgotten him. But watching her, he knew she'd be a wonderful mother to their babies.

Down, boy, Jordon thought, trying to deny his feelings though his heart told him differently. He could deny it all he wanted, but Starris dominated his thoughts night and day. And as his obsession with her grew, the harder it became to leave her at night and go home to his big, empty bed. He could barely stand to be away from Starris, and it was his obsession with her that had prompted his insistence that she accompany him today. To distract his thoughts, he said, "I'll check on the girls." Jordon walked away so quickly, he missed Starris' reply of okay.

Later that afternoon, Starris moved through the house in search of her daughter. Although in his mother she had sensed reserve, the rest of Jordon's family had been warm and receptive of her and Dani. She recalled Jolie's remark that she'd receive lots of presents, and the child hadn't exaggerated. Starris had never seen so much given to one little girl. "Make that two little girls," she amended. With Dani, Jordon and his family had been just as generous. Starris peeked in the family room, reminding herself to have a talk with Jordon later. While she appreciated the gesture, they could not accept the stereo system or the two-thousand-dollar savings bond.

She turned from the room and walked to the stairs. When overwhelmed, her daughter always sought solitude. Suddenly, Starris smiled when she heard the faint sound of lullabies being sung by Dani. She climbed the stairs and moved toward the room that had been converted into a nursery for the day.

"There you are, angel." Starris entered the room and sat on the bed beside Dani.

"I heard them crying, Mama, and came up to see. I wasn't doing anything to them. Honest."

"I know, angel. Would you mind if I held one of them?"

Dani shifted one of the babies to Starris. "You can hold Tyrone. He's being a little fussy."

Starris took the baby. "How do you know this is Tyrone?"

Dani gave Starris one of those teenage "you're an idiot" looks before she responded. "All you have to do is look at them, and you can see the difference."

"They're identical twins, Dani."

"No, they're not," Dani countered. "Look at Tyrone's right eyebrow. See how it's thinner than the one on the left and look at this dot on Terrence's cheek."

Starris leaned over to peer at the mark. "You mean that tiny mole?"

"Yeah. Tyrone doesn't have one. And you know what else?"

"No," Starris said as she examined Tyrone's cheek. "Tell me."

"When Tyrone gets mad, he makes a fist and waves it in the air, and he bumps a lot. Terrence stiffens his legs and kicks."

Dani's observations astounded Starris. She had held the babies for an hour and hadn't noticed any of the things Dani had mentioned. "You're so smart, angel, and a very perceptive young lady."

Dani raised Terrence up and laid her cheek against his, then she cuddled him in her arms once more and adjusted his blankets around his legs. "Mama?"

"Yes." Starris picked up a pacifier and stuck it in Tyrone's mouth when he began to fuss.

"Almost all the people who came to the home wanted babies. I asked Mrs. Johnson about it, and she said it was because babies were soft and lovable. She said children like me were more trouble than we're worth. How come you didn't want a baby?"

On more than one occasion Starris had wanted to slap Mrs. Johnson, the director of the children's home, after hearing some of the comments she had made to the children. After losing everything in their little lives, the last thing they needed was someone caring for them who had no compassion. Starris was still waiting for the Department of Social Services to act on the written complaints she'd filed against the woman.

"Danielle, I chose you because I fell in love with the prettiest little girl I'd ever seen as soon as I met her."

"But I was so mean to you, Starris. I called you names, and I even tried to hit you. Why would you want someone like me to live with you?"

"Oh, angel," Starris sighed. She situated Tyrone in her arms so that she could put her arm around Dani. "There is no someone like you. There's only you. Remember how you showed me all the things that make Tyrone and Terrence different and unique?" Dani nodded. "Well, you're unique, too. I'll admit that you were pretty horrid that first day. But I didn't see a little girl being mean to me. I saw a little girl who had a lot of love and no one to give it to and because of that, she was mad. Since I had a lot of love, too, I figured that we could love each other."

Dani put her head on Starris' shoulder. "I do love you, Mama."

"Thank you, and right back at you, kid." Starris gave her a squeeze before saying, "I think we should take these little guys to their mom and dad, then we can rejoin the party." Dani looked uncertain and Starris knew why. "It's a bit much to handle, isn't it?"

"Jolie has such a big family. But I like them," Dani quickly added. "And not because they gave me presents, either. I used to think that I wanted a big family like Jolie's, but you know what?"

"What?"

"I like that it's just you and me."

"Really. Well, I like that it's just you and me, too."

A shadow moved outside the door, and neither heard the footsteps that moved down the hallway.

"Having a dad would be really nice, though," Dani said, sneaking a sly look at Starris, "and maybe a sister."

Starris rose and laid Tyrone on the bed. She reached into a baby bag for a new diaper. "Would it now? And can I assume that you already have someone in mind to play the dad and sister in this family?"

Dani watched Starris and rose to follow suit. She laid Terrence down and reached into the bag for a diaper. "Starris, do you like Mr. Banks?"

Starris bent her head to her task, hiding her flushed cheeks. "Yes, Dani. I like Jordon. But we haven't known each other that long, so don't get your hopes up. Sometimes these things don't work out."

Dani pressed the tabs of Terrence's diaper closed and lifted the baby. "Oh, it'll work out, Mama. You'll see."

I'll see, all right, Starris thought as she wrapped Tyrone in his blanket, lifted the baby and followed Dani from the room.

Doreen stood waiting when they reached the bottom of the stairs. "Starris, I wonder if you would you mind helping me in the kitchen."

"I'd be happy to help, Mrs. Banks. Just let me take the baby out to Denise, and I'll be right back."

"Danielle can take the baby, can't you, child?"

"I can do it, Mama."

Starris placed Tyrone in Dani's arm. "Okay, but go slow, angel."

"I will."

Starris followed Doreen into the kitchen, watching as she tied a white apron around her waist. "Hand me those strawberries, would you, dear?"

Starris retrieved the colander and brought it to Doreen. She picked up a knife and began helping to slice off the green stems. Several minutes of silence followed.

"I heard you and Danielle talking, Starris. What I don't understand is, if you like your life the way it is, why are you here with my son?"

Appalled, Starris almost sliced her thumb. She could hardly believe that Doreen Banks had been eavesdropping outside the door or that she had the audacity to admit what she'd done. Though her disposition leaned in the opposite direction, Starris chose to endure this test to her outrage. She did not, however, hold her tongue. "What you heard was a private conversation between me and my daughter. That you would deliberately listen without making your presence known is something I find extremely distasteful, Mrs. Banks."

Doreen continued to cap the strawberries as she responded. "I didn't set out to deliberately spy on you or Dani, and we both know she's not your daughter. In fact, Dani reminds me so much of my granddaughter. Not in looks, mind you, but their mannerisms are so similar, and..." Doreen's voice trailed off.

"If there is something you wish to tell me, Mrs. Banks? I would appreciate your getting to the point."

Doreen laid down her knife. "My point is this: J.R.'s first wife was a cunning little thing, and she fooled us all with her sweet and loving act. Everyone took her retiring reserve for shyness, and Jordon gave Gloria one hundred percent of his heart. Once she had my baby's heart, that evil woman tried to ruin his life. I won't let it happen again."

"Mother! That's enough!" Jordon stormed into the kitchen.

Doreen saw the anger and embarrassment that blazed in her son's eyes, and cowered. "J.R., please. I was just..."

"I know what you were doing, Mother, and what is between Starris and me has nothing to do with you. You had no right to say those things to her, and you will apologize."

"I will not apologize!" Doreen turned to glare and point her finger at Starris. "That woman is not the one for you, Jordon! Can't you see through her act? She's just like Gloria, and I'll not have my family hurt again."

"Starris is not Gloria, and at this point in time, we are nothing more than friends!"

His words did nothing to appease his mother. "Friends? You brought her here for our approval, J.R., but you won't get it from me. She's not good enough for you!"

"What in the world is going on in here?" James stepped into the kitchen, and seeing the tears and distress on his wife's face, he hurried to Doreen's side. "The two of you can be heard down the block."

"Your wife is overstepping her bounds."

With those few words, James knew the extent of his son's anger. "Son, you calm down. I don't know what's happening in here, but we'll work it out. We always work it out."

Doreen wrenched herself from her husband's arms. "We won't work it out unless J.R. gets that woman out of my house! I don't want her around my family. She'll use J.R. and hurt Jolie."

"Sugar, how can you say that? You don't even know Starris. She seems like a wonderful person."

"She's not a wonderful person! She doesn't want you, J.R. I heard her say it! You're setting yourself up to be let down again. She'll hurt you, and she'll hurt my granddaughter, too."

They heard a muted cry, and three pairs of eyes turned to stare at Starris. Dealing with his parents, he'd forgotten all about her, and never had Jordon seen the kind of raw and open anguish that twisted her face. Heedless of his mother's cries to stop, Jordon couldn't cross the room fast enough.

"Star, I'm sorry. My mother is upset. She didn't mean it." He went to pull Starris into his arms.

She hugged herself as if trying to hold her body together. "Your mother is right. I'm not the woman for you."

Starris ran from the room as if dogs were on her heels. At the back door, she stopped. If she went out there, she would have to explain her emotional state to a backyard full of people. She turned and headed in the opposite direction and ran smack into the middle of Jordon's chest. His arms formed a viselike circle around her.

"Let me go," she cried. "I-I have to get out of here."

"No, baby girl. I'm never going to let you go."

His words, meant to reassure her, did not. It should have been a time of carefree happiness when they got to know and learn about each other. It should have been time when they were uncluttered with past hurts and open to a new love that could fill their lives with joy. They were not uncluttered, and past hurts were still there, stifling any chance of their being together. The things his mother had said reminded Starris that she could never be woman enough for Jordon. She wasn't woman enough for any man.

"Will you please take me home? I should never have agreed to come. Dani and I don't belong here."

Jordon knew that Starris was in no mood to listen, but he had to try. He wanted her, and he admitted that want to his heart, body and mind. He didn't care what his mother said. If Starris only loved him for a little while, he'd take whatever she had to offer and deal with the hurt later. It was too soon for her to walk out of his life; he wouldn't let her. "Star, you belong with me and wherever I am. I don't want to lose you, and I don't want to lose Dani. Not now. Not before we've had a chance to find out what we could mean to each other. Give us at least that chance. The things Gloria did hurt my family very badly, and my mother is still reacting to that hurt. Just let me explain."

Starris shuddered, but held back her tears. "No, Jordon. It doesn't matter. Please, will you get Dani for me and take us home?"

CHAPTER 9

Tension filled the car, and Jordon's angry grip on the steering wheel tightened. He was at his wit's end and hurt because Starris refused to listen to him. Added to the hurt was her insult of sitting in the backseat with Dani. He'd even lost his patience with the girls and their unrestrained questions.

When the car pulled into her driveway, Starris wanted to run into the house and give in to the tears she'd been holding in for what seemed like hours. She would have done just that if not for the birthday presents she had to help unload and take into the house.

Jordon gripped the boxes in his hands when Starris told him to set the things anywhere and began to thank him profusely for a lovely day. His jaw hardened when she came toward him and tried to take the boxes from him.

"Jolie, help Dani take these things to her room."

"She doesn't have to do that. It's been a long day, and we're all tired."

"You heard me, Jolie. Move!"

The girls scrambled like jackrabbits, gathered the boxes and left the room. Even Starris jumped at the voice that sounded like a boom of thunder. She trembled when the glittering black eyes turned back to her. Because she wanted Jordon to leave before she broke down in front of him, Starris renewed her resolve. She would not let him bully her into anything. "I don't want to have this discussion with you, Jordon. Please go home."

"Well, that's too damn bad, because we're going to have it!" He grabbed her arm and led her into the kitchen. As soon as the door closed behind them, Jordon started pacing in front of her. Actually, it was more of a prowl, and Starris remembered laughing when he'd once described some of the subtle things he'd done in the courtroom. Little things like body movements meant to intimidate the witness into folding on the stand. She wasn't laughing now, and the intimidation worked—she was terrified.

Jordon stopped abruptly and turned menacing black eyes on her. "In one week," he stated with ominous calm, "you and I will begin a working relationship. We need to clear the air before that happens."

"I've been thinking about that, Jordon, and I don't think it's a good idea for us to work together. We've been involved on a personal level, and that kind of situation is never good in a working environment. It just causes problems all around. I'm not an interior decorator and while I appreciate your giving me the job, I think it's best if you hire someone who knows what she's doing."

The quaver he heard in her voice gave way to the lie. Starris wanted the job. She'd already shown him preliminary sketches and had been perusing catalogs and books on the subject all week. His mother's words had hurt her very deeply if Starris was willing to give up her job, a job she needed, just to get away from him.

"I see." Jordon walked around the kitchen as if looking for something. At the counter, he began lifting items, holding them in front of his face in close study, then setting them back down. Just as Starris began to wonder if he planned to say anything else, Jordon suddenly slammed down a bottle of dishwashing liquid. His voice, however, sounded placid and unperturbed. "What about Danielle?"

"Dani?"

"Yes, Dani. Or have you forgotten that you need a job in order to keep your daughter?"

The "mother protecting its cub" guard went up. Starris stuck out her rounded chin in a stubborn tilt. "I never forget anything that has to do with my daughter."

Noting the defensive stance, Jordon decided to try a different method to bring Starris around. "Baby, my mother didn't mean any of the things she said to you this evening."

"Your mother expressed herself quite eloquently. It is not necessary for you to clarify her words."

His eyes narrowed. He didn't want to fight with her. All he wanted was the chance to explain his mother's behavior. But by the tone of her voice, Jordon knew that an argument was exactly where they were headed. Well, if an argument would make her see reason then argue they would. "Then kindly explain to me how you can so blithely throw away a job that would ensure that you keep your daughter permanently."

"You're not the only game in town, Banks. I'm an educated and highly qualified individual. I'll find another job."

Jordon spotted a holder filled with wooden utensils. He chose a large spoon, flipped it in his hand and began beating the handle against the counter. Less agitated now that he had something to do with his hands, he asked, "When?"

Rattled by his cold stare, and to get away from his towering presence, Starris found a seat at the breakfast nook. "When what?"

"When will you find another job?"

"As soon as I can."

"You've been seeking employment for three months. What if it takes another three months? Do you think the Department of Social Services will let Dani stay in your home? It doesn't matter how much you love or want to care for her. As a ward of the state, Dani's welfare is its primary concern." Jordon put the spoon down and crossed to where Starris sat. He was playing hardball. If keeping Starris meant using Dani as his trump card, then he would do it. Bracing his hands on either side of her body, Jordon leaned down. "If you turn down this job and word somehow gets out, Child Welfare may come and take Dani from you. Is that what you want, Starris?"

It was then that Shelby's words blared in her head. "Jordon is the one person you don't want for an enemy," and the tears she could no longer hold back slid down her cheeks. Starris bit down on her bottom lip to stop them; the tears continued to flow. "You wouldn't tell them, Jordon. You're not the kind of person who would stoop so low as to have my child taken away."

"You don't know what I'll do, Starris, because you've decided to end our relationship before we've had a chance to begin. But as an individual, that is your right." Jordon leaned down even closer. "Now, let me explain my rights. You signed an employment agreement to work for ROBY, Inc., and I will do anything necessary to ensure that you fulfill your obligations under the terms of that contract. So, if it is your intention to break that contract, then I'd advise you to get a very good attorney."

"You can't do this. It's not fair!"

"Fair? I asked for an opportunity to explain my mother's behavior, and you did not accord me that chance. Now, you want to talk about being fair."

"But—that's different, Jordy."

The tears and the use of his pet name almost broke him, but Jordon willed himself to stay strong in the face of adversity. What Starris did next brought him to his knees.

Driven by desperation and cracking under the emotional strain of the evening, she made a last bid to sway him. She stood, placed her hands on his shoulders and aimed her mouth for his. Blinded by tears, she missed and the kiss landed on his chin. Undeterred, she continued to land feathery kisses on his cheeks and along the long column of his neck. She flicked her tongue against his skin until Jordon trembled in her arms.

He gripped her tightly, holding Starris flush against his body. His swollen arousal pushed into her thigh as his mouth came down on hers. He used his tongue to poke and prod until Starris opened her lips and let him inside. Electrifying heat raced through his veins when she pressed herself closer and rubbed her body against his. A dynamic sense of excitement filled Jordon. Finally, he'd get to sample the body he'd dreamed of for so long.

One second later, his elation evaporated as guilt and remorse took its place. Starris was offering her body, but not for the right reasons. Until now, she hadn't allowed him more than a few spine-tingling kisses, and that she was willing to do this let Jordon know just how far he had pushed her. Starris was acting purely on a reckless instinct to save her child, the child he had more or less threatened to take from her.

Jordon wrested his mouth away and struggled to catch his breath. Contempt for himself and what he'd done made him push Starris away. When had he become such a vile individual? Had his wife's betrayal affected him so deeply that now he would act just like her? *You're no better than Gloria,* Jordon thought.

Hopelessness filled Starris when he moved across the room. "Please, Jordy. Don't do this. You have so much, and you have Jolie. Dani is the only thing I have. I'll do anything you want, just please don't take my baby from me."

It was too much. They had been walking an emotional tightrope, and his finally broke. Jordon was back in her arms like a shot, and Starris held on to him, sobbing her despair.

Jordon's hands framed her face. He used the pads of his thumbs to brush the tears from her cheeks. "You listen to me, Starris Gilmore. I would never do anything to cause you to lose your baby. I was terrified of losing you, Starris, and I said what I did out of anger. But that in no way excuses my behavior. Please, will you forgive me?"

Drained, both literally and figuratively, Starris wilted against Jordon, and if not for his strong hold, she would have fallen to the floor.

"Don't cry, Star. I didn't mean any of it. I swear. If you don't want to work for me, okay. I'll make sure you find another job, and I'll do whatever I can to ensure that you keep Dani. Just please, don't put me out of your life. I know that sometimes we bring out the worst in each other, but we also bring out the best. Give us a chance to make that best, better."

She had been on a roller-coaster ride all day long. It had taken her to the top, plummeted her to the bottom and now Jordon wanted to take her to the top again. Starris wasn't sure if she could handle the skyrocketing highs or the depth-defying lows. She had to think, and she couldn't do it in Jordon's arms. She stepped away, moved to the counter and plugged in the coffeemaker. She filled the glass pot with water and poured it into the dispenser, then measured the appropriate amount of coffee and flipped the switch.

Living with Lonnie had been one low after another. When she had kissed Jordon, she knew it was a desperate act, but she had wanted to kiss him, too. She stole a surreptitious glance at him, afraid of the control he had over her emotions. She cared too deeply, and giving in to Jordon would be giving him the power to hurt her, the way Lonnie had. She stayed at the counter until the coffee percolated, then filled two cups. Without thought, she added sugar and cream to both and carried them to the table.

Jordon stared at the brew like it was a witch's concoction. He handed the cup back to Starris and said, "Thanks, but I like my coffee strong and black, just like my woman, woman."

The comment earned him a giggle, and the sound gave him hope. He left the table and moved behind Starris. Wrapping his arms around her, Jordon leaned down and kissed her cheek. "Baby? Can we start over?"

Starris set the cup down and turned in his arms. "This would be the third time."

"Third time's a charm." His lips brushed against hers. "Say yes, baby girl, and let's show my mother and everyone else that we belong together."

When her eyes changed, Jordon knew he'd made a mistake mentioning his mother. One thing he had learned about Starris was to read her eyes. They changed color with her mood, green when happy or angered, gray when melancholy or depressed and somewhere in between when nothing in particular occupied her mind. Right now, they had darkened to gray because of the hateful words his mother had said to her. He released Starris and picked up his cup. "Let's sit down."

When she was seated at the table, he wrapped his hands around his cup and tried to sit still. Watching him, Starris went back to the counter. "Why do you need it?" she asked, returning and handing the wooden spoon to him.

"It's a habit. I had so much energy, my father used to give me a pencil so I would sit still long enough to listen to his lectures."

"And the basketballs?"

"Same reason. Listen. If I promise that you will never have to see my mother again, will you still see me?"

Starris picked up her cup and sipped the hot drink. She wouldn't be the cause of Jordon losing his family. She couldn't do that to him or Jolie. "You're not serious, Jordy, and even if you were, I would never let you become estranged from your family because of me. There's too much love there. However, if you'll promise me that our relationship will stay on a professional level, then I will fulfill my contract with ROBY."

"What about us?"

"We've known each other less than a month. There is no us."

"There could be if you'd forgive me for the things I said earlier."

Starris set her cup down. "You're forgiven," she said sincerely.

"Thank you for that at least." Jordon stared broodingly into his cup, then directly into her eyes. "Tell me something. How do you propose we take our relationship from personal to professional?"

"I don't know. We just do."

"I am not a machine, Starris," Jordon snarled, then more calmly added, "and neither are you. Emotions are not dictated by the mind, and we can barely keep our hands off each other as it is. Professional means no more evenings together, no more dates, and most importantly, no more kissing. Is that what you really want for us? I know I don't."

"I can take it if you can," Starris replied caustically. His words had sounded awfully condescending to her. "Now, you have my offer. Take it or leave it."

Take it or leave it? It didn't sound like much of an offer to him. Jordon observed the determined set of her jaw. Starris was back in charge and no longer letting her emotions dictate her actions. If he wanted to see her again, then he had no choice but to take the deal. *Face it, Banks, you blew it big time.* However, there was an upside to this. He would see Starris every day, and he could use that time to his benefit. He smiled and extended his hand, sure that one day Starris Gilmore would be his.

What, no argument? Starris eyed his hand suspiciously, thinking that Jordon's smile had come too quickly to be sincere and, after seeing it, she'd heard the faint sound of a gong as it beamed into her heart. She shook the hand he offered wondering what she was letting herself in for with Jordon Banks.

Two little girls moved swiftly but quietly away from the kitchen door and made their way back up the stairs to Dani's room.

Jolie plopped down on the bed, her eyes fixed on the Janet Jackson poster taped to the ceiling. "Do you think they're kissing?"

Dani rolled her eyes heavenward. "Jolie, this is serious."

"I am serious." She bit down on her thumbnail. "I wish there were some way we could see."

Exasperated with her friend's preoccupation with sex, Dani whipped around. "Jolie, what does kissing have to do with anything?"

"Because, if your mom and my dad are kissing, then we would know for sure that they've truly made up."

Dani shook her head. "I don't think they are. Starris said they had to keep their relationship on a professional level. I'm not sure what that means, but I don't think they'll be kissing anymore."

"Damnit!" Jolie uttered.

"Jolie! You know we are not allowed to say that word!"

"So what? If you don't tell, they'll never know."

Dani plopped down on the bed beside Jolie. "Okay, here's the plan. Your dad and my mom will be working together every day, and he'll be coming over here to pick you up. We'll just make sure that they have to spend time together here, too, if you know what I mean."

Jolie's face broke into a feminine version of her father's smile. "I know exactly what you mean."

The next morning, Starris had just dropped a raspberry Tea-Sickle into a cup of hot water when her telephone rang. Surprised by the call, but pleased with the caller, she responded enthusiastically to the greeting from Denise Banks-Pullman.

"Now, before you say anything, Starris, you should know that my mother didn't mean any of the things she said to you. Yesterday was such a strenuous day with the family and all. I guess she just cracked under the pressure. Please accept my apology on her behalf and please don't take anything she said too personally. I swear to you that my mother is usually a very sane person, and nice, too, once you get to know her. And once she gets to know you, I'm sure she'll like you as much as the rest of us."

"Wait a minute, Denise. How do you know what was said between your mother and me?"

"The whole family knows. Well, the immediate family anyway. Roz and I would like to take you to lunch. There are some things you should know that will help explain our mother's behavior."

A sleepless night had given Starris time to rethink her position. She did want to know what had prompted the things Mrs. Banks had said to her. She wouldn't be human if she weren't at least curious. She already knew it involved Jordon's first wife, but since she hadn't given him a chance to explain, it certainly wouldn't be right to get the information from his sisters. If she wanted to know, Jordon was the person she should ask.

"Denise, I really appreciate your call, but I'm going to pass on the lunch. I don't know what these things I should know are, but if they concern Jordon, then I'd rather he tell me."

"I'm sure my brother will, in due time. Roz and I just want to lay the groundwork, so to speak."

Since she had already stated her position on the matter, Starris decided to divert the conversation. "How are Terrence and Tyrone? Those are the cutest twins I have ever seen, and Dani fell in love with the boys."

"Okay, Starris, I can take a hint. Roz and I would still like to have lunch with you one day soon. I promise we won't talk about my brother, except in very general terms."

Starris sighed. "That would be great, Denise."

Starris said her goodbyes and had no sooner hung up the telephone when Rosalyn called to repeat her sister's request. She gave Rosalyn the same response and after again agreeing to have lunch, hung up the telephone. Her tea was cold by the time she returned to the kitchen. Starris dumped it down the drain and went to awaken Dani.

As surprised as she was by the morning calls from Jordon's sisters, words couldn't describe the horde of emotions that flashed through Starris when she returned home from dropping Dani at a friend's and saw a strange car parked in her driveway. When she got out of her white Corolla, her world tilted even more when the door of the black Lexus opened and a regal-looking Doreen Banks stepped from the car. Taking a deep breath to fortify her inner strength, Starris slowly approached Doreen, wondering if Jordon's mother intended to take up where she'd left off the prior evening. "Mrs. Banks?"

"I'm the last person you want to see right now, Starris, and I know that. I came because I owe—" Doreen glanced around as if she didn't want to be overheard. "Can we go into the house, Starris?"

"But Mrs. Banks…"

Doreen's grip on her purse tightened, and Starris saw the lines of strain around her mouth. As hard as it was for her to face another confrontation, it had been even more difficult for Doreen to make the one hour drive to see her. "Sure," she said. "Please, it's right this way."

Starris didn't feel nervous as she led Jordon's mother into the house or when Doreen followed her into the kitchen after her offer of coffee. Her hands shaking as she filled the pot with water, the spilled coffee grounds on the counter and the broken mug in the trashcan were all evidence that Doreen's surprise visit had petrified Starris. Pouring coffee everywhere but in the cup proved the final straw, and when her breathing accelerated, Starris set the pot down with a bang and tried to blow through the attack.

Doreen dropped her purse and hurried around the counter. She held Starris loosely in her arms and rubbed her back. "It's okay, child. Just breathe slowly. That's it. In and out."

Once Starris had calmed enough to walk, Doreen led her to the table and sat her down. She returned to the counter, poured two cups of coffee and brought them to the table. "I added a little cream and sugar. I hope that's all right, Starris."

"It-It's fine, Mrs. Banks." Starris stared into the depth of her coffee cup. She could only imagine what Jordon's mother thought of her now after she'd just disgraced herself.

"Starris, I would first like to apologize for my behavior yesterday. I was very much out of line and am embarrassed beyond belief over my atrocious behavior to a guest in my home. Please forgive the things I said and know that you are welcome in my home any time, and please call me Doreen." That said, Doreen picked up her cup and took a sip of coffee.

"Thank you, Mrs. Banks—I mean, Doreen." Since there seemed to be nothing else she could say, Starris folded her hands demurely in her lap and waited.

"I didn't only want to apologize, Starris. I also want to explain, although there isn't an explanation in the world that can adequately dismiss such rude behavior on my part."

"An explanation really isn't necessary. Your apology is more than enough."

"No, child. You do deserve an explanation." It was a few moments before Doreen asked, "Have you ever been married, Starris?"

"I was married for six years. I'm divorced."

Doreen nodded. "Has J.R. spoken to you about his first wife?"

Starris wasn't sure she wanted to hear what Doreen had to say, but knew the choice had been taken out of her hands. She shook her head no.

"I'm not surprised. My son prefers to forget that period in his life. I, however, will never forget." Doreen's ebony eyes dulled with her memories. Then she jiggled her shoulders as if shaking them off and peered at Starris. "J.R. played professional basketball. He was a Denver Nugget. Did you know that?"

"Yes, ma'am," Starris replied, wondering where the conversation was leading. The wait was becoming nerve racking.

"J.R. has also been a divorce lawyer, a high school guidance counselor, a financial planner, and he played the saxophone with a band in a jazz club. Now, he's involved with this ROBY thing. J.R. can't seem to settle down. I don't know. I guess it's his way of avoiding having to deal with what happened with Gloria."

"Doreen, please."

"No. No. I know I'm beating around the bush. You see, Starris, J.R.'s first wife, Gloria, was an immoral, vindictive woman. She tried to ruin my son's life and that of their child's. Of course, at the time, none of us knew those things about Gloria. She was so shy and had such a sweet personality that we all loved her from the beginning." Tears filled Doreen's eyes, and she wiped them away as she continued. "But Gloria wasn't sweet or shy. She was evil, so evil she put her own child in an orphanage."

Starris' cup clattered to her saucer. She couldn't have possibly heard correctly. "What did you say, Mrs. Banks?"

"It's true, Starris. That evil woman took my grandchild and left her on the doorstep of a children's home in Atlanta. How could a mother do that to her own baby, her own flesh and blood? And poor J.R. When he learned what Gloria had done to his child, he was sick, just sick."

Starris felt sick herself and disgust for Gloria Banks filled her. Why did people have children they did not want? Dani's mother had done the same thing to her, and it was something

Starris couldn't begin to understand. What was the world coming to when people threw away children? "I don't know what to say, Mrs. Banks. It had to be an awful time for Jordon, and for you."

"When I overheard your conversation with Danielle, I panicked. I don't want my baby hurt like that ever again."

"I never knew Gloria, but I don't think I'm anything like her."

"Of course, you're not," Doreen stated pragmatically. "Anyone who would take a child into her home to love as her own has to have a heart of gold, which is something Gloria never had—a heart, I mean."

God sure had a way of working things out, Starris thought. Somehow he'd brought two girls with similar beginnings together, and they had become the best of friends. Dani knew how she'd come to be at the children's home. Starris wondered if Jolie knew what her mother had done. She didn't think so since Dani had never mentioned it. "Does Jolie know what happened to her?"

Doreen shook her head. "Jordon has never told her. He doesn't speak of Gloria either. He doesn't want Jolie to have any doubts that she is loved and wanted. I suppose one day he'll have to tell her, though. Jolie is starting to ask about her mother. Now that she's older, it's getting harder to avoid her questions. But the family has a tacit agreement to divert her whenever she brings up the subject. But I don't think we'll be able to keep it from her much longer."

The expression on Starris' face clearly showed her confusion. "Mrs. Banks, you said when Jordon found out. I don't understand. How could Gloria have done something like that without Jordon's—" She stopped. Curiosity had almost gotten her again. "No. If Jordon wants me to know about his marriage, I'm sure he'll tell me."

For a few minutes, the women sat quietly sipping their coffee until Doreen's voice brought Starris out of her musings.

"You're pretty, just like Gloria," Doreen observed.

The compliment set her teeth on edge. Starris didn't care to be compared to a woman who'd thought so little of those who had loved her, but she smiled graciously and said, "Thank you, Doreen, and you can set your mind at ease. There is nothing going on between your son and me. Jordon will be my employer, and our relationship will remain strictly professional."

For the first time since her arrival, Doreen smiled. "You think so, huh?"

"Yes, ma'am. Jordon and I have discussed the nature of our relationship."

"And J.R. agreed to this"—Doreen waved her hand through the air—"this arrangement?"

Starris frowned. "Yes, he did. We both agreed it would be unwise to bring a personal relationship into a business environment."

Doreen chuckled with amusement. "You really don't understand why J.R. brought you to my house, do you, Starris?"

"We came for the girls' birthday party."

"You're right of course, but I've said enough for one day." Doreen rose and retrieved her purse. "And I've taken up too much of your time."

Starris followed the older woman to the door. She stumbled back at Doreen's unexpected turn and unblinking stare. "I'll say one thing. My son sure has a knack for choosing beautiful women."

Before Starris could respond to that comment, Doreen stepped onto the porch and headed for her car.

Starris followed her to the end of the walkway. "Doreen, how did you know where to find me?"

"My granddaughter and I share a close relationship. It's been a lovely visit, Starris. I'm sure we'll be seeing each other again soon. I'll also be interested in hearing how this—business arrangement between you and my son works out. Goodbye, Starris."

"Goodbye, Doreen."

That evening and the next, Starris waited for Jordon to show up at her door. When he didn't, she called him; her repeated messages with his answering service were not returned. Tuesday, she took Dani to her favorite pizza joint and attempted to grill the child as to the whereabouts of Jolie and Jordon. The effort proved fruitless; Dani didn't know anymore than Starris. Missing Jordon brought on another sleepless night and her rash decision to show up unannounced at his house the next day; he wasn't at home. Jolie, according to Alice, was in the Springs visiting her grandparents. She did not offer an explanation for Jordon's absence and, after a long chat discussing everything but what she really wanted to know, Starris left for home. Jordon didn't call.

When it finally sank in that Jordon wasn't going to show up or return her calls, Starris felt decidedly blue. For the remainder of the week, she kept busy by continuing to educate herself on the decorating business and forcing herself not to think about Jordon.

On Sunday evening as she readied herself for bed, Starris felt a definite improvement in her mood. Monday morning, she would begin her first day working at ROBY, and she'd see Jordon. When she did, Starris planned to renegotiate their agreement. A seven-day absence was all it had taken to prove that she couldn't take it. Monday would be another new beginning for them, one in which they would find a way to make each other happy on a personal and professional level. Happy with that thought, a smile stayed on her lips as Starris closed her eyes for the night.

That same evening, Jordon sat on the crest of the hill and let his gaze sweep the wide expanse of shimmering lights before training his eyes on a spot far off in the distance. He'd been sitting for hours, having taken up his position at the start of what had been a magnificent fiery sunset, full of the vivid oranges, pinks and purples that had followed the sun in its descent behind the Rocky Mountains.

However, most of its awe-inspiring effect had been lost on Jordon who sat with his eyes narrowed in concentration. From his place on the hill he couldn't see Starris or anything that resembled a house, but he felt her, just as sure as if he was sitting on the couch beside her. Had she missed him at all during the last seven days? Cuffing the collar of his jacket around his neck and shoving his hands into his pockets helped modulate the cold wind that had chased away the heat of the day, but not the cold ache that lay deep in his heart.

His flight from the city had been sudden, prompted by another sleepless night of yearning to have Starris in his bed.

It was an attempt on Jordon's part to again desensitize his feelings, find his core and rebuild his rapidly changing view on the purpose of women. It was also an attempt to convince himself that the kick in the teeth Starris had delivered didn't hurt as much as his heart told him it did.

Nelson liked to tease him about his most-eligible-bachelor status and the women who tripped over themselves trying to capture the elusive heart of Jordon Banks. He rarely dated, and when he did, it was with the understanding of no promises, no future and no complications. Never had he brought a woman to his house, and never, except for professional reasons, had he let a female outside of his family near his daughter.

Starris Latrice Gilmore. A woman so complicated and confounding Jordon couldn't believe he'd actually begged to be a part of her life. Even more upsetting was that Starris, whose sharp tongue had scraped his ego on numerous occasions, had rejected him. It hurt, and that's why he had retreated to the mountains, to clear his head and regroup.

Orchestrated by the crickets, the air filled with the nightly sounds of a woodland concert. Jordon lay back on the grass, stretching his cramped legs straight out in front of him. Close to the ground, the musical interlude rose in adoration of the night. Its melody straining to reach the twinkling glitter decorating the black velvet above him only to be snatched away by a gusty breeze and carried off into the night. The music and its unplanned path mirrored his relationship with Starris: gone with the wind.

Jordon rose to his feet and walked back to his campsite. Squatting, he threw some wood on the fire and stoked the blaze with a stick. The newly stirred heat hit him flush in the face, immediately warming the frigid planes, but not easing the sculpted features set in determination. He reached for the tin coffeepot and filled his cup, his face awash by the light of the leaping flames. Six days of clean mountain air had cleared his head, and he had a plan. Starris wasn't looking for love, and neither was he. But he did want her in his bed and before she finished decorating his offices, Starris Gilmore would admit that she wanted him, too.

CHAPTER 10

Her first day on the job didn't go exactly as Starris had envisioned. In fact, it came nowhere close. Jordon had chosen Denver's Five Points area for the ROBY offices because most of the boys in the program lived within walking distance. She had erred in her decision to take the highway, and it had taken more than fifty minutes for her to drive the distance. Starris hadn't minded because her thoughts were solely on Jordon. She looked forward to being in his arms again once she told him that she had changed her mind about their relationship. She parked in the empty space next to the silver Seville and walked across the parking lot, fully expecting Jordon to meet her at the door with a kiss.

Dressed in gray tailored trousers, the sleeves of his white shirt rolled up to his elbows, he was at the door, but he wasn't waiting to kiss her. "You're late, Miz Gilmore. In the future, please report to work on time." Jordon turned. "Follow me."

Starris stared at his back as Jordon walked away from her. It wasn't the greeting, so much as his voice, that chilled her. Yet, she was so very aware of his spectacular build as he moved stealthily down the hallway.

Jordon stopped and turned to face her. He placed his fists on his waist and waited, working to keep his face from breaking into a smile as he watched Starris make her way slowly toward him. The yellow rayon skirt of the business suit rode her slender hips with the sensuous movement of silk. With her hands behind her body, the jacket fell open to display an outline of breasts covered by a navy blouse. When she reached his side, luminous hazel eyes stared up to meet his, and the tip of her tongue poked out to run along her bottom lip.

Jordon shoved shaking hands into his pants pockets. "This is Selma Reynolds, my personal assistant. Let her know what you need."

Starris tilted her head to the side, and her breath halted in her throat. Selma was a stunningly beautiful woman, but Starris barely had time to say a proper hello before Jordon stalked off and she had to run to catch up with him.

"This is your office, Miz Gilmore," he said with a nod of his head. "I'm right across the hall should you need me." Jordon excused himself and walked quickly to his own office. He closed the door and leaned weakly against the wood. This was going to be harder than he'd thought, and he didn't know how long he would be able to keep up the pretense.

Her second jolt came later that afternoon when Jordon opened her door without knocking. Starris was about to point out his lack of courtesy when a woman moved from behind his tall frame.

"Miz Gilmore, I'd like you to meet Lisa Mason. Ms. Mason has just relocated to the area from Atlanta. Lucky for me, she's accepted the position of job acquisitions director before someone else snapped her up. Ms. Mason starts with us tomorrow."

Starris' heart plummeted. Job acquisitions director, the position she wanted. She glanced at Jordon, whose smile looked a little wolfish to her. Swallowing her pride, Starris rose to her feet. "It's nice to meet you, Ms. Mason, and I know you'll enjoy working here at ROBY."

"Thank you, and please call me Lisa."

As Lisa turned to smile at Jordon, Starris took a moment to size her up. ROBY probably had an EEOC policy, but Starris was sure having a to-die-for figure probably hadn't hurt Lisa Mason's shot at the job, and she couldn't stop the rush of jealousy that ran through her knowing that Jordon intended to surround himself with beautiful women. How closely would they be working together? Starris wondered before shaking her head. It was an immaterial thought and one that had no place in a professional relationship. And it looked as if that was all she was going to have with Jordon. She'd blown her chance for a personal one.

"What do you do here, Ms. Gilmore?"

Though she kept her voice perfectly normal, Starris felt the heat of another wave of jealously. "Oh, I'm not employed as a staff member of ROBY. Mr. Banks hired me to decorate the offices. I'll only be around for a few weeks. Which reminds me, now that you've been hired, we should set up a time to talk about your office."

Starris felt the heat of Jordon's stare and refused to acknowledge his attempt to draw her eyes. "Perhaps, Miz Gilmore, you and I should meet first to discuss the overall feel I'd like to project, then you and Lisa can discuss individual distinctions and tastes."

Starris stared at her desktop. "Of course, Mr. Banks. I'm available whenever you are for that discussion."

"Fine. We'll set aside some time tomorrow morning." Jordon waved his hand toward the door. "Lisa, if you'll follow me, I'll show you where you'll be hanging your shingle tomorrow."

Starris watched the two of them go. The tears in her eyes burned, but she refused to let them fall. The job she wanted was gone, but she'd find another place at ROBY; that or she'd better start perusing the want ads for another job when this one ended.

The next three weeks passed so fast, Starris barely noticed the time. From her reading, she had learned that for her interior designing wasn't so difficult. In fact, many members of the profession had started their careers as fashion or graphic designers. She already had a sense of style and color, and her background had uncomplicated the process. And when you considered that thousands of women decorated rooms every day, Starris felt confident she would do a good job pulling together the offices of ROBY. Still, she had read every book she could get her hands on, scoured the stores looking at office furniture, and several times, had collaborated with Shelby to discuss fabrics and patterns.

Sometimes she became so engrossed in her work, Jordon had to remind her that it was time to pick up the girls. However, her favorite time of the day was the thirty minutes she spent with Jordon in the mornings. They shared coffee, doughnuts and discussed their schedules. Only then did she let her guard down enough to relax and enjoy being with him.

At the office, he lived by her decree and was the epitome of professional correctness. The "Miz Gilmore" bit was a little much to handle. His exaggerated pronunciation grated on her nerves. Combined with their near brushes at touching, standing close enough for her to smell his cologne, and the clothes that fitted his physique like a second skin made Starris much more aware of Jordon as a man and not her employer. His amused expression told her that Jordon knew his effect on her and that he was doing it on purpose.

At home was another matter. The girls' plan to stall their parents in the evenings hadn't worked beyond the first three days. Starris had seen through the ruse and established rules to stop the lost-and-found searches that never started until Jordon's arrival and the movies they never put into the VCR until six-thirty. Then, to the girls' delight, Jordon began arriving with bags of takeout. They ate their meals at the table amid laughter and teasing as the girls shared the details of their day with him. Despite Starris' efforts to maintain a separation between them, a routine of sorts had developed. After dinner, Starris washed the dishes, and Jordon sat in the living room checking homework.

More and more they were acting like a family, and more and more Starris wondered about Jordon's motivations. But after weeks of trying to deflect the effect of Jordon's charms, Starris felt her resistance slipping, and she sometimes felt like a mouse in a maze, caught at an impasse with no idea of which way to go. And then there was...

"Starris, I need twenty copies of this proposal."

The pencil in her hand almost snapped in half, but careful to hide her animosity, Starris looked into the face of the elegantly tall, vivacious and beautiful Lisa Mason. The woman had been a thorn in her side since her first day on the job. Lisa's security with her femininity didn't bother Starris. It was standing in the glare of that confidence and knowing she could never measure up that made Starris feel so inadequate.

She ran a hand through the thick curls that haloed her head. She'd had her hair cut yesterday and liked the more manageable style. Last night, Jordon had stared at her all through dinner and left shortly afterward claiming a migraine. While she hadn't understood his reaction, she thoroughly understood the reason behind Lisa's behavior. The morning doughnut ritual continued and hadn't expanded to include other staff. The decision had been Jordon's, and he hadn't asked Starris for her input. Though she tried to remain on amicable terms with the woman, Lisa had all but openly declared that the fight for Jordon Banks was on.

A set of gold bracelets clinked together when Lisa raised a red-tipped hand to fluff her mane of ebony hair and crossed the office. Stopping in front of the desk, she slapped a three-page document onto its surface.

Starris glanced at the papers, then back at Lisa. Smiling sweetly, she picked them up and held them out. "Then I'd suggest you find the copy machine located just down the hall."

"Look, Starris," Lisa huffed. "I'm rather rushed this morning, and Jordon has Selma tied up on a project. Now as I understand it, he said that we were a team and as such you would be at my disposal. You are part of the team, aren't you?"

Starris knew Jordon had said nothing of the sort, and she wasn't about to play Lisa's little cat-and-mouse game. While she did have feelings for Jordon, she was not up to fighting over a man who did not belong to her. If Jordon wanted Lisa Mason, he was certainly free to pursue her.

Keeping her smile in place, Starris rose from her chair. "Yes, Lisa. I am part of the team. Jordon's. If you need an assistant, take it up with him. In the meantime, I'm pretty busy myself, and I'd appreciate it if you would leave my office."

Lisa's brown eyes boldly surveyed the surroundings. Starris cringed inwardly at her blatant possessive stare. Though he'd told her she could spend most of her time working from home, Jordon had provided her with a fully equipped office. The only problem was that Jordon had given her the office directly across the hall from his. He'd even arranged the furniture so that she had no choice but to see him every time she lifted her head.

His deliberate attempts to make her want him had shaken Starris badly enough that she had returned to the office one evening and rearranged her office furniture. The next morning, the furniture was back in place, and he'd yelled so much about safety and being in the area after dark, Starris hadn't touched the furniture again. Still, she liked her office, and for another few weeks it was her office, which meant she still had the right to toss Lisa Mason out on her butt.

Lisa sauntered toward the door. "This is a nice office, and it has a particularly pleasant view," she stated, letting her eyes drift to the man sitting just across the hall. "Enjoy it while you can because when you're gone, I'll be moving my things in here."

Starris picked up a folder and moved to the door. "I'm sorry, Miz Mason. I don't have time for this meeting right now. Jordon is waiting for me."

Crossing the hall, Starris felt an immense sense of satisfaction. Knowing she had Lisa's full attention, she stated loudly, "Jordy, I've finished the design for the lobby wall." She turned, smiled again and closed the door sharply in the face of Lisa's prying eyes.

With her arms loaded down with the large box of paint-brushes, Starris walked quickly through the warm May sun-shine and entered the building. In her office, she set the box on her desk. In a few minutes, Jordon would come through her door, and she didn't want to see him. Last night, they had made love, in her dreams. Upon waking, several minutes had passed before she was able to bring her heavy breathing under control and rid herself of the touch of his hands on her body. Still feeling remnants of the sensations imprinted by the dream, she knew there was no way she could sit through thir-ty minutes of staring at Jordon without revealing how much she wanted him to make love to her.

"Good morning, Miz Gilmore."

Jordon's voice brought Starris out of her reverie. She turned to face him without her usual smile. "Morning, Jordy." He set two cups of coffee on her desk and the box she knew contained raspberry and cherry doughnuts. She watched him pour his long frame into a chair and open the box. Starris took a deep breath and moved away from him. "I don't have time for coffee and doughnuts this morning. I need to get the rest of my things from the car and start painting the lobby."

Today, she had dressed in black. Black walking pants, black sleeveless top and loafers. A hot-pink headband provid-ed the only spot of color and held back the curls of a much shorter hairstyle. The cut enhanced the beauty of her facial features and while still long and thick enough to bury his hands in, Jordon didn't like it. The girls' hair had also been trimmed and fashioned into a style that only emphasized the similarities he'd begun to notice between them. Had she warned him beforehand, he would have told Starris how he felt. Jordon frowned. When she belonged to him, he'd lay down the law: no more haircuts for any of his girls.

Taking his time, Jordon looked over the doughnuts before selecting a fat cherry-filled sweet. He raised the doughnut to his mouth and cocked a brow in her direction. "Sit down, Star. Your coffee is getting cold."

Starris sighed and tried again. "Jordon, I really need to get started. The men are coming to lay the carpet first thing in the morning. The wall has to be dry before they get here."

Jordon removed another doughnut from the box. His baby loved to eat. It still amazed him how Starris could put away all six of the doughnuts he bought for her each day and not gain an ounce. His lips curved into a teasing grin as he held out the raspberry treat. "I chose this one just for you, Miz Gilmore. Don't let it go to waste."

Jordon had been heaping heavy doses of sensual titillation on her for weeks. Her agitation rose, and wringing her hands, Starris looked from the doughnut to Jordon. "Stop it, Jordon Banks! We have a professional relationship. Stop bringing me doughnuts and stop trying to make me fall in love with you!"

Jordon's grin only widened as he watched her march from the office. He counted to five, then held the doughnut out in front of him. Starris returned to the office, snatched the doughnut from his hand and marched from the office again.

Jordon picked up his coffee and rose from the chair. His smile faltered when he heard the low, throaty voice coming from the doorway.

"Jordon, I need your input on the Rochester proposal. If we present this right, I think we can get them to take four of the kids."

"In a minute, Lisa," he replied, but it was obvious his thoughts were elsewhere.

"But I need your help now. I have a ten o'clock meeting."

"I said I'd be with you in a minute." The voice sounded pleasant, but the look in his eyes sent a direct command to back off, which Lisa heeded.

Jordon returned to his office and went to the window where he stood watching Starris lick the jelly from her fingers as she crossed the parking lot to her car. "You don't have to love me, Star," he murmured. "But soon you'll admit that you want more than a professional relationship with me."

At her car, Starris opened the trunk and ducked her head to reach for the three cans of paint located in the back.

"Hello, gorgeous."

Startled by the deep male voice, Starris sprang up and bumped her head. She turned seeking the owner of the voice, her fingers rubbing the spot where a sharp pain throbbed.

"I'm sorry," the man apologized. "I didn't mean to frighten you." The briefcase in his hand suddenly hit the ground, and he rushed toward her. "Are you all right?"

"Yes," Starris replied. "But you shouldn't sneak up on people like that."

The man's eyes widened. "There's blood on your hand."

"What?"

"There's blood on your hand." He removed a white hand-kerchief from the breast pocket of a steel-gray suit. "Here, let me see." Using his fingers, he gently pushed aside the ringlets from her forehead. It wasn't a gusher, but it was bleeding. "Come over here and sit down." Taking her hand, he led Starris to his car, then lifted and sat her on the hood. He placed the cloth against the wound, applying firm pressure.

"Now, I suppose you're going to sue me," he said, removing another handkerchief from his back pocket. He gave it to Starris. "Use that to clean your hand."

She took the cloth. "Sue you? Why would I sue you?"

He smiled. It was a nice smile and one that suited his arresting features, but it had nothing on one of Jordon's smiles or Jordon's classic good looks. Starris shook her head to dispel the thought.

"Are you getting woozy? Here hold this." He brought her other hand up and placed it on the cloth on her head. "I have a phone in my pocket."

"Wait," Starris said. "Who are you calling?"

"An ambulance. I'd rather be sued than be brought up on murder charges. When they see how beautiful you are, I'll be put away for life. What hospital do you use?" Starris started to giggle. "Great. Now you're getting hysterical on me. Look, miss. If you would just give me a number, we can get some help here. Never mind, I'll call my doctor."

Starris brought her hand down and looked at the cloth. She turned the cloth over and rubbed her head again. Nothing. When she looked up, the man was furiously dialing and apparently having trouble if his curses and banging on the phone were any indication.

"Hey. Look, it's okay."

The man apparently didn't hear her. "Damn, the battery is dead. Can you walk, or should I carry you into the building?"

"Will you look at this? I'm not bleeding anymore."

He laid the telephone on the car. "Never mind, I'll carry you."

When he went to lift her, Starris put both hands on his shoulders. "Stop! I'm fine. I'm not woozy, and I'm not hysterical. Look at the cloth!"

The man didn't get the chance. Spun around, a fist landed on his jaw throwing him back against the car.

"You son of a bitch! By the time the police get here there won't be anything left of you to carry away."

"Jordon!" Starris leaped from the car when she saw his fist rise again. "Jordon, stop!"

Jordon put the fist in the man's chest and held him down. "You move, and I'll kill you. Come here, baby." Starris walked into his open arm. She felt his rigidity as soon as he pressed her against his body. "Are you all right?"

"Jordon, I'm fine. He was helping me."

"She's right," the man added, trying to sit up. "I was trying to help."

"I told you not to move!"

The man rubbed his jaw. "This is the very last time I look at a beautiful woman," he grumbled.

Jordon looked down at Starris. She didn't look any worse for wear except the bump and scratch on her temple. Her full, lush lips seemed to lure him, lips whose softness had haunted his dreams, lips that he hadn't kissed in weeks. Of its own accord, his hand ran up and down her arm, caressing her tenderly. He saw the response that fired in her eyes and unable to resist, lowered his head and laid his mouth on hers.

As soon as her arms came up to encircle his neck, both were moaning, lost in a passion denied. Starris opened her mouth, and Jordon plunged in his tongue to delve the warm recesses of her mouth. It was like food to a starving man, and the kiss felt good, so good. Both forgot the man on the car as Jordon's hands spanned her slender waist and pulled Starris closer.

Like a drug, his touch intoxicated her, and Starris tried to get closer to the hard, muscular body and show Jordon with her lips how much she had missed him.

They sprang apart when the man on the car coughed. "I'm sorry to bust up this little rendezvous. But, miss, if you're not hurt, I really need to get to my office."

Her cheeks burned with embarrassment. "Oh, God. Jordy, we owe this man an apology."

"An apology! That man just tried to rape you!"

"No!" Starris and the man had yelled as one.

"I hit my head on the car. He was trying to help."

The man pocketed his cell phone, and keeping his eye on Jordon, retrieved his briefcase. "Skip the apology, bro. I'm willing to forget about this, if you are. I hope the two of you can work this out, but I have to go now. There is a client sitting in my office at this very minute." He moved by Jordon cautiously. "Miss, I apologize again for scaring you. If there are any medical costs associated with your injury, please have the bills sent to my office."

He started to walk away. "Wait," Starris called. "Who are you?"

The man jogged back to her and extended his hand. "Paul McCabe."

Starris slipped her hand into his. "Starris Gilmore, and this is Jordon Banks."

"Starris. That's an unusual name. But I like it. It's nice to meet you, Starris." Jordon folded his arms, his stare hostile. "And you, too, Mr. Banks, although I wish it had been under different circumstances," he said, rubbing his jaw again. He reached into his pocket and pulled out a business card. "Take this, Starris. My address and telephone number are there, in case you do decide to sue." Paul chuckled at his joke, stopping when Jordon snatched the card out of his hand.

"She won't need this. She has medical insurance."

"He's right, Paul. I do have insurance. But thank you for the offer, and you don't have anything to worry about on that other front."

"My wife will be pleased to hear that. Gotta run."

Starris watched him sprint across the parking lot and enter a building with a sign out front that read McCabe and Peters, Accountants. He worked right next door.

Calmer now that he knew the married Paul McCabe posed no threat to his turf, Jordon still scowled when he saw the smile on Starris' face. He jammed his hands into his pockets. "Don't you have some work to do, Miz Gilmore?"

Miz Gilmore? A few minutes ago, Jordon had practically made love to her in the parking lot. Now he was back to calling her Miz Gilmore? She turned to let him have it and saw the mockery in his eyes, daring her to bring up the kiss. She knew there was nothing she could say because she'd been just as aggressive in returning the caress. Well, she didn't have time to play games with Jordon today. She had to get the lobby painted. "Yes, I do, Mr. Banks. Please excuse me."

Jordon watched the swaying hips walk away from him, his hands itching to hold her body against his again. With a growl of sexual frustration, he followed Starris to the car. He lifted the paint cans and waited until she'd closed the trunk, then trailed behind her to the building. His dark brows knitted together as he followed Starris. Putting his hands on her had been a mistake. Agreeing to keep their relationship professional had been an even bigger one, and he was paying a high price for his efforts.

Unbeknownst to either of them, a pair of misty brown eyes had also watched the proceedings in the parking lot. Lisa whisked away her tears and firmed her mouth into a determined line. The battle for Jordon Banks had just escalated to world war proportions, and Lisa would do anything to ensure that Jordon and Starris would not end up together.

Jordon left the paint cans in the lobby and stalked through the reception area to his office. He stood in the middle of the floor studying his surroundings. The pale, shell pink walls had been a little sissified for his taste until Starris had shown him how the navy carpet, maroon baseboard, and executive gray furniture pulled it together. Starris had completed all the offices. In a couple of weeks, the rest of the staff would begin to filter in, and ROBY would be back in business.

A maroon Lucite counter had been installed in the reception area, and Starris planned to finish the wall logo today.

Tomorrow, when they laid the carpet and delivered the furniture, the lobby would be complete. That left only two rooms, the conference room and the boys' meeting hall. After that, he would lose his daily hold on Starris, except to see her when he picked up Jolie in the evenings. Jordon turned from the window and sat at his desk. His plan was taking too long to work. It was time to turn up the heat and bring Starris out of denial while he still had her all to himself. He reached for the telephone. "Lisa, I'm available now."

Starris dipped her brush in a can of black paint and tried not to look down the hallway again. She'd already gone down there once because she wanted to speak to Jordon about what had happened in the parking lot. Finding his door closed, she hadn't knocked. He'd never closed it before, and she knew it was a sign that he didn't want to be disturbed. She slapped the brush against the wall. She couldn't worry about Jordon and his moods. She had a job to do and had been pushing herself to get the office done as quickly as possible. Once she'd fulfilled her commitment to Jordon, she would concentrate on her designs while looking for other employment. Paint fumes rushed her, and Starris moved away from the wall. She first leaned against the counter, then folded her arms, laid her head down and closed her eyes.

"Starris? Are you okay?"

She opened one eye and peeked up to see Paul McCabe. When she saw his look of concern, she hurriedly stood straight. "I'm fine, Paul."

Light brown eyes scrutinized her. "You're not, and I'm calling a doctor."

"No! It was the paint fumes and the bump on the head. I think I just need a couple of aspirin."

"Do you have any?"

"Yes. In my purse. It's in my office, just down the hall."

"I'll go with you," Paul said, taking her arm. "What happened to that Jordon guy? I wouldn't have left you if I had known he wasn't going to make sure you were okay. But after the way you two kissed, I just naturally assumed…" His voice trailed off.

"This isn't Jordon's fault. I'm fine, really. Or I will be once I take two Advil."

Jordon ran his fingertips swiftly across the tops of the manila files in his desk drawer and shoved it closed. He swiveled his chair toward his credenza and made a quick check of his briefcase. Frowning, he buzzed his assistant. "Selma, do you have the Calvin Saunders' file?"

"No, Mr. Banks. Have you checked your desk files and your briefcase?"

"Yeah."

"Well, perhaps Ms. Mason borrowed it."

"Perhaps," Jordon replied, more to end the conversation than in agreement. Lisa had no reason to be in his files, especially those for the kids. Hearing a male voice, Jordon left his desk. Thunder rained in his face when he saw Starris walking with Paul McCabe. She tried to smile, but a wave of pain worked its way through her head. It was so strong, she grimaced and squeezed her eyes shut. Jordon rushed forward. Paul already had her in his arms by the time he reached them.

"Point out where I can lay her down and call an ambulance," Paul instructed.

Keeping his jealousy in check, Jordon led the way into his office. Placing the call, his eyes never left Paul McCabe as he tended to Starris. As soon as he ended the call, Jordon went to the couch and knelt down. "Thank you for your help, Mr. McCabe. I'll take care of her now."

Paul leaned against the desk, reluctant to leave until he knew Starris had gotten help this time. "I'll stay, if you don't mind."

Jordon capped his temper and rose to his feet. "There is no need for you to stay, McCabe. I said I'd take care of her, and I will. Starris is not going to sue, and she has medical insurance, so there's nothing for you to worry about."

"I'll stay just the same."

"Jordy?"

Jordon rushed back to Starris. "Baby, why didn't you tell me how badly you were hurt? You know I would have taken you to the doctor had I known."

Tears sprang to her eyes as another spear of pain sliced her head. "Could you please not yell at me right now. I-I need some aspirin."

"I'm sorry, Star. I'm just so worried about you. I know it hurts, but no aspirin. You're going to lie here until the paramedics come. They're on their way and will be here in a minute. You can hang on that long, can't you, baby?" Starris nodded. Big mistake. She raised her hand to her temple. Jordon picked her up and sat on the couch with Starris on his lap. "Good. That's my girl."

These two are in love, Paul thought, observing the tender care Jordon used as he ran his fingers over the bruise before placing light kisses on her face. When Jordon steered her head to his chest, Paul ran a hand over a head of brunette curls. Starris was in good hands, and he didn't belong here. "Tell Starris I'll check on her later. I want to know how she's doing. After all, it's my fault that she's hurt."

"Starris will be fine," Jordon responded, his voice tight. "Thanks for your help, and give my regards to your wife."

At the door, Paul laughed. "I'd love to. But my wife is somewhere in the South of France. We're divorced. I'll check on Starris later."

Watching him go, Jordon tightened his arms possessively around Starris. He kissed the top of her head with the uncomfortable feeling that Paul McCabe was about to become a major problem in his life.

Later that night, Jordon returned to the office to pick up some files he'd forgotten to take with him earlier in the day. Three signed contracts he'd negotiated had been delivered to ROBY, and he wanted to match boys to the jobs that evening so his staff could begin preparing them for their new positions.

Walking down the hallway, Jordon suddenly stopped. The door to his office was closed, but a light spilled out from underneath, and Jordon distinctly remembered shutting the lights off before leaving. A tingling sensation ran down his spine as Jordon debated whether to go forward or call the police before it hit him that it was probably just the cleaning crew. Continuing forward, he placed his key in the lock, but the door was already unlocked and opened when he pushed. Stepping inside, Jordon stopped again when he saw Lisa sitting in the chair behind his desk. Evidently she hadn't heard him because Lisa didn't look up when he entered. "Burning a little of the midnight oil, Ms. Mason?"

Lisa's head snapped up, and the papers in her hand fell to the desk. Panic flashed in her eyes when she saw Jordon standing in the doorway. What was he doing here at this time of night? Holding eye contact, she slowly crumpled a piece of notepaper under her palm and took a deep breath to calm her quaking nerves. "Jordon! You scared the dickens out of me."

"Sorry," Jordon said, walking farther into the room.

Lisa rose from the chair and nervously waved her hand in a circle. "I was working on a proposal for Melcher and Company and couldn't find the file. I thought I might have left it in here after our meeting this afternoon." She moved from around the desk and shrugged her shoulders. "I don't see it, so I guess it must be on my desk somewhere." She turned for the door.

"Ms. Mason." Jordon dropped his briefcase on the desk and took a seat in his chair. "How are the negotiations with Melcher and his people going?"

Lisa swallowed. "Well, I haven't been able to get them to take a meeting with me yet."

"What have you done so far?"

"Well, I've made daily calls, but the furthest I've been able to get is to his assistant. She's the stopgap, because she schedules all of his appointments."

"How do you plan to proceed?"

"Well, I think I'm wearing her down. Last week, I sent her a ROBY T-shirt and a flyer. When I called today, she said she liked the gift, and this time she actually looked at his calendar before telling me that Melcher is booked solid for the next month. I'll continue to work on her, though, and see if I can get in any earlier."

Jordon nodded. "That's probably best. Melcher and his assistant have worked together for twenty years, and he trusts her judgment implicitly. If you can win her over, he'll take a meeting with you. But let me know if you need help on this one. I'll make myself available."

Lisa smiled. "Thanks, Jordon."

"So, how are you settling in to our fair city?"

"Well, Denver's not Atlanta, but it has its good points."

"Have you had a chance to take in any of the sights?"

"No. Not yet. I've mostly been setting up house and acclimating to the altitude."

Jordon laughed. "Yeah, a lot of folks forget that it's harder to breathe when you're a mile up in the sky. But you'll get used to it, and soon I expect you'll be like one of us natives, trolling the mountains, camping and skiing. I prefer camping myself."

"Oh, do you and your wife go camping a lot?"

For one split second, Jordon's face hardened. He quickly composed his features. "I'm not married, Ms. Mason. My wife died several years ago."

"I'm sorry," Lisa said.

"No need to be. We were divorced before her death."

"Oh." Several seconds of silence passed before Lisa said, "Well, I'll let you get to work. I'm finished for the night, so I guess I'll see you in the morning."

"Have a good evening, Ms. Mason."

With that, Lisa left Jordon's office.

CHAPTER 11

Had Jordon only known how much of a problem the accountant from next door would become over the next few days, he might have done something about it before his mind became strapped by the fierce jealousy he felt every time he saw Paul McCabe. How the man made any money was beyond Jordon since he was always in the ROBY office bothering Starris. He viewed McCabe as arrogant and an outright pest, and if Jordon had his way, he'd bodily show the man the door and bolt Starris inside.

Standing in the doorway of his office, Jordon watched Paul hold the ladder as Starris climbed down. His jaw hardened when Paul put his hands on her waist and helped Starris down the last few steps.

Paul folded the ladder and propped it against the wall. "Why does Jordon let you do this? If you need a lightbulb replaced, you should call building maintenance. It's their job."

"Jordon doesn't let me do this. Had he seen me on that ladder, he would have hit the roof, and building maintenance is way too slow."

"Yeah? Well, next time call them. Your being up there made me nervous."

"Okay." Starris moved to the reception desk.

"Let's go to lunch, Starris," he said, walking up behind her.

"No, thank you," she replied, picking up her to-do list. "I still have a lot to accomplish before I pick up my girls."

"Then I'll go with you, and we can all go out for ice cream."

At the clank of bracelets, Starris breathe a sigh of relief. Lisa's opportune appearance was just what she needed. "Why don't you ask Lisa out for ice cream?"

"If I was looking for a self-centered, all-about-me woman, I would ask Lisa."

"Ask Lisa what?"

Both turned at the sound of the sultry-sounding voice. Dressed from head to toe in strawberry red, Lisa raised perfectly curved brows in question.

"Nothing," Paul mumbled.

"Well in that case, Paul, be a love and take this box to my car."

"Yes, your highness," he said with a mocking bow. "Don't go away, Starris. I'll be right back."

"Seems like you have the Midas touch when it comes to men, Starris. Paul's absolutely smitten with you."

Unwilling to get into a verbal spat, Starris turned back to her list. "I'm busy, Lisa. Good luck on your meeting with Hiram International."

"And just how in the hell did you know about that?"

Flashing green eyes rose to engage equally bright brown ones. "Jordon mentioned it in our meeting this morning. Why? Is there a problem?"

"I thought those meetings were to discuss your work, not mine! And I don't appreciate having what I do around here dissected by a couple of amateurs."

Starris' temper vaulted to hot. "I am not about to stand here and debate this with you, Lisa. My conversations with Jordon are none of your business. But I will say this: He is very concerned about your performance—or lack thereof. He'd already done the preliminary work with the Rochester Group, and they were all set to sign the contract. Yet somehow you managed to botch it up. And three companies pulled out of negotiations with ROBY last week. If I were you, I'd be very concerned about my job. Jordon will not tolerate your incompetence much longer. So instead of worrying about my conversations with him, I'd suggest you figure out a way to get some contracts into this office unless you want to find yourself standing in an unemployment line."

Lisa stood fuming in the wake of Starris' comeback. However, Jordon and the reappearance of Paul prevented her from responding.

Walking up, Jordon almost laughed when he saw the look of indignation on Lisa's face. She had walked into a land mine when she decided to take on Starris. Humorous though it might be, Starris was correct. He was concerned about Lisa's poor performance and had planned to meet with her later that day. Now, maybe he wouldn't have to. If she was as smart as her credentials made out, she'd take Starris' advice, because if she didn't start delivering soon, Ms. Mason would find herself looking for another job. Jordon held out an envelope. "This is a copy of the signed contract for Hiram, Lisa. Be sure to tell him to expect Michael Brown on Monday."

"I will, Jordon."

"Mr. McCabe," Jordon said, acknowledging Paul's presence before he walked away.

Lisa sighed as she watched Jordon disappear down the hallway, then cut her eyes to Paul and Starris. Seeing their amusement, she flipped her hair, straightened her shoulders and marched out the front door.

Paul laughed. "Seems like her highness has been taken down a few pegs," he observed.

Starris batted her lashes flirtatiously. "Why, Paul, whatever are you talking about?"

He threw a knowing glance her way. He'd seen the animosity between the two women, but right now he had other things on his mind. "When do we leave to pick up the girls?"

"Don't you have something to do at your own office?"

Paul slanted a glance down the hall. Starris had told him there was nothing between her and Jordon Banks. He didn't believe her. The way they had kissed and cuddled the day of her accident hadn't look like an employer-employee relationship to him. Jordon had also made it clear that Paul was not welcome at ROBY, and if Starris had been wearing Jordon's ring, Paul might have made himself scarce. But she wasn't, and he was willing to keep trying in the hopes of wearing her down. He stared longingly at Starris. "Nope. I'm free for the afternoon, and I've decided to devote that time to my favorite hobby."

Starris turned and braced her back with her hands, stretching her body. Paul almost groaned in frustration. "And what hobby is that?" she asked.

"You."

Starris felt warmth enter her cheeks. Paul McCabe had been relentless in his pursuit, and so far she'd been able to hold him off. "Paul, I'm not interested."

He crossed to her and picked up her hands. "How do you know you're not when you haven't tried the flavor? Why are you holding out on me? Is there another man?"

"Paul, please. I'd like to be your friend, but you're making it very difficult. If you're going to keep up this line of talk, I'll have to ask you not to come to the office anymore."

That wouldn't be good, since the only time he saw Starris was at the office. "Okay, Starris," Paul conceded. "I'll behave myself today, but as for the future—well, we'll see."

Satisfied that he would cool it, at least for today, Starris smiled. "Want to see the boys' meeting hall? I've gotten all but one wall finished, and I'm stuck for an idea. Maybe when you see what I've done so far you can help me come up with something."

"Sure. I'm interested in anything you've had a hand in."

There was a dark glint in Jordon's eye as he stepped out of his office and watched Paul and Starris make their way down the corridor. He followed. All she wanted from him was a professional relationship.

Professional!

Starris used the word so much Jordon had come to hate hearing it. She didn't want him, and knowing that he had tried to stay out of her affair with McCabe. He had even managed to convince himself that his only interest was her safety, because the man showed signs of being a deranged individual. But this had gone on long enough. It was time to put a stop to this Paul McCabe foolishness.

Jordon entered the room just in time to observe Starris drop her hands from Paul's shoulders. Kissing? Now, they were kissing! He strode over to Starris and seized her arm in a bone-breaking grip. "Starris is late for a meeting, Mr. McCabe. Please excuse us."

In his office, Jordon sat Starris in a chair, then moved to the windows. *You're an idiot, Banks,* he thought as he waged a fight to master his emotions.

From her chair, Starris felt the heat radiating from his body. She frowned in confusion. What had she done to make him so angry? She went to him and placed a light hand on his back. "Jordy, what's the matter? What did I do?"

Jordon swallowed hard. Every bit of self-control he'd exercised for the last few weeks had fled in the blink of an eye when he saw Starris in the arms of another man. She had to think him the biggest fool on earth. And if she was laughing at him, Jordon didn't think he could take it on top of the humiliating spectacle he'd already made of himself.

"Jordy, please. Why are you so angry with me?"

When he did finally turn around, he wasn't prepared for the worry registered in her eyes. He examined the exquisite face in front of him. "I—oh, to hell with it," he cried, closing the distance between them. He took her face in his hands, held it still and lowered his head. His hands found and cupped her breasts, squeezing gently before encircling her buttocks and pulling Starris against his body. When she struggled in his arms, Jordon held her tighter, wanting her to feel the effect she had on him.

Seconds later, he released her and stepped away. Jordon brought a hand up to the bottom lip Starris had bitten and shot her a stony glare. "What the hell was that all about?"

Starris turned away and groped for composure. When she was able to face Jordon again she folded her arms across her chest. "It was about not having an out-of-control lunatic groping me."

"An out-of-control lunatic!" Jordon jammed his hands into his pockets. "Is that what you think I am, Starris? Other than kissing, I haven't laid a hand on you since we met."

"Ha! Then what do you call what you were doing just now?"

Jordon's shoulders slumped forward as he regarded Starris through hooded lids. It had finally come to a head, and the games were over. By the time this showdown was done, Starris would admit she had feelings for him or hate him for making her see the truth. Jordon geared himself for the battle. "Look, baby," he said in a tone that conveyed the word was no endearment. "It was just a kiss and you enjoyed it as much as I did. What is your problem anyway?"

Starris' chin immediately tilted arrogantly. "How dare you, Jordon Banks. How dare you insinuate that I have a problem just because I don't want your hands on my body!"

Blood rushed to his head. "Is that so! Then why is it that every time I touch you, you melt in my arms, begging to be taken to bed. I'm the one using all the self-control around here, lady. You tell me you want a professional relationship, then turn those sexy eyes on me tempting me to kiss you. Even now you're staring at me like you want to be taken to bed. Deny it, Starris. Tell me that you don't want me, if you honestly can."

She turned to hide the tears in her eyes. She couldn't deny what Jordon said because she did want him. She wanted Jordon to love her as she loved him. She wanted Jordon to ask her to stay and work for ROBY. She didn't want the professional relationship she had insisted on either. Why couldn't Jordon see that? Why couldn't he help her? Starris wanted so many things, and she didn't know what words to use to ask him. Even if she did know the words, how could she? If she asked him to make love to her, Jordon would expect her to know what she was doing. That's when he would learn the truth, a thought that scared Starris so badly her body began to shake.

Jordon rushed to her side. He held Starris in a loose embrace and lifted her chin with his finger. This was not the first time he'd seen this look on her face.

Stark fear!

Something was scaring Starris to death. He enfolded Starris in his arms and walked her to the couch. Lowering them both, Jordon took her face in his hands. "What is it, Star? What has you so afraid that it won't let you show your feelings for me?"

Tell him, Starris. Tell him, or you'll never have a chance to be with him. "I can't," she said as she pulled away and tried to stand. "It's too hard for me to talk about, and I have to pick up the girls."

Jordon concealed the hurt caused by her words. Starris still didn't trust him, and he couldn't blame her. If someone had threatened to take Jolie from him, he wouldn't trust them either, no matter what they said or did later. Somehow, he had to make Starris believe that he would never do anything to harm either of them. "The girls are in school for another three hours, and I'm not letting you leave this office. The professional relationship is over. What's between us is personal, and it's going to stay personal, because that's the way I want it. Something has you hurtin, and very badly. I want know what it is, Starris. You can trust me. No matter what's happened between us in the past, I'm here for you."

When Starris didn't respond, Jordon had to work to keep his frustration at bay. He was going to break through today, but to do that, he needed to exercise patience. "Star, do you like making love to me?"

"We haven't made love, Jordon. So, I can't answer that question."

He didn't laugh, but a tiny smile appeared on his face. She was so persnickety. "I'll rephrase the question. Do you like kissing me?"

"Yes."

The confidence he heard in her voice pleased Jordon. "Starris, do you remember our first date when I told you that we wouldn't take this relationship to the next level until you were ready?"

"Yes." The word sounded like a hiss of air.

"Well, I think you're ready. Only your mind won't release you to take the next step. Would I be correct in assuming that your ex-husband has something to do with this?"

Starris' eyes widened in alarm. "No!"

"It was Lonnie, Starris. What did that man do to you?"

Recalling her marriage sent the expected kick of revulsion shuddering through Starris. And after starting and stutter-stopping several times, she finally cleared her fears and told Jordon what he wanted to know. At twenty-seven, she had wed Dr. Lonnie Gilmore, a man ten years her senior. Though she had told him, Starris didn't realize until they entered their honeymoon suite that because of her age, Lonnie hadn't believed her when she'd said she was a virgin. Enraged and under the influence of too much reception champagne, he'd all but ripped the clothes from her back and fallen on top of her. When he discovered that she was, indeed, untouched, Lonnie had cursed a blue streak.

"I was stunned," Starris said. "I had been taught that most men preferred virginal brides. But Lonnie wasn't most men. He had a voracious sexual appetite and was not in the habit of introducing ingenues to the practice of making love. He wanted someone who already knew what to do in bed. He never helped me or told me what to do, and I didn't know how to do anything but lay under him while he brutally took what he wanted while calling me vile names.

"It was humiliating, and Lonnie didn't confine his insults to our bedroom. From that first night, no matter how hard I tried, I couldn't do anything good enough to please him. He trashed my art, my cooking and cleaning, and used every opportunity to degrade me, especially in front of others. He told me that he'd only married me because of my money. He used my trust fund to set up his private practice and spent what was left on other women. I didn't care, because then he left me alone. But it got worse. Lonnie started telling me about his escapades and comparing the women to me. He said I was cold and frigid and that I would never be able to satisfy a man because I would never be a woman. Then one day, he brought one of his women into our home, and I woke up. It had finally dawned on me that I didn't have to take Lonnie's abuse, and I left."

Jordon's jaw clenched in fury. Although he'd considered the rape theory, knowing he was right did nothing to abate the white anger that assailed him. Fervently, he wished for five minutes in a locked room with Lonnie Gilmore. Instead, he reached for Starris and brought her to rest against his chest. "It's not true, Starris. Nothing that man said to you was true. You are a woman, and you are capable of loving and receiving love.

I'm living proof of that, and the way you respond to me sets my body on fire."

Starris laid her hand on the side of Jordon's face. "You've never tried to make love to me. All we've done is kiss. In bed, you're going to be disappointed, and I don't want to live the rest of my life thinking about you with other women and knowing you're with them because I couldn't be the woman you needed. I'd rather let you go now. At least this time, I'll have good memories."

Words were not going to convince Starris. For years, she'd lived with the lies and had ingrained them into her mind until she fully believed every one of them. He couldn't tell Starris, he had to show her. Jordon brought their lips together. Starris responded immediately as the flame of passion engulfed and burst into a forest fire within her body. She parted her lips, and Jordon took time to explore the soft layers inside her mouth.

Moaning with desire, Jordon rested his hands on her shoulders and laid his forehead against hers. "I think it's time for us to move to the next level," he said, his voice a strained whisper. He stood, bringing Starris with him. "Come on, baby. Let's go."

At noon, Jordon left a note on the reception counter giving the staff the rest of the day off and locked the office door. Driving through the streets of Denver tried his strength of will like no other endurance test he'd ever faced. He tried to keep his mind focused on anything other than the woman sitting at his side. It was impossible, and after stopping to make a quick purchase, he stole a kiss to keep himself from incinerating. As he pulled into the driveway, his thoughts centered on the white sleigh bed.

When the door closed behind them, Starris' nerves went into a tailspin. She felt her heartbeat spiral and tried to breathe slowly in the tension-charged air. *Not now,* she prayed. The praying and breathing didn't help, and Starris knew that any second she would start to hyperventilate.

Jordon heard the erratic puffs and turned to face her. Overwrought almost to the point of incapacitation, Starris shook like a leaf and looked as if she was about to hit the floor in a dead faint. Seeing her state effectively cooled Jordon's desire. He took her to the couch and sat her down. He stood over her and pushed her head down between her knees.

"Calm down and breathe slowly, Star," he instructed. "Baby, it's going to be okay. Just breathe."

When the attack passed, Starris hugged herself and wouldn't look at him. "I tried to tell you, but you wouldn't listen."

Jordon didn't respond and long minutes passed as he thought back on their conversation in his office. In every other area of her life, Starris displayed confidence in her abilities. As a lover, she believed herself inept. He knew differently. Every time he took her in his arms, Starris had shown him that she knew exactly what to do. But years of abuse and being told that her efforts were pathetic at best, repulsive at worst, had destroyed any hope she had ever harbored of being a good lover.

Jordon sighed and left the couch. Starris watched him pick up the telephone. "Alice," he said, "I need you to pick up the girls from school. I'm at Starris', and we've encountered a situation that needs to be resolved this afternoon. If you need either of us, call here." He hung up the telephone and looked at Starris. "Baby, how about some lunch?"

In the kitchen, Jordon put his hands on her waist and leaned over to kiss Starris on the mouth. She returned the kiss, then ordered him back to his stool. Jordon went, reluctantly. He propped his elbows on the counter and braced his chin on his fists as he watched Starris move around the space. He sucked in air when she bent over to pull something out of the refrigerator. She returned to the counter and set the green and red peppers, cheddar cheese, and ham next to the eggs and onion and reached into the drawer for a knife.

Jordon watched her chop the ham into small cubes. "Know what?"

"No. What?"

"You have a very sexy behind."

"Thank you," Starris said, feeling warmth creep slowly up her neck. She knew what Jordon was doing. The situation to be resolved was the two of them making love, and he was giving her time to get used to the idea, for which she was thankful. So far, their conversation had centered on general topics, but Jordon never let them stray too far from their real purpose for being at her house.

"Can I help?"

"Nope. It won't take me but a minute to whip this Western omelet together. Do you want toast or homemade biscuits?"

"You make biscuits from scratch?"

"Um-hmmm. Dani loves them, and I also make some of the best corn bread you'll ever eat, at least according to my friends."

"You don't have to ask me twice. I'll take the biscuits. But I could have sworn that Dani told me you couldn't cook."

"Why would Dani tell you that? As much as I like to eat, I'd better know how to cook."

Jordon frowned in thought. "Well, I know she said something about cooking."

"She probably said that I didn't like to cook." Starris laid the knife down. "Jordon Banks, is that why you've been bringing takeout food over here?"

"Yeah. I didn't want to take a chance on your poisoning me or my daughter."

"Well, there's no chance of that happening. After church on Sunday, I'll cook dinner for you to put your mind at ease."

Jordon chuckled. "This is great," he said.

Starris bent down to get the cheese grater. "What's great?"

"My woman can cook, and she has a sexy behind."

Jordon had wolfed down the pan of biscuits, but the omelet sat on his plate barely touched. Sitting on his leg, Starris raised his head and captured his mouth again. His tongue mated with hers in a sensuous dance that left them both weak and breathing laboriously. Jordon cupped her cheek in his palm. "Are you still scared?"

Starris shook her head. "I'm not scared, Jordy. You make me feel like I can do anything."

He swept a kiss along the curve of her jaw that ended with her lips. "You can do anything, including making love to me."

"I want to make love to you. Will you show me how?"

Jordon lifted her hand and placed it on the front of his pants. "Do you feel that?" She nodded. "That's what you do to me. And you can do it with a look or a touch. You're a gorgeous woman, Starris, but it's not that. I've met a lot of gorgeous women. It's you, and only you can do this to me. And now that you've gotten me in this state, what are you going to do about it?"

Starris kissed him once more and rose from his lap. She took Jordon by the hand and led him up the stairs to her bedroom. With Jordon's encouragement and sweet words of appreciation for the things she was doing ringing in her ears, Starris' fingers fumbled to unbutton his shirt. When her hands met bare skin, she rubbed her palms over his smooth chest, followed by her mouth and tried to snuggle her body up against his. Jordon shivered under her onslaught and when she reached for his belt buckle, he clasped her hands and trailed his lips down her chin.

Using his tongue, he worked the pulse at the base of her neck and removed her blouse and the lacy cloth underneath to reveal her breasts. He moved his hands to her hips, slid her shorts down her legs as his mouth moved lower to place tiny, hot kisses along her shoulders. He moved lower still, taking the shorts with him and leaving a teasing trail of steam just above the voluptuous swell of her breasts.

Starris rose to her toes and pushed her chest forward, wanting to feel his mouth on her body. Jordon placed a kiss on each swollen tip and moved lower still. She cried out her frustration as Jordon, breathing harshly now, delved his tongue into her belly button. "Jordy, please."

"Starris. Starris." It was the only response he could manage. Finally reaching his destination, Jordon molded his hands to her bare buttocks and pulled Starris forward. She held on to his shoulders, her nails digging as her mouth emitted pants that would have been squeals of delight if Starris could have found her voice. His hands skimmed the soft, brown flesh of her bottom. His manhood pushed against the front of his pants, hardening with almost unbearable pressure. Jordon intensified his efforts to pleasure Starris and drive away her doubts. Then Starris would know that she was a woman, all woman.

"Ooohhh," she moaned, and her knees buckled.

Jordon gripped her hips as Starris found herself lost in a world she had never known. When she calmed, he raised his head, resting on her belly as he endeavored to catch his breath. When he could stand, Jordon leaned down and gazed deeply, lovingly into passion-dazed hazel eyes. "That, Starris, was your first orgasm, and I hope you enjoyed it because it only gets better from here."

Still quivering with desire, she leaned weakly into the hard body. All this time, she had thought it was her. All this time. "I thought it was me," Starris murmured as she sobbed against his chest.

Jordon cupped the back of her head in his hands. "Starris, it was never you. You just needed to find the right man to help you unleash your natural passion." Jordon grinned "So what do you think? Have you found the right man?"

"Yes, Jordy."

Jordon sighed deeply. "Good, because I know I've found the right woman, and this right man needs his right woman very badly right now."

She watched as Jordon quickly stripped off the rest of his clothes and prepared himself, gasping when he swung her up in his arms and placed her reverently in the bed. She reached for him as soon as he climbed in beside her. "Jordon," she murmured. *"Merci."*

"You're welcome," he replied, flicking his tongue to touch the surface of her nipple before taking the bud into his mouth. The rough movement of his tongue quickly sent a scorch of heat straight to the heart of her womanhood, and Starris threw back her head in wild abandonment. "Jordy! Sweet Jordy," she cried.

He moved to the other breast. This woman was incredible, and Jordon felt proud that he was the one who would introduce Starris Latrice Gilmore to the wonders of making true love. He cradled her body next to his, and for long minutes just held Starris against him. Every now and then he placed a tiny kiss on her cheek, her nose and her lips. The kisses grew more frequent and when Starris turned toward him, Jordon closed his eyes, waiting for her natural instinct to take over.

He didn't wait long before he felt the silken stroke of her hand on his chest. Her fingers played in the sparse gathering of curls and ran over a dusky nipple. When she laid her head on his chest, Jordon held his breath and tried to keep his body's reaction in check as her tongue encircled his nipple, lapping gently.

His heart raced. "Yes, baby girl. That's good. I like that."

His encouragement pleased Starris. She had no idea what she was doing, but apparently she was doing something right. She took a chance and enclosed her mouth around his nipple, sucking gently. She heard his deep groan right before Jordon lifted her head and kissed her deeply. "You are an intuitive lover, Starris."

"I don't know what that means, Jordon."

He touched the tip of her nose with his finger. "It's means that if I let you, you'd have me writhing on this bed in ecstasy."

She pulled away, and seeing that his words hadn't helped, Jordon continued. "Star, don't mistake what Lonnie put you through for making love. It was a sexual ordeal that bordered on rape. He took you time and time again, uncaring of your feelings or lack of fulfillment. That's not going to happen today. After today, you'll understand how it feels when two people really make love. And I'll help you through this because I want you to thoroughly enjoy your first time. And no matter what you think, this is your first time."

He drew her back down and fitted his mouth to hers, flicking his tongue at the seam of her lips with increasing pressure as her response level rose. She moaned and granted entrance to his probing tongue while enjoying the smooth feel of his lips. Jordon released her lips and placed Starris beneath him. His mouth found hers again, then moved lower to worry the rapid pulse in the hollow of her neck.

She sighed dreamily and rubbed her hand across the taut muscles on his back. When she felt his mouth move lower and capture one of her nipples, Starris bucked with pure joy. She framed his head, directing his movements back and forth between her breasts. Guided by her hands, Jordon followed her lead. Starris might not think she knew how to make love, but she knew what she liked, and he happily gave in to her demands.

His hands began roaming the span of her stomach, matching the growing intensity of her hands on his back. By the time Jordon eased himself inside Starris, they were both reaching for the pinnacle that would douse the flame burning inside them. Jordon loved Starris slow, then fast, then slow again all the while whispering in her ear how wonderful she was and how good she made him feel. A scream accompanied his name as Starris cried out her release. A few short seconds later, Jordon followed.

Totally astounded, Starris snuggled closer to Jordon's warm body. She laid her cheek on his chest. In wonder, she listened to his even breathing. This felt good, really right and making love with Jordon was the most incredible experience she'd ever had. She'd been right to give her heart and body to Jordon. Only love could make her feel this good.

Jordon enclosed her in his strong arms and settled her closer against his body. "Starris?"

"Hmmm."

"Is Starris your real name?"

"Yes. Why?"

"Well, it's just that it's so unusual."

Starris smiled as she explained. "I was born in a taxi cab on the streets of Paris. When they removed my mother from the car and placed her on the stretcher, the first thing she saw was stars, hence the name."

Jordon rolled to his side, facing her. "Well, I think it's the prettiest name I've ever heard and it fits the prettiest woman I've ever met."

"Merci."

For a few minutes, it was very quiet in the white sleigh bed. "Jordon?"

"Yeah," he replied sleepily.

"Do we have time to make love again?"

CHAPTER 12

"Dani, do you ever wonder about your mom? I mean your real mom."

Dani sat on the bed beside Jolie. "No."

"Why not?"

Danielle's face took on a hard expression. "Because I hate her!"

Jolie's eyes widened in horror. "But, Dani, why?"

Dani left the bed. "I don't want to talk about this, Jolie."

Moving to her friend's side, Jolie placed a comforting arm around Dani's shoulders. "We're best friends, Dani. And that means you can tell me anything."

Dani wiped the tears from her cheeks. "I know." She sighed and went back to the bed. She sat and fixed her eyes on a poster on the wall. "Sometimes, I don't hate her. Sometimes, I wonder why she didn't love me and why she left me in that place. Sometimes, I don't care."

"I know what you mean," Jolie said, leaning back on the white dresser. "You wanna know a secret?"

"Yeah."

Jolie bit down on her thumbnail, then shrugged her shoulders. "I was an orphan once, too."

Dani shook her head. "No, you weren't, Jolie. Orphans don't have any parents, and you have your dad. You've always had your dad."

"Dani, if I tell you something, something that's really important, do you promise not to tell anybody, not even your mom?"

"What is it?"

"Swear first."

"Okay, I swear." Dani lifted her pinkie and the two girls hooked fingers. Then Jolie sat on the bed.

"Okay. No one knows I know this because I overheard Nommy and Auntie Roz talking one day. And I heard Nommy say that when I was little, my mom put me in an orphanage. That's where my dad found me."

"But why? If your mom didn't want you, why didn't she just give you to your dad?"

"I don't know for sure. I didn't hear any more, and every time I ask, they never tell me anything. They think that I'm still a baby and that I can't handle it, I guess."

This time Dani did the consoling. "Doesn't it make you mad, Jolie?"

"Not really. Because I do have my dad, and he loves me. And I have everyone else in my family. Sometimes, I wish she had lived so that I could ask though."

"Your mom?"

"Yeah. But she's dead, so I can't."

"Yeah. Me neither. I don't know if my mom's dead or alive. But I don't care because Starris is the best mom in the world, and she loves me."

The ringing doorbell halted their conversation. Working in her office, Starris listened to the thumping footsteps running down the stairs.

"We'll get it," the girls called out.

Starris waited, then left her office when she heard whispering on the other side of the screen.

"It's okay, Brit, she'll do it," Dani said.

"I'll do what?" Starris asked, walking up on the girls.

"Hi, Miss Starris," Brittany replied. Brittany was Mrs. Smith's daughter. They also had a son, and since she had Dani, they had agreed to watch each other's children when the need arose.

"My brother fell off his bike and hit his head on the street. He was bleeding, and Mom took him to the hospital. She told me to come over here. Is that all right?"

"Of course it is. You can stay here as long as necessary."

"There was a lot of blood, and Mom was crying. Do you think he's okay?"

Starris hugged Brittany. "I'm sure your brother's fine, Brittany. Why don't you girls go up to Dani's room. I'll bring up a snack in a little while."

Starris waited until the girls went up the stairs and into Dani's bedroom before returning to her office. Thirty minutes later, she saved the changes to her Quad-E proposal and prepared the promised snack. She climbed the stairs with the tray and stopped outside Dani's door. The conversation she overheard sent a chill of fear down her spine.

"Now, go to the mirror, Dani."

"Okay."

The girls stood together at the dresser. "Now, don't smile, Dani," Jolie admonished.

"I'm trying not to."

Jolie's eyes moved back and forth between herself and Dani in the mirror. "I don't think we look like sisters, Brittany. Except for our color, nothing is the same."

"Wait a minute," Brittany said, rising from the bed. "Let's fix your hair. Dani, do you have another hair bow?"

"In my drawer," Dani replied, followed by a great deal of giggling.

"There now," Brittany said a few minutes later. "See, I told you. You do look like sisters."

"I still don't see it," Jolie said.

"That's because you don't want to," Brittany replied, miffed. "You're the same age. You have the same birthdays, and the same middle name. I'll bet you have the same Mom and Dad, too."

"So what?" Jolie flopped down on the bed and pulled a teddy bear into her lap. "It doesn't matter. When my dad marries Starris, Dani and I really will be sisters."

"Yeah. But what if your dad is already Dani's father. Both of you were left in orphanages when you were babies, right?"

"No," Dani responded quickly to keep her friend's secret. "Jolie isn't an orphan, and she was born in Atlanta. I've been in Colorado my whole life."

"I suppose you never heard of airplanes, stupid. What if both of you were really born here and Jolie's Mom and Dad had a fight and she was so mad that she left you in Colorado. Then she took a plane to Atlanta and left her. That would explain why the two of you look so much alike." Brittany moved to the CD pile and began flipping through the selections. "I'll bet that's what happened. Jolie's dad is really your dad, and you have the same mom, too. He probably just hasn't told you yet."

"It is not!" Jolie yelled. "My dad is my dad, not Dani's."

Brittany turned around. Her face held a smirk. "If it's not true, then why are you getting so mad?"

"Because you're telling lies!" Jolie broke down in tears.

Dani moved to the bed and put an arm around her shoulders. "Leave her alone, Brittany."

"She's just a big crybaby. It's not my fault you guys have the same parents."

"I'm not a crybaby," Jolie mumbled, wiping her eyes. "You're just stupid, and no one cares what you think anyway. Right, Dani?"

"That's right, and if you don't stop saying those things about me and Jolie, I'm telling my mom."

Starris gripped the tray. She knew she should have put a stop to the conversation before it had gotten as far as it had, but immobilized, she could only stand rooted to the spot. Everything she'd thought, her neighbor's daughter had just voiced, and if Brittany saw it, other people would, too. Jordon's mother had seen the similarity. Doreen hadn't mentioned it again, but Starris was sure she had. Even Alice had once commented that the two girls looked a lot alike.

Starris took several deep breaths, then turned and walked down the hall. In the kitchen, she set down the tray and went to sit in the breakfast nook. What was she going to do? Parental rights had been terminated, but what if Jordon didn't know about Dani? She knew how he felt about family and the hellish nightmare he'd gone through to get Jolie. If Jordon had fathered Dani, he'd want his daughter. And if he did, where would that leave her? The doorbell rang, and Starris sighed with relief, glad to put off seeing the girls until she had more control of herself.

That night, Starris told herself all kinds of things to keep from seeing the truth. Dani and Jolie really didn't look alike. Dani had brown eyes and dimples. Jolie was a female version of Jordon. The circumstances of their infancy were a coincidence. If they were twins, they'd look more alike. Her mind derided her efforts. Fraternal twins didn't look alike. Identical twins shared an egg. Fraternal twins shared the womb. Twins ran in Jordon's family. He was a twin himself. Starris prayed. "Please, Lord. I love Jordon, but I don't want to fight him for my daughter."

"Well now. Who do we have here?"

Dani and Jolie turned to see Lisa standing in the doorway. "Hello," they offered. "Who are you?"

"Might I ask you that same question? I don't remember Jordon hiring two lovely ladies such as yourselves."

"I'm Jolie Banks, and Jordon is my dad."

"He is," Lisa responded, walking farther into the office. "And you are?"

"I'm Dani, and Starris is my mom."

"Is that right?" Lisa remarked. "When I first saw the two of you sitting there, I thought you were sisters." The comment earned her a curious stare from the girls. "My name is Lisa Mason. I'm pleased to meet both of you."

"Do you work for my dad?"

"Yes, I do."

"What do you do?" Dani asked.

Lisa sat on the edge of the desk. "Has your father explained what we do here at ROBY?"

"You train teenage boys and get jobs for them," Jolie answered.

"That's right. And my job is to meet with companies and try to convince them to hire some of our kids. I do other things, but that's the most important part. What are the two of you doing here today?"

"We're waiting for my mom," Dani answered. "She needed to get something from the office."

"Oh," Lisa remarked. "You must take after your father's side of the family, Dani. You certainly don't look anything like Starris."

Dani shrugged, and turned back to the computer screen.

Lisa watched them defeat a gruesome monster, then asked, "Is Starris your real mother, Dani?"

"Yes," the child answered without hesitation. "She adopted me."

"My mom's dead," Jolie volunteered. "But when daddy marries Starris, she's going to be my mom, too."

Lisa slipped from the desk. "How did your mother die, Jolie?"

"Girls? I found I what needed. Are you two ready to go?" Starris rounded the corner and stopped when she saw Lisa in her office. "Lisa! My goodness, you startled me. What are you doing in here?"

Starris could have sworn Lisa's red lips thinned before she smiled. "Sorry. I've been getting acquainted with the girls. Now, if I remember correctly, Dani belongs to you and Jolie to Jordon. Interesting."

"And why is that, Lisa?"

"Well, it's uncanny how much they look alike. Why, they could pass for sisters."

Responding to an alarm inside her head, Starris turned to the girls. "Dani. Jolie. Get your things, it's time to go."

"But we just got to a good part in the game," Jolie complained, pointing at the screen on Starris' computer.

"I'm sorry, sweetheart. We really need to go. Shut down the computer, please."

"I hope you aren't leaving on my account."

Starris reached for her purse on the desk. "Not at all, Lisa. We have a busy afternoon. See you tomorrow."

A knowledgeable gleam entered Lisa's eyes as she watched Starris hustle the girls to the door.

The following evening, Starris slipped into the meeting hall and took a chair at the back.

Jordon walked to the front and looked out over the group of boys and men seated around the room. "Last week we talked about goalsetting. Each of you were to look within yourselves, talk with your mentors and write down at least three lifetime goals. How many of you completed that assignment?"

Every hand in the room, except one, went up, and Calvin Saunders rose from his seat. "Mr. Banks, I thought about what you said, then I talked to my cousin and what he told me makes sense. Realistically, the chances of any one of us going to college is slim to none. I mean, look at us. You guys, the mentors I mean, already got yours. How are we supposed to get ours? Who's going to come down here and help us?"

Calvin Saunders aspired to be a lawyer, and he was smart enough to reach that goal. Instead of concentrating on that goal, Christopher Mills, a police detective and Calvin's mentor, spent a great deal of his time getting the boy out of one minor scrape or another. Unfortunately, Calvin's only male influence, until ROBY, had consisted of an unemployed cousin with five children by three different women. To combat the negative image within his family, Jordon had teamed him with Christopher, determined that Calvin Saunders would make it. "Mr. Saunders, why should anyone come down here and help you?"

"Because they owe us, man!"

"Hmmm," Jordon toned. "Who, exactly, is the they you speak of, Mr. Saunders?"

"The white man, G! You know, the ones that made our people slaves and who own everything. We built this country, but do we have anything to show for it? We grew the cotton, the tobacco and the sugarcane, but do we own any factories? And how many inventions did we come up with that we never got credit for? Hell, we even laid down our lives for this country, but does anybody give a damn? They owe us, man. All of us. They owe us big time."

Jordon frowned. "We? Us?"

"Come on, G. You know what I'm talkin' 'bout. The black man and woman. If it wasn't for us, there would be no America. And now that we've built this country, there's no place in it for us. The black man is hassled, imprisoned and killed just because of his skin color. Hell, this goal-setting exercise is a bunch of crap. Everyone knows the only way a brother can make it is to tap his feet and sing a tune or put his game on the court. With the way people in this country treat the black man, my lifetime goal is livin' long enough to see my twenty-first birt'day."

Jordon looked at Nelson. "Want to handle this one?"

Nelson crossed one leg over the other and smiled. "No, my brother. I believe it's your turn tonight."

Jordon nodded in acquiescence. Calvin did have a few things right: the black race had been held in slavery, and if not for the contributions of African-Americans, there was no question America would not be the powerhouse it was. African-

American males also received more than their share of harassment, and the number of them in prisons grew daily. However, there were a couple of things Calvin did not have right, as Jordon was about to point out.

"Mr. Saunders, most of what you've said is true. The black race did help build this country, and it was done under the yoke of slavery. However, there are a few perceptions that I believe we should correct. First of all, Mr. Saunders, if you are afraid for your life, you should not look to the white man. Most young, black men killed today are murdered by other members of the race. Second, the *we*, as it pertains to you and me, have never been in slavery. It was our ancestors who labored in sweat, and in many cases, gave their lives for the survival of the race. And we have survived, Mr. Saunders, and done so in the face of all obstacles. Of the men sitting in this room, none are singers, and only Mr. Reeves and myself have played basketball."

Calvin gripped his elbows, seemingly unconcerned that his pants were about to fall to his knees. "Well, there you go, G. That just proves my point. If not for your game, where would you and homeboy be today?"

"Mr. Saunders, if we are to continue this discussion you will address me by my surname. For future reference it is not G, but Mr. Banks. However, you have posed a fair question, and you should know that while Mr. Reeves did play basketball in college, he holds a master's degree in engineering. I did play professionally, but I also earned a bachelor's of liberal arts and a law degree. Every other man in this room pursued the path of higher education, and all are successful."

Calvin did not look impressed. "Yeah? Well, I guess if I came from a middle-class background, grew up in the suburbs and had parents with money, I'd be able to go to college, too."

"That, Mr. Saunders, is not a fair statement. Mr. Reeves grew up in small, mostly black township right outside of Raleigh, North Carolina. His father worked in a cucumber factory. I grew up right here in Five Points. My father painted houses. Mr. Warner, please relate to Mr. Saunders the circumstances of your childhood and why and how you obtained your college education."

Richard Warner stood. "I'd be happy to. I grew up in Brooklyn, New York, as the oldest of nine children. My family lived in grinding poverty on the tenth floor of a building owned by a slumlord. By the time I was fourteen, most of my running buddies were dead from gang warfare or drugs. I decided that I wasn't going out like that. So, I went to the library and, after doing a little research, I discovered that there was a great deal of scholarship money available, but never used. I chose my profession, concentrated on my studies, and won a full scholarship to Howard University. Today, I am a professor of science at Denver University."

"Thank you, Mr. Warner. Dr. Lewis."

Nigel Lewis stood. "I grew up in Choctaw, Alabama, as the seventh of ten boys in a family of sharecroppers. We worked from sunup until sundown culling rice paddies. But I was bright and always bragged that I was going to college. You see, I wanted to be a doctor. Everyone told me it was a foolish pipe dream and that my time would be better spent working harder in the fields. But there was this doctor who came through the county about once a month. His name was Dr. Phipps, and he was a black man. Dr. Phipps told me to hold on to my dream and never give up, and he gave me some of his old medical books. I read those books cover to cover so many times they fell apart in my hands. I also worked for anyone who would pay me an extra dollar until I'd saved enough money for my first semester in school. I got in and even managed to win a small stipend. I still had to work every day of the eight years I attended school. Today, I am a pediatrician, and I have a successful private practice."

And so it went until each man had related his story.

Calvin, who had taken his seat and listened attentively to the men, rose again. "I get it, Mr. Banks. These men made it, and I extend to them my props. But what does that have to do with me and the rest of my homeboys sitting in this room?"

"This is what it has to do with you, Mr. Saunders. Our ancestors, who were held in slavery, never had the mind-set of a slave. They were strong-willed people, beset with tremendous obstacles, and yet they still managed to forge the way for you, one who is not held in slavery. Now, there are two paths that you can take in life, and each path leads to a different door. At the end of one path, you can open the door and find success and the other—well, let's just say it doesn't lead to success. Our ancestors did not have a choice; you do, and the decision is yours to make. How will you decide, Mr. Saunders? What will be the course of your life?"

Starris rose from her chair and left the room. Now, she knew what to do with that last wall.

CHAPTER 13

Two afternoons later, the girls were in Dani's room, and Starris willed herself to focus on the silhouette she had begun to outline on the placard. She was nervous, and rightly so, because before leaving the office, she had slipped her proposals outlining a marketing campaign for ROBY and using Quad-E in the sister program into the inbox on Jordon's desk. Along with the marketing plan, she had included several sales pieces, a press release and a list of businesses she thought would be receptive to working with the organization. Since he didn't seem to take her professional abilities seriously, she hoped that he'd read the material and discuss it with her in more detail. Then he'd offer her the job of the recently posted marketing director, a position for which she qualified, unequivocally.

Starris laid down her brush when the telephone rang and reached for the receiver. She hoped it might be Jordon, but it wasn't. It was Jim Stephenson, Dani's caseworker.

"Good afternoon, Starris."

"Hello, Jim."

"I wanted to let you know that I'm going on vacation, but before I left, I wanted to give you some good news. Now, mark this date down. Dani needs to be in court on June fifteenth, and so do you. You're both on Judge Laughton's calendar, and on that date, he will approve the adoption of Danielle Kathryn Carter by Starris Latrice Gilmore."

Starris stood to her feet, speechless. She bit down on her lip, but a tear slid down her cheek.

"Starris, are you still there?"

"Yes," Starris answered in a watery voice. "I'll have Dani in court on the fifteenth. And Jim, thank you. Thank you very much."

"You're welcome."

Numbed, Starris left her office and walked into the living room. She sat on the couch, her eyes fixed on the entertainment center, but seeing nothing. On June fifteenth, Dani would officially become her daughter. Once that happened, no one could separate them—ever—and thoughts of all she had gone through to get the little girl circled through her mind.

Her journey into the child-welfare system and the legal quagmire of the adoptive process had begun eighteen months ago. Starris had become a cottage friend, and two Saturdays a month spent the afternoon with the twelve little girls, ages seven to ten, who resided in Cottage Three of the children's home.

The day she met Danielle had not been one of her regular visits and why she had gone to the orphanage had, at the time, been a mystery to Starris. Now, she knew it was to meet the little girl that would one day be hers. Actually, two events had guided Starris to the orphanage that day. That morning, the mail had brought the final decree for her divorce from Lonnie Gilmore and her angry outburst at the Quad-E meeting had gotten her placed on censure, again.

When she arrived, Jan Cummings, one of the counselors on duty, had cheerfully introduced her to the new addition at Cottage Three.

Starris leaned down and offered her hand. "Hello, Danielle. My name is Starris Gilmore, and I'd like to be your friend."

Danielle Carter, who lived by the motto "strike first before you are struck," regarded Starris with contempt. An angry line formed over beautiful brown eyes before Danielle turned to Jan and said, "Get this ugly bitch outta my face. I don't wanna be her friend."

Verbally, Starris hadn't responded to the caustic insult served by the tall, too-thin little girl. She pulled Dani into a bear hug and held on while the child struggled to free herself. Thirty minutes later, Dani had finally given up the fight and started sobbing, and for two hours Starris had rocked and soothed the little girl until she fell asleep in her arms. Then Starris had gone to find Jan. Starris could still recall their conversation word for word.

"Danielle Carter is a 'special needs' child, a category reserved for older children generally above age five; sibling groups; and those with medical, physical, emotional or behavioral challenges, and because they make up the largest group, all African-American children in the child-welfare system nationwide."

Jan had gone further to say that someone had left Dani in a basket on the doorstep of the children's home. The unsigned note pinned to the blanket said the baby was one week old and that her name was Danielle Kathryn. The infant was given the last name Carter, and Dani had been a ward of the state ever since.

"Why wasn't Dani made available for adoption? Most people who want to adopt want infants."

"Because of the note," Jan replied. "The juvenile judge at the time refused to grant termination of parental rights. In the best interest of the child, he ruled to leave the door open in case one of the birth parents returned to claim the baby."

For the second time that day, Starris exploded. "It's been ten years!" she yelled, outraged at the thought of a child allowed to languish in an overcrowded, underfunded system because of a simple legal decree. "Don't you think that if anyone wanted that child they would have shown up by now?"

Jan raised both hands as if warding off an attack. "Whoa. Don't shoot the messenger, Starris. I agree that, in Dani's case, parental rights should have been terminated long ago. However, I am not her caseworker, and Danielle is just one of thousands who has slipped through the cracks. We have so many children, and with the increasing daily influx, it is not unusual for one social worker to have a caseload of two hundred or more kids. We don't have enough people, of any race, willing to be foster parents or adopt these children.

"Some who are willing drop out under the strain of a system and legal process that can be trying at best, damned difficult and insensitive at worst, and that can stretch the process out for years. Add to the mix do-gooder organizations that fiercely oppose all attempts to reform the system. They operate under the misguided belief that they are protecting families when what they are actually advocating is that these children grow up in a cold, unfeeling system of bureaucracy rather than a warm, loving home with people who genuinely want to care for them. The fallout is the thousands of children who grow up unloved, insecure, emotionally deficient, bitter and angry. And when they reach the age of eighteen they are dropped from the system and left to fend for themselves." By the time Jan finished speaking, she'd worked herself into a fuming snit.

Still angry herself, Starris banged her fist down on the desk. "Well, Danielle is getting out of the system. I'll adopt her. Who is her caseworker?"

Jan smiled and patted Starris on the arm. "Good for you, Starris." She left her chair and went to a file cabinet, returning with a thick, manila folder. "Now, I'm not allowed to do this, and if anyone asks, I'll swear we never had this conversation, but there are some things about Dani you should know. After hearing them, if you still want to pursue adoption, then I'll give you the name and number of Dani's caseworker. Agreed?"

Starris nodded. "Agreed."

Jan opened the folder. "You understand that I cannot violate the confidentially of Dani's court appearances by revealing specifics, and it would also be best if you kept what I'm about to tell you to yourself. Let the caseworker reveal this information in his own way. Do you understand what I'm saying?"

"I do."

"Okay then. I've already told you that Dani was abandoned here at the home. She has also been termed 'unadoptable,' a word we no longer use in favor of the more politically correct labels of 'waiting' or 'special needs' children. Dani's behavior is incorrigible. She steals from the other children, lies about it, then brazenly wears or uses the stolen property in public. If the children say anything, she beats them up. She is disruptive in group to the point where she is no longer allowed to participate, refuses to follow the rules of the cottage and uses rough language for shock value. She does poorly in school, if she attends at all. Because of that and because she's a runaway, right now, the counselors walk her to school and back. However, Dani will leave the school grounds and return right before the bell rings. Emotionally, Dani is a very angry child, and the doctors have her on daily doses of Ritalin to suppress her violent outbursts. She is unresponsive except to fight all attempts to help her. She is also insecure and has very low self-esteem."

Starris fell back in her chair. "That's a whole lot of labels to tag on one little girl. Maybe it's this place. It's so cold and unfeeling. Maybe Dani just doesn't want to live here."

Jan closed the folder and rested her hands on top. "Starris, Danielle has been in ten foster homes since the age of seven, and she's run away from every one of them. Her caseworker, except for mandatory court visits, has pretty much washed his hands of the matter. He simply has too many cases to keep trying to help a child who doesn't want to be helped. Still interested?"

Interested? Starris was more interested than ever. After what she'd just heard, she should be running for the hills, but something deep inside Starris told her that she and Dani were supposed to be together. "What is her caseworker's name?"

"Jim Stephenson." Jan reached for a piece of paper. "This is his number and the address for the Department of Social Services. Here is a word of caution: When you meet Jim, don't be put off by his manner. Jim has worked in the system for more than twenty years and has dealt with just about every imaginable situation, from simple neglect to harsh physical abuse. He may seem impatient and uncaring, but hold your temper and try to win Jim over. Once you do and he's convinced that your intentions are sincere, he can be your best friend in working your way through the process. Good luck, Starris."

It had taken three weeks to get an appointment with Jim Stephenson, and when she'd met him, he had seemed brusque, rude and very opinionated. Starris knew she couldn't even start the adoptive process until the judge terminated parental rights. So, while her almost daily visits with Dani had forged a relationship, she'd had to employ a lot of patience, pestering and friendly prodding to get Jim Stephenson to take her seriously. When he did, he had virtually walked her through the opening steps of adopting Dani.

Termination of parental rights had been granted at Dani's very next court appearance, and Starris had filed her petition to adopt. After the hearing, she'd completed the paperwork to foster parent and, a few weeks later, brought Danielle home. Abhorred by the thought that Dani had been drugged, the first thing Starris did was throw all of Dani's medication into the trash. The first few weeks had been rough, and she'd even spent an entire night looking for Dani after she'd taken off. But for the past ten months, Danielle had lived with Starris during the waiting period, a specified amount of time, mandated by law. The courts wanted to make sure that Starris could provide a good home and that Danielle had adjusted to the new environment.

Colorado's waiting period was six months to one year, and because of Dani's past history, Jim had insisted on a full year of adjustment. Dani had done so well and her behavior changed so drastically that after seven months Jim convinced the judge to waive the remaining five months. One week later Starris had lost her job, and a postponement of a final decision had been placed on her case.

Now, a little more than five months later, Starris' grandest wish was coming true. If not for Jordon and the job he'd given her, this day would not have been possible. His role and the thought that she was finally going to finalize Dani's adoption made Starris so happy that she lowered her head to her hands and burst into tears.

Alice squeezed Starris' hands. "That is wonderful, dear. I'm so pleased for you and Dani."

"Thank you, Alice. Now, you're sure you don't mind?"

"Not at all, child," Alice replied sincerely. "Tonight's my bingo night. So, really you're helping. What room do you want to start with first?"

Starris rose and hefted two of the bags on the table. "I think the family room since it's the one that needs the most work."

In a grumpy mood when he pulled into his driveway, Jordon waited for the girls to climb from the car. They raced for the door; he followed more slowly, still trying to figure out what had been so important that Starris couldn't attend the girls' play. She'd been so closemouthed when he had questioned her that he couldn't help thinking it had something to do with Paul McCabe.

The girls had Alice surrounded when he walked through the door. They were full of questions about the whereabouts of Starris. After clapping her hands for attention, Alice said, "I've already told you that I'm not sure where she is. Now, stop pestering me with questions. I'm late for bingo."

Alice didn't have the look of someone telling the truth, and seemed almost flustered to Jordon. "Are you sure you don't know anything?" he persisted.

"All I know is that she left this for Dani." Alice handed Dani a white envelope, then went to the closet and pulled down her hat. She settled it on her head. "I'm sure Starris will be along shortly. Jordon, you have the girls. Good night."

"Wait," Jordon said when she reached the door.

"Can't stop. I'm driving tonight, and I don't want to keep the ladies waiting. Have a good evening."

They watched the door close behind Alice, then turned to stare at the white envelope in Dani's hand.

"Open it, Dani," Jolie said.

Dani let her backpack slide from her shoulder to the floor. All three were on edge as she slowly opened the envelope and read the message on the card inside. "My darling, Danielle—a room bathed in white and full love is where my angel will find her dove." Dani looked to Jordon. "That's all it says." She handed him the card.

Jordon read the card, then turned it over looking for another message. He looked up and saw the confusion in the girls' faces. Okay, it was time for him to take charge. "Well, now. What we have here is obviously some kind of clue."

"And if we figure it out, it will lead us to where Miss Starris is, right, Daddy?"

"You mean like hide-and-seek?" Dani asked.

"That's exactly what it is," Jordon said, chuckling. "Hide-and-seek. Starris is somewhere in the house, and it's up to us to find her." He led the way to the steps and sat down. Dani and Jolie followed. "Okay, let's go over this again."

"I know," Jolie said, when he'd read the card again. "Hospitals are white. Maybe Miss Starris is at the hospital."

"No, sweet pea," Jordon quickly assured her. "Starris is somewhere in the house or on the grounds. Now, we have eleven rooms to search, and we'd better get to thinking." Jordon had already figured out the clue. There was only one room in his house that had anything white in it.

Dani sat up after a few minutes. "I know what room it is," she said, standing. "Come on."

Jordon and Jolie followed her up the stairs. She went directly to Jolie's room. Starris wasn't there, and nothing seemed out of place.

"Wait a minute." Jolie pointed her finger. "What's that?"

"A dove," Dani cried. She ran to the bed and picked up the stuffed bird. She pulled off the envelope attached to its wing. Dani open this one eagerly. "My darling, Danielle—if you found this you're very smart. Now, don't give up until you've found my heart. In a room downstairs, it's very dark and not appropriate at all for something that barks."

This clue threw Jordon. Except for the kitchen, every room downstairs was dark. But Dani hadn't finished reading. "You can't type when you only have paws. You'd better hurry, something might get gnawed."

A dog! Starris had put a real, live dog in his study. Jordon led the way this time. They heard the little yaps as soon as he opened the door. Jordon sighed with relief when he saw the little fellow safely penned inside a cardboard box. Dani ran and picked him up. "This is what I've always wanted, but Starris said we couldn't get a dog until…We have to find Starris!"

Jolie searched the box. "Here's another envelope, Dani."

"Read it."

"Go down the hall to the place where there's foom, but don't stop there, I'm not in that room. Foom? What's foom, Daddy?"

"A made-up word that rhymes with room, I guess." Jordon took the card. This was kind of fun. "In a special place that's not in the house, my little bitty will find something pretty."

"The gazebo!" Jolie yelled.

"How do you know it's the gazebo, sweet pea?"

"Because Miss Starris says that you grow weeds and the gazebo is the only thing in the backyard that can be considered pretty."

Humph! Now, Starris was turning his daughter against his agricultural efforts. They needed to have a chat about that little matter. Jordon looked up smiling though. "Well, let's go."

They tromped down the stairs and into the kitchen. "Something smells good," Jordon remarked, stopping to peek in the pots. He rubbed his stomach. "How about we take time from our expedition and have a little snack?"

The girls looked horrified. "Without, Mama?" they both asked at once.

"Sorry," Jordon said. "I must have lost my head there for a minute. Lead on, troops!" Jordon did, however, snatch a piece of corn bread before he followed the girls through the patio doors. Since Dani had the puppy in her arms and Jolie carried the dove and the cards, Jordon had to take the large bouquet of wildflowers Starris had left on the bench for Dani. He also managed to read the card. "Now return to a place that is cozy and warm. There I am waiting for you to see, because we're going to be a family."

Jolie, the only one who hadn't caught on yet, finally put it together. "Dani, I know what your mom is trying to tell us. You're going to be adopted!"

Jordon found himself jogging behind the girls as they ran back inside the house and into the family room. Holding on the puppy, Dani waded through the balloon-strewn floor and into Starris' open arms. Jordon held Jolie's hand to give them a private moment.

"Is it true, Mama? Am I being adopted?"

"Yes, it is. Mr. Stephenson called this morning. We have an appointment with Judge Laughton on June fifteenth. That's the day you and I will adopt each other." Dani didn't respond, and Starris felt a shiver of disquiet pass through her. "You do still want to adopt me, don't you, Dani?"

"Mama, I... Mama..." Dani put her head on Starris' chest and sobbed.

"It's okay, angel. I cried, too."

For a few minutes, Jordon let Starris hold her daughter, then gave Jolie a tight squeeze. "I'd say by the looks of this room that we are about to have a celebration, and I can't wait to get another piece of that corn bread."

Starris looked up. She released Dani and walked toward Jordon. "Another piece?"

He backed up with his hands in the air. "Now, Starris. I do have an explanation. It was just sitting there on the counter, calling my name. I tried to resist. Honest! It was a fight to the bitter end, and I had no other choice but to eat it. By the way, it is the best corn bread I've ever eaten."

⁓

A few nights later, Starris sat comfortably in the warm circle of Jordon's arms. She laid her head on his chest and let her eyes rest on the girls. They sat side by side, cross-legged on the floor, bent over with their elbows up to support the chins resting on their fists. The adults had no interest in the pay-per-view movie they'd ordered for the girls, who had done some fast talking to get their parents to approve the PG-13 flick. Other than a couple of "damns" and "hells" and a drawn-out fistfight, the feature had been acceptable. However, the movie was almost over, and with the end would come the noisy chatter that had preceded it.

Jordon gathered Starris a little closer and leaned down to kiss her lips languidly. "Our reprieve is almost over," he whispered.

"I know," she groaned good-naturedly. "It seems like the movie just started."

Jordon nudged her cheek with his nose. "Since we've been such agreeable parents this evening, perhaps we can convince them to go up to Dani's room. Then you and I can sneak down the hall and have some of our kind of fun."

He let out a grunt of air when Starris gave him a friendly poke in the ribs. "We spent most of the afternoon in bed, Jordon," she whispered conspiratorially. "Don't you ever get enough?"

His brows rose in jest, "Of you? Never!"

A pair of chestnut-brown faces spun in tandem and frowned at the couch. Jolie and Dani put their finger to their mouths. "Shhh!"

"Busted," Starris said, laughing.

Jordon gave her a gentle push and sat up. "It's not me, it's Mom."

Another poke followed that statement as Jolie rolled her eyes. "Sure it is, Daddy."

The girls turned back to the television, and Jordon pulled Starris back into his arms. A few minutes later the movie ended and two dark heads came together in a shared whisper. Jolie and Dani rose to their feet. They picked up the half-eaten bowl of popcorn and their glasses. "We're going to take this stuff to the kitchen and then go up to Dani's room," Jolie informed their parents.

"Yeah," Dani added. "Thanks for ordering the movie, and we'll stay out of your hair for the rest of the night." They left the room amid a wave of sudden giggles.

"Think they know what's going on between us?" Jordon asked with real concern.

Blushing furiously, Starris buried her face in his chest. "How could they? We've been so careful."

"It might be that glow of love in your eyes every time you look at me."

Her head came up with a jerk; the remark had hit so close to home Starris couldn't look at Jordon. "I-It." She stopped and took a deep breath. "My eyes do not glow," she said defiantly.

"But you are in love with me."

Starris twisted her head in disbelief. When she saw his teasing grin, she reached for a pillow and belted him in the face. Jordon grabbed the weapon and tossed it out of reach.

"You have a thing for pillows," he said, laying Starris back on the couch. He covered her body with his and quickly worked his hands beneath her top to caress her lovingly while his tongue made delicious swirls at the base of her neck. "If I didn't know better," he murmured raggedly. "I might think that you weren't in love with me at all."

"Shut up and kiss me, Jordy." To which he responded with an enthusiastic smack on her lips.

Sitting up, Jordon left the couch and crossed to the stereo. He flipped through the collection of CDs, and after selecting a Miles Davis disc, pushed play and returned to the couch. He placed his sock-clad feet on the coffee table and dimmed the lamp. Starris laid her head on his thigh and closed her eyes, content with the music and knowing he was with her.

With his fingers gently playing in her hair, Jordon knew the exact moment Starris totally relaxed, and her nesting movements and soft breathing made him smile. He felt rather cozy himself, and the more time he spent with her, the more he thought of Starris and Dani as his family. The sound of giggling reached his ears and for a moment Jordon let himself think of Dani and Jolie as the sisters they claimed to be. Sometimes when he looked at them, he could almost believe it was true. And this wasn't the first time he'd had the thought.

"Baby? How did Dani become a ward of the state?"

Starris stifled a yawn with the back of her hand. "She was abandoned at the children's home. No one knows where she came from or why she was left there. The workers there didn't even know her last name, and with so little information they couldn't trace her background. I can't imagine anyone leaving a wonderful child like Dani to fend for herself."

Frown lines settled between his eyes. "But I thought Dani's surname was Carter."

"That name was given to her at the home. There was a note pinned to her blanket listing her first and middle name, birth date and nothing else," Starris replied sleepily. "I guess it doesn't matter. When the adoption goes through we've both agreed to change her last name to Gilmore."

Why her remark bothered him, Jordon couldn't say right away. Starris was a Gilmore, so it followed that she would want her daughter to share her name. It didn't seem right to Jordon, and when it finally occurred to him why, a chill traveled the length of his spine. Gilmore meant that Starris still had a connection to her ex-husband, a man who had treated her badly. Jordon wanted that tie severed permanently, and the only way he could think of to make it happen was to exchange her name for another—his! Aghast, Jordon cleared his mind of the thought, but the next words that slipped from his mouth shocked him even more. "Jolie was in the system once, not here, but in Atlanta."

"I know," she said quietly.

Flabbergasted, though he knew he shouldn't have been, Jordon stared down at her. "Which one, Roz or Neecy?"

"Neither. It was your mother."

Jordon's heart stopped. "My mother!"

"Calm down, Banks. It's no big deal. Your mother came to see me and offered a very gracious apology for her behavior, which I accepted equally as gracious. She even invited me back to her home for another visit. Jolie came up in the conversation." She took one of his hands in hers and patted it gently. "I'm sorry about what happened to her and to you."

After first gripping her hand tightly, Jordon released a deep breath, and his body lost its stiffness. His ex-wife was losing her hold on him, and he knew it was due to the woman lying beside him. "Thanks, I appreciate that. I suppose my mother told you about Gloria, too."

"No, she didn't," she said almost too quickly.

"She didn't? Well, since she did share Jolie's story, I might as well tell you about my wi—Gloria, too." Starris heard the hard edge in his voice, and sat up, but his hand gripped hers again. "I want you to know, Starris, because I don't want anything standing between us."

She nodded, and he continued. "Gloria and I met during our junior year in college. She was so pretty, I fell like a ton of bricks. We married during our senior year, and it took only a couple of months for me to learn that I really didn't know my wife. The first lie was that she hadn't come from a large family, as she'd led me to believe. Gloria grew up in an orphanage in Atlanta, which is why I suppose she ended up doing what she did with Jolie. She'd always wanted a large family so she just made one up. Her shyness and vulnerability turned out to be a cunning ruse that she used to hide a devious personality. In college, Gloria attended all of my games. I thought it was because she loved me, but she was only interested in my earning potential. Once I was drafted and I signed that contract, she stopped pretending. The wives of the other players accompanied them on the road, and I begged Gloria to come with me. She absolutely refused, which led to a lot of fights."

Cloaked in memories, a sadness entered his voice, and Starris laid her hand on his arm. "There's no need to go on, Jordon. I understand."

He looked down at her. "No. I don't think you do. And you need to hear the rest, because it explains why I will never love or allow myself to fully trust another woman again."

Shocked into silence, Starris struggled to hold back the rising sea of gloom as the underlying message of his words struck her. Only a fool made the same mistake twice, and she was that fool, for she had fallen in love with Jordon Banks, a man who, like her ex-husband, would never love her. Hiding her pain, Starris forced herself to listen as Jordon continued his story.

"We were playing in Chicago when I was tripped during the game. As soon as the doctor saw the X rays of my broken ankle, we both knew I'd never play professionally again. In the span of a few seconds, my basketball career was over. I didn't think anything could hurt worse than that, but I was wrong. Gloria wasn't at the airport the day I came home, and when I arrived at the house, I understood everything. The woman who had taken vows and pledged herself to me was in our bed with another man. I was so angry I wanted to kill her. I opted for throwing her out of the door. About eight months after that Gloria was found murdered. About a year later, my lawyer received a letter. That's when I found out about my daughter."

The immense anger that rose inside Starris shocked even her. She forgot her hurt to deal with the objectionable actions of Gloria Banks. It was bad enough that people had children they didn't want, but to selfishly use them as a means of revenge was an atrocity. Starris was glad that Jordon had found his daughter and equally glad that he'd made it possible for her to get Danielle out of the system.

Jordon gave her a mirthless smile. "So you see, our daughters both had dubious beginnings and share more than just a middle name and birthday. Have you noticed how much they look alike at times?"

Now Starris was aghast. All her worst fears were coming true. She tried to rise, but Jordon's hand held her down. "What is it, Starris?"

She stopped struggling, realizing that to continue would alert Jordon to how much his comment had affected her. "Nothing, except that I wanted to get up," she said with amazing calm. She looked at the hand holding her down, then up at him. "That is, if it's okay with you."

She's lying, Jordon thought, releasing her. The easy-flowing air had filled with tension, her tension. He wanted to know why. "Since you didn't know Gloria, it must have been my comment about the girls."

Starris released a shaky laugh. "Well, yes and no. Yes, because there are times when I've noticed similarities, and no because I've chalked it up to their being best friends. They're together so much, they'd naturally take on some of the same mannerisms."

Jordon's expression turned thoughtful. "Yeah, I guess you're right," he finally agreed, though not satisfied with her response. "When you think about it, they really don't look anything alike."

It sounded as if he wanted to say more, and Starris leaped to her feet before he could voice his thoughts. She wandered over to the stereo and haphazardly flipped through the discs. She changed the music without bothering to look at what she put on and continued to traipse the room, one arm wrapped around her waist, the other hand pulling at the hair on her forehead. She had wondered when Jordon would notice what she and others had seen and what she would say when he did. Now, she knew, and a cord of fear struck deep. She also knew that she needed to discourage the conversation somehow. "What are you planning for the open house?"

He watched the wandering through narrowed eyes. "What open house?"

Starris returned to the couch. "The open house for ROBY?" Jordon continued to look puzzled. "To announce the opening of your new offices?"

His face cleared. "Oh, that. Yeah, the open house," he repeated, knowing he hadn't given the matter any thought at all. "I'm planning a little something."

"What?"

"What, what?"

"What do you have planned?"

Jordon leaned forward and peeked at her sideways. "You really want to know, for truth?"

"For truth," Starris responded, though she already knew the answer.

"Nothing."

"I'm not surprised," she muttered under her breath.

Mildly irked, Jordon grunted. "I'll get Lisa to handle it on Monday."

It figured that Jordon would look right past her to someone else, and that the someone would be Lisa Mason, really made Starris see red. "Why not me, Jordon? I can do this. Let me plan the open house. I'll plan a party that will knock your socks off."

The brow rose. Starris was getting worked up about this, and he really didn't have much faith in Lisa. "All right, baby. The party is yours."

But Starris was still talking and didn't hear him. "I'd plan a catered affair, black tie and diamonds. We can invite representatives of the companies already under contract to ROBY and some that have good potential. Oh, and we'll invite all the mothers, too."

Jordon reached up and yanked her down. "It's yours, Starris. And I have faith that you'll do a wonderful job. Only let's tone down the black tie and diamonds and go with a little music, a light dinner and business suits. I'd like the boys and their families to come, but I wouldn't want them to feel uncomfortable. Now can we go back to doing what we were doing before all this talking started?"

In her eagerness to convince him, Starris realized that she had gone a little overboard. "Thanks, Jordon." That she had successfully diverted his attention didn't make her feel any better. Wrapped in his arms, she could almost make herself believe that Jordon hadn't meant what he'd said about love and that everything would work out. Deep in her heart, Starris didn't believe that. By his own admission, he would never fully trust her, therefore their relationship had no future, the end was inevitable.

Too weary to keep thinking about a future that did not include Jordon, she leaned back and let his kisses consume her thoughts. But she made a mental note to contact her lawyer and Jim Stephenson. She needed to know how to protect herself in the event that she had to fight the man she loved in court for her daughter.

CHAPTER 14

The following Saturday, Starris added another group of doodles to the design on her pad and tuned out the highly annoying voice of Carlotta Eldridge. Most meetings, she paid the woman little attention; today was worse than usual. For one, she was still on public censure. It would be another two weeks before she could speak at the meetings and present her proposal. Two, she was furious with Jordon Randolph Banks.

Since he hadn't said anything, she had asked him about her marketing plan. He claimed he hadn't seen the document. Sure he was lying, she'd point-blank asked him for the job as marketing director. He'd turned her down, offering instead that she redecorate his home. The circles on Starris' pad became bigger and bolder as anger, in tandem with her thoughts, seeped into her drawing. She was qualified enough to decorate his offices! Qualified enough to watch his child! Qualified enough for him to take to bed! But when it came to working with him, she wasn't qualified. Realizing what she was doing, Starris drew in a breath of cleansing air and laid down her pencil. To free Jordon's grip on her thoughts, she lifted her eyes to the poster hanging on the beautifully decorated wall in Carlotta Eldridge's great room and forced herself to reread the four Quad-E principles she knew by rote.

Enrichment—stay abreast of your chosen profession; it will enrich your mind.

Empowerment—comport yourself as though you have authority; it will be empowered.

Endurance—endure and overcome all obstacles in your path; you will find success.

Entrust—the Lord is our provider. Entrust yourself to his care; He will provide.

She and her friends had had mixed feelings when they'd received invitations to join the group, because other than a dinner/dance and small scholarship fund, Quad-E had no real purpose. Despite their efforts, nothing had changed, and she and Pamela had already decided not to renew their membership. Starris looked at the poster again, keeping her face impassive as she added the fifth E she and Pamela had written.

Eldridge—do not cross Carlotta. If you do, all the enrichment, empowerment, endurance and entrusting in the world won't save you.

She swiftly brought her attention back to the meeting when she realized the room had suddenly grown quiet and that all eyes were staring at her. She directed her eyes to the head of the rectangular table and met the angry glare of Carlotta Eldridge.

"For the benefit of those whose minds may have been elsewhere, I'll repeat my former statement. Lisa Mason," Starris snapped to attention as Carlotta bent forward to read from her notes, "the job acquisitions director of ROBY, called to personally invite our group to join them at a special event to announce the opening of their new offices. Now, ROBY is a group that works with the young men in our community, and I have accepted the invitation on behalf of the membership. Also, please note that I will be making a special announcement at this event that is sure to garner Quad-E some positive press. The function will be held in the meeting hall at ROBY. Dress is business cocktail, and the function is scheduled to begin at seven, so please be on time." This statement she made with her eyes on Starris.

Starris felt the tips of her nose flare slightly. She'd only been a couple of minutes late, but leave it to Carlotta to reprimand her before the entire group. Starris didn't dwell on the thought, wondering why Lisa had gone around her to invite Quad-E to the function, especially since she'd already sent an invitation to Carlotta.

Pamela raised her hand.

"Yes, Ms. Shaw."

"Is it possible for you to tell us the nature of this special announcement?"

Carlotta's pushed-out mouth looked like two wrinkled prunes as she weighed her answer to Pamela. Lately, several of the younger members seemed restless and impatient with the governing body of Quad-E. Her eyes wandered around the table, landing in turn on Starris, Pamela, Jacqueline Tyler and Shelby Reeves. Especially those four.

They were beautiful, yes, which was the first requirement of Quad-E. As the creator of RavenLove, an editor of books written for African-American children, an account representative for African-American writers and a renowned fashion designer, respectively, they easily met the second of contributing in a positive way to the history of the race. However, they were not satisfied with the projects undertaken by Quad-E and took every opportunity to vent their views.

Carlotta directed her gaze to Pamela again. "Yes, Ms. Shaw. It is possible. However, the executive committee has made the decision to withhold the announcement even from the members. The possibility for press leaks is ever present, and we want to be sure the story has not become old news prior to the open house." Carlotta's brown eyes took on a glow as she looked around the room enjoying the suspense she'd just created. "But I will tell you this. ROBY is made up of a very prominent group of men. Most are eligible, all are handsome and quite a few are moneyed. With that in mind, I urge each of you to give due consideration to your attire."

Carlotta stood and closed her folder, missing the exchange of rolled eyes between Starris and Pamela. "As a final note, you should all be aware that our own Ms. Gilmore was hired to decorate the offices of this organization, and I understand that she has done a wonderful job. Please offer your congratulations before leaving. This meeting is adjourned."

Jordon placed the crystal vase of wildflowers in the middle of Starris' desk and clapped his hands together in anticipation, his excitement barely in check. Starris had done a wonderful job pulling together the open house. At this moment, she was in the meeting room finalizing the last details with the caterers. The boys, their mentors and mothers had all agreed to come. All of the companies currently contracted under ROBY had sent RSVPs, and several interested companies were sending representatives. Starris had gone a step further and sent invites to every prominent African-American in the Denver Metro area. Coffee mugs and refrigerator magnets with ROBY's new address and phone number had arrived that afternoon. As a special gift, Starris had ordered backpacks, baseball caps and T-shirts with ROBY's new logo emblazoned on the front for each boy in the program.

Jordon opened the box of doughnuts, removed two and laid them on the china plates he'd brought from home. He filled a crystal glass with orange juice and hit the switch on the coffeemaker behind him. Today was Starris' last day working at ROBY, but not her last as an interior designer. In a couple of weeks, school would let out for summer vacation. He hoped Starris would eventually agree to redo his house, keep the girls and, if he timed it right, be there waiting for him every night. Hearing the outside door open, he went to wait for Starris in the doorway of her office. When he heard more than one voice, he frowned.

"I've been asking you out for weeks. What do I have to do to get you to say yes?"

"Nothing. Because I'm not going out with you. I have an escort for the open house."

"But I just gave you a dozen red roses. When a man gives a woman red roses, she's supposed to melt in his arms and do anything he asks."

"Where did you pick up that bit of nonsense?"

"I read it in one of those women's magazines and the article stated that flowers are one of the surefire routes to a woman's heart."

Starris laughed. "It's no wonder your wife divorced you, Paul McCabe. My advice is that you stop reading those silly articles and just go with your heart. Women like sincere men, and they like originality. If you're observant and a good listener, a woman will always let you know exactly how to win her heart."

Paul stepped closer and placed his hand on her arm. "Then tell me, Starris Gilmore. How do I win your heart?"

Starris moved away. "You can't. It's already taken."

"Okay, I understand. But you owe me at least a lunch before you disappear from my life."

"Why?"

"To give me the opportunity to apologize for injuring you."

"Paul, that was weeks ago. You know I've completely recovered from the incident. And I'm not going to date you."

"It's not a date," he protested. "It can be a lunch between two professionals. You have to eat, Starris. So, how about it?"

Starris drummed her fingers on the counter as she considered his request. "It won't be a date?"

"No date."

"And if I agree to have lunch with you, as one professional with another, you'll stop pestering me for a date?"

"Yes and no."

"Yes and no?"

"Yes, it will be a lunch between two professionals. And no, I won't stop pestering you for a real date."

"Well, at least you're honest. Okay. I'll have lunch with you. It can be an apology and a farewell lunch."

Paul wanted to shout for joy. "Do you mean it, Starris?"

"Yes, I do, but there is one thing. I'm supposed to pick up a package at one o'clock. Can you run me by the store before dropping me back here?"

"Anything for you. Now, don't forget. You promised this time, and I'll be here at noon on the dot to pick you up."

"I'll be here, and thank you for the roses. They're lovely."

"Not as lovely as you." Paul smiled as he stared at Starris. "I have to go. See you later."

Starris watched him leave, then headed down the hallway to her office. Only after today, it wouldn't be her office, and after the party her association with ROBY would be finished. This would also be the last day she would share breakfast with Jordon. She would miss that intimate time between them and sharing her day with him the most. Though he hadn't offered her another position, his impact on her life had been tremendous.

Jordon had shown her that she knew everything she needed to know about how to please a man in bed. For that, Starris would always be grateful, and she was grateful for the job and the money she hadn't deserved. Yes, she was grateful to him, glad that she could please him in bed and so much in love with Jordon her heart ached. She swiped at the tears in her eyes, and knowing she couldn't face him until she pulled herself together, returned to the lobby. She set the roses on the reception counter and went to the boy's meeting hall.

The room, while colorful, had no particular rhyme or reason. Starris had tossed out the corporate color scheme in favor of giving the room its own unique flavor. The east wall, an eclectic mix of colorful symbols and sayings, she hoped would inspire the boys to strive for their goals. She'd let the girls cover the back wall with thick orange and yellow stripes to which she had added large rectangles to hold a photo of each of the boys. The west wall, the one that had given her trouble until inspired by the boys' meeting had evolved into a giant staircase that led to two doors. Across the top, she'd painted the words, "Which Door Will You Choose: Success or Failure?" Sitting in the room of psychedelic colors cheered her and lifted her spirits. Starris hoped it would do the same for the boys.

Jordon Banks pitched a verbal fit as he paced the floor of his office. "Starris is sleeping with me and yet she still wants to date that woman-hungry, trying-to-get-into-her-pants creep from next door," he muttered.

It's not a date, his mind quickly informed him.

"It is a date," Jordon refuted aloud. Starris is going out with a man, isn't she? They'll be alone, won't they? Aren't those the elements that constitute a date?

They're two professionals having lunch, his head reminded.

They can call white black for all I care. A date's a date, and Starris is not going anywhere with that man! Jordon left his office to tell her just that. Halfway down the hall, he stopped and retraced his steps. He had no real claim on Starris and no right to dictate her life. By his actions, he had misled her, and the longer he let it go on, the harder it would be when the end did come. He started to fall into his chair, then retrieved his sax from the closet and stood in the window playing a deep and haunting melody. The music reflected the despondency that had gripped him and came from somewhere deep inside. As Jordon played for what could never be, he tried not to mourn what could have been, if not for the vow he'd made.

Releasing the mouthpiece, he rested his forehead against the window. *Let her go, Banks,* he thought. Since he couldn't give Starris his love, he should do the gentlemanly thing and step aside. She had a right to find love and happiness, even if she found them with Paul McCabe.

He had made a vow to never forget Gloria's betrayal and her unhinged desire to destroy not only his life but that of his child's. For more than ten years, he'd kept that promise. How had he allowed Starris to get so close to him and become an influence in his daughter's life? But Jordon already knew the answer. It was the same reason that he had to end their relationship now.

"I love her."

By the time Starris returned from lunch, Jordon had tamed his emotions and resigned himself to what he had to do. He did love Starris, but it was a love he would get over. Suspicion and fear would rule the rest of his life, and because he could never trust her, he knew it wouldn't take long for him to destroy them both. Starris entered his office like a ray of sunshine. Despite his internal conflict, Jordon smiled. In her hands, she held his vase of wildflowers.

"Your door was closed this morning, so I didn't get a chance to thank you for these." Starris set the vase on his desk and dropped into his lap.

He would miss this the most, Jordon thought, when she wrapped her arms around him and landed a smack right on his lips. All her inhibitions had disappeared, and Starris often initiated their intimacy. She even kissed him in front of the girls, who seemed to take the relationship between their parents in stride. Jolie loved Starris as much as he did. Could he really hurt his daughter this way?

"They're gorgeous, Jordy," Starris said, hopping up from his lap and putting her face in the blossoms. She inhaled deeply. "They're from the garden, aren't they?"

He wanted to ask her what happened to the roses from Paul, but refrained. "Yes, Star. They came from the garden. But you don't have to keep them if you—" Jordon clamped his mouth closed.

"Why wouldn't I want to keep them? It's a beautiful bouquet, and I wish they could last forever. But wait here, I have something for you, too."

Jordon watched Starris run across the hall to her office. This was going to be harder than he'd thought. When she returned with two wrapped boxes, he rose to his feet. "What's this?"

Starris could barely contain her excitement. "They're your office-warming presents, and I hope you like them. Here, open this one first."

Jordon took the long, narrow box. Inside, he found a nameplate for his desk. The letters of his name shaped the carved wood. But it was the contents of the second box that made his heart beat faster. Starris removed the male and female statues from his hand.

"Now, the metal is not real gold. It's a brass plating and the carvings are only replicas," she told him. "But one day I'll be able to afford the real thing, and I'll replace these." She walked to his bookcase and placed the statues on one of the shelves, rearranging the other objects to showcase the serene beauty of the figurines. "What do you think about putting them here?"

He felt her exuberance across the room, and Jordon crossed to her. He lifted Starris in the air and swung her around. "I don't want these replaced. They're great." He made a thorough examination of her mouth before releasing her.

"But you're a collector, and these are not genuine pieces."

"They are genuine because they came from you. I don't want them replaced. Ever."

"Do you really like them, Jordon, or are you just saying you do to spare my feelings?"

Jordon exhaled a deep breath and placed his fists on his waist. "Starris Latrice Gilmore, what do I have to do to convince you that I love your present?"

Jordon could swear that the gleam in her eyes brightened right before it turned wicked. He watched her walk to the door of his office. She looked over her shoulder, smiled and turned the lock. He released a breath. She crossed to the windows and looked at him again. He stared back like a deer caught in headlights, startled by the intensity of her gaze. The blinds came sliding down; the front of his pants tightened at the same speed.

Starris turned and began walking toward him. Her skirt fell to the floor, and she paused to step over the material. A few seconds later, the blouse flew over her head. Momentarily released from her spell, Jordon's gaze followed the blouse's path until it landed somewhere near his couch. His head swung back to Starris, and Jordon swallowed. She was going to seduce him. Right here in his office, in the middle of the day!

Exhilarated by the thought, desire began to ebb and flow through his body. He heard the tinkle of his belt buckle and the rasp of his zipper. He groaned when his pants glided down his legs, followed quickly by his silk boxers. When Starris lowered herself to the floor in front of him, it took exactly one minute for Jordon to fall to his knees in capitulation. Her hands stripped him of his clothes; her lips silenced his hoarse protests that he had no protection. By the time Starris finished with Jordon Banks, he couldn't have lifted himself from the floor if his life depended on it.

Some time later, his embrace held Starris trapped against his body, and Jordon endeavored to regain a normal breathing pattern. It didn't matter what he'd thought earlier. Making love to

Starris felt great; having her in his life felt even better. He loved her so much, it was worth the risk of a broken heart because he wasn't going to let her go.

At four that afternoon, Starris stood at the window watching thick, black clouds tumble in volatile play across the dark sky from the West. She sighed, knowing that in a few minutes the storm would block out the sun. She drew her brows together, hoping the rain would hold off until morning. Hardly likely, but it would be nice if it could at least wait until after the party.

The weather reminded Starris of Jordon, excitably impassioned and angered. Her behavior in his office still astonished her, and though the mellow mood that had followed afterward had digressed drastically, she'd tried to hang on to the buoyancy she'd felt after the gut-level response she'd wrung from him.

Jordon had brought her down hard when he'd again asked her to redecorate his home. Again, she had refused. Their disagreement would have inched its way to a full-blown argument had he not grabbed her by the shoulders and tried to kiss her senseless. Starris glanced down at the check in her hand, her last check from ROBY, and shook her head. Jordon was a stubborn, temperamental man, and she supposed the bonus was his way of apologizing for not giving her another position at ROBY. She had enough money now to last for a while, but tomorrow she'd start looking for a permanent job.

Starris dropped the curtain and went to her bedroom. Inside, she studied the dress she planned to wear for the party. One of Shelby's designs, tiny gold flecks speckled a black silk bodice. The gown, held up by spaghetti straps, hit her knee and dipped to a low vee in the back. Starris moved to the dresser,

laid the check down and opened her jewelry box. She removed
a pair of single-carat diamond earrings, laid them on the dresser and headed for the bathroom.

"You look positively beautiful, Starris."

She turned and couldn't help admiring the tall physique in
the navy blue suit. He had been dogging her all night. "Thanks,
Paul," she said, for what she thought was the hundredth time.

Paul grinned and raised his hands. "I know. I know. But I
can't help it. You look great. How about taking a walk with me?"

"Now?"

"Right now," Paul said, watching Starris glance around the
room. "Everything's going fine, and I'll have you back shortly. I
want to talk to you about Jordon."

Her eyes sought and found the man leaning casually against
the makeshift bar. The room faded into the shadows, and Starris
held her breath as she took in the muscular build in the tailored
black suit, white silk shirt and colorful tie. Jordon stood straight
and shook hands with the man at his side, then linked gazes
with Starris. Under the cover of one hand, he held up three fingers. Jordon had just locked up three jobs for the kids.

Paul's touch on her arm broke the almost tangible bond. She
directed her eyes back to him. "Okay, Paul. But only for a few
minutes."

Sliding his arm around her waist, Paul splayed his hand
against the warm skin of her back. Starris tipped her head and
frowned up at him. Paul winked and guided her through the
exit.

A pair of glowering black eyes followed Starris and Paul as they left the room. *This is going to end tonight,* Jordon thought. Before he took two steps, a reporter tapped him on the shoulder. Jordon glanced at the door, then gave his attention to the man and the questions he fired about ROBY.

"Sure is a looker, that one. Do you know if she's here alone?"

Jordon's haunted stare followed Starris as she glided through the tables and chairs. The gown swayed with her figure, emphasizing every womanly curve, and Jordon couldn't help remembering the things she'd done to him earlier that day. All evening, he'd watched her effect on the men in attendance, his anxiety growing with each pass she made around the room. Starris was too much of a temptress, her allure like a magnet. It was the reason he hadn't hired her on a permanent basis. If she did ever leave him, it wouldn't be because of a man she'd met through her association with ROBY. He looked down at the man by his side. Douglas Speer owned a heating and cooling company and had expressed an interest in hiring one of the boys. "She's with me, Doug. Now, about that job."

Starris stopped at the table housing her friends and plopped down in an unoccupied chair.

"You did a wonderful job pulling this function together, sister-girl."

"Thank you, Pamela." Starris slipped off her shoes. "It was fun, but I'm exhausted. I can't wait for the party to end."

Jacqueline's eyes roamed the room. "I hate to admit it, but Carlotta was right. I've never seen so many eligible men in one room in my life."

"And women," Maxie muttered darkly, her eyes on the bearded face of the man Jacqueline insisted she loved. Though the encounter with the woman looked innocent, Maxie knew all about the man's penchant for philandering. She turned to face Jacqueline. "Maybe if you left this table, one of them would take an interest in you."

Jacqueline's chin jutted forward. "I already have a man, Maxie."

Maxie looked across the room again. "Perhaps someone should tell him that."

Hoping to ward off an argument, Shelby said, "Well, J.R. certainly is pleased, and he hasn't taken his eyes off Starris all night."

"And you'd better get over that exhaustion," Manny added. "I don't believe that sleep is an option you'll have this evening."

"Manny, now that you have Christopher, isn't it time for you to get over your preoccupation with the sex lives of your friends?"

"I am over it, Shel. I just stated out loud what every one of you are thinking."

At nine-thirty, Lisa stepped into the meeting hall. Attired in a tangerine cocktail dress, her hands fiddled with the rounded bubble skirt as she scanned the crowd before touching Carlotta lightly on her arm. Feeling her intuition kick in, Starris tensed when the two women moved in Jordon's direction. She watched the introductions, and his head dip to hear something Lisa said. Her heart began a rapid beat, and she didn't understand her apprehension when he followed them to the front of the room.

Lisa stepped to the podium and tapped the microphone. "May I have your attention please." She waited until the hall quieted. "I would like to welcome our invited guests, the mentors, children, mothers and employees of ROBY. I would also like to extend a special welcome to the companies and representatives who have made all of this possible and introduce to you Carlotta Eldridge, the founder and president of Quad-E."

There was a smattering of applause as Carlotta took the microphone. "As you all know, Quad-E is dedicated to helping the community when and where we can, and our contributions are well documented. Some weeks ago, Ms. Mason contacted me and explained the vital role ROBY plays in the lives of our young men. While that work is important, there is a need that is being left unfulfilled. Our young women are just as important, and with that in mind, I have approved Ms. Mason's proposal to utilize the membership of Quad-E as mentors in ROBY's sister program. Also, I plan to donate personal, as well as organizational funds to see that this crucial segment of ROBY's agenda gets off to a healthy and productive start."

Starris gasped; then felt her anger build as Lisa retook the microphone and began to outline the Quad-E proposal she herself had spent weeks putting together. Somehow the woman had gotten a copy of the document and, distressed, Starris' eyes flew to Jordon. She watched him thank Carlotta for her support and Lisa for her efforts. Someone handed her a packet. She opened it to find the brochures she had created, the fact sheet and the press releases she'd written. Devastated by Jordon's betrayal, Starris stared at the documents, and her hopes of ever working for ROBY crashed at her feet.

CHAPTER 15

The sunlight streaming through the blinds only intensified the pain that quickly spread to her eyes, arms, legs and stomach the moment Starris opened her eyes. She had a killer headache to go along with the deep depression she'd sunk into the previous evening. She sat up, and when the room took on a decided spin, she groaned and flopped back on the pillows.

Bone-tired, she couldn't stave off the snippets of her conversation with Jordon about his wife or the events of the prior evening. Both had engaged her conscious mind through the night and deprived Starris of sleep. The cache of doubts she'd thought buried since meeting Jordon added to the noise in her head and, when Shelby's warning joined the melee, Starris rolled to her side and made herself leave the bed. None of it mattered. Jordon would never love her, and they would become enemies if he had fathered Danielle, because Starris would not give up her daughter without a fight.

Rubbing her temples, she glanced at the bed again. While she would like nothing better than to wallow in self-pity, she had things to do today, the first being to start making some calls and find out what rights she had in regard to Dani. Shoving her arms through the sleeves of her robe, she belted the garment and began moving decisively toward the door. Stopping suddenly, she spun on her heel and fled for her bathroom and the toilet.

In the kitchen later, she put the teakettle on the stove then went directly to the telephone. Five minutes later, Starris hung up feeling a little better about her position with Dani but not really reassured by Jim's words. According to Jim and Colorado law, more than six months had passed since termination of parental rights had been granted in Dani's case, which meant that no person could make a claim for the child. However, Starris couldn't help feeling that in Dani's case, the judge might make a special ruling to reinstate Jordon's rights. In two recent high-profile cases, adopted children had been returned to their birth fathers. In one, the father had not known of the existence of the child and had not consented to having his rights terminated. In the other, the father proved that he had looked for his son, and that he had been purposely misled into believing that the child had died. In both of those cases, the children had still been babies and the rulings would probably have no adverse effect.

Dani was eleven, and Starris could only hope that if something were to happen, that the judge would weigh Dani's preference heavily in his decision, if her daughter chose her. But to have a real family—well, Starris knew that it was the dream of every child in the foster-care system. And what about Jordon? No matter how the court ruled—one of them would lose, and as much as Starris knew she loved Jordon, she also knew that their relationship would not survive either outcome. She had to talk to Jordon, and she needed to do it before Dani's adoption was finalized. It was the only fair thing to do.

Feeling lightheaded and too upset to continue brooding over the dilemma any longer, Starris bypassed her usual raspberry tea in favor of a cup of weak Pekoe. She had just taken a seat in the breakfast nook and a sip when she heard voices in the foyer, and they were rising. She rose from the table and left the kitchen. The girls and Jordon, she expected. Alice, sitting in the swivel rocker, she did not. "What's going on?"

Jordon took one look at Starris and knew he'd made the right decision. She had given her all to make last night's open house a huge success, and while her morose silence during the drive home had baffled him, he'd understood when she'd declined his request to spend the night, crediting her response to exhaustion. Starris needed a break. "Alice is taking the girls to the movies. They are trying to decide which flick to see, and they'd better decide quick or in a few minutes it won't matter because they'll be late for all of them."

"Late, Jordon? Why it can't be more than what? Nine o'clock?"

Jordon quirked a brow in her direction. "Starris, it's one o'clock in the afternoon."

She looked at her bare wrist, then back at Jordon, who held up his arm for her inspection. The dial definitely said one o'clock, and Starris dropped to the couch cushion behind her.

Alice moved to her side and placed a comforting hand on her shoulder. "Are you all right, child? You don't look well."

"I'm fine," Starris replied with a shake of her head.

"Well, you don't look fine, and I believe that you should go upstairs and rest. I'll take the girls, and J.R.... " Alice said, looking in his direction. "Well, I'm sure you can find something to do."

From that moment, Alice was in charge. She ended the movie debate by removing the paper from the girls' hands and choosing the film. Jordon, she dispatched to the kitchen to brew more tea and within ten minutes, had Starris back in bed, her pillows fluffed, a stack of magazines at her side and a blanket tucked securely around the lower half of her body.

"Now, you just rest, and if you need anything, J.R. is downstairs. Although I still have my reservations, I think he should be able to handle most of your needs. After the movie, the girls and I are going shopping, then to dinner. That should give you ample time to rest and get your strength back."

Without a response, Starris watched Alice bustle through the door. She heard the rustle of activity as the girls prepared to leave, Alice giving Jordon final instructions and the opening and closing of the front door. Then golden silence. Finally, the house was blessedly quiet again.

Although she didn't remember, she must have dozed off because when she awoke, Jordon was in the room with her. He had brought up a table and sat with his head bent over a pile of documents. She lowered her eyes to the blue jeans-clad leg angled toward her. The cloth played up rather than hid the well-defined thigh. She raised her eyes to his upper body, watched the muscled arm tighten and relax with his writing. Her face reflected the sadness she felt deep inside. Such a waste, Starris thought. His ex-wife's betrayal had affected him so deeply, Jordon refused to let it go. And because he couldn't, he'd elected to live the rest of his life without love, which was even more of a waste, because in spite of what he'd done, Starris still loved him with all her heart. Rising, she wrapped herself in the robe and crossed the room.

Jordon lifted his head and glanced over his shoulder. "What do you need, baby?"

"Nothing. I'm going to the bathroom."

Jordon smiled. "Okay, but per my instructions from Alice, that's all you're allowed to do. Anything else, and I'm to get my butt in gear and take care of it for you."

Good ole Alice, Starris thought, closing the door behind her. Too bad she couldn't take care of the barrier that closed off his heart. Starris was on her way out of the room when the nausea hit, and hit hard. She leaned weakly against the door, then made her way to the bowl. Her stomach rolled, but since she hadn't eaten anything, there was nothing for it to lose, and she sat on the edge of the tub, experiencing a case of dry heaves.

Jordon stood in the entrance when she opened the door, his dark eyes scrunched with worry. "Are you all right?"

"I think so. No. I'm sure. I just need to lie down."

Without warning, Jordon swept her off her feet and carried her to the bed. After tucking her in, he stood over her staring for so long, Starris began to feel uncomfortable.

Finally, he sighed. "Are you pregnant?"

Heat flushed her cheeks, giving them back some of the color she lost with her nausea. "No," she mumbled.

Jordon sat on the bed and picked up one of her hands. "Would you tell me if you were?"

Indignation flared in her eyes. "Of course I would. I would never deprive you of your child. What kind of woman do you take me for?" As soon as the words left her mouth, Starris closed her eyes as an intense case of guilt rained over her. *Isn't that what you're doing with Dani? Doesn't Jordon have the right to know if he's Dani's father?*

Jordon stretched out beside her. "I'm sorry, Starris. I shouldn't have asked that question. It was unfair of me to compare you with my ex-wife. You're nothing like her."

Oh, but aren't I? The silent prose left Starris unable to respond, and when Jordon's lips lightly brushed her temple before finding her mouth, she let his kisses soothe her feelings of duplicity. She wasn't like Gloria. She planned to tell Jordon of her suspicions. Now just wasn't the right time.

Sensing her hesitation, Jordon leaned back on the pillows. "If you were pregnant, Star, I'd marry you."

How magnanimous of you, she thought. "Why?"

Jordon picked up her hand and kissed her palm. "Well, for one thing you'd be having my child. Second, I'd want him or her to have a real family."

She yanked her hand away. "What about love, Jordon?"

"I'd love my child," he said defensively.

"Oh, I see. But not the mother."

Hearing the pain in her voice, Jordon sighed. He did love Starris, but he couldn't tell her. He was too afraid of the consequences of putting himself in a vulnerable position again. "Love is not a necessary ingredient for marriage, Star. If two people have mutual respect and make a commitment to each other, that should be enough."

"Jordon. Love is that commitment. And without it, I would never even consider marrying again, pregnant or not. I've had that kind of relationship, and I deserve better."

She was right; she did. Only, he couldn't give Starris what she deserved. Jordon left the bed. "Why don't you try to sleep. If you need anything, I'll be working at the desk."

A week later, Jordon rocked back in his chair feeling pretty good about the way things were going in his business life. Just that week, his own efforts had garnered seven more signed contracts translating into fifteen part-time jobs and fifteen new boys into the program. Proudly, he thought about his staff, whose enthusiasm had kept the momentum going. At least he felt proud of most of them.

Since the open house, Lisa Mason had become a major problem. To her credit, she had sold Carlotta Eldridge on the idea of partnering her organization with ROBY, but after two months, she had yet to land a single client with jobs for the boys. If anything, Lisa seemed to be driving potential employers away. He seemed to spend the majority of his time trying to save accounts that she somehow managed to botch. Add to that the dissension she created among the staff, and Jordon knew it was time to let her go. But the decision went against his grain. He was in the business of finding employment for people. He sighed, the sound indicative of his vacillation. He'd give Lisa another couple of weeks. If nothing happened in that time, then he would have no choice but to fire her.

Leaning forward, he picked up one of the blue forms on his desk. It was the application completed by the men wanting to act as mentors. The coordinating director had done an excellent job, and in a few minutes they had a meeting to evaluate the men who had applied.

The application in his hand had Paul McCabe's name on it. Jordon had to decide whether to leave it in the stack or toss it in the garbage can under his desk. He had thought that with Starris leaving, McCabe would cease to be a problem. He had been wrong. Not only had the man tried to monopolize Starris at the open house, Jordon also knew they stayed in contact by phone.

Jordon let the blue form fall to his desk. On paper, McCabe would be an excellent mentor. As badly as Jordon needed qualified men in the program, he'd be a fool to throw out McCabe's application based solely on the knowledge that the man wanted his woman. However, the application wasn't the only thing that bothered Jordon. Since the open house, Starris had withdrawn from him. Despite his efforts, she wouldn't talk, and his impatience had led to a number of fights, with them dancing around everything except the root of the problem. In his heart, Jordon didn't think it had anything to do with Paul McCabe, but his head told him differently, and it was hard for him to silence the fear. Jordon pushed the thought aside, pitched the application into the trash and picked up the telephone he had no idea how many times had rung.

"Jordy! You'll never guess what happened today," Starris started before he could say anything.

Jordon's doubts dissipated like smoke. Starris had shown that she was his woman in all the ways that mattered, and it was something he'd better keep remembering. "What happened, baby?"

"I had breakfast with Paul this morning, and he has a friend who owns a small graphics studio downtown. One of his artists just quit, and the studio is in the middle of a large project for the cultural arts center. He's looking for a replacement right away. Paul told him about me, and I have an interview next week."

Jordon's fear came back in a rush. "You had breakfast with Paul McCabe?"

"Uh-huh. He called me this morning, and he thinks I have a good shot at the position."

"I offered you a job, Starris. Remember?"

"I remember. If you'll remember, I told you that I am not an interior decorator, and I don't want to be. I need to find a job in my field, at least until my greeting cards start bringing in more money."

Jordon already had a mental image of Starris. One hand holding the telephone at her ear, the other perched on her hip. The rising tone of her voice told him that this was going to be a continuation of the argument they had never finished. The one that had started with him asking her to redecorate his home. The last time he'd brought up the subject, Starris had ignited like a brushfire. For a moment, he had thought she would pick up the wooden nameplate she had just given him and beat him about the head with it. It was the thought of saving himself from sure harm that had made him pull Starris into his arms and kiss her until she calmed down.

Well, he couldn't kiss her now and, short of hanging up the telephone, which Jordon knew would be a serious mistake, he had no choice but to let the conversation ride its course, unless he could stall it somehow. His hand clenched the phone at his ear more firmly. "Would it be possible for us not to argue about this today, Star? I have three meetings this afternoon, and I'd like to retain my good mood, if you don't mind. By the way, one of the meetings is with a company from the list you gave to me."

"That's just great, Jordon."

Jordon? Ooh-kay, he thought. Distraction was not going to work. "Star, I think it's wonderful that you might have this opportunity. Only, baby, don't get your hopes up. Paul McCabe may not be on the up-and-up."

"Jordon Randolph Banks!"

Should have stopped after opportunity, Jordon thought, just before Starris exploded on him. He hit the speaker button, hung up the receiver and listened to the tirade with one ear while perusing through a folder on his desk.

"You have no reason to doubt Paul. He is an honest man and has been nothing but nice to me. Not that you'd ever notice. You were so busy giving him the eye and trying to run him off. How could you? You've never even taken the time to have a conversation with him. Paul wanted to talk to you about the mentor program at the open house. You wouldn't give him five minutes. And if not for me, he'd have never gotten an application. Are you going to approve Paul's application, Jordon? Are you?"

Jordon bent down to the phone. "I'm just reviewing it now."

"Yeah, right you are. I'll bet you've put it in the trash. Why can't you try and be friends with him, Jordon? He'll be a good mentor, and you need men like Paul. He's a professional, he owns his own business, and he's willing. And I'll tell you something else, Jordon Banks. I'm going to interview with Paul's friend, and I'm going to get this job. You just wait and see. Good-bye!"

Goodbye? Jordon dropped the folder and picked up the telephone. All he heard was the dial tone.

Jordon would have called Starris right back except that his phone began to ring as soon as he hung up the line. "Cyrus, it's good to hear from you. I'm glad you finally decided to come on board with us, and I've got just the kid to fill your slot. Joshua Stone. His grandfather was a newspaper man, too."

"That's great, J.R. I'm sure Joshua will work out just fine. We're planning to start him in research. But the reason I'm calling is to discuss Lisa Mason's visit."

Lisa had stopped by the *Denver Post* to pick up the signed contract before coming into the office that morning. Jordon hadn't known that she'd also planned to meet with Cyrus. "Lisa?"

"Yeah. I overheard some talk between Lisa and our receptionist this morning. If I'm not mistaken, I could have sworn she was implying that the *Post* might not want to work with ROBY, and more specifically you."

The muscle in Jordon's cheek began to throb. "What did she say, Cyrus?"

"Well, nothing concrete, but I think she was dropping hints that you might have a problem with alcohol and that she'd heard talk that some of the funds for ROBY were missing."

"That's ludicrous, Cyrus! You know I do not drink to excess, and every penny for the organization can and has been accounted for."

"Hold on, J.R. I'm not accusing you of anything. As far as I'm concerned, there's no story here. I just thought you would want to know. Then again, perhaps I'm wrong. They could have been talking about something else entirely."

That was hardly likely. Cyrus had been in the newspaper game since college. He wasn't given to fanciful tales or bending the truth to grab a headline. "Thanks, Cyrus. I appreciate the call, and look for Joshua to show up at four on Monday." Jordon hung up the telephone. Was this the reason Lisa hadn't delivered on any jobs for the boys? His gut instinct told him it was, but Jordon knew that he needed proof. More than an overheard conversation. Nor would he mention his conversation with Cyrus. That would just put Lisa on guard, and if she was spreading lies about him or ROBY he wanted solid evidence to present before he fired her.

Starris didn't slam down the phone, but the thought did cross her mind. She puffed out her cheeks and headed for the kitchen. She filled a glass with water and, taking it with her, she returned to the living room, sat on the couch, pulled a magazine into her lap and flipped through the pages without reading a single word.

Was there a more ornery or stubborn man than Jordon Randolph Banks? Starris didn't think so. And the man's ability to set her off seemed almost uncanny. She didn't want to work for Paul's friend. She wanted to work for ROBY and had hoped that by now Jordon would have changed his mind.

For the last few nights, he'd been voicing his dissatisfaction with Lisa Mason. Starris knew that she could handle the position hands down, but Jordon refused to even consider her for the job. She slapped the magazine closed and went into her office. There had to be a way to get through to Jordon, and she wasn't about to give up trying. She sat on her stool and picked up her brush. Somehow, she would find a way to make Jordon see her as a qualified professional. But in the meantime, she had to finish the last of five new designs requested by her publisher. And with that thought, Starris put Jordon out of her mind and went back to work.

"I'm switching Calvin Saunders from Techno-tronics to Patterson and Hill. That okay with you, Dave?" Jordon turned as he addressed his job-training coordinator.

"It's okay with me, J. R. I'd like to put Leroy Green in one of their slots, too."

"I don't have a problem with that." Jordon filled in the names and slapped the folder closed. "Okay, that takes care of the Patterson and Hill agreement. Who's left?"

"Wait a minute," Lisa said, before the coordinator could speak up. "Why are you moving Calvin Saunders? If he already has a job, shouldn't the new slot be filled with another boy?"

The narrowed gaze leveled at Lisa rendered everyone else at the table silent. "As you should already know, Techno-tronics Cable is downsizing, and Nelson has had to let some of his staff go. They may be able to resume their relationship with ROBY in the future, but as for the present, we need to find replacements for two of the three positions they contracted with us. Second, Calvin wants to be a lawyer. Therefore, it makes sense that we move him to a law firm."

"That's understandable. However, haven't Calvin's grades slipped below the acceptable C average? Which means that he should be placed on probation, not given another job."

The tension in the room mounted as Jordon rose from his chair, his towering height intimidating everyone except Lisa. Staring directly at Lisa, he made a mental note to have Selma change all the locks in his office and the files before speaking. "How, Ms. Mason, did you come by your knowledge of Calvin Saunders when you have not been given a security clearance or access to the files for the boys enrolled in this program?"

Lisa shifted uncomfortably in her chair, aware that every eye was on her. "I believe that I overheard David and one of the other coordinators talking about it."

"Is that so? Well, it just so happens that Calvin Saunders is a special case. He is in danger of dropping from the program, and I will do everything possible to see that he does not."

"But it's not fair to the other kids," Lisa complained.

Jordon surveyed the faces of his staff, then indicated the door. "I believe we've covered everything on the agenda today. Thanks for your hard work and keep it up." Jordon watched his staff gather their things. "Ms. Mason, please stay a moment."

Lisa resumed her seat. Jordon waited until the door had closed, then turned thunderous eyes to Lisa. "Never again, and I repeat never, question my decisions in front of the staff the way you did today. If you have concerns, they are best expressed to me in private, and I will deal with them at that time. Have I made myself clear, Ms. Mason?"

Lisa saw the repressed rage in his hardened his features, before cutting her eyes away to the window. "Yes, sir."

"What is the status of your negotiations with Melcher?"

"They're coming along fine. All we need is a number from them, then I'll have the contract drawn up by Legal."

"What is your timetable to have that accomplished?"

"By Friday."

Jordon picked up his stack of folders and his leather pad. "Okay, Ms. Mason. One week from today, I'll expect to see a signed contract from Melcher's people on my desk or in lieu of that your resignation as director of job acquisitions."

Starris dropped the basket of clean clothes on the counter and picked up the ringing telephone. Her face registered surprise when she heard the voice of the principal at Grandville Middle School. She glanced at the clock, which read twelve-thirty.

"I beg your pardon, Mr. Pembroke. But this is Danielle Carter, my daughter, and Jolie Banks that you are speaking of? No. No. I understand. No, please don't disturb Mr. Banks. I'm on my way."

An hour later, Starris unlocked the door and entered the house with a silent Dani and Jolie tagging close behind. She threw her keys and purse down on the wicker table by the door and continued into the living room. Without speaking, the girls followed behind her. Starris dropped to the couch at the same time their backpacks hit the floor. Jolie and Dani exchanged a solemn glance, then turned tear-filled eyes to Starris.

Jolie broke first and ran sobbing to the couch. She plopped down beside Starris and buried her face in her chest. "I'm sorry, Mama. I didn't mean to get into a fight. It-it just happened."

Starris wrapped an arm around Jolie. "Hush, sweetheart. It's okay. Everything is going to be just fine."

She looked up at Dani and opened her other arm. Dani moved to the couch and laid her head on Starris' other side.

Starris soothed her girls with hugs and words of encouragement until both settled down, then sent them upstairs to clean up. When they left the room, she let the dismay she felt show on her face. Though she had attempted to reassure Jolie, Starris knew she was playing with a blind deck. Jordon Banks had a short fuse and, after this morning's conversation, she wasn't at the top of his hit parade. When she told him what happened, Jordon would detonate like a ton of TNT. But Jolie was counting on her to run interference, and Starris would try to take the brunt of the explosion. She only hoped that her shield was strong enough to withstand the blast.

A few hours later, Jordon pulled into the driveway. He sat staring at the house feeling the heavy tension that hummed in the air whenever he was in Starris' presence lately. Jordon knew that one of them should step forward and offer amends so that their relationship could get back on track, and he'd tried to bring himself to be the one to do it, but something kept holding him back. Perhaps it was the defiance he saw when he looked into the depth of Starris' hazel eyes. Perhaps it was his own jealousy. Jordon didn't know what it was, but knew he had tired of sleeping with aching loneliness as his bedmate at night. He hadn't held Starris in his arms for more than a week now, and his need lay as a heavy weight on his heart.

Why couldn't she give up this idea to work for ROBY? Why couldn't she take what he was willing to offer her and be satisfied? He wanted Starris, and he wanted Dani, and he didn't want Starris associating with Paul McCabe, no matter how innocent he knew the association to be. Just the thought that she could speak in such glowing terms about another man made the muscles in Jordon's cheek tighten in disquietude.

Why couldn't he have met Starris first? Why couldn't she have been his wife instead of the unfaithful woman it had been his misfortune to marry? If she had, Jordon knew he would feel a great deal more secure about her, him and their relationship.

As it was, he missed the closeness they'd found in and out of the bedroom. He missed holding her in his arms and spending his days and evenings with the woman he loved. Most of all, he missed the family circle they had shared with the girls. Jordon stepped from the car and glanced at the house. He was losing his family, and he couldn't let that happen. No matter what it took, that evening they were going to clear the air. When it was over, he would have all of his girls back inside the circle.

He lifted two large boxes from the backseat. He hefted the pizzas in one hand, lifted his briefcase with the other and bumped the car door closed with his hip. At the front door, he juggled his briefcase and the pizzas and stuck the key Starris had given him into the lock. He pushed the door open, stepped inside and closed it with his foot. Then he stood in the foyer looking around like a king inspecting his kingdom. No matter how many times he entered her house, Jordon couldn't get over how good it made him feel or how much it felt like home.

Frowning when he didn't hear the usual murmur of voices, he affected his deepest, manliest voice and said, "The man of this house is here, and I've come bearing gifts of food. Where are my girls?"

Starris hurried around the corner. He saw the strain on her face and knew something had happened. Jordon dropped his briefcase and slid the pizza boxes onto the table before crossing to Starris. "What's wrong? Where are the girls?"

Starris put a hand on his chest to stop him from moving around her and spoke quickly to remove the unwarranted look of fear from his face. "They're in the living room and physically they are fine, but we do have a problem."

His mind took that statement and flew away with unreasonable imagination. "That doesn't make sense, Star. If the girls are fine, how could we have a—?" A moment of blind insanity left him speechless and unable to reason before Jordon roughly seized Starris by the arms. "Are you all right?"

"I'm fine, Jordon." She grabbed his hand and led him into the kitchen. When he saw her quiet demeanor, he forced himself to calm down, too, and let the room's warm, inviting feelings soothe him.

Starris moved to the counter and pulled down a mug from the cabinet. She poured Jordon a cup of coffee and searched her mind for a way to break the awful news without setting him off. She moved from behind the counter and crossed to the breakfast nook where Jordon sat. By his working jaw, she knew she'd better start talking—and fast—or he might just unload on her. And she hoped that after preparing him, he would remain in a rational state when he spoke with his daughter.

A few moments later, Starris knew her ploy hadn't worked when Jordon shoved the cup roughly, causing the liquid to slosh onto the table. He leaped up from his seat.

"What! What do you mean my daughter is suspended from school for three days? They only have one week left and the school has my numbers. They can reach me any time of the day. Why am I just hearing about this? What have you done now?"

Jordon fired the questions so rapidly, Starris didn't know which one to answer first. When she didn't respond right away, he turned for the kitchen door, which galvanized her to action. She jumped up and ran over to him.

"Jordon! Where are you going?" She flinched from the enraged eyes that swung back to her.

"To talk to my daughter!"

She grabbed his arm, shaking her head no as she tried to stop his forward motion.

"Will you let go of me," he growled, trying to shake her off.

"No!" Realizing that she had just screamed at him, Starris took a deep breath. "Jordon, let me explain before you talk to Jolie. She's frightened enough as it is. She doesn't need to see you coming at her like a bee-stung grizzly bear."

Jordon jerked himself from her hands and folded both arms across his chest. For the second time that day, someone was questioning his decisions, a thought that further infuriated him. "So, it's not enough that you've alienated my daughter from me. Now, you want to tell me how to handle my own child."

Starris reacted as if she'd been slapped, and for an instant blind fury fired her gaze. Then her face softened. She couldn't afford to go toe to toe with Jordon right now. She had promised Jolie she'd talk to him, and no matter how unfair his remark, she had to keep her temper. "I'm not sure what you mean by that, Jordon. I would never presume to tell another parent how to raise his child. However, there is something you need to know before you talk to Jolie. It will help you to understand why she was suspended. So, the sooner you sit down, the sooner I'll let you out of this kitchen."

Jordon looked at the closed door and back at Starris, clearly uncertain of what to do. He dropped his shoulders in resignation and returned to his seat. Starris went to the sink for a dishcloth and picked up the wooden spoon before going back to the table. She handed it to Jordon and mopped up the spill. The drumming started when she sat across from him again. Since he looked no calmer than before, Starris thought it best to state what she knew about the incident in as few words and as quickly as possible.

"The school called this afternoon and asked that I come down. When I arrived, the principal told me that the girls had been in a fight. From what I understand, the other girl started it, and Jolie acted in defense of herself and Dani. Apparently, this other girl found out that Dani had been left on the steps of the children's home. It seems she had been teasing Dani the entire morning and announced it to as many of the other kids as she could."

Starris stopped to catch her breath, noting that the drumming on the table had increased in tempo.

"Go on," Jordon said.

"Well, at lunch this girl followed Dani and Jolie to their table and teased Dani so much that she was in tears. Jolie asked her to leave Dani alone. She also said that she was Dani's sister and that you were her father. The other girl called

Jolie a liar and slapped her, which made Dani mad and all three of them ended up rolling on the floor. You know the school's policy on fighting: zero tolerance. And immediate suspension for all three regardless of who started the fracas."

The rapping on the table stopped. "Why didn't someone at the school call me? I am Jolie's parent."

"I asked them not to. You're so busy at ROBY and the girls had already admitted they'd been in a fight. There was nothing to do, Jordon, except bring them home."

The few seconds he stared at Starris seemed like an eternity. She tried not to wilt. The spoon fell from his hands and clattered to the table. Jordon stood. "I see," he said, and left the kitchen before Starris could move from her chair.

"Get your things, Jolie Kathryn. It's time to go."

Behind Jordon, Starris gave Jolie a smile of encouragement.

"Daddy, I'm sorry. I didn't mean to get into a fight."

"I did not ask for an explanation. I told you to get your things. We'll discuss this at home."

"But, Daddy."

"Now, Jolie!"

"Yes, sir," Jolie mumbled.

"I'm sorry, Jolie," Dani whispered, turning to help her friend gather her belongings. "What's your dad going to do?"

Jolie peeked over her shoulder and shrugged. The tears in the girls' eyes tore at Starris. She placed a light hand on Jordon's arm. "Please, Jordy. Don't be too hard on her. I've already talked to her, and Jolie realizes the mistake she's made."

Jordon threw her hand off and whipped around. "When I need advice about my daughter, I will not be coming to you. I'll make alternate arrangements for Jolie's care when she's allowed back in school." Uncaring of the three shocked gasps, Jordon turned and held out his hand. "Let's go, Jolie."

"Jordon, please don't do this. The girls made a mistake for which they are very sorry. I'm sure nothing like this will ever happen again." She looked to Dani and Jolie for confirmation.

"Daddy, I like staying with Miss Starris. I promise not to get into anymore trouble in school. It's not Mama's fault. It's ours. Right, Dani?" Jolie turned to her friend with tears and a plea. "Right, Dani? Tell Daddy you're sorry, too."

Dani swiped her hands across her eyes. "I'm sorry, Mr. Jordon. We won't get into anymore trouble."

Jolie turned back to face her father. "See, Daddy. Dani promised, too. Can I still stay with Miss Starris?"

Her request fell on deaf ears as Jordon hardened himself against the crocodile tears falling from his daughter's eyes. "I said let's go."

Starris couldn't let him do this. Couldn't he see how much he was hurting the girls, hurting her? "Jordon, don't rip the girls apart like this. Why don't we sit down and talk, the four of us?"

Tired of having his authority challenged, Jordon stalked to his daughter and took her hand. As soon as the words left his mouth, Jordon knew he would regret them later. "There is nothing to discuss. I made a mistake letting Jolie stay here with you. She needs a stricter and more regulated environment, the kind of environment you can't seem to provide."

He moved toward the door, all but dragging a crying Jolie behind him.

"Mama," she wailed. Jerking free of her father's hand, Jolie ran to Starris and wrapped her small arms around her neck.

"I'm sorry, sweetheart. I tried."

Jordon removed Jolie's arms and kept a firm grasp on her as he started for the door again. Picking up his briefcase, he hustled them both out of the door.

Starris ran to the door and watched him settle Jolie in the car. When the car lights disappeared around the corner, she closed the door and returned to the living room. She tried to take Dani in her arms.

Dani wrenched away. "This is all my fault," she screamed.

"No, angel. It's not your fault."

"Yes, it is. I can't do anything right!" Dani ran up the stairs. Starris flinched when she heard the boom of her bedroom door.

Starris looked around, feeling desolate and empty, then moved to the stairs and sat down. She didn't understand Jordon's unreasonable refusal to sit down and talk. The girls were wrong, but he'd acted like they had committed armed robbery. And by removing Jolie from her care, Jordon had done what he said he would never do. He had taken her baby away.

CHAPTER 16

Jordon's regret came much quicker than he could have imagined. It started in the car with Jolie's stubborn refusal to look at or speak to him and the tears she cried the entire way home. At the house, she jumped from the car and ran to the door. She pushed by Alice, not stopping until she was up the staircase and inside her room. Jordon entered the house just in time to hear her door slam and receive a look from Alice hot enough to burn toast. He felt himself crumble under the stare.

"J.R., what happened? What did you do to my baby?"

Jordon loosened the suddenly too-constricting tie around his neck. *Another female challenge,* he thought. "Jolie is not a baby, and why do you always take her side? You don't even know what happened and already you assume that I'm the bad guy."

"That's because you usually are," Alice replied smugly.

Jordon emitted a soft grunt. "Well, I'm not the bad guy, and it will take too long to explain. Right now, I need a drink."

"Then I'll ask the baby."

Alice was halfway up the staircase before Jordon thought to stop her. "Damn," he muttered. Once Jolie poured out her heart to Alice, he could pretty much chuck anything he had to say. Since the day he'd brought the two-year-old child home for good, in Alice's mind, Jolie could do no wrong. By now, his daughter had probably convinced her that he was an ogre.

He strode to the library and directly to the paneled bar. Grabbing a crystal decanter and a glass, Jordon poured a tall Scotch and knocked back the drink. He poured another and took the glass with him to the couch. Setting the glass down, he removed his jacket, flung it on a chair and sat heavily on the couch. He was not wrong. Any decision he made regarding the welfare of his daughter was right, regardless of what others thought. It had been more than nine years, but Jordon couldn't let go of the hellish year he'd gone through to get his daughter out of the child-welfare system. The files on him and Jolie were closed and probably long forgotten. But that they had once been active still had Jordon looking over his shoulder. Rising, he left the library and headed up the stairs to change for dinner. When he'd gotten Jolie back, Jordon had vowed to be the best parent on the planet, and he would let nothing—not even Starris Gilmore—put him in jeopardy of losing his daughter again.

At the dinner table, Jordon looked at Jolie's empty chair, and his heart dropped. Alice had taken a tray up to her room, a violation of the rule that said, unless sick, all meals were eaten in the dining room. His troubled gaze traveled down the table to his housekeeper.

Alice's pinched features were evidence of the fact that he was in the doghouse. He'd tried to converse with her earlier. The banging pots and pans in the kitchen and her monosyllabic responses at the table let him know that he'd blown his chance to explain, and any attempts to do so now were futile.

"Alice, will you please pass the butter?"

The butter sailed down the table. Jordon reached out to stop the dish just before it went over the side. "Thank you."

"Welcome." Alice sliced him with her eyes again, picked up her fork and resumed eating her dinner.

Jordon sighed. "Dinner tastes wonderful this evening, Alice. This chicken is particularly good. Did you do something different tonight?"

"It's a shame the baby can't be here to enjoy it, now isn't it?"

His patience snapped. "I didn't send Jolie to her room. She's up there voluntarily. And you're encouraging her defiant behavior. The rule is that we eat at the table together, unless one of us is ill."

"And what would you have me do, Jordon Banks? Let the baby starve? She was hungry and much too upset to break bread with the man who broke her heart. And what you did to that lovely young woman and Dani." Alice tsked her tongue. "I'll say this for you, J.R. When you set out to hurt people, you do a fairly good job of it."

Dark brows lowered over eyes filled with distress. "I have never in my life set out to hurt another human being. I love my daughter and certainly would not do anything to hurt my little girl. What I did today, I did out of love and concern for Jolie. So don't you sit there and try and accuse me of doing something wrong when I only acted in my daughter's best interest."

Alice picked up her tea, taking her time as she slowly sipped the sweet liquid. She set the glass on the table. "You are wrong, Jordon."

His utensils fell from his hands to his plate with a loud clatter. "Wrong!"

It was all he had time to say before Alice stood. "Yes! You are wrong. You took the only mother Jolie has ever known from her today and Dani, whom she loves like a sister. If that's not wrong, then I don't know what is!"

"Starris Gilmore is not Jolie's mother!"

"Humph," Alice snorted. She drew herself up as tall as her five-three height allowed, and folded her arms under two large mounds of bosom. "After the way you acted and the things you said to Starris, she never will be either. So put that in your pipe and smoke it, Mr. Banks." Alice left the table. At the door of the dining room, she paused. "If you want anything else, you know where the kitchen is. I'll check on Jolie before I retire to my room. Good night, J.R."

He watched Alice march off, straight backed and full of silent reproach for him. "The next child I have will be a son," Jordon muttered. It was something else he regretted saying a moment later when the thought conjured images of Starris pregnant with his child. Jordon threw down his napkin and pushed away his plate. Because of his anger and rash behavior, he'd said some horrible things to Starris, and his words had all but accused her of being an unfit mother.

"She's the only mother Jolie has ever known, and you took her away." Alice's words coming back to haunt him raised Jordon's guilt meter to high. Not only had he hurt Jolie and Starris, after his bold declaration, Dani's stricken face had looked as if he'd ripped her heart out.

Jeez, Banks, he thought, when you screw up, you go for the big time.

He'd rescued Jolie from the system while she was still young enough for it not to have any lasting effects. Other children, whether under the care of child-welfare authorities because of abuse or neglect, had feelings of abandonment, of being unwanted and unloved, and the emotional and behavioral problems associated with those feelings were inherent in the system.

Dani had spent most of her life in that system. Starris had taken the little girl in and provided a loving and secure home. Jolie and Dani had formed a bond so strong they considered themselves sisters. Plus, Jolie had said that he was Dani's father. Something he'd begun to think and feel himself.

A sheen of sweat covered every inch of Jordon's body. He was wrong, and somehow he had to rectify what he'd done. If he didn't, Jordon knew the four females in his life would never forgive him, and he could only hope to fix this mess before his mother found out. Otherwise, he'd be dealing with a fifth unforgiving female.

Jordon's doorbell chimed just as he rose from the chair. *Too late, Banks,* he thought, falling into the chair when he heard the voices in the foyer.

"Papiér! Nommy!"

Dread filled Jordon as he listened to Jolie's running footsteps descend the stairs and imagined his daughter throwing herself, sobbing, into the arms of her paternal grandparents. Jolie had declared war and had swiftly retaliated against him. His daughter had called in the big guns.

"Where is that son of mine?" he heard his mother ask.

Jordon's first thought was to run. The house was so big, if he kept moving he could elude them for hours. With Alice and his parents in Jolie's corner, he didn't stand a needle in a haystack's chance of winning this battle with his daughter.

A few minutes later, Jordon raised his hands in surrender. "All right," he growled, pressured by the four pairs of eyes pinning him to his chair. "I was wrong. I will call Starris tomorrow and apologize. If she's willing, Jolie can continue her after-school care with her. I hope this makes the four of you very happy."

James placed his hand on his son's shoulder. "It might be best if you made the call and apologized to the woman tonight, son."

Jordon looked around the room, scanning his brain for a reason to put off the harrying prospect of hearing the blistering tongue of Starris Gilmore. "If Jolie's behavior this evening is any indication, Starris is having her own problems with Dani. I'm sure the last person she wants to hear from right now is me. I'll do it in the morning."

Jolie poked out her lips. She censured her father with rebellious glare and looked to her grandmother. "Make him do it now, Nommy. Tell Daddy to call Miss Starris and apologize tonight."

As soon as it can be arranged, that phone comes out of her room, Jordon thought. Before he could respond to Jolie's latest burst of defiance, Doreen Banks held out her arms to her granddaughter.

"Baby, come here to Nommy." She enfolded Jolie lovingly in her lap. "Your daddy has said that he will apologize to Starris and," she said, shooting a warning look in her son's direction, "I'm sure he'll keep his promise." Doreen stood and took Jolie's hand. "Now, you come with me. I have something special for you in the car."

Overjoyed now that she'd gotten her way, Jordon watched his daughter skip happily at her grandmother's side. Alice shot him a "serves you right" look and followed the pair from the room.

Jordon turned to his father. "Papiér, I need a beer. What about you?"

James smiled. "Son, I've been waiting for you to ask."

In his study, Jordon grabbed two bottles of Coors from the fridge, screwed off the tops and handed one to his father, who sat on the couch.

He took a swig from his own bottle before dropping his frame to the cushions. "How'd you do it, Papiér? How did you manage to survive all these years in a house full of females?"

James lowered his bottle and swiped his mouth with the back of his hand. "J.R., I've been married to your mother for forty-one years, and surviving is about all we men can do. You just have to learn to duck and move. That's the key to surviving, and if you get caught in a standstill, nod your head yes to anything they say, then run. Otherwise, they'll nail you to a wall, and if that happens, all you can do is pray." James laughed. "You're just out of practice, son. But if what I'm hearing about this Starris Gilmore is true, I'd advise you to get good pair of running shoes."

"That's not funny, Papiér. I need real advice here."

"And that's exactly what you're getting, J.R. Duck and move."

In the companionable quiet that followed, James watched the frown ease from Jordon's face. He tipped his bottle of beer to his mouth, then squirmed into a comfortable position on the sofa. This was the only room in the house with furniture that made sense. James had understood his son's need to change things following the divorce and the aftermath with Jolie, but he hadn't understood why Jordon had given that simpleton decorator a free hand. J.R. hadn't seemed to care what the woman brought into his house, and after an apparent psychic experience during the initial tour, the flutter-head had decided his son had once lived as a French prince, and that he should be surrounded by pieces from the era. James had tried to speak with his son, but at the time Jordon hadn't been in the mood to hear it.

He looked around the study, his eyes reflecting pride as he gazed at the wall of basketball trophies and plaques, and his pride over his son's accomplishments glowed in his eyes. Jordon had grown into a fine man with many talents. He founded the DownTown Stock and had propelled not only himself and his family, but several of his friends to millionaire status, and he was the driving force behind ROBY. James just wished his son would stop kicking himself over his mistake with Gloria and find another woman who could make him happy.

"Starris is an unusual name, at least one I've never heard before. Tell me more about this Ms. Gilmore."

Jordon shared a very close relationship with his father, but after what he'd done this evening and the uproar it had caused, Starris was not a subject he felt inclined to discuss, even with Papiér. Sensing his son's hesitation, James said, "J.R., it's been a long time since you've opened yourself up to the possibility of loving someone. Now, I readily admit that I've met Starris only once, but if there's a chance that she's the one who can make you happy, I think you'd be a fool to throw that chance away."

"Papiér, Starris and I are not in love. We are friends. I like the woman, and she's a good influence on Jolie, but that does not mean that I have any intention of forming a permanent tie with her or any other woman."

James rose to his feet. Jordon had stood seven inches taller than him since the age of sixteen, and James felt the need of the advantage of height for his next words. "You may say that you're not in love with Starris, Jordon. But the facts state otherwise. If you didn't have feelings for the woman, you wouldn't have let her anywhere near your daughter. The only other woman you've ever let get this close to you was Gloria."

"Yeah, and look where that landed me," Jordon muttered.

James sighed wearily. "Son, Gloria had us all fooled, but you can't let the actions of one woman color your judgment for the rest of your life. You are not happy, Jordon, which is why you involve yourself in so many projects. Work cannot replace love. The sooner you realize that, the sooner you will find the happiness that you deserve."

"Yoo-hoo! Where's my baby?"

No, Jordon thought. He needed to have a serious talk with his daughter. Jolie Kathryn Banks had definitely gotten out of hand, and it was time to rein her back in.

Both men looked up as Rosalyn Banks sailed into the room. A woman of sophisticated tastes, feminine wiles and a stubborn streak that could outlast a mule, Rosalyn glided over to her father. She kissed his cheek, then patted her black locks into place and narrowed black eyes on her younger brother. "Where's the baby?"

Jordon examined his sister. Sometimes, he wondered when the scrawny, eyeglass-wearing, braces-sporting girl he'd grown up with had changed into the gorgeous woman who stood in judgment of him now. "Why are you here, Roz?"

"I received an urgent call from my niece that all is not right in this house. Jolie said that she was locked in her room and that you wouldn't even allow her to have dinner."

James, who seemed to think the whole affair extremely funny, sat on the couch and laughed until his eyes began to tear.

Jordon, who'd had enough of the evening's antics, leaped up, snorting. "And you believed her!"

"Do I look like I came down with yesterday's rain, J.R.?" Rosalyn responded testily. "Of course I didn't believe her. But Jolie sounded so sad, I just had to make sure that everything was all right."

"Jolie is a spoiled brat, and the three of you rushing up here at her beck and call is not helping matters."

James, taking offense at the statement, rose from the couch again. "I beg to differ with you, son. I am not at the beck and call of my granddaughter."

Glowering eyes turned toward him. "Yeah? Then why are you here, Papiér?"

James, who seemed to be having trouble gathering his thoughts for a moment, scratched his head. "Well, Jolie called your mother, who then ordered me to drive her up here."

The words *duck and move* entered Jordon's mind. Apparently, his father had slowed down in his old age. "Well, all three of you can go home and let me deal with my daughter."

James and Rosalyn began to speak at once. "I think it would a good idea if you waited until tomorrow, son. Give yourself a chance to calm down," James advised.

"Remember, J.R., Jolie is just a baby. She doesn't have a mother and…"

That's it, Jordon thought. "Just stop it, the both of you. Listening to you two, you'd think I was going to murder the child. I am not the one who was suspended from school for three days, and any punishment I elect to give Jolie Kathryn, she brought on herself."

"How are you going to punish her?" Rosalyn asked, her voice filled with concern.

Jordon frowned. He hadn't exactly thought through the how, since he rarely punished his daughter. Then, as if enlightened, he said, "Restriction. That's it. Jolie will be grounded to the house for two weeks and no allowance this month either. Yeah," Jordon continued on a roll. "And I'll give her extra chores. That ought to keep her focused. Now, let me see, what else."

"Um, son."

"I know," Jordon said. "No television. I'll take that set out of her room for the entire time of her suspension."

James heaved a sigh. "Don't you feel that's going a little overboard, son? And you know your mother will never let you get away with it."

As if on cue, Doreen Banks entered the room with a miserable-looking Jolie in tow.

When Rosalyn saw her mother, she relaxed knowing that Doreen Banks had things in hand. "Hi, Mom."

"Hi, baby."

"Auntie Roz!" Jolie ran to Rosalyn and threw her arms around her waist. "Auntie Roz, you came."

"Jolie Kathryn," Doreen admonished. "What did we talk about upstairs?"

"Oh, yeah," Jolie replied. She walked over to her father. "Daddy, I'm very sorry for getting suspended from school, and I promise I'll never get into a fight again." She looked at her grandmother.

"And."

Jolie shifted her feet from one to the other. "And I'm sorry for the trouble I caused between you and Miss Starris, and thank you for changing your mind and letting me stay with her after school."

"That was very nicely done, Jolie." Doreen cocked a brow in her son's direction.

Jordon returned the stare. What was he supposed to say? He couldn't remember one time his mother had ever let him off with just an apology. The rule about parenting was true. Grandparents had one set of rules for their children and another set for the grands.

"Jordon Randolph Banks, your daughter has just apologized to you. Don't you have something to say?"

Jordon tried to hang on to his resolve. Jolie had acted like a brat, and she deserved to be punished, but with the three adults and his daughter's contrite face looking on, he gave up. "I accept your apology, Jolie, but I want you to understand that your actions today were a big disappointment to me. I won't have my daughter acting like a hoodlum, and I guess you know what to do the next time you're in a situation like that."

"Yes, sir," Jolie said. "Nommy said that I'm to go straight to the principal's office and if that doesn't stop the problem, then I'm supposed to tell you and Miss Starris and that the two of you would take care of the problem because that's what parents are supposed to do."

And Starris? Parents? Jordon shot a quick glance at his mother, wondering what else Doreen Banks had said to his child. He decided not to broach the subject. "Good. That's exactly right. Now, I can't let the matter of your suspension go so easily. What you did today showed bad judgment, and you must accept the consequences of that action. Therefore, for the next two weeks…"

James and Rosalyn suddenly came down with coughing jags, and Jordon rolled his eyes. "For the next two weeks you will forgo your allowance. Is that clear?"

"Yes, sir."

Sighs of relief could be heard around the room, and Doreen clapped her hands together. "Well, now that everything's been settled, I think it's time for Jolie to go to bed."

"But Nommy, I got suspended, so I don't have to go to school tomorrow."

Doreen tried to hide her smile. "That's nothing to be happy about, young lady. However, it also means that you and I have time for some more girl talk."

"Wait for me," Rosalyn called. "Jolie, did I mention that I brought a surprise for you?"

Watching the women leave the room, Jordon just shook his head. He sat on the couch next to his father. "Does it ever change, Papiér?"

James picked up his bottle of beer and leaned back on the sofa. "All I can say is duck and move, son. Just duck and move."

"Angel, please come out and let's talk," Starris pleaded through the door for the umpteenth time. "I promise I'll speak to Jordon again and try to get him to change his mind."

Starris received no response, and pushing the hair from her forehead in defeat, she left Dani's door and headed down the hallway for the stairs. "Thank you very much, Jordon Banks," Starris muttered, clopping down the steps with heavy feet. Dani had been holed up in her room for four hours, and nothing she'd said had persuaded her daughter to open the door. When she reached the bottom, Starris sat on a step, glancing over her shoulder every time she heard a noise in the hopes that Dani had come out of the room.

Pigheaded, Jordon Banks. That's what you are, a stubborn, hardheaded fool. She had expected Jordon to be angry when he learned of the girl's suspensions, but never had she imagined that he would react by hurling insults at her and tearing the girls apart. The man was just plain impossible. Was it any wonder that they argued all the time?

Hearing the doorbell, Starris rose from the step. She walked to the foyer with the thought that if Jordon had come back to apologize, it was too late, because she was going kill him. Starris looked through the peephole and groaned. How in the world had Paul McCabe discovered where she lived?

The doorbell rang again, and she opened the door. "What are you doing here, Paul?"

"Don't be upset, Starris, and before you ask, Chad did not give me your address. I sort of peeked at your résumé, and I know that was wrong, but I wanted to make sure everything is okay."

"What do you mean...?"

Paul held up his hand. "I came by earlier. I heard the shouting."

"Oh." Starris blew out a breath and directed her eyes over his shoulder.

Paul laid his hand on her arm. "Is everything okay?"

Starris opened the door wider. "Come in, Paul."

He grinned. "Thanks."

Starris preceded him to the living room. "Have a seat."

After thanking her again, Paul sat on the couch and watched Starris pace the room. "You seem agitated. Why don't you sit down and talk about it."

"I am not agitated. I'm mad." Starris threw up her hands and turned for the couch. She stopped when she saw Dani at the top of the stairs. Danielle looked geared for battle, from the mutinous expression on her face to the wintry stare she fixed on Paul McCabe. Dani stomped down the steps and stood at her mother's side.

Starris placed an arm around her shoulders and smiled, hoping it would melt a little of the frost. She nudged Dani forward. "Angel, I'd like you to meet someone. Dani, this is Paul McCabe. He works in the building next to ROBY, and he's a friend. Paul, my daughter, Danielle."

Paul rose and stepped forward. "Hello, Danielle. Your mother has told me a lot about you and you're just as lovely…"

Both adults looked on, stunned, as Dani ran from the room and up the stairs. They flinched when her door slammed.

Mortified, Starris turned to Paul. "I'm terribly sorry, Paul. As you've probably guessed, we've had somewhat of a problematic evening."

Paul, quite out of his element, nevertheless held his own and nodded. "There's no need for you to be sorry, Starris. I understand."

"Thank you." She glanced up the staircase again, then waved her hand. "Sit down and relax. I'll get us something to drink."

Paul watched Starris leave the room, then turned when he heard a noise behind him. The child looked angry, Starris was upset, and Jordon Banks was responsible. However, regardless of the feelings he had for Starris, he couldn't place himself in the middle of a lovers' quarrel. At this point, all he could do was offer an ear. And only if Starris allowed it.

Starris observed the stare-down Dani had initiated with Paul, but didn't go to her daughter. Dani had already rejected her, and though she understood, Starris hoped that she wouldn't resort to past behavior to express her anger. When Dani turned and entered her room again, Starris continued into the living room. She would try and talk to Danielle later.

Rising when Starris walked in, Paul removed the tray from her hands. After seating her, he poured two glasses of white wine and handed one to Starris. He sipped the Chablis appreciatively before asking, "What happened here tonight, Starris?"

Very close to tears herself, Starris ran a weary hand over her brow. If he hadn't asked, she wouldn't have said anything. But he had, and she spilled the story of all that had transpired in her home that evening. When she finished, his worried look was almost more than she could bear, but Starris held back her tears.

"Regardless of what he's done, you love him."

The question or statement—Starris couldn't decide which—distracted her momentarily, before she hopped up from the couch. "No!" She tramped the room, swinging her hands wildly through the air, then balled one of them and struck the other with a resounding thud as she ranted. "Jordon Banks is a loudmouthed, insufferable moron! He's inflexible, he doesn't listen, and he always thinks he's right. Well, he's not right, and the way he treated those girls today was horrid. The man needs to have his head examined. Why, you'd think our girls were bank robbers or something."

Paul crossed his legs and sipped his wine. He watched Starris pace in front of him and listened as she let her words propel her to fury. He'd known Starris would be a passionate woman. Jordon Banks was a fool not to know what he had. Paul drank from his glass again as Starris began to wind down.

She sat on the couch with a thump, and Paul smothered a grin when she attempted to display indifference after the emotional tantrum he'd just witnessed. He angled his body toward her and leaned down to capture her eyes with his. "And yet, despite all you've said, Starris, you are in love with Jordon Banks. The lucky bastard."

Starris opened her mouth, then closed it, unable to tell a lie. She slumped back against the couch and crossed her arms. Even if she did love the mule-headed jerk, they could pin her to stakes, and she'd never admit it. She leaned forward, a glimmer of warning in her eyes as she faced Paul. "I don't want to talk about Jordon Banks. I want to talk about Chad. Do you really think I have a shot at this job?"

"According to Chad, you're the top candidate."

"I hope so," Starris said. "I really need this job."

Paul frowned. "Well, I don't understand why Jordon didn't hire you on permanently at ROBY."

Whether it was his words or a delayed reaction to Jordon's actions that evening, Paul would never know, but he wrapped his arms around Starris when she leaned her head on his chest and burst into tears.

The expression on Dani's face turned to stone as she watched her mother and Paul through the banister spokes. She and Jolie would never be sisters now, she thought, rising from the step to go and answer her ringing telephone.

"That's great, Jolie, and I'm glad your dad changed his mind, but we have a serious problem."

"Not anymore, Dani. Not only can I stay, but Daddy's promised to apologize to Mama tomorrow."

"Tomorrow may be too late," Dani replied morosely. She pulled her legs Indian-style beneath her. "A man came here tonight."

"A man!"

"Yes, a man, and he's in love with Starris. I think she likes him, too."

Jolie, who was lying on her back with her feet propped against the wall, suddenly bounced up. "This is terrible news."

"Tell me something I don't know. What are we going to do? I don't want this Paul McCaber, McCob or whatever to be my father. I want your dad to be my father."

"Paul McCaber. Oh, that sounds so sexy," Jolie groaned.

"His name is McCabe, and will you please get serious, Jolie! This is not about sex or boys, which is all you ever think about. We've got to do something, or your dad and my mom will never get married."

Jolie crossed an arm over her flat chest and paced in front of her bed. "Boys and sex are not all I think about, Dani. And I know how serious this is."

Both girls were quiet for a few minutes, their brows furrowed in hard thought. Jolie lay back on her bed, giving up. "Well, I don't know what to do, Dani."

"Hold on," Dani whispered, rising. "I think I hear something." She moved to the door and after listening, slipped through and peeked over the railing. Horrified, she ran back into her bedroom and snatched up the phone. "It's worse than I thought," she wailed to Jolie. "I think Starris is letting him kiss her."

"How do you know?"

"I just saw them. We have to do something, Jolie!"

"Okay, Dani. I think I have it. Remember how much fun we had that day you spent the night?"

"Yeah."

"And remember how much fun my dad and your mom had?"

"Yeah, they were kissing all the time when they thought we weren't watching. But how is that going to help us now?"

Jolie heaved a sigh and her voice rose several octaves. "Don't you see, Dani. What we have to do is get my dad and your mom together and let love take its course again."

"How do we get them together? They're both mad at each other."

"They won't be for long," Jolie answered. "Remember my dad promised to apologize. I know," she suddenly said. "I'll get him to do it in person. All I have to do is think of a way to get him over there."

Jolie started when she heard a knock and cringed when Jordon poked his head around the door. "You are not to be on that telephone, young lady."

"But Daddy, you didn't say I couldn't use the phone. You said I couldn't have my allowance for two weeks."

"After the stunt you pulled this evening, you're lucky I don't take that phone out of your room, permanently. Now, tell Dani good night and get ready for bed."

"Yes, sir." Jolie placed the receiver at her ear. "I have to go, Dani."

"Don't forget. You're going to bring your dad over here tomorrow, and make it early."

Jolie looked at her father unsure if after tonight she could pull off their scheme. "I'll try. Goodbye, Dani."

CHAPTER 17

"What in the hell do you think you're doing!"

Paul rose from the chair and directed his gaze toward the door. For two cents, he'd punch Jordon Banks right in the mouth. Better yet, he'd do it for free. "If you must know, I'm doing a favor for a friend. And before you decide to display any he-man heroics, Lisa let me in."

Jordon's long strides quickly brought him across the room. "What friend?"

"Starris." Paul turned his back to Jordon and opened a drawer. He pulled out a stack of folders and laid them on the desk.

Jordon's confusion mounted. "Why didn't Starris come herself? Why did she send you?"

"Come on, Banks. I know you're a fool, but I never figured you to be stupid, too."

Jordon dropped his large frame into a chair. "She confided in you."

Paul turned, his eyes glittering with renewed anger. "Not only did Starris tell me everything, she cried in my arms for an hour last night."

"Last night." Jordon closed his eyes, unable to stop the feeling of betrayal that stole over him as images of Starris lying in Paul's arms refused to be blocked from his mind.

"Yes, last night." Paul moved from behind the desk. "You know something, Banks. If I didn't know it would upset Starris even more, I'd knock you on your ass right this minute. Maybe you are stupid. You'd have to be to let a woman like her get away from you."

Jordon rose from his chair. "I think you'd better leave, while it is still possible for you to do so."

"I am leaving, but I think you should know that despite what you and Lisa have done, Starris still loves you. I intend to change that."

"Lisa? Now, I think you've gone dense, McCabe. There is nothing between Lisa Mason and myself. And I'd advise you to forget any thoughts you've entertained of stealing Starris. She's mine." And only in that moment did Jordon Banks comprehend just how much he wanted that statement to be true.

"I wouldn't be too sure about that, Banks. Starris is not the type to take a backseat to another woman or wait around while you make up your mind. Let her go. I'm sure you'll have your hands more than full with Ms. Mason."

"Why do you keep bringing up Lisa Mason? She is my employee and nothing more. Starris knows that."

"And I suppose you had nothing to do with the announcement at the open house, either."

"What announcement?"

"Look, Banks. You and Lisa might have fooled everyone else, but Starris worked for weeks on that proposal to match ROBY with Quad-E, and she planned to approach you and Carlotta Eldridge last week. But before she could, you and Ms. Mason took her idea and presented it as your own. You even had the balls to use the materials she created. You don't deserve a woman like Starris; she's way out of your league."

Jordon's mind reeled under the weight of Paul's accusations and, picking up the stack of folders, he strode from the office without another glance in Paul's direction.

Before Starris could get around the screen, Dani had run down the stairs to answer the pealing doorbell. She opened the door, then stepped back to let Jordon inside the house.

At first stepping around her, he stopped. He set the folders on the table and pulled Dani into a hug. "Li'l bit, I owe you an apology. Yesterday, I acted in haste, and for that I can only say that I'm sorry. I truly didn't mean to upset you or your mother. Do you forgive me?"

Dani tilted her head. "I forgive you."

"Thank you."

Starris watched the scene with mixed feelings. His apology to Dani was a step in the right direction, but she didn't want to see Jordon or listen to anything he had to say. "Why are you here?"

Jordon just stopped himself from shivering in the frigid wind of her greeting. He loved this woman and felt ashamed at the bleakness he'd put in her eyes. "I brought the files you wanted from the office."

"I sent Paul for those."

"I know." Jordon's body quaked with nerves. This was not going to be easy. "Baby, can we talk?"

"I think everything that needed saying, you said yesterday. Goodbye, Jordon."

He caught her arm when Starris turned away. "I'm sorry, Star. Yesterday, I spoke in anger, and I didn't mean any of it."

Starris removed his hand from her arm. "You know something, Jordon, Lonnie Gilmore was a pitiful excuse for a man, but the one thing he taught me is that anger brings out the truth in people. Regardless of what you feel now, I think you meant the things you said yesterday."

Jordon winced at the despondency he heard in her voice, wishing that she'd give him the dressing down he deserved. At least then, he'd know that he had a chance. "Baby, please. Let's talk this out. I regret everything I said to you, and if you're willing, I'd like you to continue watching Jolie."

Hope sprung eternal in Starris, but Jordon needed to understand that she would not tolerate what he'd done. Not from him. Nor from any other man again. "What you did yesterday, and the things you said, hurt me and the girls very badly, Jordon. I took six years of abuse from one man, I'll not stand for it from another."

"I understand, Star, and I swear it will never happen again. Now, I won't ask that we start over. We've done that too many times. Let's just move forward and try to be the best we can be for ourselves and each other." He held out his arms and prayed that Starris would come to him.

She let him sweat it out for a few moments. When she saw grim lines form around his mouth she stepped forward. "I accept your apology, and Jolie is always welcome in my home whether we're together or not."

Jordon hugged her tight. "Oh, we're going to be together, so if you're thinking otherwise, forget it, babe."

Starris poked him in the ribs. "Don't be too sure about that, Banks. You have a few bad habits that will need to improve before—"

Jordon kissed her, and Dani silently left the two adults alone.

The following Friday, Jordon looked up when his office door opened. He rocked back in his chair. "I hope that envelope contains the signed Melcher contract."

Lisa, who had waltzed in unannounced, stutter-stepped to a halt. Sensing the restrained tension, she took in the austere planes of Jordon's face and tightened her lower jaw. "That's why I'm here, Jordon. Melcher and his people have decided not..."

"Stop." Jordon picked up a manila folder and rose from his chair. "Tell me about Quad-E."

"What do you want to know?"

Jordon moved to the window and looked down on the street. "Let's start with your proposal and the strategy you used to convince Carlotta to team up with ROBY." He turned. "Though you have recounted your verbal conversations, I've never seen the actual proposal. Why don't you get it, and we'll discuss our next move."

Lisa's lips twitched with indecision. "I can't."

"I beg your pardon, Ms. Mason?"

"I mean, I didn't submit a written proposal to Carlotta. I pitched to her over the telephone."

"Now, that is interesting." Jordon moved back to his desk. He opened a folder and took out the contents. "Come closer, please." With trepidation, Lisa walked to the desk. "As you can see, this is a copy of a proposal prepared and ready to submit to Carlotta Eldridge. Remarkably enough, your name doesn't appear anywhere on it."

Lisa squeezed her eyes shut. "What exactly are you implying?"

Jordon sat in his chair. "I am not implying anything, Ms. Mason. I am stating quite plainly that you are fired."

"Fired! You have no grounds."

"Plagiarizing the work of another employee is ample grounds, Ms. Mason. Add to that your lack of performance on the job, and I think any court in the land will back me on this decision."

Lisa crossed her arms and lifted her chin haughtily. "You have no proof, Jordon Banks. That proposal could have been written by anybody, at any time."

"This proposal is proof, Ms. Mason. You should also know that I obtained this copy from Paul McCabe, not Starris. She has had several conversations about this proposal with both Mr. McCabe and Shelby Reeves. Both are willing to sign affidavits stating that fact. Now, if you'd like not to add the further embarrassment of being escorted from this office by the police, then I'd suggest that you gather your personal belongings and leave these premises immediately."

It isn't fair, Lisa thought, as she marched out of Jordon's office and let her anger propel her down the corridor to her own. Jordon Banks thought he could call the shots, and he didn't seem to care who he stepped on in the process. Entering her office, she went to her desk and began slamming her things together. "Jordon Banks might think he has all the power," she muttered. "But we'll just see about that." Suddenly tired, Lisa sank into her chair and removed her purse from one of the drawers. From it she lifted a small vial. Staring at the powder through the brown glass, she told herself that she only kept it as a reminder of her past and that she really didn't need the drug. But it was just getting too hard. She'd been planning the downfall of Jordon Banks for years. She'd worked against Jordon for weeks, doing everything she could think of to ruin his reputation the way he'd ruined her sister's and thereby get custody of Gloria's child. Nothing she'd done had made one bit of difference. Everything was falling apart, and Lisa was at a loss as to how to reverse the situation in her favor.

With a sigh, Lisa screwed the cap off the vial and dumped the powder on her desk. She'd only do a little, just enough so that she could think. Think of a way to stop Jordon Banks dead in his tracks.

Later that afternoon, Lisa pulled up to the curb and quickly scanned the bobbing faces of the scattering children in the school yard until her eyes found the two little girls standing beside the bicycle rack. Watching them, she tried to repress her memories. Dani and Jolie looked so happy, just the way it should be when you were a child. Not like her own childhood, where pain and poverty had been constant companions. When Starris arrived, Lisa slunk down in her seat. She watched with envy as Dani and Jolie ran to Starris and she enfolded them in a big hug. Lisa could almost feel the love they shared, and a tear she did not bother to wipe away streaked the makeup on her smooth, brown cheek.

Except for Gloria, no one had ever loved her like that. That's why she wanted Dani. She knew that raising Gloria's child would fill the deep and dark void she lived with since they'd taken her sister away. But she had no real legal recourse in regard to Dani. According to the lawyer and private investigator she'd paid, too much time had passed and everyone, including Dani's caseworker and the judge, was in Starris' corner.

Unable to continue watching the happy scene, Lisa sat up and started her car. She drove away slowly, her mind gripped with thoughts of revenge for Jordon Banks. She might not get Dani, but she wasn't leaving until she found a way to make Jordon Banks feel the same torment he'd put her sister through.

After escorting Lisa from ROBY's office, Jordon sat in his office feeling antsy. He wanted to talk to Starris, but she'd already left to pick up the girls from school. Since it was the last day, he'd already agreed to let Jolie spend the night with Dani and knew that Starris planned to stop by his house so that his daughter could get her things before taking the girls home. But Jordon couldn't wait to tell Starris of the afternoon's events and apologize for his unwitting role in Lisa's duplicity. Picking up his car keys, he left his office, stopping only long enough to let Selma know that he'd be out of the office for the rest of the day. If he left now, he could meet Starris at the house, apologize and take them all out to dinner.

Pulling into the driveway, Jordon was surprised to see Lisa standing in front of his house. Furious at the thought that the woman actually had the nerve to show up at his residence, Jordon flung open his door and stepped from the car.

Lisa hurried forward. "Jordon, I need to talk to you, and it's important."

Jordon placed his fists on his waist and attempted to remain calm in the wake of his anger. "I believe I made myself quite clear this afternoon, Ms. Mason. Our association has ended. There is nothing left to discuss. Now, kindly remove yourself from my property, or I will call the police."

"Oh, but there is." Lisa reached into her purse and took out a gold envelope. She held it out in front of her. "We need to discuss this, and we can do it standing in the middle of your driveway or we can go inside the house. The choice is yours, but I'm not leaving until you look at the papers inside this envelope."

By the look on her face, Lisa meant business, and indecision coursed through Jordon's body. His first thought was to call the cops and have Lisa Mason arrested, but he knew that the police would not get there in time to remove Lisa before Starris and the girls arrived. And he couldn't risk placing his family in harm's way should Lisa prove to be dangerous. He needed to deal with this situation himself. "You have five minutes," Jordon stated as he turned for the door.

Inside the house, Jordon led the way to the library, then stepped aside to let Lisa enter before closing the doors behind them. He watched Lisa's eyes open in astonishment, and her gaze roam the room before she turned back to face him.

"Nice digs."

Jordon was not amused. "You now have four minutes, Ms. Mason. And you should know now that nothing you say will change my decision regarding your employment with ROBY."

A smirk formed on Lisa's face. "I'm not here about that job, and I think that if you read these papers, it will be quite obvious what I want."

"I'm not going to read anything. So if this is the only reason for your visit, then I suggest that you leave the same way you came in."

Lisa moved to the couch and gracefully lowered her body to its cushions. She tossed the envelope onto the table and leaning back, stretched her arms along the back and directed a pointed stare at Jordon. "Well, then I guess that I'll be here awhile, because until you do read those papers, I'm not going anywhere."

With that statement, Jordon's patience snapped, and he moved to the bar. Anger singed the air as he picked up the telephone receiver and punched a number into the keypad. "This is Jordon Banks of 125 Mockingham Lane. There is an intruder in my home."

Lisa's body stiffened, and a trickle of sweat worked its way down her spine. Jordon Banks was not bluffing, but she had come too far to back down now.

"No, she doesn't appear to have a weapon. However, I'd like her removed from the premises."

The rest of the conversation lasted no more than a few seconds, and Jordon hung up the telephone. "The police are on the way, Ms. Mason. It would be best if you weren't here when they arrive."

Lisa jumped up from the couch, her eyes burning with the loathing she felt as she pinned a hostile stare on Jordon. "Gloria was right about you!"

Jordon's spine snapped straight. "Gloria!"

"Yes, Gloria," Lisa screamed. Her pain-filled voice faltered to a murmur as she continued. "My sister, Gloria Banks."

A myriad of thoughts rushed through Jordon's brain, and feeling himself sinking into a dark undertow of grief, he grabbed the edge of the bar for support. His breaths became short, jerky pants, and Jordon fought to keep his head. With effort, he managed to look up, only to see the specter of his wife standing before him, mocking him. He looked away, telling himself that it wasn't true, that it couldn't be true. Gloria had no family. She'd spent her entire childhood as a ward of the state of Georgia.

Through the haze in his mind, he heard Lisa say, "It's true. I am Gloria's sister."

Jordon's gaze returned to Lisa. His jaw tensed as his dark eyes took on a hard glint. He shook his head. "You are mistaken, Ms. Mason. My ex-wife had no family," he finally said with quiet indignation. "Gloria was an orphan."

Lisa's rage spilled over, and she lashed out in hatred. "Gloria may have been an orphan. But she did have family. Me! I searched for my sister for years only to find that you, the man she loved and trusted, had turned her out into the streets. Gloria had nowhere to go when you forced her to leave her home, and by the time I found her, it was too late. But Gloria did leave me something, a letter that I received a year after her death. In it, she told me about the abuse and your affairs with other women. She said you used her, then tossed her aside when you didn't want her anymore. You killed my sister, Jordon Banks! Just as surely as if you'd pulled the trigger yourself. And I intend to see that justice is served."

Jordon slowly crossed the room, his face ashen. "Justice has already been served. If you are Gloria's sister, then you should know that she lied to you. I did not violate my marriage vows, and I did not abuse your sister. The reason I divorced Gloria is because I found her in our bed with another man!" Still breathing harshly, Jordon turned away to calm himself. Lisa stood directly in front of him when he turned back. Though his insides tightened with anxiety when he saw her tears, his conscience was clear. "I feel no guilt where your sister is concerned, Ms. Mason."

"Liar!" Despite the tears in her eyes, Lisa's aim proved true when her palm connected with the side of his face. "That's what Gloria told me you'd say!"

Jordon grabbed her by the shoulders. "It's the truth, Lisa!"

She broke from his hold and backed away. "I don't believe you! Gloria was afraid of you and that's why she hid her children from you. She begged me to find them before you did because she didn't want you to corrupt their minds against her. And she was right. You don't deserve to raise either of my sister's children."

Jordon rubbed the side of his face, his eyes constricting in anger. "Lisa, that makes no sense. Your sister sent a letter to my lawyer telling me exactly where to find my daughter, and Jolie is with me, where she belongs."

Lisa backed away from Jordon, stopping only when her legs hit the table behind her. "I'm not talking about Jolie. It has taken me years to find Danielle, the child you didn't want, and I won't let a stranger raise my sister's child." At Jordon's shocked and pain-stricken eyes, Lisa snatched up the envelope and threw it at his feet. "It's all there. And you may want to read it because you'll be subpoenaed when I take you and Starris Gilmore to court and sue for custody of my niece!"

"You can't be serious, Lisa. Danielle doesn't even know you, and if what you say is true, I'm her father!"

Lisa's laugh sounded hollow even to her, but she bravely kept up the front. "By the time I'm finished, no court in the land will award Danielle to you, Jordon Banks, and I'll probably get Jolie in the bargain, too."

Snatching up her purse, Lisa ran to the doors. She pulled them open, raced through the house and out of the front door.

A marked police cruiser pulled up behind Christopher Mills when he stopped his jeep in front of Jordon's house. Christopher had barely cut his engine when he saw the slender, black woman run from the house and to her car.

Christopher and his partner leaped from the jeep. "Check the house," he yelled, heading for the woman. Lisa had already started her car by the time Christopher reached the door. He reached for the handle, just as Lisa hit the gas. She barreled down the driveway, squealing to a halt when Starris turned her car into the drive.

Turning the wheel quickly to the right, Lisa veered onto the lawn and out into the street, her thoughts only of the look on Jordon's face when she'd dropped her bombshell. Tears still brimmed her eyes, but the smile on her face was more brilliant than the sun. Her plan hadn't worked perfectly, but the sense of revenge that coursed through her now felt oh so sweet. And while she hadn't been able to get Danielle, Lisa felt sure that Gloria would be proud of the pain and disruptive chaos she'd just caused in Jordon Banks' life.

Christopher ran back to his jeep, stopping when he saw Starris get out of her car. When she bent over to say something through the window to the girls, he called to his partner, "Stop her from going inside."

"Where are you going?"

"After the other one!"

Christopher pulled into the street and quickly spied the silver Honda. The vehicle was moving at a rapid speed and narrowly missed hitting another car when it continued through a stop sign at the corner. Christopher shook his head. He knew the woman was oblivious to what was happening around her, and also knew that he had to stop her before she killed somebody. In the next instant, Christopher realized that he wouldn't have the opportunity to catch and stop the car. The light controlling the north and south flow of traffic had turned red. The car in front of him didn't stop, and Christopher clinched his jaw when a big yellow moving van barreled into the side of the silver Honda.

Jordon sat at his desk, staring at the gold envelope. Drumming his pencil on the arm of his chair, he attempted to rein in his emotions. Nothing Lisa Mason had said could possibly be true. But the proof was in the envelope, and he only had to open it to find out for sure. With a trembling hand, he finally leaned forward and picked it up. His pulse quickened as he slowly lifted the flap. Jordon removed the papers inside, and his whole body went numb.

He'd seen the small, neat scrawl enough times to know that the handwriting belonged to his ex-wife, and tears blurred his vision as he read the words. Except for the lies she'd told regarding him, every fiber of his being told him that the things she'd said about Danielle and Jolie were true. The letter dropped from his hands, and he reached for the second piece of paper. The words were unclear. He wiped his eyes with the back of his hand and focused on the document:

Mother: Gloria Leanne Banks. Father: Jordon Randolph Banks. Name of child: Danielle Kathryn Banks.

"Bitch!" The word hissed through his lips as the birth certificate fell from his hands. Jordon closed his eyes and tears slid unheeded down his face as he relived every painful moment his ex-wife had caused in his life. How much longer was he going to be punished for marrying the wrong woman? How much longer would Gloria Banks continue to haunt him from the grave!

Wracked with despair, Jordon doubled over. "Oh, Dani," he whispered. "Li'l bit, I'm so sorry."

The cop holding Starris in a loose embrace tried to tighten his hold. "You can't go in until we've checked out the house. We don't know what happened in there yet."

Starris continued to fight and, breaking free, she made a dash for the front door; the cop followed. Starris ran directly to Jordon's study. When she didn't find him, she turned and headed for the library. She came to a sudden halt when she saw him doubled over in his chair.

The cop pushed her aside. "Sir! Are you all right?" Jordon didn't answer, and the cop rushed forward. "Sir, are you hurt?"

Jordon raised his head and all color drained from her Starris' face. She'd never in her life seen pain of such magnitude. A wave of dizziness hit, and Starris gazed around the room, fighting to stop the tension she felt rising in her chest. She couldn't panic now. Jordon needed her. With a will of iron, Starris held back the attack and after inhaling deeply, she moved forward. "Jordon," she said in a voice laced with a modicum of calm she managed to pull from an inner reserve, "what happened? What was Lisa Mason doing here?"

CHAPTER 18

An hour later, the two officers and Christopher had left. Starris sat in a chair trying to digest everything she'd just learned about Lisa Mason. It hadn't surprised her that Lisa had stolen her Quad-E proposal and tried to take the credit or that Jordon had fired the woman—too late to Starris' way of thinking. But it had shaken Starris to her core to learn that Lisa Mason was, or rather had been, the sister of Jordon's ex-wife.

She studied Jordon from across the room. Although she knew the revelations and the afternoon's events had shaken him, especially learning that Lisa had died in the car crash, the pain she'd seen earlier was gone, and he seemed to have pulled himself together. Starris rose from her chair. "Jordon, what are you going to do about Dani?" Jordon didn't respond. "This is not something that can wait, Jordon. The adoption is scheduled to be finalized in a few days, and I need to know what you plan to do."

Starris saw his agitation as Jordon glanced nervously around the room and wished she could go to him. But rooted to the spot where she stood, Starris didn't move. She tried to think of ways to combat any response he might make, but with her anxiety growing by leaps and bounds it was impossible for her to think clearly. He was going to take her daughter. Starris knew it as sure as she knew her name.

Jordon began to pace. Starris had asked the question he'd been asking himself for the last hour. What was he going to do about Danielle? With everything that had transpired that day, this was the last thing Jordon wanted to think about. But it was the only thing he could think about. Because of a sick mind bent on total revenge, his daughter had spent ten years in the child-welfare system believing that no loved or wanted her. He was Danielle's father. Somehow he had to find a way to make up for all the years he hadn't known that she was his daughter. But what about Starris? Starris had been the one to rescue Dani from the system. Starris had lavished his daughter with love, and for all intents and purposes, Starris was Danielle's mother, a mother Dani loved and expected to grow up with. Jordon clenched his jaw. He couldn't just wrench Dani away from the only mother she'd ever known, and though it cut through his heart like a knife, Jordon gave the only response he knew he could make. "I want to bring my daughter home."

Brokenhearted, disappointment surrounded Starris like a cloak. She crossed her arms over her chest as if trying to hold back the pain. She'd known what his response would be before she'd asked the question. But to hear Jordon say the words was almost more than Starris could bear. "She's my daughter, too, Jordon."

Anguish flashed in Jordon's face. "What do you expect me to do, Starris? Although I didn't find out until today, I am Danielle's father, and I want my daughter."

"No!"

Two sets of startled gazes swung in tandem. The girls, whom neither adult had seen enter the room, sat on the couch. By the stricken look on their faces, Starris knew they had heard everything. "Danielle, Jolie, come here," she said.

Danielle jumped to her feet, her fury evident in the fisted hands she held stiffly at her sides. "He is not my father. He's not!"

Dani ran, almost knocking down Alice in her rush to get out of the room. Starris gasped and turned bewildered eyes from Alice to Jordon before hurrying out of the room after her daughter.

Immobile, Jordon could only stare at an astounded Alice. *God,* he thought, *would this day never end?* He made a move to go after Starris, but was stopped by the hand on his arm. Jordon looked down at Jolie. "Daddy, is it true? Are Dani and me really for-real sisters?"

Jordon felt his heart lurch as he stared into the face so much like his own and yet so much like Dani's, too. There were so many similarities. How many times had he looked into the faces of his daughters and seen them? How had he not known that Dani was his own flesh and blood? Pulling Jolie into a tight embrace, Jordon hugged his daughter. "Yes, sweet pea. You and Danielle are sisters, and right now you and I are going to go and find your sister."

On the lawn outside the house, Starris attempted to hold on to Dani as the child fought for freedom. Pushing herself out of Starris' arms, Dani's eyes blazed with anger, and she struck out with her hands. "You're going to leave me with them," she stated accusingly. "You said you would never leave me, and you lied! You're just like all those other people who lied. You never loved me, Starris. But I don't care. I don't care because I never loved you either!"

Starris grabbed Dani by the shoulders and pulled the girl to her. Picking her up, Starris sat in the grass and wrapped her arms around Dani, rocking and soothing her daughter. Wasn't it ironic, Starris thought, that she and Dani would end their relationship exactly as it had begun. This time though, it didn't take nearly as long for her to calm the little girl, and when Dani quieted, Starris looked down into her tear-stained face, her heart breaking for the second time that day.

"Angel, I want you to listen to me very carefully. I did not lie to you, and I don't want to leave you. I'm sorry that you found out about Jordon the way you did, but he is your father and while that may be hard to accept right now, I think that if you give him a chance, you'll find that Jordon loves you as much as I do." When Dani hiccuped a sigh, Starris bravely continued. "Do you know what that means, Danielle?" Dani shook her head no. "It means that you have a family now, Dani. You have a father and a sister and a grandmother and a grandfather. You have aunts and uncles and cousins. All of these people will want to love and take care of you. And you know what?" Starris stopped and sought within herself for the strength to go on. She lifted her hand and wiped the tears from her cheeks. "That makes you a very lucky and special little girl."

Dani ducked her head. "I don't want to be lucky or special, Mama. I want to stay with you forever and ever."

"Oh, angel." Starris said, taking Dani's face in her hands. "I want to stay with you, too, forever. But I can't. Jordon is your father, and Jolie is your sister. They love you, and I'm sure that they will want you to come and live with them."

Dani buried her face in Starris' chest. "But what about you, Mama? Who's going to love and take care of you?"

Starris smoothed her hand over the thick mane of hair. "I'll be all right, Dani, and even though you and I can't be a family like we planned, I want you to remember that I will always love you. No matter where you are or where you live." Starris kissed Dani's cheek. "Who knows," she said, "it will take a while to get this all straightened out and afterward maybe your father will agree to let you come and visit me every once in a while. As for…"

Starris never finished what she wanted to say. Gripped from behind, Dani fell from her lap when she was yanked to her feet. She left the ground when Jordon raised her to eye level, his face so full of anger, Starris cringed.

"What do you think you're doing?"

"I-I was just telling—"

Jordon cut her off with a glare, and lowering Starris to the ground, he gripped her by the arm and headed for the door.

If she could have figured out a way not to enter the house, Starris would have. But Jordon pulled her along until they were inside. He gave Alice the briefest of explanations with a promise to sit down with her later and left the girls to her care. After watching her shuttle them off to the kitchen, he took Starris by the arm again and practically dragged her up the stairs to his suite. Jordon pushed Starris none too gently down to the bed, then began to pace the floor. She watched him in wary silence and thought it best that for once she hold her runaway tongue.

Finally, Jordon stopped in front of her. "Would you mind explaining that little scene down in the yard?"

Starris crossed her arms as a little of the defiance she'd worked to control rose to the surface. "What scene?"

Jordon ignored her question and sat on the bed. He took one of her hands in his. "Are you planning to leave Dani here with me, Starris?"

Surprise lit her eyes. "No."

Jordon heaved a sigh and shook his head. "If you are not leaving Dani, then I don't understand the tearful goodbye scene?"

Starris stood. "Jordon, I cannot play your little mind games right now. It's been a horrible day. I just want to get Dani and go home."

Jordon stood. "You're right. It has been a horrible day. One of the worst I've ever experienced in my life. But you and Dani are already home."

Her mind went into a chaotic spin, and Starris sat heavily on the bed behind her. "Jordon, I have to get out of here. Now that I know that you plan to take Dani, I need to figure out what to do next."

"Take Dani! Starris, you are Danielle's mother, at least the only one she's ever had. I would never take her from you, even if I had known that I'd fathered her. Although, you do realize that we now have a problem."

"No, we don't," Starris said, shaking her head. "That's what I was explaining to Dani. You're her father, Jordon. She has a wonderful sister and your family to take care of her now. Dani doesn't need me anymore."

Nonplussed, his gaze flew to her face. "That's ridiculous, Starris. Dani needs you more than ever now. You can't be planning to walk out of your daughter's life. Not now when she needs you the most. Not when I need you."

"Jordon, you don't need me, and it's probably best that I step out of the picture as soon as possible. Dani needs time to adjust to you, to Jolie and to her new family and environment. My hanging around will only prolong that process." She looked around for her purse, then remembered that it was still in her car. "Dani's caseworker is Jim Stephenson. He's the person we need to talk to about this, only he's on vacation right now." Starris rose, knowing that if she stayed in the room another minute, she'd break down in tears.

Jordon let Starris get as far as the door, before he swept her off her feet. Lifting her higher in his arms, he took her mouth in a blistering kiss, then stared savagely into the startled hazel eyes. "You aren't going anywhere," he growled, striding purposefully to the bed. "And neither is Dani."

As soon as she hit the mattress, Starris scrambled to her knees, then off the opposite side of the bed. "You can't kiss this away, Jordon. I know you're Dani's father, but she is legally a ward of the state. Until we talk to Jim and he's says differently, she has been assigned to my home, and I am responsible for her care."

"Dani is my daughter, and I want her in my home."

Starris' eyes flashed fire. "You can't move her in here just because you wish it!"

His gaze smoldered with scorn. "I can and I will."

"No, Jordon. You won't. Jim will be back in town next week. I'll leave a message for him to call me. Until then, things stay as they are. You and Jolie are welcome to visit with Dani as often as you like. But until I'm told differently, Danielle will continue to live with me."

Jordon ran a hand over his face. "Star, it took me a year to get Jolie out of the system, and the things I had to endure just to prove that I was a fit parent turned my stomach. I will not submit to any more psychiatric evaluations, blood tests or home visits. And I won't put Danielle through it either. And speaking of Dani, the only reason she's living with you is because you filed a petition to adopt. If you go to the Department of Social Services, the very first thing they will do is remove her from your home." Jordon fell to the bed. "There has to be a better way. Danielle is my natural-born child. I shouldn't have to prove that I'm good enough to be her father."

Starris moved to his side and sat beside him. "Jordy, I'm not trying to hurt you or Dani. I'm trying to do what is best for everyone. You'll get your daughter, but we have to do it the right way."

"I'd rather let you adopt Dani than go through that night-mare again."

They sat quietly, each with their own thoughts until Jordon suddenly looked up and said, "Unless we tell them, DSS will never know that I am Dani's father. You could go ahead with the adoption, and once it has been legally approved, marry me. Then we'd both have custody of Danielle."

Although his reasoning did have merit, without his love, Starris knew she couldn't even consider marrying Jordon. Not under those circumstances. "I'm sorry, Jordon, but the answer is no."

Jordon wrapped his arm around her and leaned his head down. "I don't think you understand, Starris. I want my daughter, and I won't deal with the child-welfare system to get her. So, you have two choices. Either you marry me or you'll never see Danielle again."

Her head jerked up. "You can't possibly mean that, Jordon Banks."

He released her. "I can and I do."

Heartache moved swiftly across her face, and tears filled her eyes. Starris wiped them away when they ran down her cheeks. Marry him or lose Dani. That was his solution to the problem, his ultimatum. It was unfair, and Jordon knew it. Starris firmed her shoulders and met his obstinate stare with her own. "What about Dani?"

Jordon left the bed and sat in a chair across the room, his face impassive, his eyes unfathomable. "What about her?"

"Dani loves me. How do you think she'll feel about you when she finds out that you kept me away from her?"

"Starris, Danielle is a child. Sure, she'll miss you at first and she may even shed a few tears, but in a few months, she'll wish you never existed. I'll make sure of it."

Now he was being deliberately cruel, and Starris, who'd had enough for one day, jumped to her feet. "I will not let you do that to me or to Dani, Jordon Banks. I'll see you in hell first before I let you teach my child to hate me!"

Jordon rose from his chair. "And a few minutes ago, you were prepared to give your daughter away. Come here, Starris." When she crossed her arms in defiance, he went to her. "Don't be angry, Star. I'm sorry for what I put you through just now, but I had to make you see what you're doing, not only to Danielle, but to yourself. That little girl loves you and, after all this time, I don't believe that you'll be able to give her up as easily as you think."

Starris reached for him, and he enfolded her in his arms. "You're right, Jordy. I can't give up Danielle. She's my baby."

His lips came down on hers, then kissed away the tears on her cheeks. He again lifted Starris and carried her to the bed. Lying beside her, Jordon took her in his arms again and let her cry. Her tears lanced his heart, and he held on for both their sakes. When she quieted, he cupped her face in his hands. "Star, Dani belongs to both of us, and I won't let you lose or leave your daughter. Marry me, and we can both have her."

Starris squeezed her eyes shut. What was she going to do? She loved and needed her daughter. And she loved and needed Jordon. Only he didn't love or need her. He'd only offered to marry her so that she could keep Dani. Starris wasn't sure it would be enough to keep them together. Lonnie hadn't loved her either, but the mistake she'd made was in letting him know that she did care for him. She wouldn't make that mistake with Jordon. She would learn to keep her feelings to herself.

She felt Jordon's fingers on the buttons of her blouse and his mouth trailing up her neck. Starris felt the passion begin its flow and tried to stave off the feelings. When his hands pushed open her blouse, she turned to face him, her face reflecting her resolve. "Okay, Jordon. To keep Dani, I'll marry you."

A short while later, Starris marveled at her actions as she rubbed her hands over the thick shoulders, then down the smooth skin of Jordon's brown chest. Never in her life had she imagined that she would have the kind of power that could make a man cry out in pleasure. While she might not have his love, she reveled in her mastery of his body and the pure joy she saw expressed in his face. Jordon gripped her slender hips, and she lowered her head, capturing his lips. He rolled her onto her back and took command of their lovemaking. His movements became frenzied as he tried to merge their bodies and each cry of his name from her lips rippled through him exhorting Jordon to give up more and more of himself. And Jordon gave himself to Starris, the whole of what he was, piece by heart-rending piece. When he had nothing left to give, Jordon slid his hands beneath Starris and held on tightly when the shout of her name mingled with his as their worlds collided in cataclysmic rapture.

Drained of his essence, Jordon lifted himself and fell to his side on the bed. Barely able to breathe, he reached for Starris and buried his face in her neck. "I love you, Starris, and I swear I'll be the best husband you'll ever find."

A nanosecond later, Jordon's jaw clenched together like a steel trap. He closed his eyes, unable to believe the words that had left his mouth. Once, he'd given his heart to a woman, and she'd nearly destroyed him. He had just given Starris that same power, and now that he'd said the words, there was nothing he could do to recall them.

Too moved to speak, Starris left the bed. In the bathroom, she stood in the mirror, stupefied, as the enormity of his words hit her. Jordon loved her, and she wanted to believe him; she truly did. But as much as Starris loved him, she couldn't return the sentiment. His words, however genuine they had sounded, were nothing more than a delayed manifestation of the shock they had experienced that afternoon. In his right mind, Starris knew the word love would never pass through Jordon Banks' lips.

She swiped away her tears and returned to the bedroom. Jordon hadn't moved, and she waited until he looked her way. "You didn't have to say that, Jordon. And please don't think that you have to express something you don't really feel. It's enough that you are willing to marry me so that I can continue to be Dani's mother."

Jordon continued to stare while trying to slow the runaway beat of his heart. With effort, he rose to his feet. "Then what Paul McCabe told me isn't true."

Starris felt her knees weaken. "What do you mean?"

"According to Paul, you do love me."

Starris wanted to deny it, but said, "Well, we both know that love ain't all it's cracked up to be, don't we?"

Jordon skirted the end of the bed and slowly closed the distance between them. He stopped only inches away, close enough for her to feel the heat emanating from his body. "Say it, Starris."

"I don't know what you want me to say."

"Yes, you do, and we've reached the final level. I am not Lonnie, and you are not Gloria. They are a part of our past and it's time to lay that past to rest. Once we do that, we can learn to trust each other and believe in love again. I want to believe, Starris, and I do. You once told me that you would not marry again without love. Well, I love you, and I want you to be the mother to Dani and Jolie and any children we have in the future. I want you for my wife, and I will love you until the day I die. Tell me that's what you want, too."

"Jordy, please."

He took her in his arms and skimmed his lips along the line of her jaw until he reached her ear. "Say the words, Star, and make them real for both of us."

She searched the depth of his dark eyes. There she found the truth. Jordon did love her, and she let those eyes and his hands, warm and loving as they massaged her back, soothe away the doubts and her fears. Starris wrapped her arms around his waist. "I do love you, Jordon Randolph Banks, and I always will."

EPILOGUE

"Othello."

"No."

"Okay. What about Einstein? Now, he was a smart man."

"Forget it, Banks. We are going to name this child Jonathan."

"Fine." Irked, Jordon turned away and seated himself in a chair across the room. "The least you can let me do, Starris Banks, is choose my son's middle name."

Starris gazed down lovingly at the baby in her arms. She gently brushed a finger along one of his soft cheeks until he opened dark gray eyes and stared up at her. "Hello, Jonathan," she cooed. Then she shot a warning glare at her husband. "You can choose the middle name, Jordy. As long as it's not Othello, Wilfred, Einstein or any of those other awful names you've come up with in the last twenty-four hours."

"I like Jonathan, Daddy," Jolie said, seating herself beside Starris on the bed.

"It figures. You women always stick together."

"Daddy?"

Jordon looked first at the small hand tugging at his shirt, then into the brown eyes of his daughter. "What is it, li'l bit?"

"Don't be mad at Mommy. My name used to be Carter and you gave me the name Banks. When we adopt Einstein and he belongs to us, you can pick another name for him, too."

Jordon drew Dani into his lap and smirked at his wife. Starris glanced away hiding her smile. Dani had taken to backing up her father's causes in an effort to show her loyalty and how much she loved him. Starris knew it would take a while longer before her daughter felt secure enough in their love to truly become herself again. She and Jordon had agreed to monitor the situation, but to give Dani all the time she needed to find that security and feel comfortable in her new family setting.

Jordon kissed her cheek. "We don't have to adopt Jonathan, li'l bit. He's already a Banks and he belongs to us—all of us."

"Oh," Dani replied. She snuggled against his chest.

Jordon's eyes slipped back and forth between his daughters still looking for the similarities, but as Starris had pointed out, they were few and far between. Exactly one month after Starris adopted Dani, they had married. Since the wedding and the move into his home, Jolie had clearly shown that she was the dominant twin. Jordon felt sure, however, that soon Dani would come into her own. Then Little Miss Jolie Banks would find herself on the other end of the ordering-about stick.

Somewhere along the way, Jordon's misguided views had been adjusted in regard to women. Starris had taught him that all women were not alike. She kept him constantly on his toes, never knowing what to expect, except to know that she would always love him and that he was the number one priority in her life. Still, he did like to tease her just to see the green glow in her eyes. "I suppose that since you've had a baby, you'll want maternity leave, too."

"Of course. All phases of the marketing plan have been launched, and my assistant can handle anything that may arise during my absence. Besides, I might just give up that job, and you might want to think about promoting her to marketing director. I need to concentrate on my children, redecorating the house and fulfilling my contract. They've only given me six months to create a whole new line of cards for RavenLove."

Jordon gathered Dani a little closer. "I gave you that job after you pestered me for weeks, Starris Banks. Now, you tell me to find somebody else. Forget it, babe. You have eight weeks, then I want you back on the job."

Her heart turned over. "But I just gave birth to your son, Jordy. How can you be so unfeeling?" She saw his grin and pursed her lips. "When I get my strength back, Banks, you're going to pay for that one."

"When you get your strength back, I want another son. Next time make it twins. Then with my boys backing me up, I'll have the final say in my household again."

"No you won't, Daddy. Mommy is the mother, and she runs our house. Doesn't she, Dani?"

Tilting her head, Dani looked up at Jordon before her gaze traveled to the bed. She studied the baby in Starris' arms for a few moments, then lifted thoughtful brown eyes to her mother's face. She looked at her sister. "I don't know, Jolie. I'm just a kid. Me and Einstein are going to do whatever Mommy and Daddy tell us to do."

Jordon laughed. "Good answer, li'l bit." Shining black eyes sought and found those of his wife and Jordon basked in the love that flowed between them. "And I'm going to do whatever Mommy tells me to do because I love her and I trust her to take care of us."

ABOUT THE AUTHOR

When a college history professor asked, "Who in this room thinks that they could be President of the United States?" **Wanda Y. Thomas** immediately raised her hand, then looked around to see that she was the only person with a hand in the air. As a twenty-four year veteran (or casualty-her words) of the cable television industry, Wanda has worked in various Administrative and Affiliate Sales & Marketing Management positions. In 1994, God led Wanda to the dusty desert and decadent city of Las Vegas, NV. "Though God may have had a hand in it," says Wanda. "It was actually a home shopping network, which relocated about 100 people from across the country to Las Vegas, and then laid us all off within a month." That experience and the lessons learned prompted Wanda to review the goals on her life's list; and to pursue the one that said: write a book and get it published.

Currently writing for Genesis Press, Inc and their Indigo Romance line, Wanda's first novel *Truly Inseparable* was released in hardback form in October 1998, and in soft cover in December, 1999. Her second, *Forever Love* was released in November 2000, and a third, *Subtle Secrets* was released in June 2001 and was nominated by Romance In Color in the categories of Book Of The Year and Genesis Press Release of the Year. Wanda was also nominated as Author of the Year. Wanda is single and lives in Denver, Colorado with her teenaged son.

2007 Publication Schedule

January

Rooms of the Heart
Donna Hill
ISBN-13: 978-1-58571-219-9
ISBN-10: 1-58571-219-1
$6.99

A Dangerous Love
J. M. Jeffries
ISBN-13: 978-1-58571-217-5
ISBN-10: 1-58571-217-5
$6.99

February

Bound By Love
Beverly Clark
ISBN-13: 978-1-58571-232-8
ISBN-10: 1-58571-232-9
$6.99

A Love to Cherish
Beverly Clark
ISBN-13: 978-1-58571-233-5
ISBN-10: 1-58571-233-7
$6.99

March

Best of Friends
Natalie Dunbar
ISBN-13: 978-1-58571-220-5
ISBN-10: 1-58571-220-5
$6.99

Midnight Magic
Gwynne Forster
ISBN-13: 978-1-58571-225-0
ISBN-10: 1-58571-225-6
$6.99

April

Cherish the Flame
Beverly Clark
ISBN-13: 978-1-58571-221-2
ISBN-10: 1-58571-221-3
$6.99

Quiet Storm
Donna Hill
ISBN-13: 978-1-58571-226-7
ISBN-10: 1-58571-226-4
$6.99

May

Sweet Tomorrows
Kimberley White
ISBN-13: 978-1-58571-234-2
ISBN-10: 1-58571-234-5
$6.99

No Commitment Required
Seressia Glass
ISBN-13: 978-1-58571-222-9
ISBN-10: 1-58571-222-1
$6.99

June

A Dangerous Deception
J. M. Jeffries
ISBN-13: 978-1-58571-228-1
ISBN-10: 1-58571-228-0
$6.99

Illusions
Pamela Leigh Starr
ISBN-13: 978-1-58571-229-8
ISBN-10: 1-58571-229-9
$6.99

2007 Publication Schedule (continued)

July

Indiscretions
Donna Hill
ISBN-13: 978-1-58571-230-4
ISBN-10: 1-58571-230-2
$6.99

Whispers in the Night
Dorothy Elizabeth Love
ISBN-13: 978-1-58571-231-1
ISBN-10: 1-58571-231-1
$6.99

August

Bodyguard
Andrea Jackson
ISBN-13: 978-1-58571-235-9
ISBN-10: 1-58571-235-3
$6.99

Crossing Paths, Tempting Memories
Dorothy Elizabeth Love
ISBN-13: 978-1-58571-236-6
ISBN-10: 1-58571-236-1
$6.99

September

Fate
Pamela Leigh Starr
ISBN-13: 978-1-58571-258-8
ISBN-10: 1-58571-258-2
$6.99

Mae's Promise
Melody Walcott
ISBN-13: 978-1-58571-259-5
ISBN-10: 1-58571-259-0
$6.99

October

Magnolia Sunset
Giselle Carmichael
ISBN-13: 978-1-58571-260-1
ISBN-10: 1-58571-260-4
$6.99

Broken
Dar Tomlinson
ISBN-13: 978-1-58571-261-8
ISBN-10: 1-58571-261-2
$6.99

November

Truly Inseparable
Wanda Y. Thomas
ISBN-13: 978-1-58571-262-5
ISBN-10: 1-58571-262-0
$6.99

The Color Line
Lizzette G. Carter
ISBN-13: 978-1-58571-263-2
ISBN-10: 1-58571-263-9
$6.99

December

Love Always
Mildred Riley
ISBN-13: 978-1-58571-264-9
ISBN-10: 1-58571-264-7
$6.99

Pride and Joi
Gay Gunn
ISBN-13: 978-1-58571-265-6
ISBN-10: 1-58571-265-5
$6.99

Other Genesis Press, Inc. Titles

A Dangerous Deception	J.M. Jeffries	$8.95
A Dangerous Love	J.M. Jeffries	$8.95
A Dangerous Obsession	J.M. Jeffries	$8.95
A Drummer's Beat to Mend	Kei Swanson	$9.95
A Happy Life	Charlotte Harris	$9.95
A Heart's Awakening	Veronica Parker	$9.95
A Lark on the Wing	Phyliss Hamilton	$9.95
A Love of Her Own	Cheris F. Hodges	$9.95
A Love to Cherish	Beverly Clark	$8.95
A Risk of Rain	Dar Tomlinson	$8.95
A Twist of Fate	Beverly Clark	$8.95
A Will to Love	Angie Daniels	$9.95
Acquisitions	Kimberley White	$8.95
Across	Carol Payne	$12.95
After the Vows	Leslie Esdaile	$10.95
(Summer Anthology)	T.T. Henderson	
	Jacqueline Thomas	
Again My Love	Kayla Perrin	$10.95
Against the Wind	Gwynne Forster	$8.95
All I Ask	Barbara Keaton	$8.95
Ambrosia	T.T. Henderson	$8.95
An Unfinished Love Affair	Barbara Keaton	$8.95
And Then Came You	Dorothy Elizabeth Love	$8.95
Angel's Paradise	Janice Angelique	$9.95
At Last	Lisa G. Riley	$8.95
Best of Friends	Natalie Dunbar	$8.95
Beyond the Rapture	Beverly Clark	$9.95
Blaze	Barbara Keaton	$9.95
Blood Lust	J. M. Jeffries	$9.95
Bodyguard	Andrea Jackson	$9.95
Boss of Me	Diana Nyad	$8.95
Bound by Love	Beverly Clark	$8.95

Other Genesis Press, Inc. Titles (continued)

Breeze	Robin Hampton Allen	$10.95
Broken	Dar Tomlinson	$24.95
By Design	Barbara Keaton	$8.95
Cajun Heat	Charlene Berry	$8.95
Careless Whispers	Rochelle Alers	$8.95
Cats & Other Tales	Marilyn Wagner	$8.95
Caught in a Trap	Andre Michelle	$8.95
Caught Up In the Rapture	Lisa G. Riley	$9.95
Cautious Heart	Cheris F Hodges	$8.95
Chances	Pamela Leigh Starr	$8.95
Cherish the Flame	Beverly Clark	$8.95
Class Reunion	Irma Jenkins/	
	John Brown	$12.95
Code Name: Diva	J.M. Jeffries	$9.95
Conquering Dr. Wexler's Heart	Kimberley White	$9.95
Crossing Paths,	Dorothy Elizabeth Love	$9.95
Tempting Memories		
Cypress Whisperings	Phyllis Hamilton	$8.95
Dark Embrace	Crystal Wilson Harris	$8.95
Dark Storm Rising	Chinelu Moore	$10.95
Daughter of the Wind	Joan Xian	$8.95
Deadly Sacrifice	Jack Kean	$22.95
Designer Passion	Dar Tomlinson	$8.95
Dreamtective	Liz Swados	$5.95
Ebony Butterfly II	Delilah Dawson	$14.95
Echoes of Yesterday	Beverly Clark	$9.95
Eden's Garden	Elizabeth Rose	$8.95
Everlastin' Love	Gay G. Gunn	$8.95
Everlasting Moments	Dorothy Elizabeth Love	$8.95
Everything and More	Sinclair Lebeau	$8.95
Everything but Love	Natalie Dunbar	$8.95
Eve's Prescription	Edwina Martin Arnold	$8.95

Other Genesis Press, Inc. Titles (continued)

Other Genesis Press, Inc. Titles (continued)

I'll Paint a Sun	A.J. Garrotto	$9.95
Illusions	Pamela Leigh Starr	$8.95
Indiscretions	Donna Hill	$8.95
Intentional Mistakes	Michele Sudler	$9.95
Interlude	Donna Hill	$8.95
Intimate Intentions	Angie Daniels	$8.95
Jolie's Surrender	Edwina Martin-Arnold	$8.95
Kiss or Keep	Debra Phillips	$8.95
Lace	Giselle Carmichael	$9.95
Last Train to Memphis	Elsa Cook	$12.95
Lasting Valor	Ken Olsen	$24.95
Let Us Prey	Hunter Lundy	$25.95
Life Is Never As It Seems	J.J. Michael	$12.95
Lighter Shade of Brown	Vicki Andrews	$8.95
Love Always	Mildred E. Riley	$10.95
Love Doesn't Come Easy	Charlyne Dickerson	$8.95
Love Unveiled	Gloria Greene	$10.95
Love's Deception	Charlene Berry	$10.95
Love's Destiny	M. Loui Quezada	$8.95
Mae's Promise	Melody Walcott	$8.95
Magnolia Sunset	Giselle Carmichael	$8.95
Matters of Life and Death	Lesego Malepe, Ph.D.	$15.95
Meant to Be	Jeanne Sumerix	$8.95
Midnight Clear (Anthology)	Leslie Esdaile	$10.95
	Gwynne Forster	
	Carmen Green	
	Monica Jackson	
Midnight Magic	Gwynne Forster	$8.95
Midnight Peril	Vicki Andrews	$10.95
Misconceptions	Pamela Leigh Starr	$9.95
Montgomery's Children	Richard Perry	$14.95
My Buffalo Soldier	Barbara B. K. Reeves	$8.95

Other Genesis Press, Inc. Titles (continued)

Naked Soul	Gwynne Forster	$8.95
Next to Last Chance	Louisa Dixon	$24.95
No Apologies	Seressia Glass	$8.95
No Commitment Required	Seressia Glass	$8.95
No Regrets	Mildred E. Riley	$8.95
Nowhere to Run	Gay G. Gunn	$10.95
O Bed! O Breakfast!	Rob Kuehnle	$14.95
Object of His Desire	A. C. Arthur	$8.95
Office Policy	A. C. Arthur	$9.95
Once in a Blue Moon	Dorianne Cole	$9.95
One Day at a Time	Bella McFarland	$8.95
Outside Chance	Louisa Dixon	$24.95
Passion	T.T. Henderson	$10.95
Passion's Blood	Cherif Fortin	$22.95
Passion's Journey	Wanda Thomas	$8.95
Past Promises	Jahmel West	$8.95
Path of Fire	T.T. Henderson	$8.95
Path of Thorns	Annetta P. Lee	$9.95
Peace Be Still	Colette Haywood	$12.95
Picture Perfect	Reon Carter	$8.95
Playing for Keeps	Stephanie Salinas	$8.95
Pride & Joi	Gay G. Gunn	$15.95
Pride & Joi	Gay G. Gunn	$8.95
Promises to Keep	Alicia Wiggins	$8.95
Quiet Storm	Donna Hill	$10.95
Reckless Surrender	Rochelle Alers	$6.95
Red Polka Dot in a World of Plaid	Varian Johnson	$12.95
Reluctant Captive	Joyce Jackson	$8.95
Rendezvous with Fate	Jeanne Sumerix	$8.95
Revelations	Cheris F. Hodges	$8.95
Rivers of the Soul	Leslie Esdaile	$8.95

Other Genesis Press, Inc. Titles (continued)

Rocky Mountain Romance	Kathleen Suzanne	$8.95
Rooms of the Heart	Donna Hill	$8.95
Rough on Rats and Tough on Cats	Chris Parker	$12.95
Secret Library Vol. 1	Nina Sheridan	$18.95
Secret Library Vol. 2	Cassandra Colt	$8.95
Shades of Brown	Denise Becker	$8.95
Shades of Desire	Monica White	$8.95
Shadows in the Moonlight	Jeanne Sumerix	$8.95
Sin	Crystal Rhodes	$8.95
So Amazing	Sinclair LeBeau	$8.95
Somebody's Someone	Sinclair LeBeau	$8.95
Someone to Love	Alicia Wiggins	$8.95
Song in the Park	Martin Brant	$15.95
Soul Eyes	Wayne L. Wilson	$12.95
Soul to Soul	Donna Hill	$8.95
Southern Comfort	J.M. Jeffries	$8.95
Still the Storm	Sharon Robinson	$8.95
Still Waters Run Deep	Leslie Esdaile	$8.95
Stories to Excite You	Anna Forrest/Divine	$14.95
Subtle Secrets	Wanda Y. Thomas	$8.95
Suddenly You	Crystal Hubbard	$9.95
Sweet Repercussions	Kimberley White	$9.95
Sweet Tomorrows	Kimberly White	$8.95
Taken by You	Dorothy Elizabeth Love	$9.95
Tattooed Tears	T. T. Henderson	$8.95
The Color Line	Lizzette Grayson Carter	$9.95
The Color of Trouble	Dyanne Davis	$8.95
The Disappearance of Allison Jones	Kayla Perrin	$5.95
The Honey Dipper's Legacy	Pannell-Allen	$14.95
The Joker's Love Tune	Sidney Rickman	$15.95
The Little Pretender	Barbara Cartland	$10.95

Other Genesis Press, Inc. Titles (continued)

The Love We Had	Natalie Dunbar	$8.95
The Man Who Could Fly	Bob & Milana Beamon	$18.95
The Missing Link	Charlyne Dickerson	$8.95
The Price of Love	Sinclair LeBeau	$8.95
The Smoking Life	Ilene Barth	$29.95
The Words of the Pitcher	Kei Swanson	$8.95
Three Wishes	Seressia Glass	$8.95
Ties That Bind	Kathleen Suzanne	$8.95
Tiger Woods	Libby Hughes	$5.95
Time is of the Essence	Angie Daniels	$9.95
Timeless Devotion	Bella McFarland	$9.95
Tomorrow's Promise	Leslie Esdaile	$8.95
Truly Inseparable	Wanda Y. Thomas	$8.95
Unbreak My Heart	Dar Tomlinson	$8.95
Uncommon Prayer	Kenneth Swanson	$9.95
Unconditional	A.C. Arthur	$9.95
Unconditional Love	Alicia Wiggins	$8.95
Until Death Do Us Part	Susan Paul	$8.95
Vows of Passion	Bella McFarland	$9.95
Wedding Gown	Dyanne Davis	$8.95
What's Under Benjamin's Bed	Sandra Schaffer	$8.95
When Dreams Float	Dorothy Elizabeth Love	$8.95
Whispers in the Night	Dorothy Elizabeth Love	$8.95
Whispers in the Sand	LaFlorya Gauthier	$10.95
Wild Ravens	Altonya Washington	$9.95
Yesterday Is Gone	Beverly Clark	$10.95
Yesterday's Dreams, Tomorrow's Promises	Reon Laudat	$8.95
Your Precious Love	Sinclair LeBeau	$8.95

Order Form

Mail to: Genesis Press, Inc.
P.O. Box 101
Columbus, MS 39703

Name _____
Address _____
City/State _____ Zip _____
Telephone _____

Ship to (if different from above)
Name _____
Address _____
City/State _____ Zip _____
Telephone _____

Credit Card Information

Credit Card # _____ ☐ Visa   ☐ Mastercard

Expiration Date (mm/yy) _____ ☐ AmEx   ☐ Discover

Qty.	Author	Title	Price	Total

Use this order form, or call 1-888-INDIGO-1

Total for books _____
Shipping and handling:
 $5 first two books,
 $1 each additional book _____
Total S & H _____
Total amount enclosed _____
Mississippi residents add 7% sales tax